PLAYING WITH FIRE

Winner of the RT Book Reviewers' 2015 Award
for Best Contemporary Love & Laughter

A *Publishers Weekly* Best Book of 2015

A *Washington Post* Best Romance of 2015

"Meader packs the flawless second Hot in Chicago romance with superb relationship development and profane but note-perfect dialogue."
—*Publishers Weekly,* starred review

"Steamy sex scenes, colorful characters, and riveting dialogue . . . a real page-turner."
—*RT Book Reviews*, Top Pick Gold

"A smart, sexy book."
—Sarah MacLean, *The Washington Post*

"Hot, sexy, wonderful."
—Beverly Jenkins, *The Huffington Post*

"I absolutely love Meader's voice and the easy flow of her dialogue, the growth of the characters, and the actual plot of the story. And, oh my God, is Eli Cooper one sexy alpha male."
—*Heroes and Heartbreakers*

"When it comes to writing hot, sexy heroes and strong, independent women, no one does it better than Kate Meader. Her Hot in Chicago series is a scorcher."
—*Harlequin Junkie*

"Ring the alarm because Kate Meader has once again turned up the heat in her newest scorching sizzling sexy read, *Playing with Fire*. It's definitely getting hot in Chicago."

—*Four Chicks Flipping Pages*

FLIRTING WITH FIRE

"Sexy and sassy . . . I love this book!"
—#1 *New York Times* bestselling author Jude Deveraux

"Sexy, witty, and hot, hot, hot. Kate Meader will make you fall in love with the hunky firefighters at Engine Co. 6."
—*New York Times* bestselling author Sarah Castille

"Get your fire extinguisher handy—*Flirting with Fire* is HOT and satisfying!"
—*New York Times* bestselling author Jennifer Probst

"This book is everything you want in a romance: excellent writing, strong characters, and a sizzling plot that keeps the pace up throughout the story."
—*RT Book Reviews*, Top Pick

"Extremely romantic and undeniably entertaining."
—*Single Titles*

"If you're a fan of contemporary romances or are looking for a great romance, I highly recommend Kate Meader's *Flirting with Fire*. I do have to warn you, Kate and I are not responsible if you decide to visit Chicago to look for your own Dempsey brother."

—*Literary, Etc.*

ALSO BY KATE MEADER

SPARKING
THE
FIRE

KATE MEADER

Pocket Books

New York   London   Toronto   Sydney   New Delhi

Pocket Books
An Imprint of Simon & Schuster, Inc.
1230 Avenue of the Americas
New York, NY 10020

This book is a work of fiction. Any references to historical events, real people, or real places are used fictitiously. Other names, characters, places, and events are products of the author's imagination, and any resemblance to actual events or places or persons, living or dead, is entirely coincidental.

First Pocket Books paperback edition October 2016

POCKET and colophon are registered trademarks of Simon & Schuster, Inc.

For information about special discounts for bulk purchases, please contact Simon & Schuster Special Sales at 1-866-506-1949 or business@simonandschuster.com.

The Simon & Schuster Speakers Bureau can bring authors to your live event. For more information or to book an event, contact the Simon & Schuster Speakers Bureau at 1-866-248-3049 or visit our website at www.simonspeakers.com.

Manufactured in the United States of America

10 9 8 7 6 5 4 3 2 1

ISBN 978-1-4767-8593-6
ISBN 978-1-4767-8596-7 (ebook)

To Nicole Resciniti, *agent, cheerleader, and friend.*
I heart you, lady.

PROLOGUE

Once upon a sultry summer night . . .

Her nipples sensed his presence before every other part of her.

The drop-dead gorgeous Marine.

Though Molly Cade wasn't 100 percent positive that he was one of the few and the proud, there was just something about him that screamed Devil Dog. The tan line where the crease of his strong neck met those shoulders to rival Atlas. The ramrod military bearing. The Semper Fidelis tee.

He might have been a wannabe who never made it past boot camp or was bounced for insubordination, but Molly didn't think so. Likely, he was a just-returned. Barely a month, she'd bet. Even twenty feet out from her usual spot at the end of the hotel bar, she smelled sun and desert and all-American honor oozing from his pores.

She pushed her *I'm not here to be picked up* glasses higher on the bridge of her nose and turned to the bookmarked spot in her copy of *Macbeth*. Too keyed up to focus, she saw nothing but a mess of blurry words. A glass of Pinot Noir sat untouched on the bar, her hormones scrambled in anticipation of the night ahead.

She braved another peek. Most guys alone in a virtually empty hotel bar would be engaged in one of three activities:

1. Playing with their drink/coaster/phone to while away the time
2. Bugging the hell out of the bartender with yarns about sports/women/glory days long gone
3. Checking out the talent in the hopes of finding a warm, equally desperate partner for the evening

The Marine did none of these things.

He drank a Coke. Not a Jack and Coke, either, and not from a highball glass. He drank from an old-timey, hourglass-shaped bottle that greeted his sensuous lips in a way that made her jealous. Of a bottle. Watching the swallow of that smooth, tan throat was like witnessing a lascivious sex act.

"Can I get you a drink, honey?"

Molly's fingers stiffened on the book in her hand. So unsubtle, so unimaginative, and so unlike her Marine. The unwelcome new arrival now blocked her pleasure-filled sightline. She'd noticed him lurking on the short side of the L-shaped bar, and apparently her refusal to meet his gaze wasn't enough of a deterrent—he had finally made his move.

"Got it covered, thanks."

The guy whose pickup lines needed work inclined his greasy forehead toward the open book in her hand and added fetid body odor to his list of offenses. "Shakespeare, huh? Pretty classy."

"I'm studying for a test and I really need to get back to it."

"Maybe I can help you bone up."

Real original, bud.

"You heard the lady." At last. The clichés were off the charts tonight, but there was comfort in them, and in twisting them deliciously later.

"It's none of your—" The words stalled in Stink Boy's throat as he realized how much trouble he would be in if he finished that sentence. "Okay, got it." He backed off, away from the loaded weapon about to blow in his sweaty face. Away from the Marine.

Though the bones in her body ached with the need to look up at her savior, she resisted the urge. "Thanks," she muttered, as diffident as a wallflower in her spectacles and conservative, high-necked silk blouse.

"I'll let you get back to your book, miss," he said, words she could barely hear above the thunder in her blood and the throb between her thighs.

"You could join me if you like." She lifted her gaze to meet shockingly clear blue-gray eyes. Magazine-cover, must-be-Photoshopped blue. Mama, he was a big 'un. Six three if he was an inch, the proverbial tall, dark, and badass.

"Don't you need to study?"

She leaned in, then remembered that her wall-flower role required a modicum more reserve. Edging back, she owl-blinked as if the idea of a big, burly man in her personal space felt threatening. "Well, I just said that to . . ." She gave a wave to fill in the rest. "Really, I'm reading it for fun."

Molly braced for the smartass comment about Shakespeare and fun making strange bedfellows. The Marine assessed her coolly like he might a roadside IED, an enemy combatant, maybe a revolver held to his temple. In the week since she had first seen him at the other end of the bar, his expression had never changed, except when . . .

He lowered his large, masculine frame to the stool beside her. Five seconds passed before the bartender placed the Marine's half-finished Coke before him. *Extra tip for you, good man.* His left hand curled around it like he needed it to anchor his body and keep him at a safe distance.

If he placed his right hand on her leg, Molly would part her thighs.

"Tell me something fun about *Macbeth*," he said, desert grit in his tone.

Fun? She could talk about it for hours, but the fun aspects of that might be lost on the just-off-the-copter serviceman she had picked up in a bar. She elected to go for the more commonly known facts about the Scottish play. "It's supposed to be cursed. Unfortunate accidents and ghoulish deaths have been associated with the play throughout the centuries."

"Sounds hilarious," he deadpanned.

Encouraged by his good humor, she went on. "Billy Boy apparently used the spells of real witches in the text. 'Double, double, toil and trouble. Fire burn, and caldron bubble.' "

" 'Cool it with a baboon's blood,' " he continued. " 'Then the charm is firm and good.' "

Well, then.

Shock that the gorgeous Marine was quoting Shakespeare beyond the two lines everyone and his aunt knew left her dumbstruck. Laugh lines feathered out around his eyes. She wanted to kiss them.

"It can read, y'know," he said, dry as dust.

"And I thought it just propped up hotel bars and kept the Coca-Cola Company in business." She shifted in her seat. Crossed her legs. The sexy front slit revealed the tops of her stockings and the lace-trimmed satin garter. Oops.

When his hold tightened on the bottle, a flood of moisture pooled between her thighs.

His phone buzzed in the pocket of his jeans. He ignored it.

"You don't want to get that?"

He remained silent. After three more chirps, his phone followed suit. Terrorized into voice mail.

Six days ago, she had watched as he engaged in Activity No. 1 for Lone Men in Bars: scrutinizing his Coke bottle while he waited for a date to arrive. That night, Molly had worn shorts and a light summer sweater, having just completed the third week of her run in *The Who's Tommy* at Chicago's Ford Oriental Theatre around the corner. The strains of the show's get-up-and-sing closing number still echoed in her tired brain, the standing ovation with it. *Gazing at you, I get the heat* . . . All she'd wanted was a glass of wine at the bar to relax her before she headed to her sterile hotel room.

Then she saw the Marine.

First date was her best guess: he wore a likely bor-rowed jacket that fitted a little too snugly over his broad shoulders, stiff, unbroken denim, and loafers. Not like how he was dressed tonight, with his faded-to-touchable-softness tee, jeans that looked like an old friend, and boots that competed with his weathered face for mileage. Six nights ago, his date hadn't shown. Every night since, he'd sat at the other end of the bar, drinking a Coke and ignoring his phone.

Pretending to ignore her.

Now those relentless blue eyes pinned her to the spot, never leaving her face, even with that garter reveal. She knew he'd seen it. Every muscle in his body affirmed he'd seen it. Her gaze dipped below his trim hips, above his muscular thighs, and lingered. She was actually leering. The intriguing bulge expanded as she watched, turning the pulse between her thighs painful.

He was speaking and she had missed what he said.

"Excuse me?"

"It's been nice talking to you, miss."

What? Oh, Marine. "You, too."

He stood, careful not to brush against her accidentally or give her any relief whatsoever—the tease!—and left the bar, an empty Coke bottle his legacy.

Two minutes later, Molly headed toward the elevator without a backward glance. The show's final performance had been tonight, and she had to pack her bag, print out her boarding pass for her 6 a.m. flight back to LA, and read the sides for her audition. Coming in overly rehearsed would be disastrous, but neither did she want to appear too blasé about her big chance to play movie star Ryan Michaels's love interest in his next shoot-'em-up extravaganza. Summer popcorn fare, not her cup of tea at all. But twenty-four-year-old theater actresses looking to make it in Hollywood couldn't be choosy.

With this role, she might finally get her break.

In the elevator, she pressed the button for the twelfth floor and pushed thoughts of the hot Marine to the back of her mind. A pleasant diversion for the final week of this gig in Chicago, but that was all. The doors closed—

A large hand separated them, and they sprang apart.

"You forgot your book, miss."

Miss. Oh boy, that politeness masking a brute did it for her. As did that muscle factory with the keen blue-gray eyes and kissable laugh lines.

"Thanks." She pushed the glasses she never wore to the top of her nose and held out her hand for the book.

He stepped inside, dropped the book to the ground, and had her pinned to the elevator wall before the doors closed. All that masculine heat seared through her silk blouse, hardening her nipples to pleasurably painful buds.

"A garter," he whispered against her lips, his granite-hard body covering her like a sex blanket. "You know that ain't fair."

"You in those jeans ain't fair, soldier."

"I told you not to call me soldier." He took swift possession of her mouth and punished her for her infraction. She knew former marines didn't appreciate the moniker, more evidence that he was late of the Corps. Not only that, he had the body of one, and without a doubt the stamina, too.

Five nights of her nameless lover worshipping her

with his mouth, hands, and cock were confirmation enough.

"Know what else isn't fair?" she whispered when he let her up for air. "I left my panties in my hotel room."

He groaned. "All night you're sittin' there with no panties on? And there I was thinking you couldn't beat that tight little dress you wore last night or the leather skirt the night before. Sexy librarian might be the hottest yet." His fingers teased the inside of her thigh, then higher until he found her soaking and ready.

"This for me?" Coarse, workingman fingers abraded her plush folds, teasing, easing. Maddening.

"Nope. Shakespeare always turns me on."

He huffed a laugh, but his next words held no traces of humor. "Gonna need to take you here. Again."

They'd already done it once in the elevator this week, a quick, furiously blissful fuck two nights ago when she'd worn a leather skirt and blond wig borrowed from wardrobe at the theater. She'd been raiding the costume racks all week in anticipation of these nightly trysts—it was the least the company could do after the pittance of a salary they'd paid her for the show's run.

She should have been tired of him by now, but when she was in this hero's strong arms, familiarity only bred hunger and a dangerously heightening affection. The temptation to tell him more fluttered in her chest like a panicked bird. Her plans. Her dreams. She wanted to ask if he knew more than four lines of Shakespeare or had an opinion on sunshine all year-round.

Snap out of it, Mol.

The doors opened before he could make good on his sensual promise. They stumbled out of the elevator—or she stumbled out in a lust fog—and he held her steady with his big, blunt hand cupping her ass as he marched her to the room. For the last five nights, their room.

She fiddled with the key card, put it in the wrong way, then not quickly enough to get green for go. *Come on, come on!* His hand over hers stilled her nervous motions.

"Our last night together." Not a question.

"Yes," she whispered, the word a puff of longing she was unable to disguise.

Against her rear, she felt him, huge and ready. Against her back, the beat of his heart found a rhythm with her own. In this space, they existed as one. All he knew about her was that she liked dressing up in sexy costumes to lure near-mute marines into her web and that she was free after 10:30 in the evening. And one other thing: come tomorrow, Chicago, and the best week of her life, would be a distant memory.

But they still had tonight. She still had a few precious hours to watch that sexy-stoic expression of his light up in ecstasy as he rocked in the cradle of her body.

With the hand not dwarfing hers, he tunneled in her dyed-for-the-role auburn hair and directed her to face him. So hard to read, but an expression she hadn't seen before played on his brutally handsome face: regret. It fled so quickly she suspected she'd imagined it.

"Then let's make it a night we won't forget," her

tall, dark, badass marine said before he claimed her mouth in an unforgiving kiss and pressed the hand holding her key card into the slot.

The lock clicked, the door opened, and like the last two people on Earth, they fell inside.

♦ CHAPTER ONE

Five years later . . .

"You can go right in, Lieutenant Fox. He's waiting for you."

Wyatt Fox nodded curtly at Kathy, the firehouse's perky admin, as he stood outside the cap's office contemplating his next move. The going-in part was a foregone conclusion—he had been summoned, after all—but how he would handle what lay behind that door was still up in the air. Normally he would have knocked. Raised his right hand, curled his fingers into a fist, and rapped his knuckles on the door. But he had a pass to just waltz in, so mercifully he didn't have to complete even that simplest of motions. He didn't have to be reminded that the tendons in his shoulder were shredded like Mini-Wheats after he'd wrenched it during a tricky rescue two weeks back. It was either that or let that shithead—sorry, *citizen*—take a header off the LaSalle Street Bridge.

Suicide attempt averted. Three months off squad his reward.

Unless he could persuade the cap that it wasn't as bad as all that.

He gripped the doorknob with purpose, ignored the wince even that small action produced, and strode in like a man without a care in the world.

"Fox."

Captain Matt "Venti" Ventimiglia lifted his gaze from a file on his desk. A pretty cool cat, he wasn't one for small talk, which Wyatt appreciated, especially as his own family could talk the hind legs off a herd of mules. Sitting at the dinner table with the Dempseys—his cobbled-together foster family—was like an episode of *The Brady Bunch* on steroids. And now that the rest of them had hearts-and-shamrocks happy-ever-afters to call their own, it approached Disney to the nth degree at every gathering.

Wyatt took a seat.

"At least three months, according to the doc," the cap said.

Good, straight to it. "Docs can be wrong."

"If you push it and make it worse, then you could be looking at six months or more."

"I'm not good at sitting around." As if that was a valid enough reason to put him back on active duty. It was a family trait, both Dempsey and the original. His biological father, Billy Fox, was never one for letting the grass grow under his itchy feet, always keeping Wyatt and his half brother Logan on the move. Needs must, when you're trying to stay one step ahead of the law.

The cap sniffed. "You hear about Dave Kowalski?"

The subject change gave Wyatt pause, but as he wasn't having any luck going against the tide, he figured he'd swim with it for a while.

"Hollywood Dave? Word's out that he's looking

at ten weeks in traction." Kowalski was the Chicago Fire Department's designated consult for that TV show about firefighters, the one where the station bunk room looked like the Ritz (nope), fires broke out every ten seconds (hardly), and everyone was screwing their coworkers (if only). Years with his nose permanently wedged in the asses of his actor pals had apparently dulled Dave's reflexes to mush because he'd neglected to step out of the way when a roof had caved in on him last week. If Venti was trying to compare their situations . . .

The cap smiled a crooked grin, knowing that Wyatt's mind had crashed that particular gate and was hurtling down the track.

"They need someone to fill in for him."

Wyatt scrubbed a hand across the two-week growth on his jaw. Usually he'd have to stay clean-shaven to ensure his mask retained the proper seal, so he was enjoying the only perk of rehab—the pleasure of ignoring his razor. Add a hunting rifle, a haunch of hog meat, and a cabin in the woods, and you had the makings of a profile worthy of the FBI's Most Wanted list.

"Before you shut it down," Venti continued when Wyatt remained silent, "let me tell you it's not for the TV show. It's an eight-week movie shoot, starts in less than a month, July through August. You know how the city is always looking for revenue and to up its appeal for production companies. Cade Productions asked for someone from Engine 6 to be the consult."

Something pinged in his chest. As a firefighter—a rescue squad firefighter—Wyatt had learned long ago that his instincts were that guardian angel on his shoulder, keeping his ass in one piece. But the reason behind this hitch in his lungs was escaping him this second.

"Why Engine 6?"

Venti grinned and waited a beat until Wyatt got it.

"Because of Alex. They think they'll get more play if they have an in with America's Favorite Firefighter."

Last year, his sister, Alexandra Dempsey, had made a name for herself slicing up the Lamborghini of some rich D-bag who'd insulted the family during a traffic accident run. And as if that wasn't enough, she'd gotten herself involved with Eli Cooper, Chicago's mayor, who proceeded to tank his campaign and subsequently lose his reelection bid to prove he loved her. The whole mess had Hollywood written all over it, but his sister had turned down offers to have her romantic shenanigans immortalized on-screen. Looked like the vultures were looking for another way to skin that kitty cat.

"Might be better to keep these movie people on a short leash, don't you think?" Venti offered with a cocked eyebrow, reading Wyatt's mind. Or at the very least recognizing that "Don't mess with the Dempseys" was as ingrained in Wyatt as it was in the rest of his crazy motherfucking family.

Wyatt sighed. There was logic here, but hanging with Hollywood types and artistes was not how he wanted to spend his rehab. It was the kind of thing his brother Gage would enjoy, he of the billboards and firefighter calendars and all-around exhibitionist tendencies. Kid had never met a camera he didn't want to bang.

He was just about to offer Gage's services instead

when something Venti had said poked his brain matter like a Halligan through termite-ridden drywall.

"Back up a sec. What's that about production companies?"

"The city wants to encourage more production companies to come here—"

"No, the other thing. The name of the production company that asked for the consult from six."

Venti squinted. "Cade Productions. Headed up by that actress who had all that trouble last year. The public divorce from Ryan Michaels, the hacked photos, the 'I'm so exhausted' rehab." The captain was well known for spending more time reading *People* than *Fire Engineering* magazine. Anyone who dared touch the latest issue before Venti laid his eyeballs on it had better find latrine duty enjoyable. "This is supposed to be her big comeback."

The ping now ratcheted up to a full-on four-alarm. "And is she in the movie? Molly Cade?"

That garnered more than a squint from Venti; it earned a skin-penetrating stare because Wyatt had sounded . . . animated. He didn't do animated for anything or anyone.

Except for Sean and Logan, his foster father and biological brother, both long gone. For Roni, very much alive and vexing.

And once, for Molly Cade.

A smile spread slowly across Venti's face. Asshole. "I believe she *is* in the movie. Fan of Ms. Cade's work, are you?"

Big fan. Of how hard her tongue had worked when wrapped around his cock. How good her curvy body had worked his until every one of his atoms had exploded in the kind of pleasure he'd never experienced before or since. They had crossed paths at a strange time in Wyatt's life. In the intervening five years, whenever he saw her on the screen, a cavalcade of what-might-have-beens marched through his brain. Ridiculous, for sure. Oscar-nominated actresses who commanded multimillion-dollar paydays weren't exactly his usual diet.

But . . .

Molly Cade was in his zip code. Or soon would be. Dubbed America's Sweetheart in all those dumb romantic comedies when she wasn't playing a macho loser's helpless love interest in the latest summer popcorn movie, her one step outside her wheelhouse had yielded that Oscar nod for some indie film. And then it had all turned to shit for her in the last year.

Not that he had kept track of her starry life or anything.

But before that, before she was *the* Molly Cade, she was the one woman who had snuck under his skin and burrowed in for the long haul. It would be mighty interesting to see if she had the means to make him itch like before. Come alive like before. Keeping her and her production company out of his sister's orbit would be a bonus.

He met Venti's gaze squarely, not caring what the cap might think about his sudden about-face.

"When do I start?"

"You have to admit, he has a great ass."

Molly turned to the maker of that bald statement and gave her the slitty eyes. Calysta Johnson—bestie,

gal Friday, and fellow ass connoisseur—remained
oblivious to Molly's glare, too busy ogling the *ass*-
ets of Gideon Carter, costar on Molly's latest movie
venture, *Into the Blaze*. Molly followed Cal's gaze
to where Gideon the Idiot stood just as . . . *sigh*, he
rang the antique firehouse bell affixed to the wall of
the Robert J. Quinn Fire Academy on Chicago's West
Side. For the third time in ten minutes. At the clank-
ing din, he whooped like a frat pledge and nudged the
ribs of his right-hand dickhead, Jeremy.

"Sure, great ass. Pity it's on his shoulders."

Cal chortled. "If I was ten years younger—"

"Or had a brain injury."

"—I'd be all over those perfect globes." Cal was
equal opportunity when it came to her dating interests. Men, women, and IQs below seventy were all
fair game. Grinning, she aimed a glance past the hulking steam-powered engine in the lobby and checked
her phone again. "Our contact is late."

"You make it sound like a special military op. We're
just meeting the Pabst Blue Ribbon–drinking, pot-
bellied hose hauler who's going to make sure this movie
is more authentic than a Ken Burns documentary."

Cal squeezed Molly's arm. She could always tell
when Molly was nervous. "Hon, this is going to be
a huge success. Your ticket back onto the A-list, into
the fickle public's hearts, and their big fat wallets."

"I don't care about being A-list or making bank on
the first weekend. I just want"—Molly balled her fists
and placed them on her hips—"I just want people to
hear my name and not think 'Ryan Michaels's pa-
thetic ex' or 'Her tits look bigger on the screen than
they do in those hacked photos.' "

"Well, they do look bigger. That's the magic of Hollywood."

Molly barked a reluctant laugh. Thank God for Cal, who always managed to shred the invites to the pity party.

"Speaking of photos, did you see them?" Cal jerked her chin to the west wall, where a battery of frames hung in a grid. They both moved toward them.

The Wall of the Fallen.

Feeling a touch ghoulish, Molly studied the pictures. Faces shone back at her, some smiling, most not, all of the men dressed in their CFD uniforms. Each of them someone's father, brother, son, friend. Their courage and sacrifice enveloped Molly to the point that the shitstorm she had endured this past year paled in comparison.

With reverent slowness, she walked past the memorial until she came to the two she recognized: Sean Dempsey and his foster son, Logan Keyes.

Sean was that stereotypical hale and ruddy-faced Irishman with a twinkle that not even his grim official photo could dull. Beside him, Logan stared out from beyond the grave, a hint of a smile teasing the corner of his mouth. A real heartbreaker, no doubt. Nine years ago, they'd given their lives, spawned a legion of bar tales, and inspired a family of foster kids to follow in their footsteps. One of those kids, Alex Dempsey, was as well known for her on-camera and romantic exploits as she was for her bravery. Her story of fierce familial loyalty, headline-grabbing heroics, and a love for the ages—the movie poster was already designed in Molly's mind—would add the human interest element to *Into the Blaze*'s pulse-pounding action sequences.

Unfortunately, Alex and the CFD had stonewalled Molly's efforts to tell it. Months of no calls returned preceded a sternly worded letter from former Chicago mayor, now hotshot lawyer Eli Cooper, informing Cade Productions that Firefighter Dempsey's story was not for sale.

Six months of fighting tooth and nail with Ryan's lawyers for her rights and dignity had soured Molly on smooth-talking lawyers. While the movie would still get made, its success would be assured with Alex's endorsement, which is why she was here.

The Dempseys, as the foster siblings were collectively known, worked at Engine Company 6, so she had requested to meet with one of the company when the usual CFD media affairs rep was injured. It was a long shot, but if she could learn more about the Dempseys, find a way to connect with them, maybe she'd find a way in with Alex. Time was nipping at her heels, though. The adapted script was ready to go and shooting started in under four weeks. It just needed the imprimatur of America's Favorite Firefighter to varnish it with the sheen of authenticity.

This was to be Molly's comeback, and it would be spectacular.

"God, they are positively smokin'." Cal held up her phone to showcase the ripped-as-shit body of Gage Simpson, one of the Dempseys, posing in the charity firefighter calendar that had taken the city and Internet by storm last year. "Two of them in those beefcake calendars, one of them a cut boxer, the hot-tamale sister. Wonder what the mystery brother looks like."

So did Molly. Four of the Dempseys were unafraid

of the public eye, but the fifth—Wyatt Fox—remained a shadowy figure who shunned the limelight. To be fair, she hadn't looked all that hard, but no clear photos of Mr. Mysterious had come to light. Not even on Facebook.

"Probably got thrashed by the ugly stick. But the rest of 'em . . ." Cal gave a low whistle. "Must be something in the Chicago water."

As they were standing before a monument to the city's finest and bravest, Molly opened her mouth, ready to admonish her friend for her crassness, only to find Cal gaping and her gaze directed to a point over Molly's shoulder. "Or maybe it's what they're feeding them down at the firehouse," she murmured.

A curious shiver thrummed through Molly's body a split second before she heard a deep, bone-penetrating baritone. "Miss Cade?"

The shiver magnified in intensity, though that wasn't quite right. It rocket-fuel-boosted every cell in her body to the level of a quake.

That voice. It couldn't be.

She turned.

The Marine.

Her brain tried to compute the vision before her. The same uncompromising blue-gray eyes, but more distant. The same fit body, but more space filling. The same rugged features, but more bearded. (Bearded!)

He was also in the wrong place at the wrong time, wearing the wrong . . . no, no, no . . . Chicago Fire Department T-shirt that stretched taut against chiseled pectorals, the sleeve hems pushed north by biceps she remembered gripping as he pistoned those trim hips into her over and over.

Five years ago.

Five years of climbing a pinnacle of fame to that coveted spot on the A-list. Well, four years. The last year had wiped out all that had gone before. Every high, every joyful moment.

But back in a simpler time, there had been a week—six glorious, sex-filled nights, actually—with the Marine. Who was not a marine at all, it seemed, or at least no longer was.

Cal, seeing that Molly had been struck stupid, donned her personal assistant hat and stepped forward.

"Hi, I'm Calysta Johnson. I've been emailing CFD Media Affairs about today's meeting, and this is—" She motioned toward Molly.

"Miss Cade," he grated.

Oxygen was suddenly hard to come by, the floor moving beneath her feet. A thundering sound had started in her head and now echoed in her blood—and it had nothing to do with that 90 percent juice diet her personal trainer had her on. The Marine said something to Cal, maybe his name, but Molly missed it.

She had never known that name, had never wanted to. That was their unspoken agreement. No names, no history, no future. Just six nights of scorching passion and inhibitions annihilated. He had done things to her no other man had ever dared. Plumbed the depths of her pleasure and scaled her to orgasmic heights she had forgotten existed during the icy wasteland of her marriage. She used to like sex. She used to like the person she was during sex, but Ryan had drilled it out of her—literally—with his all-consuming focus on himself.

"Mol?" Cal's eyes were wide with concern. "You okay?"

Molly swallowed. "Yes! I'm fine!" Squeaky voiced, about to fall over, but otherwise okeydokey.

She met the cool gaze of the Marine. "Mr. . . . ?"

"Fox. Wyatt Fox."

Hello, seren-freaking-dipity, it was him. Not just him from all those years ago, but *him,* the elusive Dempsey. How was it possible that the man who had lit her on fire, body and soul, was also the man who could get her closest to her heart's desire—a straight shot at his sister?

Wyatt Fox. It suited him. Clean, masculine, not a syllable wasted. Like James Bond, if 007 included cowboy-marine-firefighter in his stable of personae.

Fox. Wyatt Fox. License to thrill—and send your panties plummeting.

A manic giggle bubbled up from somewhere deep, the same place where illicit laughter in church originated. The wicked, don't-you-dare-Molly kind of giggle she had never been able to smother in front of her gran whenever Pastor Morrison delivered his sermon with a booger hanging from his nose—every Sunday, without fail, at St. Peter's Episcopal Church in New Haven, Missouri.

She held out her hand, and to distract from her tremble, she parted with that giggle. Wily move, she thought.

He stared, no doubt wondering if she had lost her mind. *Don't worry, Marine, that train left the station long ago.* Only now was she starting to put the splintered mess back together again.

Drawing on Serious Molly, she cleared her throat, though she was quite enjoying this giddy version. It had been a while. "Mr. Fox. Thanks so much for meeting with us today."

No reaction. What—so—ever.

This was priceless. The one guy on the planet who could probably map all her freckles and he didn't remember a single one—or her! But that was their game, wasn't it? Each night, they would circle each other in that hotel bar like predatory strangers, as though they hadn't already memorized every inch of each other's bodies, the pulse points, the weak spots, every breathy sound.

Could he be reverting to their previous dynamic? Is that why he was looking at her like she was nothing to him? Or had she truly made so little impact?

He dwarfed her hand in his giant one, squeezed once, and let go. As if her touch offended him.

She was reading far too much into this.

"Miss Cade."

The third time he'd called her that. Something in his voice was hot-wired to the dampening center between her legs. "Molly. Call me Molly."

The prickle of heat on the back of her neck could mean only one thing: Cal was staring at her and compiling a list of questions in her head to be brought out later over a bottle of Pinot.

"Hey, do you guys . . . know each other?"

Or, why wait? Just get it out now and clear the air.

Not a muscle moved in the Marine's face, not even an eyelash, but then . . . then . . . yes! A slight rise of his eyebrow, like the ghost of a breeze fluttering practically invisible molecules. He *did* remember. The enormity of his reaction, and what it meant, smashed her to the ground.

He was feigning ignorance, allowing her the freedom to admit or deny.

For the past five years, her life had not been her own. A Faustian bargain she had made knowingly, of course. Hello fame, good-bye privacy. But those hacked photos infecting the Internet, that *violation,* had not been her choice.

Her heart clenched at this small gesture of gallantry. So perhaps banging Molly fifteen ways from Sunday before she was famous might not be worth bragging about, but any other guy would be salivating at the chance to compose a headline of "Hot Nights in the Sack with Molly Cade!" Instead, the Marine was giving her the choice whether to reveal their past affair.

Tears pricked her eyelids at the unexpected kindness.

All things considered, however, this prior connection could not get out. She was trying to rehabilitate her sorry rep, not create more gossip for the gutter rags. Which is why she really should not have said in answer to Cal's question about whether they knew each other, "Depends on your definition of *know.*"

One razor-straight eyebrow shot up, hovered near his cocoa brown hairline, and lowered slowly. How gratifying to be able to throw him like that. He had always been so unshockable.

"We had some mutual interests once," Wyatt said, a pagan gleam in those blue-gray eyes. "Bars. Shakespeare." Sexy pause. "Elevators."

Heat rose to her cheeks. *Point to you, Mr. Fox.*

"How long have you been with CFD?"

"About four and a half years. Signed up after I left the marines."

So she'd been right about his military service, and he'd joined the family business after they'd met. It was strange to think of him with a family. With the Dempseys.

Inward mental shake. Did she think he sprouted fully formed from Lake Michigan, ascending in a seashell like a male Venus with maybe a fig leaf—or a Cubbies cap—over his manly magnificence? Toting a fire hose instead of a trident? No, that was Neptune. Or Poseidon. Whatever.

She savored the glorious image for a moment while another giggle gathered inside her. No man had ever exhibited the capacity to unhinge her like this, not even Ryan. With him she had been starstruck, but never man-struck.

Desperately, she turned to Cal with a helpless shrug of *I think it would be best if you speak now.*

Cal had witnessed several breakdowns from Molly in the past year, so this latest turn did not surprise her. Deftly, she picked up the conversational slack. "I understand our original CFD contact is injured, Mr. Fox. I hope he's okay."

"He'll make it. And it's Lieutenant Fox." He crossed thick-as-oak-branch forearms over his immense chest, a move that made his biceps bulge indecently.

Oh. My.

Directing his stark gaze back at Molly, he said, "This isn't my usual gig, but as long as you do as I say, we should get along fine."

Somehow, she found her producer voice. "Already bossing my crew around?"

"Who said anything about your crew?"

All the blood she needed to stay upright rushed to her face in remembrance. Back then, the man had held on to regular conversation as if every word cost a sliver of his soul to speak it. But he had been expressive in other ways. Throaty commands. Raspy instructions. *Touch me. Suck me. Take it all, baby.* Every order designed to maximize their joint pleasure.

A loud clanging sound cut through the sexual tension as thick as the lust fog in her brain. Gideon was at it again, playacting about thirty feet off near the museum's entrance.

"Hey," Wyatt said quietly, forcefully, and with what sounded like great restraint.

Gideon raised both hands, all innocence, because the brass bell had clearly rung itself. If he didn't quit playing the part of a ten-year-old trapped in a thirty-year-old's body, Molly was going to shove that bell in a very uncomfortable place. He was definitely not her first choice to play Macklin Chase, the heroic fireman who loses his best friend and has to deal with the soul-shattering consequences, but the studio refused to green-light the project without him. Apparently, some suit at Sony thought he projected the appropriate gravitas.

Some suit should have seen him mooning the cast and crew at yesterday's meet and greet.

"He with you?" Wyatt asked Molly.

"Yes. One of the actors." Just in case Wyatt cared if she and Gideon were together.

Which by the look on his face, he did not.

A bemused Cal shook her head at this exchange and cleared her throat. "In any case, Lieutenant, we appreciate you stepping in at the last moment. I'm not sure if Captain Ventimiglia told you, but our original plan was to spend a day at the academy observing the trainees, giving the actors a feel for the typical job of a firefighter. I understand that you'll be meeting with our tech people tomorrow."

"Uh-huh. So you want to learn the ins and outs of life in the CFD in two hours."

"Well, we realize that we can't cram years of knowledge into such a short time." Molly offered her most persuasive smile, feeling on a more sure footing. That smile was her fortune. "But we were told we could watch a class and then maybe ride the truck from your firehouse for a day. At Engine Company 6."

Ancestral seat of the Dempseys.

He didn't take the bait. "Not sure watching the class is going to help much," he said with another squint. He really had that Old West gunfighter thing down. "Doing will give you a better feel for the physical endurance and skill set needed to be a firefighter. Ladder drills, hauling equipment, the smoke box. How's your stamina?"

Pretty damn good, if you recall.

There was that imperceptible eyebrow lift again, henceforth known as a Wy-brow. He did recall.

Before Molly could answer, Cal cut in. "There are insurance issues. We can't let the talent climb ladders or enter smoke-filled boxes."

Wyatt stepped forward, right up close, and addressed Molly. Of course he smelled incredible, because how hot he looked wasn't already sending her hormones into a Wyatt-fueled frenzy.

"You want to make this movie as authentic as possible, feel what it's like to come home with smoke pumpin' out of your pores, grime in your hair, your muscles ragin' and your body itchin' to find release?"

Yes, yes, all of that. She blinked, swallowed, and nodded when really she wanted to ask more about the body-itching-to-find-release part. And those dropped g's. She remembered that coming out more, how his vocabulary contracted, when he was losing himself inside her body.

"Well, you'd need to train for a year, then spend three more in a firehouse."

She was glad to hear that humor as dry as the California brush in August threaded through his graveled voice. So laconic you had to rewind your brain to check for the joke.

"But if you let me do what you're paying me to do, I can give you a damn good approximation of it. You interested in what I got to offer?"

"Yes," she whispered, and then more forcefully, "Yes. I want to make it real."

"Good." Without missing a beat, he spoke to Gideon. "Touch that bell again and I'll take an ax to your hand."

Gideon stepped back, looking suitably chastened. Maybe he wasn't such a bad actor after all.

"Don't worry, Miss Johnson," Wyatt said to Cal. "I'll take care of your talent. With me. Now." So decreed, he turned and strode toward the entrance to the academy barracks, housed next door to the museum.

Cal wagged her finger at Molly and gestured at Wyatt's departing back with a murmur of, "Lucy, you got some 'splainin' to do."

I know, I know.

"But while we're on the subject of Great Butts of Western Civilization . . ." Cal made a box gesture with her hands, composing Wyatt's very fine ass in her imaginary viewfinder. "Cut that one out, frame it, stick it in the Met."

"No. Bronze it." And another more crucial part of his anatomy, Molly thought, before her manic giggles finally got the best of her.

CHAPTER TWO

Wyatt's heart pounded so loud it was a wonder the whole damn academy didn't shake with the vibration. Five years. Five years of her face on that big screen, sometimes as a brunette or a redhead, but more often as her natural blond—information he knew intimately—and she was here. Looking more stunning than he'd imagined in his fevered dreams. She'd scraped her honey-colored hair back off her face and shoved it under a Cubs baseball cap. Sunglasses sat perched over the brim, ready to descend and protect her anonymity once she hit the streets. Her features were largely unchanged: perky nose, cupid bow lips, sink-into-me eyes in that unusual violet-gray shade, but it was her eyebrows that had always set her apart. Those brows transformed her girl-next-door looks into something wild. Feral.

Unknowable.

He had wanted to know her that first night he saw her, sipping from a wineglass at that hotel bar downtown, swinging one long, tan leg back and forth. That leg had mesmerized him like a pendulum used by a hack magician in a hypnosis trick.

A week later, he'd woken up from whatever spell she'd put on him to find her gone.

He stopped at the entrance to the training facility. Turned. Molly snapped her gaze north and blushed furiously while the assistant laughed.

Checking out his ass, it would seem.

He couldn't remember the last time a woman had done that. Though he'd need eyes in his ass to be able to say so with certainty.

"A new class of recruits starts up tomorrow, but in the meantime, you can see the facility. Then visit a firehouse."

Molly's eyes burned brighter at the mention of the firehouse visit. If she had done her research, she would know by now his Dempsey connection and that his mission was to keep her on a short leash. A cheeky lift at the corner of her mouth told him they were on the same page, along with something else.

Challenge accepted.

Suddenly his brain locked up. He'd had some crazy notion of showing her and her crew around. Maybe boost her up a ladder. Check out *her* ass. But now he realized that he couldn't just pretend. Walk around with these strangers and act like he and Molly meant nothing to each other.

"Wait here." Sixty seconds later, he returned with company in tow. "This is Lieutenant O'Halloran. He's going to continue the tour."

The graceful column of Molly's neck bulged on her swallow, and Wyatt couldn't help the thrilling surge in his chest that enjoyed her obvious disappointment.

"Is there something wrong?" Miss Johnson asked.

"I need to speak with Miss Cade alone, so the lieutenant will be taking over."

She looked at Molly. "I'm not sure—"

"I figure that since you're the producer," Wyatt said to Molly, "we should probably discuss some of the logistics about our time together."

Color spotted her cheeks at his words, which had sounded mighty intimate. Totally his intention. Without waiting for an answer, he headed toward O'Halloran's office, the thud of his heart finding a triumphant rhythm with the *click-clack* of her heels behind him. Once she arrived, he took a few necessary distancing steps back to the desk and waited.

She leaned against the closed door, but he knew better. That was the least casual lean he'd ever seen.

The urge to pin her to the wall punched holes in his chest.

"You've changed," she said.

"You haven't."

A small sound erupted from her. So her life was a million miles away from five years ago, but fundamentally she hadn't changed. That energy in her body still rippled the air. It fired him up now, a feeling he hadn't enjoyed in a while. A feeling he hadn't craved in a while.

He took a moment to survey the rest of her, his gaze roving up and down her length in a way he hadn't permitted himself outside, around her people. A bright yellow top clung to her breasts above white pants that stopped halfway down her calves. One of those casual looks that probably took a couple of minutes and a boatload of money to throw together. She stood almost a foot shorter than him, but that had never been a problem, given most of their conversations had been horizontal. The years had filled out her curves, and she wore those few extra pounds of plush well, especially below the flare of her hips. The ass that dethroned JLo, or some shit. Her shapely figure had its own press corps.

A woman like this was built to be bedded, and often.

She kicked off from the door, like she needed to propel herself forward into the room. Into this conversation. The momentum brought her to O'Halloran's display shelf with his league hockey trophies and the signed baseball from the White Sox's game three during the 2005 World Series.

"So what did you want to talk about?"

"Think we should lay things out. Clear the air."

Her fingers grazed the edge of the shelf. "What you did out there—well, I'm grateful." She raised her eyes, the color of a summer storm over the lake. "I appreciate your discretion. It's not something I'm used to in my business, where everybody is looking to take a piece. You could have . . ."

"What could I have done?" Bragged about sucking begging moans from her gorgeous lips? Reminded her how he'd made her come repeatedly until she'd nearly passed out? Told the world about every filthy thing he had done to her?

"Oh, I see," she said, a flash of anger in her eyes. "You'd rather unnerve me in private."

She wasn't wrong.

"You want to lay things out," she said into the taut silence. "Clear the air."

Yes, but not how she imagined. They didn't need to talk about what had happened all those years ago because it was here, between them, fueling this organ-crushing torrent of sexual energy. Those memories were as vivid now as if they were projected onto the wall.

"You want to use my sister's story for your movie."

She betrayed no surprise at his plain speaking. "Busted."

"You thought maybe you could work your Hollywood charm on some poor sap from Engine 6 and get the inside track."

She picked up the baseball. Turned it over. Put it back. "You've got me."

"And now that the poor sap is me, maybe you're thinking our past connection will work in your favor and I'll be eating out of your"—he paused—"hand."

"Nothing gets by you, soldier."

He'd let her have that one, even though he'd told her once he didn't like the term.

"You've done your research on my family."

Her face softened, positively transformed. But then, she was a great actress. "I have. Loyal, generous, big-hearted, prepared to do violence when necessary. You're a TV series waiting to happen." She canted her head. "Or a movie."

"You're also aware that my sister doesn't want her life to be made fodder for Hollywood."

"And you're here to play junkyard dog."

"I'm here to play your worst nightmare if you try turning my family's life into a circus."

She crossed her arms over those gorgeous breasts that were once so sensitive to his touch. "Sounds like they're doing a pretty good job of that themselves. Luke punching out a CPD detective in your family's bar, Alex cutting up a VIP's car in the guise of a rescue, Gage on every billboard—"

"They tend to think with their hearts." In Gage's case, his dick. "Now, we're just trying to keep everything on an even keel. No drama, no shenanigans, and especially no headline-grabbing encounters."

She narrowed her eyes, considering. "You took this job on to keep me out of your family's way."

"You could say that."

"What else could I say?"

"That maybe I was curious."

"And now?"

Still curious. But no way was he getting involved with this woman and her crazy life. What had he been thinking? He had enough drama to cope with at home, and if he had any chance of making things right with Roni, Molly Cade needed to be deep-sixed to a locked recess of his brain.

Which shouldn't be a problem. There was a reason why he was the go-to guy when hands were shaky and the world was in flames: Wyatt Fox kept the coolest head in the CFD. In the marines. In the game of life.

"Curiosity satisfied."

She smiled, and *hell-oh,* that smile made a big ole liar of him. The inability to be satisfied had been the hallmark of their affair. More often than not, one of them would wake the other with kisses and rubs and sucks, their need greedy. Grasping.

That he may have miscalculated gnawed at his gut. No matter, he refused to fall under her spell again.

"You might have thought you could work your charms on some starry-eyed tech consult or, failing that, the guy you spent six nights balling in a hotel room a few years ago, but I'm here to tell you, I'm the gatekeeper. And the gate isn't opening in this lifetime or the next."

"Well, good thing we cleared that up," she said in a way that hinted the waters between them were still murky. "I'm ready for that tour now."

She grinned, a cheeky stretch of her wicked mouth. A conqueror's smile. God, he remembered that. But last time he'd seen it turned on expressly for him, he'd been inside her, quickly wiping the grin off her face and replacing it with ecstasy.

He joined her at the door. Save for the moment he'd leaned in to shake her hand earlier, this was the closest he'd been to her in five years.

Resignation assaulted him hard. "You haven't heard a word I've said, have you?"

"Oh, I heard. But you see, I've spent several years listening to people telling me what to do. Agents, publicists, directors, my ex-husband. I created my own production company so I could call the shots. Divorced Ryan so I wouldn't have to listen to his whining about how my career was overshadowing his. So while I appreciate that you have a job to do protecting what's yours, I also have a job to do, ensuring this is the best firefighter movie ever made."

In her voice, he heard the frustration of a woman who had been to hell and back, and was ready for a change of scenery. However, in resolving to redirect her journey, she had placed herself on a collision course with his needs and the needs of his family.

That was going to be a problem.

"I'd like to spend a day with the CFD recruits doing what they'd normally do," she announced imperiously. "Don't concern yourself with the insurance issues. I'm the producer, so I say who on the crew does what."

Fine, he'd let her flex her diva muscles. It wouldn't take long to establish who was top dog here.

"You can join the class tomorrow," he said, all accommodation.

She narrowed her gaze, clearly suspicious at the ease with which she'd achieved victory. *Enjoy it, babe, as it will very likely be your last.*

After a lengthy pause, she nodded and stepped away from the door. "After you," she said. "You know where you're going."

That he did.

He left the office and walked ahead, then stopped and turned. Those violet-hazed eyes jerked up from a spot about two feet below his neck to meet his. More of the blatant ass ogling. Getting to be a habit, that. Another gorgeous blush suffused her cheeks.

"Enjoy the view while you can, Molly, 'cause from here on out, I'll be watching *your* ass."

Leaving her townhouse for the summer in the upscale Gold Coast neighborhood on Chicago's North Side, Molly nodded at Terrence, her bull-necked bodyguard. To be honest, security was unnecessary, but the studio was anxious to ensure nothing TMZ-worthy tainted the shoot. Thankfully, the press hadn't figured out where she was staying, and with her wraparound sunnies and blond hair tucked into a Cubbies baseball cap (blending in to the max, though she was a Cardinals girl to the bone), she looked like a typical Chi-Town dweller.

In LA, the studio would usually hire a town car

to drive her to and from the set, but this summer, she was endeavoring to take back her independence, one car ride at a time. These solo rides in the rented Lexus—a hybrid in Nebula Gray Pearl—allowed a few moments' reflection before she had to call up her game face.

She'd need it for Wyatt Fox.

The man was going to present quite the challenge, to both her professional plans and her sanity. She felt a smile tug at her lips. Well, immovable object, meet willpower to rival any amount of gunfighter squinting and intimidating silences.

After a coffee pickup at the nearest Starbucks drive-through (Terrence had a weakness for Green Tea Crème Frappuccino), she arrived at the Quinn Firefighter Academy and parked around back. Checking her phone, she discovered that Cal had sent several text messages urging Molly to call her, stat.

She pressed one on her speed dial and her friend picked up on the first ring. "What's up, Cal?"

"Gideon the Idiot strikes again."

Molly groaned. "What now?"

"Jimmy Kimmel broke his collarbone during one of the *Late Show* stunts and you know what brahs they are."

"You mean he has to hold Le Kimmel's hand while he recuperates in LA?"

"Close. He's stepping in to host for the next two weeks. The studio said it was okay because he doesn't really need to be here for prep."

This unwelcome news dragged a growl from Molly. Of course, the actors wouldn't be doing their own stunts but, eager to promote team building and full-scale immersion, Molly had wanted them all to attend the fire academy boot camp.

"Tell me the rest of them are here."

"Yeah, they should be," Cal soothed. "And Mol?"

"Uh-huh?"

"Give the sexy firefighter a big old smooch from me." On a chuckle, she hung up.

Molly drummed her fingers on the steering wheel, considering. Analyzing. Scheming.

Maybe Cal was onto something.

Molly used to have wiles: a flirty smile for a casting director, an eyelash flutter for a maître d'. So she was a little rusty—with A-listers, the name is enough. But Wyatt Fox stood in her way. Starting up "something" with him was a terrible idea, but maybe a little Missouri farm girl charm would melt the ice in those flinty eyes and carve out a path to Alex Dempsey.

Once inside the training facility, she was relieved to see several of the film techs, stunt doubles, and the actors who would be playing her firefighter family on set. Standing head and shoulders above them was Wyatt, looking bearded, muscled, and capable.

Capable. Better to assign him that rather benign description than all the other possible words that could enter her head. Grabbable. Kissable.

Fuckable.

He zeroed in on her, as if sensing exactly what was running through her sex-starved mind. Her memories were bad enough, but now he was adding that beard to the mix. Since when had she turned into such a facial hair ho? She had a career to salvage, a reputation to rebuild, and men—or one sexy bearded man—was the last thing she should be thinking about.

Except in the context of her mission, the Molly Cade Charm Offensive. A little flirting, a little smiling, a little banter (emphasis on *little;* the man seemed to be surrounded by a charm-repelling force field).

"Hey, guys," she said to the crew, averting her gaze from those crystal blues she could drown in if she got too close. She chatted innocuously about today's plan. The actors were seeing it as a fun primer on the job of a firefighter; Molly intended to take it more seriously than that.

She was here to impress.

"Okay, I'm going to pair each of you with a firefighter trainee," Wyatt said, and proceeded to do so with everyone but her.

"I hope you're not thinking of leaving me out," she said, instantly peeved.

"Miss Johnson mentioned we need to be mindful of insurance issues for the A-list talent." *Sarcasm noted, Marine.* "So you're with me, Hollywood."

"Watching my ass?"

"Not letting it out of my sight."

That was sort of bantery, wasn't it? In a gruff, Rick Grimes from *The Walking Dead* kind of way. He turned back to the crew and began to issue orders to the trainees, a squadron of buff guys—no women—with grave expressions. Wyatt's demeanor was all business, as well, and after his initial flirtatious rejoinder, she was glad of it. Work now, flirt later.

"First thing is to get you all suited up." Each of the trainees helped their assigned partner with the heavy-duty bunker gear: pants, suspenders, fire-retardant jacket, and boots.

"Here, lean on me," he said as Molly inserted one

foot into the boot that wouldn't have looked out of place on a moon landing expedition. She could have used the wall, but it was five feet away and his arm was right there attached to a human wall, and what harm could it do?

Untold amounts, it seemed.

As her fingers curled around his right bicep for leverage, she immediately realized her error. That holy-crap arm had to be the thickest, warmest, most solid arm she had ever touched. Five years ago, he had just left the marines, and even then, his arm had not felt like this. Like the last defense between the United States and an invading army. She imagined him repelling terrorists with roundhouse punches and chokeholds during his deployment. And now? This arm pulled people out of burning buildings and mangled metal. It saved lives. And as much as it was a professional tool, it was also a mouthwatering thing of beauty.

Positively porn-worthy.

His tee sleeve hem had ridden up (she might have helped there) to reveal a red-inked tattoo of the intertwined letters of the CFD and *Logan* below it, set off by a Celtic ribbon. This was new. He'd not had it back then, yet Logan and Sean would have been gone four years. She'd seen identical emblems on Luke and Gage in those firefighter charity calendar pics that had busted the Internet last year.

They all carried the same ink, a branded memorial to their fallen. Wow.

"Logan was your foster brother," she said, the need for more information a potent rise in her blood.

"Biological brother."

Oh. She hadn't known that. She'd assumed they were a band of solo, motherless misfits saved by the Dempsey fostering machine. Stronger together than apart.

"You don't have the same last name."

"Half brothers. Same mom, different fathers. Sean and Mary fostered us when I was ten and Logan was eleven."

She whipped her eyes to his and found unexpected disquiet lurking there. The Dempseys' closeness was legendary, but that fraternal bond of blood would likely have been just as strong, if not stronger. To lose your brother and father figure in one fell swoop must have broken Wyatt's heart. It broke hers just thinking about it.

Unsure why, she squeezed his bicep on the pretext of needing an anchor. Maybe to give herself comfort as much as him. She didn't imagine that shiver of his beneath her fingertips.

"You're not gonna get far with one boot, Molly."

"Oh—right," she said, and quickly caught up with everyone else. She had visited a firehouse in Los Angeles and tried on the bunker gear there, but the CFD version felt like more of an encumbrance. Or perhaps *she* felt heavier in Wyatt's presence.

Stepping in close enough that he could have kissed her if he wanted, he snapped her bunker pants closed. The notion of him dressing her was unbearably erotic, especially as the previous times they'd been this close he'd been doing the opposite.

Sometimes with his teeth.

"How do you feel?"

Horny. "Heavy."

He attached tools and filled her pockets: a flashlight, shears, two different types of knives, a crescent wrench, pliers, a wedge of wood, more pliers. By the time he'd finished, she was a walking Ace Hardware and she'd lost that loving feeling.

"Standard gear before you add on breathing apparatus and bigger tools weighs about thirty pounds."

She took a breath and a couple of steps, feeling like she was wading through a waterlogged cornfield.

"Your sister must be crazy fit. And strong."

"Never met a more capable firefighter, man or woman."

Big boots to fill. A huge legacy to honor. A movie— and career—to screw up. At five four, Molly was about as far as it got from Alexandra Dempsey's physique.

Uncannily reading her mind, Wyatt said, "Firefighting is more than physicality. It's as much about stamina, instinct, and listening. You'll get a taste of all that today."

With me, he didn't have to say. They might be at odds regarding his family, but he was here to do a job, and he clearly planned to do it well. She would expect no less from this man.

After all, he had always approached every task with the utmost professionalism.

A̲n hour later, Molly felt like she'd filmed every *Rocky* movie training montage, these firefighter drills making her rigorous six-mornings-a-week personal training sessions look like a lazy stroll down Melrose. The SCBA—self-contained breathing apparatus—

hooked over her shoulders added another twenty-five pounds. She had hauled a forty-pound hose bundle from one end of the gym to the other and pounded mercilessly on a dummy simulation to bring it back to life. With every potentially rib-fracturing compression, she'd imagined Ryan, though in her fantasy he hadn't made it. So sad.

Now she stood in the academy's outdoor plaza in ninety-degree heat gazing up at two ladders propped side by side against a wall. Molly steadied her nerves. She wouldn't say she had a fear of heights, but neither was she a daredevil who enjoyed looking at the world from a hundred feet up.

"You don't have to do this," Wyatt said, closer to her than she'd thought. "No one else is."

The cast and crew were inside, availing themselves of the AC, ice-cold beverages, and the chance to rest after being put through their paces. Molly wouldn't force the actors to scale a ladder, and it was old hat for the technical and stunt crew.

She gave a stubborn shake of her head. "I want to experience everything."

"Okay, but we're going to strap you in." Above a window near the top rung of the ladder, a rope had been threaded through a pulley and was attached to a harness. He held it for her to step into and secured it around her shoulders and waist. Again, the intimate proximity made her breath wobble. "I'll be on this other ladder, moving up at your pace. Take your time, it's not a race. No one needs saving today."

"How long do you usually take to get up there?"

"Competitive, huh?"

Hells yeah, but neither was she stupid.

"One rung at a time," Wyatt instructed, grave as ever. "Feel it with your boot and keep your eyes up to grab the next rung. When you get to the top, I'll be there to help you through the window, so wait for me." Nice of him to imply she might make it up there before him. "If at any time you feel uncomfortable, tell me, and you can come back down again slowly. Candidate Hale will be taking up the slack on the rope and holding the ladder below you."

No doubt, taking a damn good look at her ass. She met the knowing smirk of Candidate Hale, one of the academy trainees. No time to be concerned with that. Today, she wasn't Molly Cade whose butt had been voted "Best Booty" by *Maxim* three years running; she was a CFD firefighter with lifesaving on her mind.

Squaring her shoulders, she grabbed a rung at neck level and placed a boot on the bottom bar. Once certain she had a secure footing, she lifted herself—and the fifty pounds of gear attached to her body—off the ground.

One small step . . .

Ten feet up, she slid a glance to the other ladder. Wyatt was poised one-handed (of course) at her level, all laid-back strength and easy grace.

"'Kay?" he asked.

"Just fine."

She took another step, and another, careful to secure her hand before her boot found purchase. All good, no problems . . . until her foot slithered on the rung. A split second of panic popped in her chest and extra beads of sweat joined the damp sheen already painting her face. It was damn hot in this gear.

"Molly, you good?"

It was a variant of the same question she heard every day from her agent, publicist, interviewers on the red carpet, and her conditioned response never wavered. *Yes, I'm fine! Absolutely fabulous. Never better.* She was an old pro at spouting the party line, betraying no cracks in her public facade. Because as soon as that fissure appeared, it would widen in the blink of a Hollywood eye. All it would take was a sighting of her in sweats and no makeup at the Farmshop in Brentwood or a whisper from a chatty studio PA about her diva reaction to a cold cup of coffee. *She's not fine,* they would say. *Bitch is losing it.*

"You good, Molly?" Wyatt repeated.

Tell him you're okay. Tell him you've got this. The words of affirmation refused to climb her throat. After the photos appeared online, those private pictures taken by her husband, *for* her husband, she had withdrawn into a shell. Just the mere thought of the violation had her hyperventilating—not full-blown anxiety attacks, according to her five-hundred-dollar-an-hour therapist—but enough to make her think carefully about whom to trust.

And included in that was whether or not to trust herself.

She stared at her hand. Strong and purposeful, it could curl around a ladder rung and a man's thrilling bicep perfectly. She didn't dare look at her feet, but she knew they could pound the living daylights out of a running path and a kickboxing bag. She trusted these pieces of her body, but the thundering piece of machinery in her chest had let her down. It was so fragile, always leading her astray.

Never again.

"Molly, climb down."

"I'm—I'm fine." *Absolutely fabulous. Never better.* Speaking the words unfroze her legs, and quickly, she scrambled up while her heart pounded. *Shut it, you lump.* Adrenaline barged through her veins and she fed off it, every fleet step a willful *fuck-you* to the people who said she was finished, her career was in the toilet, that she'd never recover. Not quite knowing how it happened, she made it to the top, practically floating.

This was the point where she was supposed to wait for a guiding hand to pull her through, but she was faced with an open window. *No one needs saving today,* Wyatt had said.

She begged to differ.

"Molly, do not—"

She did. She swung her booted foot and hardware-encumbered body over the window ledge and sat there for a second's respite. Then she pulled herself inside. Triumph soared in her chest. Yes!

The brick-walled room was empty. That state of affairs did not last long. The large, intimidating body of her firefighter mentor soon filled the space around her. And he was pissed.

At least, she assumed that was the reason behind the slight flutter of molecules around his mouth. This was Wyatt Fox's version of fury, and like every other look on him, it was thong-meltingly hot.

"What the *fuck* was that?"

CHAPTER THREE

Wyatt's muscles seethed with a rage he rarely allowed to manifest. Anger was a useless emotion. It tended to get in the way of common sense, good judgment, and doing his job. He'd always been happy to leave the blowups to Luke and Alex, but right now, he was not feeling like himself.

He was feeling like a Dempsey.

"I told you to wait."

Those violet eyes held his gaze, steadier than his heartbeat, steadier than his breathing, amazing considering that two minutes ago her hands shook on that ladder. It had taken every fiber of his being not to reach out and close his hand over the white knuckles of her fist. Soothe her through her panic.

"I had a moment, but I pushed through it."

Appreciation of her honesty warred with fury at the rush of protectiveness that placed his heart and lungs in a clamp. He was not enjoying this in the slightest. All his life, he was careful about expending emotion, choosing to channel it into other pursuits. The marines, the CFD, a not-so-friendly hockey game between fire and police. But this last year had seen moments of deviance from the path of Zen, most recently with landing a punch on Eli Cooper's jaw because the prick had made his sister cry. But even that couldn't compete with the current flood of passion that had him in its grip.

This tiny woman in bunker gear that weighed half as much as her stood before him, chin up in bravado, hands on hips in defiance. Her face bore the shiny effects of her exertion. Her chest heaved with the effort of her climb. And in her eyes, challenge shone to anyone willing to take her on.

Moving in, he roughly unsnapped her harness and pulled it off her shoulders, but left the bottom half in place.

"Disobeying orders gets subordinates killed."

"I'm not your subordinate."

She had *not* just said that.

He didn't respond, just let the words live and breathe between them. Because once she had been exactly that as he dominated her curvy body. Removing her helmet, he pushed a strand of hair that had matted to her forehead out of the way. For no reason other than to touch her and affirm to himself that she was okay.

Christ, she was a beautiful woman.

A dangerously beautiful woman.

"I had the harness," she said, the first whisper of uncertainty in her voice, likely fueled by his refusal to give her any clue as to what was coming next. Silence was as much a weapon as a fist.

Never breaking eye contact, he unhooked the snaps on her bunker jacket, undressing her with the same care with which he'd clothed her a couple of hours ago. She wore a plain white T-shirt, the lacy fabric of her bra embossing the thin cotton layer from underneath. Something within him sparked.

Kindled.

Ignited.

Hunger unlike any he'd ever known—at least not since the last time he'd been inside her—hardened every inch of his body.

As if his gaze were a touch, her nipples popped against the fabric of her tee. He bit back a groan and let the jacket fall to the floor, the clank of equipment loud in the weighty silence enshrouding them. His cock felt thick and achy.

Her tongue slid across the suckable flesh of her lower lip. "I knew I wasn't in danger. The harness . . ." She gestured to the straps crossing over the crease where her stellar thighs met her shapely hips. "And you were there, too."

He pulled on the harness rope through the window, slowly, almost teasing, until it was completely in the room. It was still attached to the hook at the small of her back.

"If I give an order, I expect it to be obeyed." Choking the nylon rope short, he twisted it so it pulled hard against her body. The jerking motion pivoted her away from him like a dancing marionette. It also drew her gasp.

"Am I gonna need to keep you on a leash?" Unable to stop himself, he yanked the rope so she was within inches of his aching body. It might have been the inherent dominance in the move or the pressure of the harness against her ass, even through the thick layer of the turnout pants—whatever, it sucked a throaty moan from her that traveled a straight line from A to B, where B stood for his aching balls.

"You're already watching my ass like a hawk," she said over her shoulder, a marked tremble in her tone. "Additional restraints seem unnecessary."

Those beautiful eyes of hers remained hidden from view, but the graceful curve of her neck had him itching to take a bite. A primal urge to bomb her every cell with sensation rocked him. He wanted to run his bearded jaw over all that silky softness. Watch the gooseflesh pleasure-prickle her skin. Hear her throaty moans, the memory of which he'd used as spank bank material for a year after their affair. She'd always been so sensitive and their role-playing games had primed them hard, the slightest touch enough to shoot them both off into a stratosphere of pleasure. A light tug of the harness might give him what he needed.

Not idly, he wondered if she could come like this.

"We have a problem here, Molly."

"Oh?" she asked, all innocence, as if she had no freakin' clue what he was talking about. As if his using the harness as a sex toy was just SOP. *Yeah, babe, this is how we roll at CFD. We strap in, climb ladders, and get frisky with nylon ropes.* She wanted to play coy? He could do that—and make her suffer at the same time.

"You've hired me to do a job," he said, moving his mouth to her ear. There was no mistaking her shiver of anticipation as his beard drew the fines hairs of her neck to a stand. Needing to retain a grip on reality, he refused to breathe her in. Her pleasure, his pain. "To use my experience and expertise to keep you safe."

"I knew what I was doing," she said, a touch of

diva swagger not quite overcoming that quaver in her voice.

"Next time I give an order"—*tug*—"I expect"—*tug*—"full compliance." Another jerk of the harness and she was flush against his body. That amazing, award-winning ass practically cuddled against the dick that could probably have snagged its own prize for Hardest Cock of the Century.

Wyatt had now entered the land of Mollywood.

Whip quick, she turned with her hands raised to keep their bodies separated, but they landed on his chest, sizzling his skin with want. Cheeks flamed, her eyes blew wide, and she moistened her lips. Christ Jesus. He felt his body bend, his head incline, his will waver.

"Wyatt," she breathed, her mouth so close to his that he wouldn't have had to move an inch to taste her. He could have swiped his tongue across the seam, indulged his craving right then. After so long, it was the one unshakeable thought combusting every brain cell.

Losing his mind, that's what she was doing to him. She was the only one capable of turning him into this beast, the Abominable Un-Wyatt. Keeping her safe? What about keeping himself safe? He couldn't get involved with her, not when so much was on the line. He had Roni to think of, and the freak show that followed Molly Cade around was not going to help that cluster at all.

He broke away, his hand still clutching the rope like a talisman. But then he made a cardinal error . . . he dropped his gaze to the swell of her beautiful tits, their perky nipples like beacons ready to dash him to the rocks.

"I can't be getting distracted when your safety is on the line."

Error number two.

She folded her arms over her breasts—a deserved punishment—and her expression turned smug. She had him, and she knew it.

"That sounds like a 'you' problem."

True, but that didn't make it any less of one. "Just remember who's in charge," he murmured, the last gasp of a drowning idiot.

"Yep. You da man." On a soft laugh, she started to wriggle out of the rest of the harness.

They both knew he was in charge of shit.

If it made Mr. Stoic feel better to think he was running the show, Molly was happy to let his dude brain go there. That oh-so-tempting pressure she'd felt against her ass affirmed that she was the captain of this voyage. And she could so ignore the silky dampness between her thighs that might have bloomed when he brought her to heel like a Texas steer.

He had checked her body with a "leash" and she had *liked* it.

"Shit." He dropped the rope and stepped out of her orbit like she leached toxins.

"Hey, bro," came a smiling voice behind her.

Spinning around, Molly barely managed to suppress a gasp on encountering the prettiest specimen of male she'd ever laid eyes on—and she'd seen Joe Manganiello up close. Dirty blond hair dipped over a strong brow, framing blue eyes that sparkled with a puckish gleam. Sun-kissed skin made her wish sunglasses were included in a firefighter's standard gear. That calendar had not done him justice. Gage Simpson was a hundred times more dazzling in the flesh.

"Not even gonna ask why you're here," Wyatt said laconically.

"I was in the neighborhood." Gage's tee read: "All men are created equal, and then some become firefighters." He held out his hand. "I'm Gage, but you probably already know that."

As cocky as his reputation, then. She clasped his hand and shook. "I'm Molly, but I'm guessing you already know that, too."

They grinned at each other, buoyed by that recognition shared by two people who know they are attractive but have no interest in each other whatsoever.

"Everyone's dying to meet you," he said.

"Gage," Wyatt growled from behind her.

"They are?"

"My sister-in-law Darcy is a huge fan. Rifle-through-your-trash, Norman-Bates-in-a-dress levels. When we heard Wyatt volunteered for this gig—"

"Was 'voluntold,'" Wyatt muttered.

"It sent everyone into a tizzy."

"It did?" Molly slid a glance to Wyatt and found a muscle in his superhero jaw working itself into a tizzy of its own. "Firefighter Fox, I had no idea your family wanted to meet me."

"It's Lieutenant, and they don't. My brother is projecting his own desperate neediness onto the rest of them."

Gage grinned. "That's only half true. So how's prep for the movie going?"

Molly opened her mouth to respond, but Wyatt

spoke first. "Moving along. Start shooting in three weeks."

"Must have your script all settled." Gage smiled again, but there was tungsten underlying it. Not such a pushover after all.

"We have *a* script."

"But you'd like to amp it up with some ripped-from-the-headlines stuff. My sister's headlines."

"It would definitely make it more appealing. Look, Gage, I just want a chance to present my case to Alex. The movie doesn't have to be an exact rendering of her story, but I want to get it right. I want to know what it's like to be a woman in this profession. What it's been like for *this* woman in particular."

She could hear it in her voice. The desperation to fight back, to climb out of the hole she'd fallen into this last year. Attaching Alexandra Dempsey's name to the project would create Julia Roberts/Erin Brockovich levels of attention.

Neither Dempsey responded with any level of enthusiasm to Molly's pitch, so she changed tack. "I recognize your sister is a very private person."

Both men snorted.

"She's not?"

Gage shoved his hands into his jean pockets. "You saw the video of Alex cutting up that car, right? My sister doesn't care who knows her business. She's too busy living and saying screw you to anyone who doesn't like it. Alex is not the obstacle here."

"It's Eli," Wyatt said. "Eli wants to protect her. Some negative things were said about her in the press back when they were dating and she doesn't care. But Eli does."

Molly met Wyatt's gaze, and a frisson of something tethered them for a split second. Did Wyatt admire Eli's protective streak? That sort of defense was something Molly had always craved in a partner, but she had never received it from Ryan. Her husband had viewed her purely as a means to an end: whatever made Ryan Michaels, Superstar, look good.

"So who'll be playing me?"

Molly blinked back to the conversation and Gage's question. "You?"

"I recognize that it might be difficult to find someone to capture my grace, charm, good looks, and je-ne-sais-fucking-quoi, but it's a well-known fact that I'm Alex's number-one brother, her daily inspiration, and the reason she cut up that car in the first place. If it wasn't for me, there would be no America's Favorite Firefighter."

Wyatt rubbed his mouth, evidently hiding a . . . smile? Surely not.

"In the adapted script," Molly said, her tone careful, "we've conflated the brothers into just two. We ended up with someone who looks more like . . . uh, Luke."

A robust laugh filled the room. Stop the Facebook updates, was that what joy sounded like from Wyatt Fox?

"Luke?" Gage exclaimed. "You have got to be kidding me. Luke's the completely charmless Dempsey!" He motioned to Wyatt. "And that's saying a lot because he's got this one for competition."

To Molly's dismay, Wyatt was still smiling. It made her a touch dizzy. "When did I overtake Luke in the charm stakes?"

"You have your moments." Gage was clearly still miffed that there were no plans to capture his daring exploits on the screen. "But now's not one of them. Dunno what you think is so damn funny."

Wyatt gave Gage's hair a friendly rub. "Don't worry, Baby Thor. If you're good, we'll let you visit the set and see how your life is not being made into a movie."

Molly perked up. "Baby Thor?"

"That's what my sister-in-law Kinsey calls him. She thought he looked like that actor from the *Thor* movies, but all fresh-faced and cute."

Gage scowled, which did nothing to diminish either his fresh-facedness or his cuteness. "I'm ten times hotter than that guy. Like to see him blitz a ladder, rescue ten kids from a burning orphanage, and look this freakin' good while doing it."

Molly caught Wyatt's eye, and again saw unmistakable humor warming those Arctic blues. What an enlightening day. The Marine had at least two weaknesses: he was still attracted to her and he was crazy in love with his family.

She would make it her mission to find out the rest.

Her phone buzzed in the pocket of her bunkers and she pulled it out. It was a text from Cal.

Call me ASAP!

Sometimes Molly questioned who was the diva here.

"Well, gentlemen, it's been a pleasure. Nice to meet you, Gage."

"Likewise, Miz Molly."

She picked up the SCBA, helmet, and jacket loaded with tools—had she actually climbed a ladder in this gear? Go, her!—and headed to the stairway that led down to the ground floor.

"Later, Lieutenant." Refusing to meet Wyatt's gaze, she felt its sensuous weight all the same, heavy on her ass. Unsurprising. Guys always checked out her tush, and she knew she still looked damn fine and award-worthy—even in bulky bunkers.

As the fading *clop-clop* signaled Molly's descent, Gage turned to Wyatt with a shit-eating grin.

"Well, well, well, most *inter-est-ing*."

Wyatt gusted a sigh, because when his brother had a point to make, there was no stopping him. Classic Dempsey trait.

"All those dates I set you up on and no joy." *See?* "Then today I walk in and the sexual tension practically cannonballs me all the way to Indiana."

Ignoring that, Wyatt circled back to the primary problem. "You didn't have to be so damn nice to her. That's not how we're supposed to play this."

"The only people who have a problem with the movie idea are you and Eli. And we all know if Alex wants it, he'll cave."

True. In fact, his sister's reaction on hearing Molly was in town and sniffing for the rubber stamp had been typical Alex. *I'm gonna challenge her to an arm-wrestling contest and if she wins, she can tell my story.* He almost believed her.

Taking on this consulting gig, he had to acknowledge that some overlap with his private life was bound to happen. He should feel guiltier about how he had stepped up here. How he had let his curiosity trump common sense.

He should.

The key was to ensure it stopped there and didn't enter the realm of complicated.

Gage was back to his favorite subject: who's sexing whom. "So, you and Molly Cade. Don't think I've ever seen you so . . . giggly."

Wyatt had never giggled in his life. "Is there a point to this conversation?"

"She makes you laugh, she pisses you off . . ."

Surely there was an unsubscribe link, an off switch, a bolt of lightning that would shut his brother up.

". . . she kept leaning into you. Spidey senses are a-tingling."

"Just a job." Been there, done that, and hell if he didn't want more.

"I worry about you being alone," Gage said, all jokiness gone.

In a family where love was so freely given, it was assumed that everyone longed for a love connection that mirrored the great precedent set by Sean and Mary Dempsey. Despite Wyatt's annoyance with the constant sugar-to-the-max levels of romance in his family circle, he supposed he wouldn't mind having a woman to come home to, a couple of ankle biters wearing him out, a life that didn't revolve around work. But remarkably, women willing to suffer brooding lugs with the charisma of a hose bundle were thin on the ground.

So he sidestepped, as he always did when faced with Gage's loving concern. "I dream of being alone."

Gage offered up a wry grin. "You'd miss us."

"Like a tumor."

Wyatt's phone chimed, and as he checked it, Gage leaned in because his loving concern often came with a side of nosiness.

"Who's Jen?"

A thorn in my fucking side. "No one."

As Wyatt declined the call, Gage eyed him carefully, a query evidently on the tip of his tongue about Wyatt's "secret double life," as the rest of the family labeled it. Three or four nights a month, he made the trip downstate to Bloomington, overnighters that fueled his sibs' curiosity. Keeping secrets from the four closest people in the world to him was not his preference, but he had no choice.

Correction. Jen gave him no choice.

"International man of mystery," Gage said. "Luke said he asked you and it's not a woman, so I assume this Jen's your handler. CIA?"

"I'd tell you but then I'd have to kill you."

Smiling broadly, Gage bounced off, leaving Wyatt to pick up the harness that had been wrapped around Molly's body. He ran his fingers along the edges, imagining the warmth of her still embedded in the nylon.

Idiot.

Shaking off that whimsy, he threw the harness over his shoulder and reflected on that cheeky grin she hit him with as she left. How the sway of her hips turned his brain to lust-mush.

The call he'd just received threw a vat of ice on that foolishness.

He'd thought he could control himself around

Molly, yet every second in her presence loosed the granite hold on his emotions one more slippery, dangerous inch.

No more. All future interaction between them would be chaperoned on the set. He would do his job and keep his hands, eyes, and needy, greedy cock to himself.

◊ CHAPTER FOUR

The Camaro's undercarriage looked like shit. Comparisons could probably be made to Wyatt's own rusty undercarriage, but he'd rather not go there.

Forty-five minutes later, he'd worked off most of the dirt with a degreaser, but a couple of defiant rust spots still made his car-loving anal side wince. He'd need to jack it up and get a steam cleaner in there. Any more time staring up at it was going to result in a full-scale rehab: engine, trans, gas tank, and subframe connectors all out so he could expose the underside and do this properly. He was halfway through restoring her—had spent two years already—but he didn't mind how long it was taking. This cherry-red beauty, a '69 ZL1, the original *fuck yeah* muscle car, deserved her time to shine.

A low engine purr perked up his ears. Sounded like Eli's Merc pulling into the spare space in Wyatt's double garage. Chicago's former mayor was touchy about parking his precious motor on the street, so Wyatt usually left the spot open when he knew Eli would be venturing forth from the tony confines of Lincoln Park to the earthier hood of Andersonville. Beck's birthday party was today, a cookout hosted by Gage, and everyone was coming over.

Not feeling ready to be social—he had a whole afternoon ahead for that—Wyatt stayed put. A car door slammed. Soft footfalls sounded.

Not Eli, and definitely not Alex, who was never subtle in announcing her presence. He turned his head and got a surprising eyeful of color: peach-colored fabric skimming gold sandals and toes painted pink with red starbursts.

He heard a caught breath, an appreciative whistle, then one raspy word: "Beautiful."

Fuck, he'd recognize that voice anywhere.

He rolled out from under the car and stood to face his visitor: Molly Cade in the flesh. She stood at the entrance to the garage, the early afternoon sun bathing her in a corona of light, looking like an angel descended to earth. He tried to blink away the vision but no amount of clenching and unclenching his eyelids was producing sense out of this mirage.

She barely glanced at him, all her attention focused on the car. Eyes adjusting, and brain catching up, he let his gaze skim her body dressed in an ankle-length dress that hugged her breasts and flared out over her waist.

He was running out of synonyms for gorgeous when it came to this woman.

"A '69 ZL1," she said by way of greeting, because apparently explaining her presence wouldn't be happening. "Is it yours?"

She wore that dress, was the barometer by which he had measured every woman in the last five years, and she had the 411 on cars?

Someone up there hated his guts.

"You know your autos."

"My granddad was a mechanic. He had a '68 RS. Blue with white stripes."

He reached for a rag on the workbench, hyperconscious of his grease-streaked appearance. Of the throb in his blood. Of pretty much everything. "What happened to it?"

"Sold when he died. It wasn't in as good shape as this." She moved toward the car and stopped.

"Go on," he said gently, curious to see how she would treat it. For some reason, knowing that was more important than knowing the why of her presence here today. What idiot questioned manna from heaven?

She traced a slender finger along the hood. "Do you drive it?"

"I've taken it out a couple of times. She's still dragging and needs a new transmission. A couple of the kids from the foster home program I work with are helping me out."

She stayed put, her hand glancing the shiny surface. "Gage chased me down at the academy the other day and invited me. Told me to park around back. He said your brother's party was a spur-of-the-moment thing and no one would mind an extra warm body."

Tossed off casually as if the owner of the body was irrelevant. Well, someone did mind an extra *hot* body. He vowed to strangle Gage at the earliest opportunity.

Needing the time to compose himself, he continued wiping the engine grease off his hands. Slowly. One finger at a time.

"Your car's here," she said after several long seconds of awkward silence. "So you live here, as well?"

"Next door to Gage. He lives in the house we all

grew up in with his guy, Brady. Alex used to live there, too, before she moved in with Eli."

At the mention of Alex, her brow crimped. "I know Gage is fine with me here and your sister-in-law is apparently a fan, but how much resistance can I expect from the others?"

Interesting that she didn't see fit to comment on Wyatt's opinion, likely because she thought that showing up looking like God's gift to the lust-struck idiot cut him from the equation. "Like we said, mostly Eli, though I'd watch out for Kinsey, who's the suspicious sort. She works in PR. And Luke and Beck are pretty gung-ho about protecting the family. If they perceive a threat, they'll come out of their corners, gloves on, fists up."

A smile curved those kissable lips. "So pretty much everyone. But guns blazing isn't your style?"

"I prefer a quiet life." And Molly Cade, whether it was a six-day fuckfest or a ten-week movie shoot, was not conducive to a quiet life.

Truth be told, he wanted to show her off, shout from the rooftops that he had once attracted a quality woman like this. But then he recalled that their past connection was a tool she was using to get what she wanted now.

"Might be best if you kept our previous acquaintance on the down low. See if you can win them over with that charm of yours. If it looks like you're using our history together to get an in, then your chances plummet."

"Is that what you think? That I'm trading on our prior acquaintance to wrap you around my little finger?"

"Woman, I know you are."

A furrow dug between her eyebrows as she wrestled with a response. And hell if the one she came up with didn't surprise the shit out of him.

She laughed.

"It *might* have crossed my mind."

Damn, she was some kind of special. He loved that she didn't try to cover.

He threw the dirty rag on the workbench. Took a step toward her. "What else crossed your mind?"

"Well, my scheme involved a lot of eyelash fluttering"—quick demo—"coquettish turns"—hands on hips with a jaunty shimmy—"and flirty touching." Her hand glanced across his right bicep, over Logan's tattoo, shocking him to a shiver in the ninety-degree heat. "You've clearly been immune so far. I was about to unload the big guns at the academy the other day when your brother showed up."

"Put a crimp in your evil plan, huh?"

She lifted one beautifully rounded shoulder. "Well, he caught up with me and put the plan back on track."

"Lucky."

"Incredibly. But then evil plans often need a little luck to succeed."

Unsure how it happened (okay, he'd gladly erased the gap), he found himself standing close enough that he could have cradled her cheek with his dirt-embedded palm and gone in for the kill. Hell and damn, she was one fine woman, her beauty arousing his beast. A shower might remove his surface grease; it would take electroshock therapy to bleach his brain of the filthy thoughts running riot in his skull.

Time slowed and he chose to let the moment ride. It was the marine snipers' motto: *suffer patiently, and patiently suffer*.

"Tell me about the big guns in this evil plan of yours."

Her caught breath moved her breasts in a way that made him swallow.

"I might have gone with the nostalgia card. Reminisce about the good ole days in a certain hotel with a certain marine."

His body hardened. Nostalgia often had that effect.

"And if that didn't work?"

"Next on my list of dastardly deeds?" She looked thoughtful. "I might have recruited my hands, see if those big muscles were as hard as I remembered."

Do it, baby. Check. Them. Out.

She did, and shit, was that a whole other level of good. Soft palms caressed his pectorals, strayed briefly to his nipples, and settled on his shoulders.

"And if the plan still came up short?" His voice had gone husky. Intimate.

"You mean, if it wasn't evil enough?"

He nodded, no longer able to shape anything close to words. Her beauty was seeping into his bones along with her fleeting touches. Those summer-storm eyes flashed with a heady brew of power and desire.

"I would have unleashed my secret weapon." She leaned in and whispered, "Operation Feel the Beard."

"That's your secret weapon?" He felt his beard every day, and he could say with 100 percent certainty that it was fairly low on his list of ways into his good graces. "I think you're overestimating the beard, Hollywood. Now, if you were to feel another part of—"

She felt his beard. Sweet effen Christmas.

Her touch was a caress that started out soft, but increased in intensity as she moved her hand over one side of his jaw, then the other. A moan of pleasure slipped out before he could stop it.

She snatched her hand back. "Not working?"

"Not yet," he rasped. Barely. "I'll let you have another shot, though."

Her fingers returned to his jaw, exploring the underside, tracing a path through the softer growth. Each time her delicate finger pads made contact with his skin, zings of sensation traveled all over his body. What would it be like if she raked the hair on his head? Everywhere else?

Her eyelids had fallen to half-mast, this beard-feel moment seeming to affect her as much as him. Gently, he tipped up her chin with a knuckle, and she seemed to bloom under his touch. Like he was sun and rain to this withered plant. But really, he was the weed who came alive when their skin connected.

Another stray thought cut through the lust haze: it couldn't possibly be as good as before. He held on to that. Needing the safety net because, if it came anywhere close to matching their previous encounters, he'd be a goner.

He should not graze the delicate line of her jaw.

He should not stamp his erection on her belly, telling her with his body what he could never say in words.

He certainly should not close those last few millimeters to her lips and take the one thing he'd wanted since the moment she had strutted back into his life.

Pity the bad ideas always felt so damn good.

"I couldn't stay away," Wyatt admitted before he could bite it back. "Took the job. Had to see you."

Her breath hitched. "To satisfy your curiosity."

"Satisfied is a word that don't make sense between you and me."

"So you lied."

"You zigged." He leaned in, breathed her deep. "I zagged." He rubbed his beard against her jaw, the truth setting him free. So good to admit his need at last. A soft sound left her throat, more than a whimper, less than a groan. Working hard not to touch her with his dirt-streaked hands, he fisted the roof of the Camaro, caging her in on either side. "Gotta do what's necessary to fight evil in all its forms."

Every primitive impulse in him fired, and he lowered his lips to hers to let her know just how evil this was. How one kiss could incite and engulf, a flashover that destroyed everything in its path. Because she had to learn.

Those soft, sweet lips of hers should have recognized the peril, but it seemed Molly Cade liked living dangerously. The hands that should have pushed him away clutched at his shoulders. The words that should have ended this before it started never came. All he heard was a low-throated moan of encouragement, and he was lost.

Any concerns that kissing her couldn't possibly live up to his memory were blasted into dust by that first, hot joining.

Better.

Sweeter.

Hotter.

God, how? Kissing her was like realizing that your world until now was monochromatic. Color sparked behind his eyelids and traveled all over his body, setting off mini-explosions of bliss. Some guys didn't bother to take the time, but Wyatt loved kissing. Loved the build. Loved that deep, wet connection, and how it mimicked what would come later when he drove into her hot, slick heat.

Her moan was the sound of amazement that, even after all these years, it could still be so good. Her palms found his face and rubbed his beard again, more sure of her power over him. She liked it. Just as she would like it when he rubbed it against her inner thighs and used it to bring her off.

There was an excellent chance he was going to take her on the hood of his Camaro. And while that might be a dream come true if he were a horny fourteen-year-old—ah hell, a horny thirty-four-year-old—it was not how a classy woman like Molly Cade deserved to be treated. Neither was it appropriate with his family due to descend any second.

He pulled away. It killed him a little.

Make that a lot.

"So, Molly, you ready to meet the Dempseys?"

"Yowza, you look gorgeous!"

Molly smiled her thanks at Gage as she walked into his backyard, prepared to wow all the Dempseys with her sincerity and nonthreatening vibes. Beautifully landscaped with roses, azaleas, and an herb garden, the space had a tall wall shielding for privacy on one side. A water feature spilling into a koi pond looked like it had been naturally formed, its soothing trickle the perfect soundtrack on a hot summer day. One corner hosted a large picnic table with colorful cushion-layered benches, while a fire pit sat in the other. Community would be important to the Dempseys, and a pang of longing hit her at the thought of them eating, laughing, and loving in this urban sanctuary.

Better that than the pangs of a different kind currently working over more sensitive areas of her body. Her legs shook because she was nervous, she insisted, and not because she'd just gone ten rounds of mouth-to-mouth with Wyatt and emerged flattened.

It was a truth universally acknowledged (and universally despised by women everywhere) that as men aged, they tended toward improvement in their appearance. Their bodies filled out. They grew into the hard planes of their faces. Some of them even had the nerve to acquire more rakeable hair. While women sagged, developed wrinkles, and had to go to increasingly longer and more expensive lengths to maintain the status quo, men cruised by, looking *distinguished*.

So it should not have surprised her that years later, Wyatt Fox would have taken the word *more* and redefined it. Lantern jaw more square. Blue eyes more devilish. Muscles more . . . muscular. And don't get her started on the beard—the man was a lumbersexual fantasy made flesh. But it was just plain ridiculous that his kiss was even better than she remembered.

One minute she'd been working her flirt, the next she was intoxicated by everything Wyatt: the rough fingers, the hard body, the damn beard. Fine, they'd made out on top of a Camaro. Time to archive that and put on her other cap: businesswoman Molly Cade. She had a family to win over.

She walked over to Gage, offered a bottle of Zin as tribute, and accepted his kiss on the cheek. On his apron was the F-word followed by a list of check boxes for *You, Me,* and *Off.* Very cute.

"This yard is absolutely amazing," she said. "Did you do it all yourself?"

"Wyatt helped, though he should have kept his efforts for the rain forest next year. Pretty sure there are velociraptors mating in the undergrowth."

"Hilarious," Wyatt said as he grabbed a beer from a cooler and held it up in query for Molly. "Where's the real chef, kid?"

"The real chef is Brady, my hot-as-fuck boyfriend," Gage explained to Molly. "He owns a restaurant called Smith & Jones in the West Loop, and right now he's in Louisiana seeing his parents for his once-every-five-years visit. Probably gator wrasslin' in his downtime. So whatcha think of Wyatt's face blanket?"

Sneaky, sneaky, tacking the question onto the small talk like that. Was it so obvious that she'd just been wandering her fingertips all over that sexy pirate jaw?

Before she could defend herself with *the beard made me do it!* Gage shook his head pityingly at Wyatt. "Might be time for an intervention, brother mine. If I checked your closet right now, would I find worrying amounts of flannel? A ukulele on your nightstand, Wilco on your iPod?"

"Shut it," Wyatt said, not unkindly. He passed her a beer. "You wanted this."

She suspected he wasn't talking about the Sam Adams IPA.

"And she's about to get it." Gage's gaze slipped past Molly to a point behind her. "Welcome to the Seventy-Eighth Hunger Games."

Two couples had walked through the side-door entrance from the street, comprising a cool blonde, an inked brunette, and a pair of tall, tatted hunks. Luke Almeida and Beck Rivera, or the Hothead and the Boxer, as she had christened them in her research. Men she could handle—she'd been handling them all her life. Women were another story. The hate piled onto her over the last year, most of it from the so-called sisterhood, kept Molly in a state of perpetual alert around women she didn't know.

You're just a gal from Missouri, Mol. Thrusting her hand forward, Molly opened with, "Hi, I'm—"

"We know!" the stunning woman with the tattoos shrieked, clasping Molly's hand. "Gage said you'd be here. I'm a big fan." She nudged the Latino streak of heat beside her. "Beck, tell her."

"She's a big fan," he confirmed with a blinding grin.

Molly's hand felt like it might drop off, the woman was shaking it so hard. Horrified, the new arrival looked down. Let go. Goldfish gaped. "So. Sorry. I'm acting like such a star fucker. Crap, I said I wouldn't swear but I'm just so fucking nervous." She made a self-deprecating face. Adorable. "Starting over. I'm Darcy and this is my husband, Beck."

"Think she knows, *querida*," Beck said, amused. "She's done her research." One hand was slung around his wife's waist while the other rubbed her stomach protectively.

"Oh, you're pregnant," Molly said. *Nice going, dummy.*

Thankfully, she'd called it. "Yeah, five months gone. I'm a body artist and Beck's worried the baby's going to come out fully inked."

"It could happen," her husband commented with a look of such love for Darcy that Molly's heart melted.

The blonde behind them stepped in, hand outstretched, all business. "I'm Kinsey, nice to meet you. This handsome devil here is Luke." Luke gave a curt nod, not ready to be won over just yet. "I love your dress," Kinsey said, genuine appreciation in her voice.

"Thanks." Molly wasn't used to that. After the fakery of Hollywood, sincerity was a rarity. She'd spent a good hour deciding and undeciding what to wear. Dior, Saint Laurent, Michael Kors—nothing seemed suitable for a low-key barbecue with the Dempsey clan. She didn't want to appear like she was trying too hard, but neither did she want to look like a schlub and be judged for not making the effort. *Us* magazine had a monopoly on the "They're Just Like Us" feature; she certainly didn't need to hear it muttered with disdain from the mouths of the women who Molly suspected, despite Wyatt's claim to the title, were the true gatekeepers to the inner circle.

For the next ten minutes, she sipped her beer and chitchatted with the Dempseys, her nerves in a jangle while she waited for Alex to show. Wyatt had disappeared, not that she was tracking his every movement or anything.

"My award-winning Gage-a-rita," Gage said, holding out an oversized margarita glass.

"Okay, before I commit to that bucket of awesome, I'm going to need to use your bathroom."

He motioned with his free hand toward the house. "Top of the stairs. No snooping in the medicine cabinet."

"Spoilsport," she muttered with a grin.

When she entered Gage's kitchen, a shower-fresh man scent tingled her nostrils. Yum. And then her stomach did back flips at the sight of Wyatt standing with his back to her, complete with deliciously bitable ass, broad shoulders, and damp hair. Only when he spoke did she realize he was on the phone. (She'd started her perusal at butt level. So sue her.)

A heated conversation was in progress, or as heated as this man was capable of. "Jen, this can't go on. We have the perfect opportunity here to make this right."

Jen? Molly edged back, reluctant to intrude.

Wyatt was still talking. "I've done every single thing you've asked. There's only so long I can keep this up."

Seconds passed, then: "I'm not threatening you. But it's been a year."

A moment later, he hung up. *Très mystérieux.* Tension barreled off him, and she had a sudden urge to touch the back of his neck, massage out the stress that phone call had put there.

With a rather clichéd interrupting cough, she made her presence known. He turned and *whoa*. Across his vast chest, a blue, red, and white target stretched taut, the logo for the Who. Butter-soft jeans clung fondly to his thick thighs. And she'd thought the vista from the back was spectacular.

"Just headed to . . ." She waved to some point above their heads.

His expression turned a few notches up on the broody scale, and wordlessly he stepped back, creating a (too) wide space for her to pass on by. Given what had happened in the garage, that distance was probably not the worst idea.

A few minutes later, Molly emerged into the yard to find that the woman of the hour had just arrived and now stood hand in hand with one of the handsomest men Molly had ever seen. Apparently the Dempseys had some sort of monopoly on sex gods, both in house and out. All this hotness concentrated in one small area? Surely there was a disturbance in the world's gravitational pull.

Alex Dempsey was even more of a knockout in person, Wonder Woman herself in the flesh with smooth olive skin and a riot of gorgeous copper-streaked dark hair. For a woman who supposedly wore her emotions on her sleeve and then liked to brag about the soiled shirt, she was remarkably unreadable as Molly approached. There was *one, two, three* seconds of slice-through-butter tension where the entire gathering seemed to hold a collective breath.

"Looks like we've got Hollywood royalty in the house," Alex said, a luminous grin breaking wide. "Has Gage finagled his way into the movie yet?"

"I was going to wait until my Gage-a-ritas got her good 'n' sloppy," Gage called out from his spot at the grill. "I know there's a walk-on part with my name on it."

"Hi," Molly said, sticking her hand out straight to mask its slight shake. She'd met actual royal personages; she'd lunched with Meryl Streep, for heaven's sake. Yet meeting this woman she admired so much was more nerve-racking than her first screen test.

Alex narrowed moss-green eyes at Molly's hand, ignored it, and went in for the hug. A tight, bone-crushing, *you're my new best friend* hug. "Shit, you are tiny. You planning to bulk up before the shoot?"

Molly loosed a breath of relief. "We'll CGI in some muscle."

"The hair, too? Eli would never forgive you if you didn't get the hair right. He's obsessed with these handfuls of sin." Alex winked at Molly over Eli's grunt of discontent. Definitely not the male reaction she was used to, which made her appreciate his attitude all the more. He was worried about Alex, and his obvious love for her refused to be diminished in the face of a Hollywood smile.

Alex hadn't agreed to Molly's as-yet-unspoken pitch, but her reaction so far definitely boded well.

"Eli, be nice to our guest," Alex said to her scowly-faced man. "Or I'll take back my yes." She held up her left hand, its fourth finger twinkling with a pink diamond ring, and displayed it HSN-style to the group. "Look what happened to me last night, family unit."

Kinsey and Darcy screamed, and even Molly found herself going a bit gaga. Love was in bloom and that was always a reason to turn into a squealing imbecile. Alex recounted the proposal, something about a domed platter at a restaurant and a letter on a legal scroll, and it all sounded like the stuff movies were made of. As if these two could get any more cinematic. Eli watched his fiancée like she was more precious to him than a million of those diamonds on her hand.

He'd be a tough nut to crack, but Molly was used to hard-asses. *Prepare to be charmed, Mr. Mayor.*

CHAPTER FIVE

So that was it. Another one of Wyatt's sibs officially shackled. Not that there had ever been any doubt about the direction Alex and Eli were heading. The guy was nuts about her, had been from the minute he laid eyes on her, and not even a punch in the face from Wyatt stopped him from going after what he wanted. Wyatt couldn't help his admiration for that. And the ice-pick gaze Eli was laying on Molly said it all—he'd protect Alex with his dying breath.

While the ladies went into nuclear meltdown over Alex's ring, Wyatt handed a beer to Eli, and they both stepped out of the fray. After a couple of drafts, Eli spoke.

"Want to tell me why I'm in such esteemed company?"

"Had no idea you thought so highly of me."

Eli snorted a laugh that didn't quite make it. "So what's going on here, Fox?"

"Gage."

That earned Wyatt the Cooper side-eye. "Yeah. Gage."

It was admittedly weak. Technically, Gage had invited her, but Wyatt had set this mess in motion when he stepped up and took that job. He'd convinced himself he was doing it to keep Molly on a leash (so *not* the time to be thinking of that harness). Bullshit. He'd wanted to see her again. He'd put his own desires before the needs of the family—of Roni—and now that lapse in judgment was coming back to bite him.

"Not sure this will help your case," Eli said.

As the only person who knew about the shit pool Wyatt was currently wading through, Eli had made a good sounding board the last few months. Keeping Roni under wraps had weighed on him, but Eli never judged. Just stowed it in the vault, assuring Wyatt that his position was weak. That, for the moment, he was playing his cards right.

"Alex wants to say yes to the movie," Wyatt said.

"She does." Eli grimaced. "And if it's what she wants, I can't stop her. But you could if you came clean about the real reason why this is a bad idea."

Keeping secrets was not Wyatt's natural inclination—he didn't have Eli's sneaky dexterity in moral gray areas—but locking down his emotions was definitely in Wyatt's wheelhouse. He had always operated at a slight remove from the rest of them, the Dempsey least likely to fit the mold. This little white lie was merely an extension of his characteristic reserve. He was the least excitable of them all, and cool heads were a necessity right now.

Whether they'd see it that way was another story.

Wyatt's greedy gaze found Molly again, ostensibly to check in on how she was doing. She'd looked pretty surprised at Alex's reaction, which had been both typical Alex and wholly unexpected. The one thing Wyatt could say with certainty is that his sister

was predictably unpredictable. Now Molly was chatting easily with everyone, charming their flip-flops
off. Even Luke seemed to be on board, if that deep,
bass laugh was anything to go by. His brother had
always been the family bellwether. So Luke goes, so
go the Dempseys.

"But aside from the obvious," Eli murmured, "it
looks like you have another problem on your hands."

Wyatt waited a beat. Then another.

"Guess all those dates Gage used to set you up on
were missing one thing."

"What's that, then?"

"Molly Cade."

Cheeks warming, Wyatt took a slug of his Coke
while Eli chuckled evilly. So, his attraction was obvious. To look at her was to want her.

He wasn't evolved enough to react to Eli's observation with grace, so he simply muttered, "Shut the
fuck up, Cooper."

Which drew an even louder laugh from his future
brother-in-law.

Molly couldn't remember the last time she'd had
this much fun: the Dempseys lived up to their billing
and then some. Staunchly loyal, gloriously profane, a
special bond that couldn't be faked. It took a singular
woman to hold her own in this sea of testosterone
and bash-you-over-the-head-Dempseyness, and both
Kinsey and Darcy had the skills in spades.

Kinsey handed her a (second) Gage-a-rita and took
a seat in the periwinkle-blue Adirondack chair beside
her.

"They're a lot to take in all at once," she said with a soothing smile. "Helps if they're naked."

Because Molly was suave like that she choked on her drink. "Excuse me?"

"That's how I met Luke. Half naked in the locker room at his firehouse after he'd pissed me off by not returning my calls. But the sight of him in that low-slung towel, all steam-fresh from the shower . . ." Her wistful sigh accompanied a shiver of remembered appreciation. "Well, my mind definitely went there. And I can see your mind going there, oh, about every other second where Mr. TDB is concerned."

"TDB?"

"Tall, Dark, and Brooding. Aka Wyatt." Darcy had appeared out of nowhere and now took a seat on Molly's other side, resting a can of soda on her baby bump. "Kinsey's terrified of him."

"I'm not!" Kinsey protested in a stage whisper. "Okay, maybe I was at first. It's just that I can usually read people really well, and Wyatt is a total cipher. It made for some awkward alone time, I'll tell ya. But the two of you . . ." She gave a crafty smile. "You seem to have a language all your own. He likes you."

"He does?" Molly sought out Wyatt, who had not paid her one iota of quality attention since they arrived, never mind that he had just ravished her mouth with the Thigh Tickler a couple of hours ago. And yes, Thigh Tickler was aspirational. "What gave it away? The squinting off into the middle distance, the scowling when he accidentally looks my way, or the determination to ignore me at every turn?"

"So you don't want to be ignored?" Darcy asked, the epitome of coy.

Molly opened her mouth. Closed it immediately. Damn, they were observant, or she was tipsy. Probably both.

She tried again. "I understand he feels threatened and his family is his primary concern. With this movie, I want to honor the CFD, firefighters, strong women." Herself. She wanted to restore the pride she used to feel in a job well done. "I can make a good movie without Alex's stamp of approval, but I can make a great one with it."

"So what's the movie about?" Kinsey asked. "And don't you already have your script locked down?"

"Yes and no. It's about Kelly Flynn, a Chicago-Irish female firefighter"—she gestured to herself—"and her struggle for respect on the job. The current script has her falling for another firefighter played by Gideon Carter."

"Dreamy," Kinsey said approvingly.

"Yeah, he thinks so, too." The women laughed softly while Molly bit her lip and glared at her Gage-a-rita. *No more tequila for you.* "The adapted script would include scenes of her run-in with bigot billionaire Sam Cochrane, who we'll rename for the movie and change enough to ensure we're not sued, and her developing relationship with the mayor of Chicago. Right now, those parts are smaller but can be enlarged if we get the go-ahead from Alex."

Darcy's mouth hooked in a wicked curve.

"*Aaaand* I just remembered that you're Sam Cochrane's daughter," Molly added. *Awk-ward.*

The glowing woman smiled. "Yep. We fell out for a while, not helped by the hate-a-thon he was waging against Beck's family. But the idea of being a granddad has softened him up." She rubbed her belly. "My little peacemaker."

Hearing that warmed Molly's insides. Family was important, and she knew all too well the regret at leaving a promise of reconciliation to wither on the vine. Memories of Molly's own tricky relationship with her grandmother Ellie MacNeill, the woman largely responsible for raising her, gushed to the fore. Molly's parents, both doctors in Medicine without Borders, had usually been out of the country on humanitarian missions. After their deaths in a car crash in Zambia when Molly was fourteen, her grandparents had done the heavy lifting, seeing her through her inconsolable grief and troubled teenage years, a combination of nightmarish proportions.

Raised strictly and expected to follow her parents into medicine, Molly had shocked everyone back in New Haven, Missouri, with her decision to become an actor. Especially Gran. Even her relatively quick success (after six years of poorly paid theater gigs and one semi-lucrative tampon commercial) hadn't swayed her disapproving grandmother. No, only when Oscar came calling did Gran finally offer a grudging respect.

Which was immediately snatched back as soon as those photos went viral. By the time the divorce was final and the furor had died down, cancer had already eaten away at Ellie's insides. Too late for Molly to make amends. Too late to go home again.

The lively conversation continued around her, and Molly fought to find her place in it.

"You know, Alex is interested," Kinsey was saying with a contemplative look toward where the guys stood around the grill, discussing meat char levels or something equally manly. "But Wyatt and Eli are the big naysayers. Not sure why they're so against it."

"Well, she'd better say yes." Gage paused in front of them on his way out from the kitchen with a plate of peach halves ready to be grilled. "This talent should not be going to waste."

Kinsey groaned. "I created a monster. The day you called me saying you wanted in on that CFD calendar shoot, I should have shut you down."

Darcy touched Kinsey's arm. "You gifted something special to Chicago, maybe the world. Let's not be greedy. Time to share."

That drew Molly's laugh. "Who am I to get in the way of what the people want? Perhaps I can find a small part for you, Gage. We always need shirtless background candy."

Gage's handsome face lit up. "Finally, someone who recognizes gym-given talent when she sees it." And then his face crumpled as his gaze slid to the gable of the house. A hulk of a man stood there, sporting more tattoos than all the Dempseys combined, biceps fighting his sleeve hems, and a buzz cut that revealed harsh planes and raw scar tissue on his brutally compelling face.

"Brady," Gage whispered in a voice filled with so much yearning that Molly's heart checked to hear it. He took a step, realized that his hands were full of fruit, and with a quick pivot, thrust the plate of peaches at Molly and made a beeline for the new arrival. The big guy dropped a duffel bag to the ground, freeing his arms for Gage's full-body embrace. They kissed lustily, with total abandon, and frankly it was the hottest thing Molly had seen in some time.

Or since Wyatt Fox's beard had zeroed in for that sexy kiss.

"Damn," she said under her breath.

"I know," Darcy said. "They're like the poster boys for hot alphas everywhere."

Gage finally removed his suction cup of a mouth from Brady, picked up his duffel, and dragged him over.

"Brady, this is Molly. She's gonna put me in the movies."

Brady nodded a not-unfriendly greeting at Molly and turned to Gage, grinning. "Your whole life is a movie, Golden."

Gage's smile could have powered the city's grid. Not relinquishing his hold on Brady, he pulled the huge man toward the house. "You guys can manage here, right?"

"Aren't you going to even pretend you have something to show him inside?" Alex called out with an air quote on the word *show*.

"Nope. I haven't seen my man in three days and we're now going to have noisy, sweaty reunion sex. May I suggest you turn up the music or use earplugs?"

On a bubble of laughter, Gage and a flame-faced Brady practically fell over each other trying to get into the house. Shaking her head, Alex joined the women around the empty fire pit and gestured with a beer bottle to the men near the grill. "Watch this. Power vacuum."

All eyes refocused on the yard's center of operations. Now that Gage had temporarily ceded his rule as grillmeister, the remaining players were eyeing the unattended grill with serious intent.

"My money's on the boxer," Darcy said.

"I'll take that action," Kinsey said. "Twenty bucks says the bare-knuckled bar brawler comes out on top."

Alex laughed. "Eli's a lover—I mean, a lawyer—not a fighter."

Molly was silently rooting for the Marine, but ten seconds and a little friendly elbow shoving later, Luke had installed himself as undisputed ruler. To seal the deal, he waved the grill spatula around like a scepter.

"*Game of Thrones* comes to a backyard cookout," Kinsey said, clearly proud that her man had emerged victorious.

Molly's heart twanged at the easy authenticity around her. She tried to imagine Ryan at a gathering like this, but the image refused to form. Her ex-husband's parties were notorious for their opulence and grandiose pretentions. The swankiest food, the hippest DJs, the best people. No one wore board shorts or Who T-shirts (unless it was ironic). No one talked about anything but who had signed on to what movie, how much less that multi-honored actress got paid compared to her less talented male costar, which studio executive had called which diva a spoiled brat in a hacked email.

Molly didn't miss it. And she certainly didn't miss Ryan's personality change when the partygoers left. *That cheek kiss was about two seconds too long,*

Molly. Are you banging him? Supposedly said in jest, but she knew better. Though anything was preferable to Ryan's suggestions on how to spice up their marriage, by inviting into their bed any one of the aspiring actress-singer-models LA vomited by the thousand. Ryan usually got what he wanted, but she had repeatedly shut down the threesome talk with a countersuggestion of her own, one she knew Ryan would never tolerate: *Maybe we should ask another guy? What's good for the gander . . .*

Sloughing off those noxious memories, she replaced them with something more pleasurable: a beard-enhanced kiss with a mountain man firefighter who took his sweet, sweet time.

Blame it on heated remembrance, the gentle ribbing of the Dempsey women, or her just-drained Gage-a-rita, but she couldn't help discreetly checking out Wyatt as he stood shoulder to shoulder with Eli. Both men were impressive in stature, though Wyatt sported a rough-hewn edge that appealed to her more than Eli's GQ handsomeness.

Eli was talking, but Wyatt's steel-blue gaze magnetized to her and locked on. At last. To be the focus of such intense regard was heady. Drugging. *Oh, think I can handle you, Marine.* She refused to break his visual hold on her until Wyatt's expression changed from sexy-stoic to one she hadn't encountered before.

Surprise—and it was not directed at her. Molly tracked his gaze over her shoulder to where a girl stood near the adjoining gate to the next backyard. In her midteens, with dark, purple-streaked hair and

serious hardware in her ears, she projected a 'tude
Molly could feel from twenty feet out.

Mischievous, surprisingly familiar blue-gray eyes
were sealed on Wyatt.

"Hey, Daddy," she said.

◊ CHAPTER SIX

Daddy?

That cheeky little minx.

Wyatt dipped his gaze to the ground and found it surprisingly intact. No giant rent in the fabric of the earth. No world-ending hell mouth beckoning. Hell was very much present and accounted for in his brother's backyard.

Roni, who must have thought her entrance would be hilarious, now looked like she might have misjudged the situation. A flicker of pain crossed her face. With her perpetually cynical view on everything, it was so easy to forget that she was just a teenager. Barely fifteen.

He moved forward, conscious of how his skin prickled with the heat of a thousand Dempsey stares.

"Daddy?" he heard Luke say behind him. Wyatt didn't dare look back, knowing his sibs were seeing exactly what he did every time he looked at her.

Roni was the spitting image of her father.

"What are you doing here, sweetheart?" He looked over her shoulder, waiting for the punch line. All he saw was her backpack. "Is your mom with you?"

"No, she's still in Seattle. Grams dropped me off. Sick of me, she said." She drew in a shaky breath and blew it out to ruffle the dark, curly hair that curtained half her face.

Shit, this was not how it was supposed to happen. He had wanted to prepare the rest of them, but Roni's mother had pinned him between a rock of secrecy and a hard place of lies.

"Wyatt," Luke said, closer now, his tone foreboding. "Somethin' you'd like to tell us?"

"Yeah." He scrubbed his mouth, snatched a breath, and instantly sought out Molly. Not sure why, but there it was. Those big eyes watched him keenly. He saw calm there and took strength from it. "This is Roni."

Luke hadn't looked at her, maybe couldn't look at her. "Your kid?"

"No." God, he wished. It would have been a damn sight easier if she was. "Logan's daughter. She's my niece. Our niece." He placed an arm around her shoulder because she had to be feeling so exposed right now. Her body stiffened at his touch, but he held on. He'd been trying to hold on for a year.

"She lives a couple of hours away in Bloomington with her mom and grandmother. At least, she usually does." He turned to her. "I'm gonna take a stab here and guess your mom doesn't know where you are." Jen had left a few days ago for an eight-week course in Seattle, getting an advanced certificate in nursing. Wyatt had tried to persuade her that now would be a good time to break the news and let Roni visit. She had refused.

She always refused.

Roni snorted. "Mom's none the wiser."

"Did you say your gran dropped you off? You mean, outside, just now?"

What the hell? That she'd been abandoned by her grandmother released a rush of rage in Wyatt's chest.

"She said I'm out of control. She can't cope with me, so now that Mom's out of town you should be the one to take me on while she's gone." An eyebrow raise accompanied that challenge, and in that moment, she looked so like Logan that Wyatt's heart cracked in half. Was it possible she had engineered this to force her grandmother's hand?

She eyed the crew warily before turning back to Wyatt. "I know you don't want me here."

"That's not true." God, how could he explain that his niece here with his people was the culmination of his heart's desire? Try that without making her mother into the villain. "Sweetheart, everyone wants to meet you. But first, I need to talk to them all and let them know where you've been all this time."

"Holy shit," Roni said.

Okay, not the expected reaction, but then he got it. Molly stood in front of them looking so damn fine he was practically bowled over by her beauty. *Holy shit* was right.

"Hey, Roni, I'm Molly. So are you a Coke or a Sprite girl?"

Eyes wide, Roni dropped her jaw at the sight of one of the most famous women in the world standing in a humble, albeit very nicely landscaped, backyard on the North Side of Chicago.

"Are you—?"

"Sure am," Molly said with a wink. "Just another day at chez Dempsey, kid."

She smiled at Wyatt, which was incredibly classy of her considering he'd done nothing but alternately scowl and ignore her all afternoon. Right now, she was the only other adult he was brave enough to look at, her outsider status the branch he clung to.

"You go with Molly for a moment while I talk to your aunts and uncles."

Without looking at him or anyone else, Roni followed Molly into the house.

Drawing a jagged breath that serrated his lungs and felt like it might be his last, Wyatt turned to his family. Expressions of hurt and betrayal greeted him. He deserved every one.

As expected, Luke spoke first. "This is where you've been sneaking off to every week. How long have you known?"

"Just over a year. Logan never found out. It was a one-night stand long before he met Grace." Logan's widow, Grace, had moved back to Boston to be with her family after his death nine years ago. "Jen—that's Roni's mom—was training to be a nurse when she met Logan at a bar on the South Side. She thought the father was someone else because she used protection with Logan. She married this other guy but they divorced a few years ago."

"Logan's strong little swimmers," Beck said proudly before his brow furrowed. "So how did she find out it was Logan for sure? And how did she find you?"

Wyatt rubbed his forehead. He could feel a head-ache coming on. "About six years back, when Roni was nine, she got sick. Leukemia." At the newly shocked expressions, he quickly put them at ease. "She's okay now. But they did some genetic testing and found out the man Jen had thought was Roni's dad wasn't her dad after all. Not that it mattered, because he's a total deadbeat drunk. Jen figured out it must have been Logan, but by then it was too late."

"Six years," Alex said, her voice shaking with anger. "She's known for six years. Why did she wait so long to tell us?"

Good question, and her true reasons would be a bitter pill for them all to swallow. "Nursing Roni back to full health was her number-one concern. At the time, we didn't rate."

"But then you found out." The beginnings of DEFCON Luke looked to be imminent. "A year ago. And kept it from us. Was it because you're his biological brother and we're not?"

"That's not it." Or at least Wyatt didn't think so, but he supposed it was possible he had subconsciously assumed the role of ultimate decider because of his blood connection with Logan. There was never any intention to keep them in the dark forever.

"Roni's grandmother got in touch with me behind Jen's back because Jen was having money problems. You wouldn't believe how pissed I was when I heard, but she had her reasons. She'd done some research since finding out Logan was Roni's dad. Knew us by reputation. How tight we were, how crazy we are about family—"

"If she knew that," Alex cut in, every word enunciated with fury, "then why the hell would she keep our niece from us?"

"Because some of the ways we express our love of family are not exactly the norm. I was working on her, getting her to come around."

"And what happened?" Alex asked, her voice more plaintive now with doubt that split his lungs apart. "Why wouldn't she want us to meet her?"

"You happened. First Luke, then you."

Alex's face collapsed in shock.

"Jen's quiet, keeps to herself, and she doesn't want to involve Roni in a whole lot of drama. Her ex was an alcoholic prick who was in and out of Roni's life, and that's when he thought he was related to her. When he found out Roni wasn't his, he cut off all contact with a nine-year-old girl who was fighting for her life." Who the fuck does that? Even now, the knowledge of how this bastard had treated Roni before and after her cancer diagnosis set Wyatt's molars grinding. "They've both been let down and, with Roni sick for a couple of years, Jen's hugely protective. She doesn't want to risk any more toxic influences in her daughter's life, not after the way her ex bailed. Above all else, she wants stability for Roni. I'd just about convinced her that meeting you all was for the best when the next thing she sees are Luke's fists plastered all over the Internet after he punches up a CPD detective in the family bar. Then America's Favorite Firefighter is using the Jaws of Life as her primary method of communication in the video that's at ten million hits and counting. Doesn't exactly scream 'stable home life.' "

Alex was still fuming. "You mean she keeps our niece out of our lives—*you* keep our niece out of our lives—and it's *our* fault?"

Wyatt knew it was messed up, but he had been trying to work this out so no one would feel hard done by. Jen might not have moral right on her side, but she had legal. Her ex was at minimum emotionally, if not physically, abusive when he drank, and that history was her frame of reference for every decision regarding Roni. Seeing the Firefightin' Dempseys, as they'd been scathingly nicknamed by the press, from the outside might give anyone pause.

"She's her mother. Her guardian. Legally, we're nothing."

Alex turned to Eli. "This woman pulls this stunt and we have no rights? How is that possible?"

"Honey, Wyatt's right, you have no standing here," Eli said. "None of you do. Your brother's been doing the best he can under the circumstances."

Aw. Shit.

Awareness dawning, Alex puffed up. "You. Asshole. You *knew* about this."

"Yes, I did," Eli said, unfazed by Alex's reaction. He'd been managing her temper for months now and he had no problems standing up to her and talking her down. "Wyatt didn't tell me, but I had background checks run on you all before we started dating."

"Of course you did." Alex was clearly ready to tear her fiancé a new one when Beck cut her off.

"Could we hold off on the domestic drama for a sec and deal with the real issue here? We've just found out that we have family. Logan's blood, our brother's blood, is running through that girl's veins, and now we have to make up to her the years she's missed out on with the Dempseys."

Wyatt sent a look of immense gratitude to his

brother. Thank God for Beck, who had always been the calm one—at least, outside of the ring. If Wyatt could win them over one by one . . .

His eyes met Luke's. They had gone through a lot together since their teens, brothers in every way that mattered. Wyatt had known the Dempsey he was closest to would not take it well, but he'd hoped to break it gently. Not that news like that was capable of being broken gently—or that Luke was capable of being reasonable about anything. And could Wyatt blame him? After Logan and Sean died nine years ago, the two eldest Dempseys had been faced with a choice. Both in the marines, one of them needed to leave and play Dempsey dad to the young 'uns, especially Gage, who was only sixteen at the time and would have been put in group care.

Wyatt had failed the test, his grief over the loss of the two men who had shaped him so heart-crushing that he couldn't bear to be around the rest of his family. Luke had stepped up, like always. Holding back this information about Logan's girl was a punch to his brother's gut. Right now? Luke's expression was far from brotherly.

And Wyatt had thought resisting the charms of Molly Cade would be his biggest challenge this summer.

Well, this was awkward. Of all the days to visit. If Molly hadn't felt like an intruder before, this sure as hell took the cake.

"Can I get you anything? Soda? Water?"

Roni sat at the kitchen table, her body language

shouting that she wanted to be anywhere but here. Dressed in black, and wearing what looked like a manga character on her tee, she rocked the stock attitude of "disaffected youth" straight from Central Casting. Stunningly beautiful, though—or she would be in about a year, when her remarkable bone structure was revealed.

Passing over Molly's offer of refreshments, the girl shifted her gaze nervously toward the backyard. "Not exactly rolling out the welcome mat, are they?"

"Everyone's just surprised to see you, is all."

Roni looked unconvinced. She locked eyes on Molly, their similarity to Wyatt's uncanny. That unholy blue. "I liked you in *Sweet Rain*. My mom didn't think you deserved the Oscar nomination, but I thought you were good."

"Thanks. It's my favorite part of everything I've done."

Roni waited. Now that she'd confessed something, Molly supposed it was her turn to explain her presence.

"I'm making a firefighter movie in Chicago and your uncle Wyatt is the tech consultant on it. So what did you do?"

"Do?"

"Well, your grandmother said you were out of control and she couldn't handle you anymore. What stunt did you pull to get here?"

She flushed. "I don't want to be here."

A likely tale. Molly wasn't so far removed from her teenage years that she didn't recall the underhanded methods she'd used to get her own way. Roni might be fronting don't-give-a-damn, but every furtive glance toward the backyard said differently. She cared. Deeply. As Molly had employed a few sneaky stunts of her own to meet the Dempseys, she could see where the girl was coming from.

Who wouldn't want to meet them?

The sound of raised voices trickled through the screen door. Renewed worry creased Roni's brow.

"People don't sound too pleased I'm here."

"They're just surprised that Wyatt didn't tell them." She cocked her head. "I suppose he has a good reason for that?"

Teenage eye roll. "My mom doesn't like the Dempseys. She thinks they're trouble."

Molly couldn't disagree with her there. "Still, seems kind of tough on everyone to keep you all apart." She had no right to be critical of this mother's decisions. Lord knew what went into making them, but at the same time, the Dempseys were so family oriented, the pros had to outweigh the cons.

"She used to be a nurse in Chicago years ago and she knew some people in the fire department who told her about them. They get into fights and go mad dog on people who piss them off. She's kind of over that since my dad"—a furious hurt froze her expression for the briefest moment—"since the guy I *thought* was my dad messed her around. But Wyatt found out about me and he visits every week, trying to play the caring father figure. Not that I need him or anything." She shrugged. "I'm all Mom's got. She's gonna kill Grams when she finds out she sent me here."

Molly suppressed her smile. Yeah, Grams "sent" her here. But more important, Molly now understood Wyatt's reluctance to support her bid for Alex's story.

No drama, he'd said. *No headline-grabbing encounters*. This girl was his number-one consideration, the reason why he was snarling at Molly's attempts to infiltrate the Dempsey defenses.

"Um," Roni said, "I need to use the bathroom."

"Top of the stairs, to the left."

Head down, she shuffled out. Wyatt walked in thirty seconds later with a querying frown.

"Little girls' room. How's it going out there?"

Tension radiated from him, the feeling of an unexploded bomb making the air heavy. "Everyone's reacting with the typical nuance and restraint I've come to expect from my family."

"It's a lot to take in."

Nodding, he rubbed his mouth. "Thanks for stepping up there. Appreciate that. I think everyone was too shocked to figure out what came next. Now I gotta call her mom and grandmother and work this out." He held her gaze. "With Roni showing up like this, it puts a different spin on things."

"You need to keep everything drama-free while she's here." Which meant that having the Dempseys attached to the movie and using them as official inspiration was not going to happen. Not when Wyatt was trying to convince this girl's mother to let her be a full-fledged Dempsey. She understood the priorities. "If you'd told me why—"

"You'd have understood?" His face remained a wooden mask, distrust tainting the air between them and unexpectedly stinging her skin. Of course he shouldn't have told her. A six-day sexfest back when dinosaurs roamed the earth did not make them bosom buddies. "When Logan and Sean died, I had a chance to step up with my family and I failed. Luke was there for me and took care of business. I can't screw this up."

"You don't have to explain." Hearing about his devotion created a well of yearning in her chest, a yawning gap she wanted filled. Completely unfair of her to want him to fill it. "If you need to get someone else to take your place as tech consult, I understand."

He looked at her hard. "That's probably for the best."

Oh. She'd offered it as a courtesy, not expecting he would truly want out. But then he'd never wanted in, had he? She was a job assignment for him, and given their past connection, his curiosity had gotten the better of his usually rock-solid judgment. Now that curiosity was sated, and apparently even a strictly professional association with her would be toxic.

That conclusion should not have hurt her heart the way it did.

The intimate conversation had erased the gap between them. His scent addictive, his mouth drew her in, and all she could think was: *Kiss me, Marine. One last time, kiss me.*

A shriek sounded from upstairs, closely followed by a gruff "What the—!" and a door slam. Wyatt and Molly exchanged puzzled glances.

Roni bounded in, her face a bright red. "I met Uncle Gage."

"*Ker-ist,*" Wyatt said, covering his face.

Soon the kitchen was filled with Dempseys drawn by the commotion, and Gage not too far behind, pulling a shirt on. His curious gaze fell on Roni.

"So, I would apologize if I knew who the hell you

were and why you're wandering around opening doors in strangers' homes."

"Gage," Wyatt said, his voice a warning. "This is Roni, Logan's girl."

"Good fuck," Gage said. "F'real?"

"What the hell were you doing?" Luke yelled at Gage.

"Scarring my niece for life apparently. Brady, too." At the horrified expressions, he held up a hand. "Don't worry, my billboards and calendar revealed far more flesh than what she just saw. Totally PG." He spoke to Roni. "How old are you, kiddo?"

"Fifteen." The first inkling of a grin brightened her previously moody demeanor.

Wyatt arced a hand in a sweep that encompassed the entire family. "This is why we can't have nice things." He pointed at Roni. "You will not tell your mother about—shit, *anything* you've seen today. She's already going to be pissed at me. Now, come here."

Tentatively, Roni walked over and Wyatt placed his hands on her shoulders. "I don't know what you did to piss off your grandmother so much she had to drive all the way from Bloomington, but you're here now and we're gonna deal."

Molly couldn't see Roni's expression, but she'd lay odds the girl was embarrassed at Wyatt's go-deep intensity. *Get used to it.*

Wyatt turned her around and held her back against his chest with his arms wrapped around her shoulders and his lips pressed to the top of her head. Such a protective gesture that Molly's heart squeezed to see it.

Ovary down!

"Veronica, time to officially meet your family. Everyone, this is Roni. She'll be staying for the summer."

Needless to say, Roni's mom was not pleased.

"Hey," Wyatt said when he answered the call she'd made before he had a chance to dial first.

"Hey? That's all you have to say? Why am I hearing about my daughter's whereabouts from my mother instead of from you?"

"I was about to call you. And Judy is the one who laid this on me without consulting anyone. She didn't even come in to talk to me. Just dumped her outside."

Jen, the queen of selective hearing, ignored that. "Did you put her up to this? I know you've wanted her with you, and the first time I'm away, you see your chance—"

"I'm gonna stop you right there. I did not tell Roni or your mother to do this." Though he suspected that Roni might have manipulated the situation and forced Judy's hand. Pride that she would find a way warmed his chest.

Jen wasn't having any of it. "You will drive her back home tomorrow."

"No."

She coughed. Spluttered, more like. "No? Do I need to call a lawyer?"

"You don't want to put her through that any more than I do. I've been very patient with you, Jen, and now the box is opened. She's here. Her uncles and aunts know about her and they want to know her better. If you fight me on this, I can't be responsible for how it's going to go down."

"You're—you're threatening me?" She sounded aggrieved and a little bit scared, as if every nightmare she'd envisioned about the all-powerful Dempseys had come true. Well, time she learned what she was truly up against.

"Jen, you're the only one who sees us as a threat. You're her mother. That's not going to change. You are doing an amazing job raising her. Let her stay for a few weeks, have her curiosity satisfied. Putting us in the forbidden zone just makes us more appealing." Christ almighty, this was Parenting 101.

"I don't like this, Wyatt." She sounded chastened, less sure. "I should come home."

"I'll keep her safe, Jen. God, I love her like she's my own. You know I do. Trust me."

At her surrendering sigh, his heart cheered in victory.

"She's become so difficult in the last few months. I've no idea what to do with her." She dragged in a noisy breath. "I'll email you a list of foods she shouldn't be eating." Which he suspected was longer than the list of what she should be eating. No problem, he'd put the chefs next door on the case. "And she has a doctor's appointment in Bloomington in a few weeks. It's just routine, but she can't miss it."

"I'll drive her myself."

"No drama, Wyatt. If I see or hear of any of you pulling your usual Dempsey crap, I'll be on a plane so fast your head will spin."

"You have my word." He'd have to make sure Roni didn't mention the presence of a certain Hollywood star at the family barbecue. Exactly the sort of spectacle Jen would not be on board with.

"Now, can I speak with my daughter, please?"

"Sure. And Jen? Thanks."

"Don't make me regret it, Wyatt."

Wyatt pressed the mute button on the phone and looked around. "Roni?"

"I'm here." She popped in from the other room, looking nervous, as well she should.

"Your mom wants to talk to you. She's pretty pissed, but I think that's understandable because she assumes you engineered this. You're going to let her shout at you and you're not going to make excuses, 'kay?"

She nodded, biting down on her lip.

"Another thing. Might be easier if you didn't mention that Molly Cade is here."

"You mean lie?"

"I mean omit."

"Okay." He handed off the phone to her and headed out back. Everyone was standing around, still in a daze over what had happened. They all looked to him for an update.

"Roni's mom is going to let her stay here for a few weeks."

"I should freakin' well hope so," muttered Alex before turning silent at Wyatt's glare.

"I don't know how long she'll be here but I do know this: it's going to be the best summer she's ever had."

"Fuck yeah, it will," Gage agreed.

"Which means we need to set some ground rules."

Everyone groaned. No one hated rules more than a Dempsey, but it had to be said. Wyatt caught Molly's eye and found her doing her utmost to suppress a grin. In his corner, that's how it felt. Like the two of them were a team.

But that had to be nixed in the face of what needed to happen.

Wyatt started a count on his fingers. "No swearing. No sneaking off to have sex in bathrooms during family gatherings."

Gage opened his mouth.

"Or anywhere else," Wyatt finished, arrowing a dark look at his baby brother.

"It was the most convenient. And all our best work is done in bathrooms." A grinning Gage threw an arm around Brady, who by the looks of it had still not recovered from the intrusion.

Wyatt went on. "No getting into fights or any drama whatsoever. We clear?"

"Of course we are," Luke gritted out, still steamed. "You don't even have to tell us that." *Unlike the family secret Wyatt should have shared* was the undertone.

"We're going to need to work up a schedule to keep her entertained and ensure someone is always with her. She looks older than fifteen but she's just a kid."

"Shouldn't be a problem," Beck said. "An army of teen-sitters. As long as she's not into One Direction or something that makes my ears bleed."

"Does she look like she's into One Direction, handsome?" Darcy asked. She had a point. Those guys were likely a little too squeaky clean for Roni, with her emo-Goth look.

"I dunno. Don't want to judge a book by its cover, *princesa*." He kissed Darcy's temple. "You've been known to belt out the Biebs in the shower."

Maybe this could work out. "She likes alt-rock. Like her dad," Wyatt said.

"Thank Christ," Luke said, then held up his hand in a gesture of mock apology. "Thank the goddess."

That concession, and the mention of Logan, had a cheering effect. Everyone broke into grins, the reason why Roni was here seeping in. She was their dead brother's girl and nothing was more important.

"She also likes hockey, so I was thinking—"

"I'll talk to Bastian," Alex said. "Maybe we can get her some one-on-one time with the league's hottest player." Eli bristled and everyone laughed. Bastian Durand played right forward for the Hawks and had a thing for Alex, about which she liked to tease Eli mercilessly.

"Best summer ever," Gage said. "I feel like we should join fists or have T-shirts made."

"Summer of Roni," Kinsey said, swiping a hand across an imaginary billboard.

"Hashtag SummerOfRoni," Darcy clarified.

On a burble of chatter about how awesome the summer would be, Wyatt walked over to Molly, who had stayed back through the discussion.

"I should probably get going," she said before he had a chance to speak. "Leave you to it."

Wyatt nodded. Much as he wanted her to stay, this summer had just taken a left turn, and if he was enforcing the no-drama rule among his siblings, he had to be the first to set the example. But he couldn't resist a few final, private moments with her.

"I'll see you out."

"You don't have to. My security followed us here."

Like he trusted them. "Let's go."

◈ CHAPTER SEVEN

The knock was soft. Reverent. "They're ready for you, Miss Cade," the PA said from the other side of the makeup trailer door.

"Be right there," she called back, careful to sound calm, sweet, and pliant. Ryan had always said never to answer—it was their Hollywood-given right as the talent to ignore "the help." What a jerk. These days she could ill afford the slightest rumor about her behavior on the set. No fodder would be given to the machine.

"Watch you don't overdo the powder, sweetheart," Gideon said to the puppy-eyed makeup artist, currently trying her damnedest to minimize the sweaty sheen that insisted on reappearing after every sponge press. Pores by Jose Cuervo.

"Sure thing, Mr. Carter," the woman said breathlessly. "Of course, you hardly need it. Your skin's flawless."

Gideon offered a smirk of *I know* and an eyebrow lift of *Let's bang later.*

"I see Ryan's been busy." He held up his phone. In the mirror's reflection, Molly saw the now-familiar silhouette of her ex wrapped around a (much) younger woman. Grasping on to his youth by having a pair of tits-in-diapers prop him up as he walked into Urasawa on Rodeo. Molly would have loved to warn her of the dangers of getting involved with a megalomaniac. How she risked having her personality whitewashed, her every decision second-guessed, her life consumed in service to the Ryan Michaels enterprise.

It wasn't so hard to believe she'd loved him once. What woman could fail to be smitten when the biggest actor in Hollywood—in the world—showed an interest? Her first big audition, and Molly had been blinded by Ryan's dazzle. He'd insisted she be hired for the film, then proceeded to shock and awe her with rare orchids, Harry Winston jewels, lavish trips. He'd set his sights on Molly Cade, Midwestern rube, and she'd fallen at his feet in adoration.

He'd liked her there.

"He highlighted his hair," Molly said blandly. The makeup artist met her gaze in the mirror, a cross between pity and vulture.

"Yeah, he's filming that new Disney project," Gideon said, eyes glittering malevolently. "Though we all know Ryan Michaels is the last person who should be representing the Mouse House." He checked out the TMZ photo on his phone again and let out a low wolf whistle. "Although I wouldn't say no to being the meat in a girl sandwich with her on one side."

Standing, Molly struggled to maintain a perilous grip on her fading calm. The nude photos had only fueled the tawdry rumors about Ryan's supposed oh-so-naughty proclivities, though that was about as daring as *their* sex life had gotten. Her husband hadn't been interested in Molly personally, just in using her as a prop. Of course it was assumed that she'd been party to his rumored drug-fueled orgies—after all, if a woman had so little self-respect that she'd allow her husband to take those photos, what else was she capable of?

For a long time, Molly had wondered if she had an existence apart from Ryan. Oh, she knew she had a career and that she inhabited her own body, but she had let him control her to the extent that she had felt transparent. A ghost of herself.

Only in the last few months had the shimmer started to coalesce into the solid form of the woman she once was. So her plan to get the rights to Alex Dempsey's story hadn't panned out—no worries, it was back to script A about the Chicago Irish Flynns with Molly playing flame-haired Kelly, the youngest daughter of firefighter royalty struggling to gain respect in a male-dominated world. Molly lived that shit every day, so it would be like playing herself. In bunker gear.

She grabbed the firefighter's jacket off the hook of the trailer door, then because she had to establish a baseline of appropriate behavior going forward, she turned back to Gideon, who was futzing with his hair. And this dickhead had earned twice as much as her regular payday on his last movie! Ensuring that the makeup artist was out of hearing range while busy rearranging her palates, Molly leaned in and whispered in her costar's ear.

"Some studio suit might have dumped you on my production but that doesn't mean I have to make it easy." She squeezed his shoulder for emphasis. "Bring up Ryan again in my presence and I'll let everyone know about your micro-penis problem. Speaking from personal experience, it's amazing what can be done with Photoshop these days. You'll be lucky if you can get a hired escort to bang you, never mind any of the crew on this movie. We clear?"

He swallowed. "Sure, Molly. Just kidding."

Uncertain as to whether she'd achieved anything apart from earning herself an enemy, Molly headed out toward the soundstage, one of several at Cinespace on Chicago's West Side. Outside the trailer, she was immediately swarmed by a bevy of crew: runners, assistants, assistants to the assistants. She already missed Cal. This morning, her friend had caught a flight to Tennessee to check in with her grandmother, who had slipped and fallen last night. She'd promised she would be back within a couple of weeks, but Molly's only thought was that Cal's grammy be taken care of. The best medical care, whatever she needed.

A week of interiors lay behind them, and today they would be filming the first action shots involving a rescue from a blazing fire. The first time the CFD tech consultant needed to be on set, too.

But it wouldn't be him.

She wondered how unclehood was treating him. It was one thing to visit weekly, quite another to have a surly teenage girl thrust upon you for an entire summer. But he had his family, that bastion of strength and loyalty. Roni was a very lucky girl.

And Molly was just a teensy bit jealous of a fifteen-year-old.

"Miss Hotshot Producer, so thrilled you could join us," her director, Mick Santos, drawled in his British accent, then hugged her to let her know he was kidding. She and Mick went way back to her second movie, an action-packed bang-bang fest aimed at teenage boys that had cemented her status as damsel in distress and the subject of masturbatory fantasies. She was trying to change the former; she saw little hope of affecting the latter.

"Charming as ever, Michael," she said, hugging him warmly.

"Okay, darling, we've got the first big rescue scene today." While he ran through the details she already knew by heart, she cast her gaze over the soundstage, taking in the warehouse set entrance where the AD had corralled the second unit that would be working on this sequence.

"So, Molly, have you met the tech consultant from the Chicago Fire Department?"

"No, I haven't."

She turned and of course, it was him, because evidently her not-so-subtle subconscious had wished for him to materialize.

"Miss Cade." Wyatt's low voice rumbled through her like a 7.6 earthquake. She blinked, looked up, looked up some more. How had he become taller in three weeks? And broader? And . . . beardier? He was really allowing freedom to reign all over that handsome face. She bet he could wreak havoc between her thighs with that lush growth.

Good Lord, ten seconds in and she'd already given herself a facial hair–inspired orgasm.

"Hello," she said, suddenly shy. "I didn't expect to see you."

"Harder to quit than I thought," he said cryptically. His blue-gray eyes seemed bluer than usual. And twinklier. All the *-er*s. "You dyed your hair," he added.

"I did." *I did? Don't use up all your witticisms in one go, Mol.* A blush stole across her body to match her newly colored auburn locks, which cemented her Irish American persona. They also happened to come astonishingly close to her hair color when they first met five years ago.

Even through the mat of hair, she could see his lips lifting. Those piercing blue eyes watched her with surprising intent. "Ready?"

Was she ready to take her life back? To make a fresh start, change the American public's perception of her, reestablish herself as the crème de la crème of the Hollywood elite?

Molly squared her shoulders and looked Wyatt straight in the eye. "Ready."

He tucked a hand under her elbow—*sizzle*—and led her to her first mark on the movie that would signal her redemption. "Trust me, Hollywood. You're gonna do great."

Four hours later, Wyatt was done with the movie-making business.

He was used to waiting around at the firehouse, sure, but he usually had entertainment or food, or, if Gage was on shift, both. Film craft required a lot of dawdling and repetition and retakes because someone had forgotten to move a cable or hit a mark or remember a line.

He'd tried to bail. Now that Roni was in the frame,

working so closely with the woman who was one, walking temptation and two, completely out of bounds, was a train wreck waiting to happen. So he'd told Venti a little white lie: that the new responsibility of his niece superseded this gig. To which his captain had grunted companionably and nodded sympathetically and finally responded with, *Tough*. Well, he'd been a bit more vocal, citing the numerous projects CFD was already consulting on and how the cap couldn't spit without hitting a god*damn* Dempsey at Engine 6. In other words, Wyatt had a built-in support network and basically, he could shove his baby-sitting excuse up his ass.

So here he was, bored as fuck, that damn temptation dangling right in front of his face in her movie-issue firefighter gear. If someone had told him before today that bunkers could look hot, he'd have laughed them right off the lot. But Molly Cade's curves could sex up a potato sack.

She was the consummate professional, though, he'd give her that. The scene they'd shot involved a tricky rescue of a homeless man in an abandoned warehouse. Molly had listened, absorbed, and knocked it out of the park. After the director shouted "Cut," she spent a few moments checking the playback on a screen before she was hustled off the set by an assistant.

That he missed her presence as soon as she was gone did not sit well with him.

"Firefighter Fox?" A girl not much older than Roni, dressed head to toe in black and holding a clipboard, approached with an inquiring look.

"It's Lieutenant."

Evidently unimpressed, she went on. "Miss Cade would like to see you in her trailer."

She gave him her back, his acquiescence a given, and who was he to argue with Hollywood? When he reached the trailer, which looked as big as some apartments, she gestured at the door. "She said to go right in."

No sign of security outside. A quick scan picked up a guy wearing a suit, an earpiece, and sunglasses (indoors, so, *douche*) at one of the catering tables chatting with some blond piece doling out coffee. Wyatt supposed the set was considered safe, but all the same, he didn't much like the ease with which he could access Molly's private sanctum. He pulled open the door and stepped in.

His timing? *Perfection.*

She was emerging from a cloud of steam, dressed in a bathrobe that unfortunately covered those dynamite legs of hers but dipped low enough to keep things interesting. Combing through her damp flames as she walked, she grimaced as she caught on a tangle, but her expression smoothed on seeing him.

"Hey, thanks for stopping by."

"Didn't feel I had much of a choice."

She raised an amused eyebrow. "Oh, did my sending an assistant come off as a diva move?"

He rubbed his thumb and forefinger together. "Just a touch, Hollywood."

She took the jibe like a champ. He'd met a lot of drama queens in his life, most of them Dempsey, and Molly Cade did not fit the mold at all.

"I wanted to thank you for today," she said. "I was

nervous about how some of the set pieces were going to go down and you made it easy for me."

"Just doing my job."

She opened a small fridge. "Water? Or I could use my diva moves and get a Coke sent over."

"I'll survive on H_2O."

She passed him a bottle. "How's Roni?"

"Driving me nuts." He took a seat on the sofa and a slug of water. Jen was right about how difficult she'd turned in the last couple of months, although this was also the first time he'd spent more than a couple of hours at a time with her. He supposed every kid went through a rebellious streak, but he had hoped Roni had outgrown hers and that surrounding herself with her family would bring out her shine. Instead, she preferred to hole up in her room, listening to music or watching videos all day. For a kid who had pulled every move in the book to land with her dad's family for the summer, she sure as shit wasn't acting like she wanted to be here.

There was something else, though, something that made him uneasy. The way she looked at him with troubled eyes the color of Logan's.

"She doesn't want to do anything. The greatest city in the world and she'd rather sit around at home."

"I was like that during my summers in high school. But then my grandparents made me get a job at Dairy Queen."

More of the so-not-diva business. Sometimes he forgot that Molly Cade had come from humble beginnings in a small Missouri town. "How'd that go?"

"It added ten pounds. All to my ass." She pointed

at her ass in case there was some confusion, then seemed to realize she had pointed at her ass. A blush climbed up her cheeks as he let his grin fly.

"Shut up," she muttered.

"Didn't say a word."

She sat in the armchair opposite, pulling her robe tighter. "How are things with everyone since the big reveal?"

"Alex is getting over it, but Eli's been shunted off to the guest room. Everyone else is coming around." Everyone except Luke. On a surface level, his oldest brother would get over it for the sake of Roni and the family peace, but the resentment at Wyatt's call would always exist between them.

He looked up to find Molly watching him carefully. A sudden urge to confide in her overwhelmed him. He tamped it down.

"I'm sorry it didn't work out with getting the Alex seal of approval for the movie."

She waved it off. "Family's more important, Wyatt. You have to protect Roni. It was a no-brainer."

Perhaps, but he realized that it meant a lot to Molly to make this movie the way she wanted, and while keeping his distance was definitely the safest option for his niece, funny how he felt like shit about it. Like he'd disappointed Molly. He suspected her last year had been filled with disappointments.

"The movie's gonna be great," he said. An inadequate tack-on, he knew.

The air thrummed between them, a crackle along a live wire, a whoosh of oxygen into a vented room. "Yeah, it will," she murmured.

But it was as if they were talking about something

else. Another missed opportunity. What else could be great if they were willing to forget themselves and pick up where they had left off with that kiss against his Camaro?

His gaze fell to her bare legs, and he quickly looked away. If he spent any time there, this was only going to end one way: with his face between her thighs.

She crossed her gorgeous legs, and he almost laughed. None shall pass.

Alrighty, then. He stood. So did she, and while she was a tiny thing, she still managed to project ten feet tall.

"I just wanted you to know that . . ." She trailed off, and that hesitancy drew him in. There was an invisible thread between them, sometimes the length of a hotel bar, sometimes as short as the inches between them now. His pulse quickened, the thud loud in his ears.

"Know what?"

"That I understand your need to keep your life ordered right now. Private. For yourself, your family, Roni."

She sounded regretful, not because she wanted to blow up his existence—something she had been doing since the first moment he had reconnected with her—but because she could never go back to that. Private. Her life was a three-ring circus with no space for a dull moment. They couldn't return to the safe anonymity of that hotel. Their time had passed.

The ache in his chest spoke his regret.

"You should go." It passed her lips in a throaty whisper. "You should—"

He swallowed that next *go* with his mouth. He

should go. He should run, not walk, away from her, but a more primal urge overtook him. The urge to haul her back to a simpler time when all that mattered was the pleasure they pulled from each other's sweaty, naked bodies.

It had been so long since Wyatt had given in to what he wanted. Since he'd even acknowledged a deeper need for something of his own.

He wanted this. Her. Plain and simple.

Her lips concurred. So much hunger in that sweet little mouth of hers, but then her life was about hunger. For success, adulation, whatever goal was waiting over that next hill. She tasted of that hunger, and of something else. A need that matched his own.

He had to get closer to her, to grind all up in her, to climb inside her. The ache in his chest spread south and his cock shot a few notches up on the granite scale. It hit her at belly button level, which was not going to be any good for her, so he cupped that Hollywood booty and raised her up until he notched right between her thighs.

The act of lifting her would normally be a breeze, but his shoulder twinged and shit, he'd have to do something about that. For the moment, he embraced the discomfort and associated the pain with this. With her. Because without it, there would be no barrier to taking her.

He found himself sitting on the sofa, not quite sure how it had happened. One second, she was a foot off the ground while he positioned himself between the heaven of her thighs, the next she had pushed him down.

Hunger in fucking spades.

The ache in his shoulder diminished while the ache in his dick burned brighter. She straddled him as they kissed, their mouths in a tangle of *yes, yes, don't stop,* and *there, right there,* and *keep that sweet, sweet grind all over my hard cock, baby.*

The comfort in touching her was shocking, and at the same time, it was a form of madness, pure and unadulterated.

It had to end.

He framed her face with both hands and held her back a few inches. Panting hard, they stared at each other.

"Molly."

"I know."

She pulled back and the thread snapped. He felt it in his chest.

"This isn't about you." *It's totally about you.*

"You mean for once I'm not the center of the universe," she said, unmistakable humor in her tone. He liked her mature take on it.

She clambered off him, and to his infinite regret, refastened the loose robe belt. "I told you to leave." There was no recrimination in her words, just a plea for him to make it easier by following instructions. Despite his years in the service, he'd never been good at taking orders.

Before him she stood, hands fisted on hips, lovely chest heaving. Six weeks left on the shoot together. This was going to be a problem.

Then she broke into a grin, shaking her head at the craziness of it all. He stood and examined his erection because it was a fuckova lot easier than watching the dazzler of a smile that urged him to forget every single reason why getting involved with her was the worst idea in the history of terrible ideas.

His hard-on refused to stand down. It wanted out and in.

Hey, buddy, sorry to get you all hot and bothered. Again.

Molly giggled. "Why do I get the impression you're having a conversation with your dick?"

"Just apologizin'."

"How's he taking it?"

"Not well."

She laughed her head off, and he'd never heard a prettier sound. Almost as nice as those throaty gasps. She was known for her distinctive laugh, the husky chuckle of a girl who knew how to have a good time. Nothing beat hearing it because of something you'd said.

He couldn't even hit the gym until his shoulder was in better shape, so that method for working her out of his system was off the table.

"I'll run it off."

"That your usual solution for sexual frustration?" She was enjoying herself far too much, but he'd let her have it. He owed her that much.

"It is."

"Run a lot, do you?"

"Lately? I could outrun the winner of the Kentucky Derby."

She liked that, he could tell. This little insight into his life, which wasn't a cavalcade of balling women and taking his sexual due as a member of the CFD. He had no idea why he felt she needed to know that, or why he wanted to tell her all the fucking things. He never talked about anything with anyone, not even with Luke, who was his closest sib.

"Lately," she murmured, "I could give that Kentucky Derby winner a run for his money, too." Hey, so sharing was contagious.

He'd seen a picture of her once in running gear somewhere in one of those beachy West Coast places. Probably a long shot, but the idea was fast growing on him, especially as tomorrow was a no-shoot day. "I usually run on the lake path. If you're free . . ."

He trailed off, and tease that she was, she left him hanging for the longest three seconds of his life.

"Wyatt Fox, are you asking me out"—she clutched her chest dramatically—"on a platonic running date?"

"No better way to tackle this sexual frustration thing than to do it together." Bullshit meter? *Zing!* Never had he wanted so much for a woman to say yes to the promise of no sex.

She considered him, a fingertip held to one perfectly plump lip. "If checking out my ass as I leave you in my rearview on the lake path helps with your chatty dick problem, Marine, then I'm happy to take one for the team." That flirty grin, the one that had won her legions of fans, lit up her face. She held out her hand. "Phone."

Wyatt handed his over and watched as she put her number and where she was staying in his contacts. Not dillydallying, she opened the door to her trailer and ushered him out. Probably worried she couldn't keep her hands off him.

Yeah, let's go with that.

"I usually run around 8 a.m. I'll meet you outside

where I'm staying. Don't be late." Order issued diva-style, she shut the door.

Fair enough.

He scanned the entry she had completed in his phone contacts, an address in the affluent Gold Coast. Of course.

But that wasn't what had him grinning broadly, exercising muscles that protested the sudden use. It was the name she'd entered, or should he say, alias.

Hollywood Booty.

Unable to contain himself, he laughed out loud. A couple of crew members shot weird looks in his direction, but fuck if he cared. He'd allow himself this little indulgence.

Just this once.

CHAPTER EIGHT

Wyatt hated the Gold Coast.

More accurately, he hated the parking situation in the Gold Coast. No one ever drove around here, which meant no one ever left their rock-and-roll parking spaces. He'd forgotten to ask Molly if she had a spot at the back of the townhouse where she was staying, so he did the hunt-and-peck parking dance in ever-increasing circles until he found something six blocks away.

Usually busy, this neighborhood was close to Magnificent Mile shopping, Northwestern University's medical campus, and the lake. Moms with strollers that probably cost more than his truck carried lattes that probably cost more than a tank of gas for his truck. He was a little early, otherwise he wouldn't have been tempted to stop at the grilled cheese stand at the farmers' market on the Museum of Contemporary Art plaza. Small cubed samples with embedded toothpicks lay on a plate. He'd had to make do with Cocoa Puffs this morning because Gage was on shift, so his stomach was already rumbling percolator-style.

"Five-year-old Wisconsin cheddar and maple-smoked bacon," the animated girl at the stand said, her eyes roving appreciatively over his standard-issue CFD shirt underneath his unzipped hoodie. "It's our most popular sandwich."

He nodded as he chewed while Grilled Cheese Girl tried what he imagined would be winning chat-up lines for the right audience.

Oh, you're with CFD!

You guys do such an awesome job.

My sister-in-law/neighbor/friend of a friend is dating a firefighter.

I should be done here by one.

And so on.

Most guys faced with this level of flirty onslaught would grin and lock that down in half a heartbeat, but Wyatt didn't have that easy way about him. Small talk, flirting, and plain old sociability were beyond him, so he usually grunted until the woman gave up. Gage liked to say that Wyatt wouldn't know passion if it hit him over the head with the Jaws of Life. Wyatt supposed that was true; passion had a habit of trumping cold, brutal decision making, and he'd choose common sense over his dick every time. Neither could he change his personality. He was destined to be Mr. Solid, the boring Dempsey. The one time he had stepped outside the dull zone—five years ago with Molly Cade—he had let his dick do the talking and trusted the conversation would turn out right. But it sure as hell wasn't the stuff relationships were made of.

Women liked guys who *communicated*.

Grilled Cheese Girl had stopped talking, beaten into silence by his own. He murmured his thanks and turned away, only to run slap bang into a petite red-head carrying flowers that practically engulfed her and a canvas shopping bag bursting with produce. Her baseball cap and sunglasses might keep her identity a secret from the rest of the market goers, but his body knew when Molly Cade was in its orbit.

"Building up your strength?" she asked, curving her gaze around his chest to the tray of samples.

"Figure I'll have to if I'm to keep up with Hollywood Booty."

She grinned, a triple shot of tropical sunshine that slammed him in the solar plexus. "I need to drop this stuff off, then I'm ready to go."

He removed the bag from her shoulder and the flowers cradled in her arms.

"Oh, you don't have to do that."

"Not a problem." Really, the notion of her body being covered by those gigantic blooms didn't sit well with him. He preferred a more comprehensive view. After freeing up her hands, he helped himself to a not-so-furtive ogle of that Coke bottle–shaped body poured into running shorts and a stretchy top that was having a hard time accommodating the glories within.

She rested a hand on her hip. "Get a good look, did you?"

He put his tongue back in his mouth. "Figure I may as well, seeing as I'll be forced to watch your ass during the run. I'm pretty equal opportunity when it comes to the female anatomy." He gestured forward with his free hand. "Right behind you, Hollywood."

The curves of her body, the perfect wave of her, gave him no small amount of pleasure, and as she moved forward, the sway of her hips and roundness of her gorgeous ass made him glad he had these flowers covering his burgeoning hard-on. But it wasn't quite enough to distract him from the guy in running gear who had moved as soon as Molly did and stayed about ten feet behind her.

"Toting your own security, then?" Wyatt asked, coming alongside her.

"The studio assigned a team. I've done a pretty good job of keeping a low profile. No press has shown up anywhere I've been. I suppose it's comforting to know the security is there, but really, I want this summer to be about . . ." She paused and clearly checked her thought. "Just about the work. Making a great product. Something I can be proud of."

"What were you going to say?"

She turned her head slightly. "I was going to say this summer was about finding me again. But that sounds like I should be listening to the Smiths and writing terrible poetry in my Hello Kitty journal."

"Applications for Club Angst are currently being accepted by my niece."

That made her laugh, and her laugh made him warm.

Walking the short distance through the market, Wyatt was on high alert despite the hired comfort of Molly's personal security team. As a woman in the public eye, Molly had to have her fair share of crazies stalking her, and in this environment she was highly exposed. He found himself invading her space, keeping close on the off chance any threat materialized.

It wasn't long before he realized the real threat was not from some loco fan, but from him. She smelled like a dream, and it wasn't some heavy, expensive scent, either. This was all her, the fresh, natural scent of a beautiful woman, the same as all those years ago. Sense memory kicked in. The tangle of limbs, the taste of her skin, the slick juncture where their bodies connected again and again.

"God, that smells good," she murmured.

He turned to find her focused on a nearby crepe stand, and the only reason Wyatt had the word *crepe* in his vocabulary was because Gage insisted on making them for firehouse breakfasts instead of pancakes like a regular person. Everyone knew that crepes were just pancakes on heroin.

His stomach rumbled. Those grilled cheese samples hadn't cut it.

"How 'bout we delay that run for a bit?"

Her lips formed a grim seal. "While I'm always up for procrastinating when it comes to exercise, I'm supposed to be on a strict diet. For the movie."

"If you want to get a firefighter's diet right, you need to chow down on about three of those bad boys." He nudged her with his elbow. "Think of it as research, Molly."

A few minutes later, they were seated on the steps of the museum with "research" in hand, hers ruined by greenery because she wanted healthy, his a Nutella-and-banana beauty because he had a sweet tooth he refused to be ashamed of.

He scarfed his down quickly, licked his lips, and took a moment to secretly watch Molly. Chewing, she tipped her face up to the sun, and a curious grin quirked the corner of her lips. He couldn't see her eyes hidden behind the sunglasses, but he'd take good odds they were crinkling with joy.

"Penny for 'em," he said.

"Tabloids would pay a lot more than that." Her smile turned self-deprecating. "Though they wouldn't be worth it. I'm just liking this moment of peace."

"They're hard to come by."

"Your family isn't a quiet bunch, are they?"

"Not one of them knows the meaning of the word." Sometimes he questioned if he was a fit for the Dempseys. They were such an effusive lot and he was far from it.

"What about your people?"

"My mom and dad were doctors. They died in a car crash in Africa when I was fourteen, and I went to live with my grandparents in New Haven, Missouri, population 647."

"And the Camaro."

"And the Camaro." She looked pleased that he'd remembered. "Granddad died just over ten years ago, Gran five months back."

"Proud of you, I'll bet."

The downturn of her mouth registered her discomfort. "She was. Before."

Before the photos. The Internet had pretty much collapsed when those hacked photos of Molly were released on some scumbag gossip site. Bad enough they were taken in the first place, but every double standard you could think of applied because she had supposedly invited her husband to do it. Private shots for her husband's eyes.

"Pretty messed up how that all went down," Wyatt said carefully.

She faced him, considering. "You think I was dumb to let Ryan take those photos?"

Had he sounded critical? He'd been going for sympathetic. "I'm in no position to judge how a man and his woman get their kicks." Ryan Michaels's woman. Thinking of Molly belonging to someone else, even in the past tense, constricted his chest uncomfortably.

"They weren't recent. They happened just after he and I were married, six months after I met him at a screen test. I'd never been the daring sort, but after you and I . . ."

"After we what?"

A flush crept up her neck, painting her cheeks with a watercolor-pink bloom. *Fuck me.* Shock barreled through him. Was she actually relating her sexual bravery in posing for those photos to her time with Wyatt in Chicago? Had another man gotten the benefit of Wyatt opening up this beautiful woman? He'd been the one to make her beg and scream and suck and beg some more and— *Way to make it all about you, shithead.*

She coughed out a laugh filled with regret. "Learned my lesson, that's for sure." She still wore her sunglasses, so he couldn't see her exact expression, but he'd guess it was as hard as the concrete steps cushioning their asses. "Did you look at them?"

"You mean, am I like every other red-blooded man on the planet when faced with naked photos of a beautiful woman?"

She nodded slowly.

"Nope. You didn't give me or anyone else permission to look at them. Besides, I've got a memory like a steel trap and the use of my right hand." Leaning in, he pulled her sunglasses forward on her nose. He needed to see right into those beautiful, haunted eyes. "I've had the privilege of kissing every inch of your body, of plunging deep inside you, and hearing your orgasm-hoarse moans. Don't need some crappy stolen photos when I've had the real thing."

A sob cracked in her throat.

"Molly." He curled a hand around her neck and pulled her close with a press of his lips to her forehead. "You've been through it these last few months, haven't you?"

"Longer than that."

So the rumors about her marriage being on the rocks for a while were true.

"Sean used to say that when you're on the floor, the only way is up."

She sniffed. "Well, the floor tastes like shit."

"Sure does, but you just keep looking up, Molly. The papers, the gossip, the fair-weather fans—fuck 'em. None of them get to define who you are. Only you do that. Remember you are fierce, that inside you beats the heart of a warrior."

It felt so good to hold her like this. Be useful. But it was more than a little self-serving. Comforting her was a sneaky way to steal his own slice of heaven.

Seeming to recognize that they were hovering on the line here, she drew back with a mental hitch of her bootstraps. Sunglasses back on, shoulders squared, tough girl to the fore.

She stood and reached for her bag of purchases but he was already there, throwing it over his good shoulder. "So you weren't tempted even just a little, Marine?"

He heard humor in her voice, and he allowed himself the luxury of thinking he might have put it there. Being splashed naked all over the tabloids was shitty, but eventually you had to put it into perspective. Wyatt was the king of perspective.

"Course I was. I'm not dead."

If her grin was anything to go by, it was the right thing to say. The guys at the firehouse had drooled all over those pics and it had taken every ounce of strength not to pummel their self-satisfied faces. Taking the high road had always been his preferred path. He didn't butt into anyone's business. He let people do their thing.

But with Molly Cade . . . why did it feel like she was *his* business?

With her bodyguard in tow, they continued in comfortable silence until they reached her three-story townhouse, one that likely cost a few million more than Wyatt had in his bank account. A wry grimace almost made it onto his face as he thought of his tiny duplex in Andersonville. Sure, it had appreciated well as the neighborhood became more gentrified in recent years, but the idea of Molly there conjured an untimely gust of want in his chest. He lifted his gaze to Molly Cade's summer rental, and he bet even this was subpar for a woman who probably had multimillion-dollar properties in Malibu and St. Tropez and other places a guy like him would contaminate by merely uttering their names on his filthy lips.

Molly in his little old house? *You're a fucking moron, Fox.*

"Did you want to come in?" She motioned to the front door once they had reached the top step.

He handed off her farmers' market haul. He didn't want to be rude after he'd carried her stuff like a lovelorn schoolboy, but going in would only make him feel lower than something she'd scrape off her shoe. "Nah. I'll wait here."

She nodded and headed inside while he used the extra moments to get his shit together and assess the surroundings. Quiet enough except for a few older folks enjoying a walk with their dogs and more moms with gold-plated strollers. The bodyguard—Farmers' Market Guy—stood across the street, chatting with what Wyatt assumed was the rest of the security team. Thick necks, thick skulls, likely thick as two planks, they sat in a black Escalade. A three-fer, which probably switched out at night. Not cheap.

He ambled over, ready to make introductions. Holding out his hand, he gripped FMG's outstretched one. "Wyatt Fox. I'm"—*what, exactly?*—"with Miss Cade."

FMG's shake was firm. "Keith Dennison. She mentioned you'd be stopping by. Said you were CFD, former corps." The guy rattled off his own unit. Wyatt wasn't surprised. A lot of marines went into law enforcement.

"You planning to run with us?"

"I've been chasing her the last couple of days." He gave a droll smile. "She won't even slow down to take it easy on me."

Yeah, he could see that. This woman would give no quarter. "We're gonna take the lake path. Probably forty-five minutes there and back. No need to follow."

Dennison slid a glance at the suit in the driver's seat, likely the team leader. An imperceptible nod followed, and Wyatt shook hands with Dennison again.

Morons, the lot of them. Wyatt could have promised that every single one of the Dempseys and the entire offensive line of the Hawks would be flanking Molly as she jogged down the lake path, and that should not have been enough to have this so-called security hand over the reins of her protection to someone not on the team. If they were slacking in this, then they were slacking elsewhere. He'd discuss it with her later.

The front door opened and for a moment, he was frozen, just flattened by the beauty of her as she hurtled down those steps. She betrayed no hesitation, either, no hitch in her step, no wavering in her stride, when the last year had given her plenty of reason to be wary about setting foot outside the door.

"Ready?" Challenge tinged her voice. Clearly not similarly affected by *his* beauty.

"I'll try to keep up."

An hour later, they were back off the lake path and winding their way homeward through the Gold Coast streets. The twinge in Wyatt's shoulder was burning like a mother now. Pushing through it with every step as he kept pace with Molly was torture.

"Not bad, Fox," she said, grinning, but her face crumpled at whatever she saw on his. "You okay?"

"Yeah, just an old football injury." He rolled his stiffening shoulder. No joy.

"Seriously, what's up?" She placed a hand on his bicep. He'd noticed she liked to touch it and he also noticed that he liked to feel it there, right over Logan's name.

"Six weeks ago I wrenched my shoulder during a rescue. That's how I'm on ass-watch-to-the-stars."

She crossed her arms, a move that pushed up her cleavage. Even through his pain, he could appreciate the hell out of that. "So you're overdoing it right now to prove you're Mr. Tough Guy/screw the docs/pain is optional, is that it?"

"Pros far outweigh the cons."

She growled her annoyance. "We're going to ice it. Now."

His mind jumped ahead to sitting on the sofa in her fancy summer mansion. Removing his T-shirt so she could look after him, maybe removing her T-shirt so he could look after her. Pros trumping cons all over the place. So embedded was he in his dirty little fantasy that they were halfway down her block before he realized it.

"Shit," she muttered.

In the time it took for their run, the population of the neighborhood had increased. Outside the gate to the townhouse, two girls Roni's age were on phones, taking photos of the front door. Selfie hunters, perhaps. At his nine o'clock, a leggy blonde in very tight shorts was draped all over the driver's side of the security team's Escalade, one leg bent behind her so her tee stretched taut against her rack and gave the suits something to look at. No sign of Dennison.

Okay, two teenagers. No biggie. Yet heat prickled Wyatt's neck, that warning he got when a shitstorm was hurtling around the corner with him in its crosshairs. Because if two girls knew where Molly was staying, then the undesirables of her fan base weren't far behind. He pulled his sunglasses down, his hood up, and tucked a hand beneath Molly's elbow.

"Let's go in the back way."

Too late. The teens were already surging forward with phones raised, snapping and gushing, and Molly smiled and obliged like the good little starlet she was. Thirty seconds with the fans and they'd be on their way, because he didn't like how exposed she was. Not one bit.

They didn't have thirty seconds.

A dark shadow split the girls apart, knocked them roughly aside, and wedged into Molly's personal space. A photographer?

An admirer.

And he was admiring his hand on Molly's forearm, especially how it gripped her tight enough to bruise.

"Molly, Ryan doesn't deserve you!" the shadow said.

Molly yanked back but the admirer held on, soulless eyes unfocused, spittle-flecked lips working to proclaim his adoration. Definitely on something, and not just the high of getting this close to his favorite movie star.

Wyatt's *don't dare fuck with me* training kicked in.

He chopped the heel of his right hand against the admirer's throat, neutralizing him with a single blow, and absorbed the sting of pain barreling all the way up to his wrecked shoulder. The admirer fell. The girls screamed. The security yelled.

Pande-*fucking*-monium.

With his left arm wrapped around Molly's waist, Wyatt carried her up the steps to her front door. "Key," he grunted.

She blinked terrified eyes at him, then over her shoulder. "The girls—"

"Will be fine." The downed target was on his knees

clutching his throat and hauling in air while the teens took photos and the security—finally—surrounded him. Not that Wyatt was looking, because his eyes were locked on Molly. But he knew two things with certainty: Wyatt's hands were lethal and teenage girls were ruthless.

"Key, Molly."

Visibly shaken, she fished it out of a side pocket of her shorts and handed it to him. He unlocked the front door and ushered her inside.

Shutting the door, he scanned the wall for the beeping alarm panel. "The code."

Her hand shook as she raised it. Her fingers slipped on the buttons. "I ca—I can't . . ." The beeping turned shriller, a countdown to drawing every dog, cop, and reporter to the house.

He curled a hand around her neck and turned her to face him. Wide-eyed, flushed, and so damn beautiful even in her terror. "You've got this."

She input the code without hesitation and the beeping stopped.

The door blew open behind them and Wyatt blocked Molly with his body, braced for confrontation. It was only one of the suits.

Good, because Wyatt's hands weren't done talking.

CHAPTER NINE

Molly was dimly aware of a door slamming, voices muted and raised, and the panicked utterances of *fuck, fuck, fuck*. It wasn't coming from her. Was it Wyatt?

His large palm gripped her elbow firmly and all she could do was stare at it, comparing it to the strange, clammy hand that had manacled her outside.

"Molly, you okay?"

She met his gaze, those crystal blue shards now on fire as he searched her face.

Her head felt too heavy for her neck, like it should roll off her shoulders and out onto the street so anyone could kick and stomp it. Behind Wyatt, Green Tea Crème Frappuccino Terrence was pacing the townhouse's foyer. The mutterer.

"Molly, you all right?" Wyatt asked.

She nodded once because anything more would detach her head. It would bounce down the steps like a beach ball and they would boot it all the way into the lake and—

"Words, babe. I need words."

I'm fine. Absolutely fabulous. Never better. "Okay. Just got a scare."

Terrence stepped forward. "Miss Cade, we need

to—" The words died in his throat, likely because Wyatt had choked them off with a huge paw around his neck.

"What the fuck was that?"

Wyatt eased up enough to let Terrence explain what the fuck that was. "Th—the guy came out of nowhere!"

"There's no such thing. Your job is to monitor every possible threat, not flirt with the first piece of ass who smiles at your fugly face. Molly's the mission and you just failed the fucking mission."

She had seen Wyatt's muted fury the day she climbed the ladder at the academy, but this was a hundred times more intense. More personal. She thought it might also be hot, but that likely meant her brain was not firing on all cylinders, because who the hell thinks that in a moment like this?

"Wyatt, it's okay." Feeling like she was moving in slow motion, she palmed his wrist, still cupping Terrence's bull-thick neck. "I'm safe now."

"We'll see." He released Terrence and said, "You be a good boy and check in with the fuckwits who hired you."

Terrence scowled. "I don't take orders from you."

"Seeing as how I just performed the job you were paid to do, I'd say you're probably the least qualified person to argue with me on this." Gently, he gripped Molly's elbow. "With me. Now."

In the living room, he sat her down—actually placed her on the sofa—and stood before her, hands on hips, jaw clenched so hard a single touch might shatter it.

"How many exits?"

"What?"

"How many exits does this house have?"

She looked around, not having given it much thought. The house had an alarm system and the studio-supplied security usually put her mind at ease. Hoping to spend her summer living a normal Chi-Town neighborhood existence in what she had thought was an urban sanctuary, only now was she starting to realize what an impossible dream that was for someone like her.

"There's the kitchen through there." She pointed behind him.

"Any balconies in the bedrooms?"

"A terrace overlooking the back garden."

He took off and was back a minute later. "This isn't gonna work."

"What isn't?" The tech consult? The jogs along the lake? Them?

Hey, now, where the hell had that come from?

"Good alarm system, but you're too exposed. Two teens and a weirdo know where you live. Won't be long before word gets out. If you have to run a gauntlet every time you step outside your door, you're going to spend your summer on a misery yo-yo between the set and here."

"I don't know how they found out. A friend of mine owns this place, but only a select few people know I'm staying here. That guy on the street . . ." She swallowed. "Is he hurt?"

"He'll live. Cops will want to interview you. Determine if charges should be made."

"I—I don't want to bring charges. Guys get too close all the time." *Ryan doesn't deserve you,* the man had said before he gripped her arm. Damn straight. "He was just an overzealous fan."

"You want to face that every time you walk out the door?"

"I can use the back entrance. Hire more security."

His expression was stoic, not buying her blasé assessment. To be honest, she didn't want to make a big deal of it, and if that meant adding more layers of cotton wool, then so be it. Wordlessly, he left the room and the sound of raised voices, or one raised voice belonging to Terrence, carried over the polished hardwood. In the foyer, she found Wyatt and her security detail in the process of pulling out tape measures for a thorough dick length assessment.

Terrence's eyes lit up in relief on seeing Molly. "Miss Cade, we need to discuss your security arrangements."

"Discussion over," Wyatt ground out. "You're fired."

"You can't do that," Molly and Terrence said in unison. Shaking her head in disbelief, Molly addressed Wyatt. "Stop bossing everybody around. We need to discuss this." She winced at how that sounded. *We.* Like she had already given him a say in the decision.

She turned to Terrence and gave him a more sympathetic look than he deserved. "I think it would be best if you waited outside. I'll call you if I need you." *If?* Jesus, she was already being brainwashed by Wyatt Fox.

Visibly affronted, Terrence opened his mouth and seemed to think better of it. He made a noisy departure that affirmed he had no stealth skills whatsoever.

Annoyed with pretty much everyone, she steeled

her spine and faced Wyatt. "Listen. I make the decisions about my safety and who I employ. I do not need some know-it-all ex-marine firefighter waltzing in here barking orders at everyone."

"Former."

"What?"

"It's former marine. Ex is for servicemen who got the big chicken dinner."

She could feel the frigid air of the townhouse's cooling system on her tongue, which could mean only one thing: her jaw had dropped open.

"In. English."

"You only call a marine ex if he was ousted on a bad conduct discharge. Big chicken dinner. I'm a know-it-all *former* marine firefighter."

They were locking horns over whether this caveman should be responsible for her personal safety on a level that was already feeling far too personal, and he was arguing over semantics?

He crossed his arms, and a lean expanse of delicious, tan skin filled her vision. Those arms had protected her ten minutes ago. Warded off evil and carried her to safety. The pleasure and pain he could deliver with those weapons thrilled and terrified her.

"This"—he waved around the townhouse foyer—"is not going to work for you. Unless you want to live in a fortress. And if you do, you'll need better security."

"The studio hired them. Said they were the best."

"They were distracted by a pretty face and didn't see the danger coming at you. They let me take you out of their sight after one conversation. Complete amateurs." He stepped in close, huge and beautiful above her, and tipped her chin up to face him. Nothing would have given her greater comfort than to sink against that chest, clearly made for her frazzled head.

"If I could be here myself, Molly, I would—"

"But you can't." She swallowed, and what emerged next sounded rusty. "And I'm not your responsibility."

Truth was, she wanted him here, filling this gigantic space with his solidity. The altercation with that fan, if that's what he could be called, had unnerved her. But that wasn't even on the table. Wyatt had his own responsibilities, and his life would be compromised by a close association with her. Most guys—and why was it that lately all her sentences started that way when she thought of Wyatt Fox?—would jump at the chance to be seen with her. But not this one.

She remembered when she was nothing, a nobody, and Ryan Michaels, Superstar, had chosen her to be his arm candy. *You're going to love the attention, Molly. We're all little whores at heart.* She had never grown to love it in the way Ryan had claimed she would, and she completely understood that a man as private as Wyatt would hate to be thrust into the limelight. He had his niece and family to think of.

Ignoring the lurch in her chest, the one that signaled regret that her life was so at odds with his, she drew a fortifying breath.

"So that's that. Thanks for your concern, but I will manage this situation myself. That's why I have people."

She knew it left her mouth sounding imperious, but sometimes that diva bitch was the only thing keeping her from falling into an abyss of woe-is-me. *Climb back onto your pedestal, Molly, where the air is clearer and your nostrils aren't filled with the intoxicating male spice of ex—no, former—marine firefighters.*

He didn't say a word, just stared at her, into her, with those eyes that could force truths and drop panties.

Neither would be happening. She was an Oscar-nominated actor, after all.

♦ CHAPTER TEN

Having made his selections, Wyatt stepped back from the jukebox in Dempsey's on Damen, the family's bar and Sean's legacy outside the firehouse. The ethereal synth opening of the Who's "Won't Get Fooled Again" flooded the air, a welcome relief from the usual diet of U2, Thin Lizzy, and Hozier that the bar's patrons inevitably chose on a nightly basis.

A long-suffering groan was followed by a *thunk* behind him. Over his shoulder, he spied Alex playing drama queen, banging her head against the bar. SOP when Wyatt chose the music.

"Jesus, Wy, we know you *act* like a sixty-five-year-old, but do you have to inflict the tunes of your old-man generation on the rest of us at every opportunity?"

He stepped behind the bar, wiping down a counter spill as he went. "Sorry, can't hear you. My eardrums are shot from standing too close to the speakers at Woodstock in '69."

Chuckling, she held up her phone, though Wyatt didn't need to look to know what filled the screen.

"So it seems not only do you need lessons in musical taste but you could do with a few pointers on how to handle the fame game."

"Worried I'm trespassing on your territory as You-Tube maven?"

"As if." She shook her head in disgust. "The hoodie, the sunnies, the ninja-ghost reflexes to disable that dickhead—no one even knows it was you! Not a single smile for the camera or a flash of your Dempsey tats. I'm ashamed to call you my brother."

He hid his smile in a draft of Coke. Mere hours since the incident outside Molly's house, and video taken by those teens of him flooring the assailant had gone viral. Slow news day, he guessed. So far no one outside of his family had identified him, which was just the way he liked it. More important, Jen hadn't called—yet—looking to use it as further leverage to pull Roni away from them.

But damn it, he'd hated leaving Molly behind. That went against every single instinct—marine, fire-fighter, and male.

Wyatt had wanted to wrap her in the embrace of his body, soothe away the fear beating in her eyes. Instead, he'd waited with her, impotent with rage, while she made a police report and insisted she was fine. She refused to bring charges, claiming "overzealousness" on the part of that fucker. The woman talked a good game, but more troubling was the fact that she was minimizing it. As if it was an acceptable by-product of being famous.

What kind of life did she lead where that was considered normal?

Luke emerged from the back carrying a crate of Newcastle Brown Ale. Wyatt moved to help but earned an Almeida grunt of "I've got it."

Relations between them had been, to put it mildly,

strained. In the three weeks since Roni made her dramatic entrance, the flurry of activity her stay had caused evened out everyone else's mood about the circumstances that had taken her out of their lives for so long. Everyone but Luke.

Luke straightened from putting the bottles in the fridge and faced Wyatt. "All the years I've known you and I've never seen you lose it once."

"You still haven't." Wyatt crossed his arms. "What you saw—"

"What the world saw."

Wyatt suppressed a nascent growl. "What you saw was a surgical removal of a threat. No tempers lost, no theatrics."

Luke cocked his head. "Will Roni's mom see it that way? Because according to you, that's the kind of behavior that kept our niece away from us in the first place."

"Hey, guys," Alex said in her mom voice, but this was past peacemaking.

Anger flared in Wyatt's blood. "Do you not believe me, Luke? Do you think I'd make that up?"

"Hell if I know." He immediately held up a hand in apology. "I know you'd never keep her from us on purpose. I just wish we'd been told."

"So you and Alex could go charging in? Jen would have hit us with a restraining order so ironclad it would have been years before we could have come within spitting distance of Roni, let alone get to know her as one of our own." Wyatt unfolded his arms, aiming to come off less defensive than he sounded. Too late. "If I could have handled it another way, I would have. She's here now and we need to make up for lost time. Present a united front."

"United front?" Sarcas-o-meter levels shot through the roof. "You just got done blaming Alex and me for why Roni was kept away from us because apparently we're magnets for drama. Yet *you* decide to go jogging with someone who has paparazzi following her around. Your face is all over the news."

"No one ID'd me and she's . . ." Fuck, he couldn't even say it. *She's my past. She's nothing. She's someone I can never, ever have.*

"You're full of it," Luke said with a sneer. "On practically every squad run and night you work behind this bar, chicks throw themselves at you and nada. Woman repelling doesn't even begin to describe it. But Hollywood comes calling and all of a sudden, Wyatt Fox's dick accepts a new mission. You couldn't take your eyes off her at the cookout."

"I know what I'm doing here," he insisted, but the words sounded hollow even to his own ears. "Molly Cade is just a job and Roni will never be in danger. Half the time she's staying at your or Beck's place anyways." Because she was in a perma-silent standoff with Wyatt. She didn't want to talk about Logan and that's all Wyatt wanted to talk about.

He missed his brother.

He also missed Luke, the man who had stepped up and shown Wyatt the meaning of family. Wyatt had tried to return the favor. When Kinsey had left Luke almost a year ago to head back to California, Wyatt told him to quit being a martyr and go after his girl. Luke laid it all on the line, told Kinsey he'd move to San Francisco to be with her, that he'd leave the Dempseys behind because she was now his number one.

It hadn't come to that, thank God, but Luke had chosen his woman—had chosen happy—and Wyatt had been so proud of his brother's bold decision. He deserved it after dedicating his life to the family when Wyatt had failed. Now it felt like Luke was testing him. *Where do your loyalties lie, Wyatt? Prove you're a Dempsey because you sure as shit haven't done much to make us believe.*

Hell, Wyatt knew getting any more involved with Molly was a catastrophe in the making. No more fun runs along the lakefront. No more holding her close as she lost her shit. No more . . . selfish indulgence.

A scowling Luke headed back down to the cellar, leaving Wyatt to grip the edge of the bar, his annoyance at being dressed down still bubbling through his heated blood. He had wanted to spend time with a goddess, and yeah, he knew that was ridiculous—and not just because it equaled hassle for his family.

Alex set a black and tan on the counter for one of the cops from District 5. Once he'd moved out of earshot, she turned to Wyatt.

"So," she said, all slyness, "you haven't explained exactly *why* you and Molly Cade are jogging besties."

"Just trying to toughen her up for the shoot."

Hilarity ensued. "What are you going to wow her with next, Wy? A rhumba with the kickboxing bag? A tango on the rowing machine in your basement?"

Suffer patiently. Patiently suffer.

"It was a onetime deal. Won't be happening again."

"She must have been pretty scared, though," Alex mused, worry he identified with threaded through her voice. He'd watched the video a couple of times, freeze-framing on an image that checked his heart cold each time he saw it: a terrified Molly as that guy tried to get all up in her business.

But Wyatt couldn't do anything except ask a couple of off-duty CPD buddies to check in on occasion. Let the diva pay her security team a fortune to keep weirdos from her door. After that kiss on the hood of his Camaro, the one he'd used to fuel every hand job since, and the sexy coda in her trailer, a line needed to be drawn in the sand.

Problem was he wanted to cross it. Again and again.

"She'll be fine. Woman like that's got plenty of resources to pay more rent-a-cops or find a new place."

With those all-seeing eyes, Alex watched him for a protracted beat before a customer grabbed her attention and let Wyatt off the hook.

Molly took a sip of a robust Malbec and ignored the townhouse's ringing landline. Again. Really, she should unplug it because nothing good was on the other end, but taking that step had all the hallmarks of panic. Surrender. She was trying to play it cool.

And failing.

Ever since the incident this morning, she'd been jumpier than a frog on a hotplate. Cal had called from Tennessee as soon as footage of Wyatt Fox, 1, Grabby Fan, 0 had surfaced on the Internet. Faced with her friend's concern, Molly had played it down—Molly's problems weren't worth spit in comparison to Cal's while she looked after her gran (who was out of the woods, thank God).

Maybe Molly should have pressed charges. She knew celebrities who had done it for less, but it seemed like an overreaction to a man who had wanted to— what? Talk? Hug? Since Ryan, she'd been trying not to sweat the small stuff or do anything that made her a target for the haters. The look on Wyatt's face when she told the detective she was *fine, absolutely fabulous, never better* said it all. Why was she accepting this as normal?

Because grasping on to normal was sometimes all she had. It's what she had wanted this summer. Now that dream felt as solid as smoke. She had a leasing agent looking for somewhere new, but these things invariably took time, even for someone with as many resources as she had.

Five minutes later, her mobile phone rang and Molly jumped half a mile into the air, spilling half her wine on her blouse. Enough! She needed to quit acting like a scalded cat.

It was a gruff Terrence. "There's an Alex Dempsey here. Says you're expecting her."

She wasn't, but she was hella glad for the distraction. "Please let her up."

Molly opened the door to find a beaming Alex in jeans, Converse, and a hoodie that barely contained her rumpus of hair.

"Top Cop here needs to work on his reflexes. *And* he got a bit handsy when he finally caught up with me." Stepping inside, she shot Terrence a withering look over her shoulder that said his genetic line might end here if he dared to lay another hand on her. "Too much, too late, dude."

Poor Terrence. He was really having a rotten day. Hiding her smile, Molly closed the big oak door behind her and made sure the dead bolt was re-secured. She hadn't used it before yesterday but now she was hypervigilant.

"At the cookout a few weeks ago," Alex said, "I mentioned I'd be happy to chat with you about the trials and tribulations of being a Vagina American in the CFD. So here I am." She looked up to the cathedral ceiling and gave a low whistle. "Nice place."

An understatement. The three-story townhouse, impeccably furnished and loaded with modern art, belonged to a movie director friend who was currently filming in London. Molly loved the neighborhood, its proximity to the lake, and how it felt like a sorority house when Cal was here. Without the pledging. And the Jell-O shots.

There might have been Jell-O shots.

But now it felt cavernous and lonely. Oppressive.

"Thanks, it does the trick." Molly was often a little weirded out by her own wealth. She didn't own this house, but she owned something four times as large in Malibu. The butt pinches she'd suffered as a cocktail waitress, even the rash she'd acquired while wearing that Lonnie the Lobster costume to hand out flyers on Santa Monica Pier, were war wounds in her struggle to the top. She had worked her ass off, and on occasion she had to remind herself that she deserved good things.

Alex was staring at Molly's chest. "Any joy juice left or are wine-stained shirts all the rage in Beverly Hills?"

Molly grinned, looking down at the mess on her blouse. It was shaping up to look like Texas. "I'll change and then we can open a new bottle. Damon's cellar can handle it."

"Damon?"

"Damon Castello. He's letting me stay while he's filming in London."

"The director? I didn't know he lived in Chicago." Alex's gaze swept over the great room that led to the full-service kitchen and humongous dining area. "You move in pretty ritzy circles, lady. Not bad for—"

"A farm girl from Missouri?"

"I was going to say a no-talent hack."

Molly's mouth dropped open.

Alex cracked up. "Just kidding! Sorry, I tend to say stupid shit to people, assuming everyone has the same sense of humor I do." Translation: *Are you a tight-assed diva or can you take a joke?* She eyed the Mondrian hanging over the fireplace. "I'm guessing that's probably an original. I've no idea what of, but I'll take a stab and say it's an original 'Look away and don't sully it with your filthy gaze.'"

"Exactly," Molly said, laughing. An earlier work of the artist, it was a bargain at a paltry $15 million. "Come check out the wine cellar and let's pick something outrageously expensive."

Ten minutes later, Molly had changed into clean clothes and was dispensing liberally from a bottle of 2008 Mouton Rothschild. "Dinner is poured."

"Hmm, fruity," Alex said after a healthy gulp.

Somewhere a French vintner's heart cracked in half. "I need to take a picture of the label to prove to Eli I drank it. He thinks I'm such a heathen because I know nothing about wine."

"Yet he's still crazy about you."

Her face lit bright, and unreasonable envy tackled Molly's heart for a nanosecond.

"I kissed my fair share of frogs back in the day," Alex said. "And then the biggest toad of all turned out to be a prince in disguise. Go figure."

"What he did for you . . . when I heard about it, I positively swooned." Molly and the rest of America. Eli Cooper's sacrifice of his mayoralty on the altar of love was up there with Edward VIII and Mrs. Simpson.

"Hey, so did I. And I'm not a swooner, I'll tell ya." Alex looked at her phone as it chirped with an incoming message. Her cheeks flushed. "The man also knows his way around a dirty text. Of course, I'm not talking to him right now after he covered for Wyatt about Roni. I'd thought we were past all that underhanded bullshit. You wouldn't believe some of the stunts he pulled to get me in the sack."

After dealing with Ryan, nothing could have surprised Molly. Most men were pretty good at looking out for their self-interest. She wasn't tipsy enough to confide that and neither did she want to put a damper on a woman so obviously in love.

So instead she used her words to defend Wyatt.

"Seems like your brother was in a pretty tough position."

Alex arched a skeptical brow. "Perhaps, but I have to wonder when he was going to tell us. Wy's always been a lone wolf, and while I don't doubt his loyalty or love, I'm also aware that he's never seemed to need us as much as we need him. Knowing him like I do, I bet he could have waited out this call forever, maybe until Roni was eighteen." She sighed heavily. "And then there's you."

Molly froze. "Me?"

"Yeah, I mean, he's clearly into you, but will he do a thing about it? You bet your sweet—"

The house phone rang on the Chippendale sideboard, cutting Alex off. Predictably, Molly jumped. She made no move to answer it, though, preferring to let Alex finish whatever she'd been about to say.

You know, about Wyatt being *into* her. OMG! She wanted to draw hearts all over her diary.

Alex frowned at the phone. "Not going to get that?"

"It's Damon's line, so I've been leaving the calls. If it's for me, I don't want to hear it." She laughed nervously as she waited for the ringing to stop . . . *five . . . six . . . silence.*

"Why wouldn't you want to hear it if it's for you?"

She drew a deep breath. "Since people have found out where I live, I've had a few well-wishers checking in to tell me how much they enjoyed my photo spread from a few months back." She left it at that, the implication obvious. Once her location became public knowledge, it was just a matter of time before someone found out the house's landline number. It might have been unlisted, but an enterprising stalker would always find a way. This afternoon, she'd picked up and the filth she'd heard spewed over the line made her skin crawl.

"After my brief hook-up with fame last year," Alex said, "I had plenty of asshats crawling out the woodwork looking to light my fire, if you know what I mean." She worried her lip. "But I didn't get any phone calls. That's not nice. It's much easier to ignore it online."

Agreed, but for now, Molly would handle it the best she could. In a fetal ball.

"I'm looking for somewhere else and the security outside puts my mind at ease." She smiled big, trying to keep the shake out of her voice. *For your consideration, members of the academy, another amazing performance from America's Fallen Sweetheart, Molly Cade.*

"The mall cops?" Alex asked incredulously. "Sorry, probably not what you want to hear, but Wy was unusually vocal about their skillset. About as upset as I've ever seen him."

The damn phone rang again, and this time Alex hopped off the sofa and made a grab for it.

"No, you don't have—"

"Hello?"

Oh, God. Molly's bones tightened in discomfort as she watched Alex's expression turn from open to curious to downright surprised.

"Whoa, hold up there, handsome! I'm guessing that crowbar of yours is *pret*-ty hard right now. Whatcha got for me? Five inches? Five and a half?"

Molly covered her face with her hands as Alex listened for a few seconds, then went on to explain exactly where the caller should shove his below-average-length penis. Anatomically impossible, but remarkably colorful.

Alex dropped the phone back into its cradle. "Who in fucktopia still has a landline these days anyway?"

"What did he—never mind. I appreciate you standing up for me, but it's really best to ignore it."

Alex's brow crimped like a corduroy swatch. "I used to think that. I got a lot of hate where I worked, most of it insidious, because I was doing something that's traditionally seen as requiring male wedding tackle. I didn't want to rock the boat or look like I needed special treatment for my lady sensibilities. So I'm the first to admit I've had a hard time finding the middle ground. Either I'm going off the reservation cutting up chauvinistic assholes' cars or I'm biting my tongue worried I'll come off as too mouthy. Being a woman is pretty freakin' hard on a regular day, but there is no good reason why you should continue to put up with the shit you've endured this last year. Scum like that"—she waved at the phone— "needs to be wiped off the face of the earth."

Molly's heart cheered at Alex's spirited inclusion of her in the sisterhood. "You want to be my publicist?"

She grinned. "Sure, if you don't mind your big comeback failing spectacularly." Her expression faded to bleak again as she cast a troubled glance up at the cathedral ceiling. "This place is on the big side for one person."

"I had a friend staying but she had to leave town for a family emergency." And now Molly was alone, hyperaware of every sound: the shrill ring of the phone, the fridge's ominous heartbeat, the dramatic whoosh of the AC as it geared up into action.

She was afraid of appliances. A new low.

Alex frowned at whatever she saw on Molly's face. "You can't stay here, girl."

True. It was time to admit defeat and check into a hotel, though that inevitably came with its own set of problems. Last year, she'd holed up in one after the photo hack occurred during a movie shoot in London and felt like she was under medieval siege, especially when a hotel employee leaked pics of her emotional coping methods, i.e., binge eating the entire room service menu.

"Go pack a bag, Molly." From Alex's expression, Molly guessed a different plan might be on the table.

"If you're offering a room at Cooper Manor, I appreciate it but—"

Alex held up her hand. "You do not want to be in the middle of me and Eli the way I feel about him right now. Besides, he's such a manipulative prick he'll have you on his side with his lawyerly tricks within the hour." She looked incredibly pleased with herself. "I have a much better idea."

CHAPTER ELEVEN

Wyatt walked into his kitchen just after nine in the morning and found Roni, her thumbs skimming a mile a minute over her phone.

"Hey, girl."

Her head snapped back at the sound of his voice. A guilty blush suffused her cheeks, and she immediately turned off her phone.

"Talking to your friends back home?" Or maybe a boy. Better not be a boy because he would very soon be not-a-boy. He'd be a eunuch.

"Yeah."

He leaned against the counter, projecting casual. "Miss them?"

"Not really. Lili's in summer school and Kat has a part-time job in her dad's restaurant. Wouldn't have seen them much anyway."

So much for the Summer of Roni. He'd assumed she would enjoy Chicago more, getting to know her family. That she had planned this all along. But she'd shut down most efforts to fill her time, opting instead to hang around Wyatt's place and fill her brain with mindless TV on her iPad. "Some of the guys I work with have daughters your age. Maybe I could introduce you."

She rolled her eyes and shot him a look of *Lame*.

Jesus, he was trying here. This was exactly how all his visits had gone over the last year. As soon as he met her and saw his brother's face shining back at him, he had made every human effort to connect. She'd demonstrated pretty much no interest, only a bored disdain. But she'd also shown up at his house this summer, so he knew there must be something she wanted—he just didn't know what.

"Okay, Roni, cards on the table here."

Her blue-gray eyes—Logan's eyes—widened.

"Time for some truth telling. You can ask me anything you want."

"Anything?"

This kid was his flesh and blood. His only living biological relative. It was a heavy responsibility and he didn't plan on shirking it.

"About your dad, his family, us. Whatever you want to know."

She considered him intently. "What difference does it make? He wasn't around."

"If he'd known about you, it would have been another story."

But he didn't, her hard expression said, and the result was the same. Just like the man she'd thought was her father had abandoned her when her parents divorced, then cut her dead when he found out she didn't share his genetic code. While she was fighting a killer disease ravaging her body. Roni was pretty much shit out of luck when it came to fathers.

She seemed to recognize that Wyatt wasn't going to let her go without some attempt at discussing Logan. "So what was he like, then? The sperm donor."

"Don't call him that. He's more than just a scrap of DNA."

Color tinged her cheeks, and he immediately regretted his testiness.

"Sweetheart, I'm sorry. I know this is hard. Logan was . . . funny. Warm." The one tasked with charming the old ladies during Dad's grifter schemes while Wyatt stood around tongue-tied and awkward. Billy Fox's constant, heart-crushing comparisons of Wyatt's uselessness to Logan's appeal should have made Wyatt jealous of his half brother, but he was impossible to hate.

"He had a way about him. Magnetic. Drew people in."

"Must be how he fooled Mom."

Ignoring that, he drew a deep breath. "He would have been a kid when he"—*he knocked up your mother*—"met your mom. Nineteen. Just joined the fire department." A year younger, Wyatt had joined the marines at the same time, needing to forge his own path. As much as he loved being a Dempsey, sometimes it suffocated him. He wanted to make something of his own.

Logan didn't understand why Wyatt would seek out separation from his family. *We landed on our feet with the Dempseys, Wy. Golden. You really wanna mess with that?* There had never been a word of recrimination from Sean that Wyatt had chosen another road, that he didn't buy into the hoopla surrounding CFD. Sean had squeezed his shoulder when Wyatt showed him the enlistment papers, those Irish eyes twinkling with pride. They didn't talk much, but they understood each other.

Which all added up to Wyatt as the worst person to be doing this; any other Dempsey would be better because he had never learned the language to emote. Logan's easy mouth would have known exactly what to say.

"I don't know what happened between your mom and dad, but I do know that if Logan met you now, he'd be so proud of you. How beautiful you are. How strong you've become. That's how we all feel."

She blew out a breath through hair falling over eyes that looked suspiciously shiny.

"Kinsey's picking me up soon to go shopping," she mumbled out of the corner of her mouth. "I need to get ready."

"Sure, sweetheart." At least she was doing something with one of the family. But had he made any progress here? 'Cause it felt like he'd slipped further into a mud pit of failure. And if she had actually asked the right questions, how would he have answered them?

Where did you guys grow up? *Crack houses and motels. Rust-bucket cars and bus depots. Everywhere and nowhere.*

What were my biological grandparents like? *Well, Grandma was a junkie, Gramps was MIA, but no worries—Logan had a stepdad,* my *dad, who taught him the family trade. How to pass a fake hundred-dollar bill. How to bilk someone out of their life savings. How to get something for nothing.*

A lineage to be proud of.

As he watched her walk out, it hit him full force: guilt at hiding Roni from his family; aching regret that he couldn't bridge the gap with his niece; sheer impotence at not being able to protect Molly properly; and to top it all off, his trusty pal, sexual frustration.

To have his desire explode like this with the one woman he couldn't use it on was one of life's crueler *fuck you*s. Christ, he needed off that shoot. Seeing her every day and having to call his lust to heel was a special brand of torture. A few strokes . . . of the rowing machine might distract him for a while.

After twenty minutes of "gentle" oar work in his basement gym, Wyatt was feeling the burn again in his shoulder. The PT had told him to ease into it, but Wyatt didn't want easy. He wanted to work it off. Punish himself.

Back in the kitchen, he opened the fridge and saw yet another reason why he was the worst guardian ever. Only coffee creamer and milk. Wyatt should be stacking the cupboards with nutritional goodness, because part of the contract in taking care of a teen was that they needed to be fed more than cereal. Thank God for Gage.

Who had better coffee than Wyatt. Usually those fun-sized one-cups with all the different flavors. Wyatt really liked the hazelnut one and he didn't much feel like loading his banged-up Mr. Coffee or heading down to the Dunkin' when there was a perfectly decent option going begging next door.

He stepped outside and that sense of failure struck him upside the head again at the sight of the pissyellow grass and jungle growth. Compared to Gage's submission for *House & Garden* magazine, Wyatt's backyard looked like a landscaping apocalypse. Mating velociraptors, indeed. Shrugging it off, he headed toward the gate separating his yard from Gage's and stopped as a sound assaulted his ears.

Assaulted was probably overstating it. It was music, the kind that was supposed to be soothing. Pipes? Waves? A flutist on a kayak? A voice droned in a bland, genderless tone: "Now raise your body to greet the sun."

Drawing closer, he peeked over the fence and the vista that greeted him did a damn sight better job than a cup of joe:

Molly freakin' Cade.

Wasn't it enough that she had a starring role in his dreams—must she haunt his waking hours, as well? Right now, the desert mirage before him was coming out of a down-on-all-fours position, pointing her very fine ass in the air. Stretchy material across her rear was currently being pushed to its limits as she held ass-to-the-sun pose.

The ethereal voice that was starting to creep Wyatt out advised deeper breaths, bunchier cores, and love for your fellow man. Well, not the last one, but Wyatt wouldn't have been surprised to hear it. Molly's bare arms, nicely tanned and toned, looked like they could hold that position forever. It had to be at least a minute he'd been standing there gaping like a horny teenager, assuring himself that the hallucination was very, very real.

"How's my form?" she asked, not breaking the pose.

"Looks great from this angle," he managed.

He crossed over into Gage's yard and walked around the purple yoga mat stretched out on the patio. "Not bad on this side, either."

Sadly, she pulled out of it and sat back, knees to her chest. "And how's your charge this morning?"

Huh. So they were going to pretend that Molly Cade's presence next door on a yoga mat at ten in the morning was completely normal. He guessed stranger things had happened.

"Surly, pissed, noncommunicative, or all of the above. She's currently inflicting her joy on Kinsey. Gone shopping."

"And you didn't want to join them?"

"Next time."

That earned him a saucy grin. She held out her hand, looking for help to stand.

He gave it, enjoying the grip on her smooth palm so much he held on and continued to enjoy it. "You do this every morning?"

"I try to. When I'm working, I manage in my trailer."

"Times, please."

"Why, would you like to join me one day? Get in touch with your chakras?"

"More of an observer. Not in a creepy way, though."

Look at him, Mr. Fucking Flirty.

"Might be good for your shoulder." Her expression shifted to concern as she reached for his bicep and rubbed. They still held hands. Music still played. Puppies should be entering from stage left any second. "How's it feeling?"

Like he would have no problem lifting her against the fence and driving in deep and true. The outside temp was cooler than average, but his blood was boiling with the heat of her closeness.

He dropped her hand. "So . . ."

"I expect you're curious about why I'm here."

"Curious? Sure, let's go with that."

"Your sister—"

"Say no more. Alex, and I'm guessing Gage, decided that this would be the perfect secluded spot for the Hollywood diva trying to dodge the paparazzi." He was pretty sure he could plead extenuating circumstances during his trial for Alex's murder. Any judge who saw that video of her cutting up Sam Cochrane's car would recognize that she had eventually pissed off the wrong person and that her demise was justifiable homicide.

Molly frowned, and he regretted his grumpiness, especially so soon after the headway he'd made with the cute rom-com banter. Girls were confusing.

"I have someone working on finding a new place," she said, "but it could take a little while. I can handle the press at my door but . . ." A flicker of discomfort crossed her face. "Believe me when I say this was not my idea."

He didn't doubt it. She had been more than clear that she didn't want his help, though her fear had been a palpable thing.

Something had changed.

A tug of war was duking it out in his chest. She was here, safe, where he could keep an eye on her. This was exactly what his primal subconscious had wanted, and though he wasn't in a position to make it happen directly, somehow the gods had smiled on him.

He'd hold off on sending Alex to her maker for now.

"You have coffee yet?" he asked.

"I was just about to one-push the Keurig."

She turned and walked into the kitchen, offering him the perfect view of her ass in those curve-hugging yoga pants. It was a good thing she was staying next door, because if he had to witness that flitting around his kitchen, she would not be safe.

Molly wasn't sure what she'd anticipated would happen once she ran into Wyatt.

Grumpiness? Of course.

Sex-in-a-beard? Undoubtedly.

But flirting? Unexpected—and incredibly hot.

Granted, he could have been reciting the phone book and she would have been mopping up the drool. Because *hello there,* glistening slab of badassery. He must have been working out. His frayed Marine Corps–emblazoned tee was damp with sweat, a bead of it trickling down his beefy arm.

She wanted to lick it.

But first, further explanation of her presence seemed necessary. "Wyatt, this is just for a night or two. I'll be out of here before you know it."

Ignoring that, he reached for a cupboard and there was no missing his pained wince. He gestured to the neat rows of stacked K-cups. "Gage has all the flavors."

"Your shoulder. Is it still bothering you?"

"Not a big deal."

"Sit down, dummy. Where are the Ziplocs?"

His eyes narrowed. "Did you just call me a dummy? And ask for Ziplocs?"

"Did you just deflect by answering a question with two questions?" Splaying a hand on his broad chest, she pushed him toward a chair. And pushed. Immovable, he dipped his gaze to her hand as if it were a foreign object and did not compute with his Terminator programming. She could've sworn she heard a mechanical whirring sound.

"You need coffee," he said, reverting to his primary directive.

"And you need to take care of your shoulder. I can't believe you're still overdoing it. Against doctor's orders, I'll bet."

"Popped a couple of Aleve. Doing okay."

"Sit. Down."

He obeyed, an amused curve to his lips, and watched while she ransacked the freezer for ice cubes.

"Ziplocs?"

"Bottom drawer on the right."

Using a dishcloth and a Ziploc bag, she crafted an ice pack. "Do I need to take your shirt off, as well?"

"My family's giving you a place to stay. Expecting a shirtless firefighter just seems greedy."

God, she wanted to have babies with that dry wit of his. She pressed her lips against a smile and called on a no-nonsense nurselike persona. "You're pissing me off."

He did the one-hand-over-the-shoulder-move and pulled his shirt off. No visible bruising, but even if there had been, she wasn't sure she'd have noticed.

How could he have become broader in the intervening years? Marines were the fittest bunch on the planet, and Wyatt had been the finest specimen she'd ever laid eyes on. These days, his muscles had muscles. She could grate parm on those abs. And whereas before his skin had been ink-free, now it showcased his service in the marines with a globe and anchor over his left pec, keeping company with that pulsing shamrock and red CFD logo on his biceps.

Annoyingly flustered, she twisted the dishcloth, tied a knot, and placed the pack over his right shoulder.

"Here okay?"

Covering her hand with his, he shifted the pack up. "More like here." Their fingers laced, the intimacy of it vibrating through her. He could have held the pack himself, but this joint venture seemed to be working. For both of them.

"Sit down," he said.

She glanced over her shoulder at the closest kitchen chair, a couple of feet off. About to hook it with her foot, she gasped when a brute hand landed on her waist and pulled her down in his lap.

"Not comfortable for you to stand," he said, as if that was an adequate explanation for why she was perched on the thickest thighs to ever cushion her ass.

"Not comfortable for me to sit," she managed.

The big hand tightened on her waist and pulled her closer so she landed in the well of his thighs. That was not what she'd meant, but it felt like a dream to be here, wrapped in the safe embrace of this man who had already taken care of her so handily.

Silent moments ticked over, the tension agonizing. Molly reached for any topic, a distraction. "How did it happen? Your shoulder?"

"Jumper off a bridge. Grabbed him and tore my tendons. Off squad for a couple of months."

He had saved someone's life. "So yesterday's heroics are just run-of-the-mill for you."

Those blue-gray eyes took her measure. "Figure I owe the universe."

"In what way?"

"What I did before in the service placed me on the negative side of the cosmic equation." At her frown, he added, "I was a sniper in the marines."

"Oh, I see." Of course. When the world was falling apart, who else would you trust to keep you safe but Wyatt Fox? But did he truly think there was some cosmic imbalance because he had killed in the service of his country?

"What you did before, those decisions you made, the lives you took, all of that saved others. I think your ledger is very much in the black, even without what you do now, day in, day out."

"You don't know what I've done."

She knew what she saw before her: a good man trying to do right by everyone. And here she was complicating his already complicated life.

"What you did yesterday, protecting me, getting me to safety—I didn't thank you. I was so frazzled, couldn't think straight."

"That happen a lot?"

"More so in the last year since . . . since everything with Ryan. Mostly it comes at me online. I've been trying to take the high road and block out the nastiness. Not make trouble, keep a low profile."

She'd allowed her husband to take photos of her and was punished for it. She'd demonstrated to all that she was a sexual being, precisely the thing they objectified daily before the hack. At once desired and despised.

She refocused her attention on the ice pack, now

squishier because it was melting from his body heat—or the heat between them. His hand trailed her thigh, calming the shake that had started up without her even realizing it.

"Whenever you're ready to stand up and take it back, you let me know."

"Take what back?"

No response was forthcoming, but she knew the answer anyway. The *it* was her. What had he said while calming her through her meltdown at the farmers' market? *Remember you are fierce, that inside you beats the heart of a warrior.* She needed to find her warrior heart and take back her life. Make the *it* about her.

He smoothed long strokes of comfort against her thigh. Caught up in the heady musk of him, she felt her body leaning in, falling under, going down. What a terrible nurse she was.

"How does it feel?" she asked, getting back to his medical issues.

"Like it could punch through steel."

So, not talking about his shoulder, then. Averting her gaze, she shifted, intending to rise, but his palm held her fast at her hip. Her nipples peaked, hardening painfully against her bra. No amount of padding was keeping those puppies from making their case. He snugged her tighter over the irresistible weight of his erection and placed the ice pack on the table behind her.

"Molly, look at me." His voice had dipped lower, and it reached inside her to a private, lonely place. Faced with such masculine pressure, she tried her best to resist.

A small, growing part of her questioned that. Would it be so wrong to let herself fall into him for a little while?

The next words out of her mouth should have been "This is crazy" or "We can't do this" or even "I'll take that coffee now." They should not have been what emerged: a rusty, whispered, desperate "Please."

His mouth took hers and every single reason why they should not do this was forgotten in the heat of Wyatt's kiss. So perfect. Combining ferocity with control, the man knew exactly how much pressure to apply, when to deepen, when to draw back. Wedged against him, all Molly could do was hold on and let him take what he needed. While he gave her everything she needed in return.

He rubbed his beard along her cheek, moving his lips down her jaw, her neck, the sensitive spot where her collarbone met her shoulder. Every part of her wailed for that rough yet soft texture. How would it feel grazing her breasts and her belly? The sensitive skin of her inner thighs? The aching heartbeat at her core? She moved in his lap, restless, needing to feel more of him against more of her.

His fingers latched on to the hem of her tee and curled beneath it. Coarse, hero-roughened hands traced erotic trails across her belly, at once too much and not enough. Up, up, up his hand moved until his knuckles skimmed the underside of her breast.

She jerked back, not sure why. Some innate instinct that said she wasn't ready.

"Could we take it slow?"

He licked his lips, savoring her taste, all while

regarding her with lust-stoked pupils. Panic flared. He was going to get pissed. He was going to call her a tease. After all, anyone who posed for those pictures—

"Slow's my best speed." His palm smoothed over her hip, away from her breasts, the movement forcing air from her lungs in relief.

For what seemed like hours Wyatt proved that slow was indeed his best speed. Feather-soft kisses alternated with sensuous nibbles. Lusty sucks traded with shiver-inducing caresses. Just when she thought she'd experienced every genus of kiss, he introduced a new one to surprise her. A gentle nip of her ear, a sexy lick along the seam of her mouth, a tender nuzzle along the arch of her neck.

"God, you're good at this," she breathed.

He lifted his lips from her shoulder. "You say somethin'? Kinda busy here."

She laughed, loving how patient he was. Ryan had never . . . *no*. Her ex had no place here, and neither did the haters. This was about taking it back, just like Wyatt said.

Her last exposure had occurred without her permission. The next one would be on her terms.

She peeled off her tee. Threw it to the floor.

And froze.

The problem with the claims to girl power and female agency is that they were often just that: claims. In the cold light of day, when you sat on a man's pillar-thick thighs and let him see you, truly see you, the claims suddenly sounded small. Undeserving. Especially when the man didn't say a word.

The moment held, suspended on the fog of her doubt. Seconds ticked. Tocked.

Her hand crept up to cover, because really this was ridiculous, and then finally, he reacted as if emerging from a trance, with a gentle push against her palm to keep her exposed to his gaze. Sheer, undiluted ecstasy wracked his expression.

"Christ, didn't think it was possible."

"What?"

"You, even more beautiful than my memories." His hand cupped one breast and molded her lace-covered flesh, dark eyes locked on his target. Relief that he enjoyed her body slipped into the ether, replaced with raw anticipation. But this was Wyatt. He took his time priming her with that rough palm, co-opting the scrape of the lace to incite her to madness.

"Please."

"Please what?"

"Taste me."

She felt his erection harden with those words, and she shifted, needing to crank up the crazy. Make him wild. He groaned, a deep, chest-filling sound. Slipped one breast free of its lacy prison, then the other. She arched into him, offering her body for his pleasure. For her own.

With that made-for-her mouth, he latched on to one pleasurably sore, dusky peak.

Yes.

That beard was a sexual weapon of its own. It tickled, teased, and increased her pleasure tenfold. His hot, wet mouth suckled and drew every heated sensation to the tip. Untold minutes were spent sipping and licking, his total absorption like that of an explorer with a new artifact.

By the time cool air was glancing across her skin, he was already lifting her onto the table.

"Wyatt," she protested, "your shoulder."

"Fuck my shoulder."

He pulled at the elastic waist of her yoga pants and drew them down to her ankles, then off. She let him, no longer needing to be in control of this, suspecting that control had left the kitchen with an arch smirk about ten minutes ago. At the sight of her silky black thong, his eyes turned molten with hunger, yet in typical Wyatt Fox fashion, he stayed on his own timetable.

Watching.

Feasting.

Planning.

Heat writhed like stoked embers in her belly. She widened her legs, knowing the scrap of silk wouldn't cover everything with that stretch. With each slow inch—yay, yoga—his breathing picked up and his eyes darkened further.

"Touch me," she gasped.

Giving in to her demand, he moved those rough hands ribbed for her pleasure along her thighs with a deliberate, torturous pace. His thumbs formed a V over her fabric-shielded core and hovered there with a light, unbearably teasing touch. Then one velvet swipe along the center line pushed the fabric into her soaking seam.

"Oh!" She shuddered.

"Now's the time to tell me to stop, Mol. 'Cause if you don't, this pussy is mine."

Stop? Was he mad? She supposed she should be annoyed by the "pussy is mine" comment, but a part of her thrilled at the crude words spoken with such possessiveness.

"Don't you dare."

On a lusty groan, he ripped her Agent Provocateur panties clean from her body. He splayed his hands on her inner thighs, pushing them apart for his viewing pleasure.

"Say my name. I need to hear it a million times over when my face is buried between your thighs."

"Wyatt."

He kissed the crease of her knee, softly, like he had all the time in the world. Then the other. It was one of those things she'd loved about him back then—how he never rushed.

He stopped. Waited.

Not so enamored of it now.

"Wyatt."

He started up again.

One thick finger slicked through her folds and separated. Pleasure snapped, crackled, and popped. He continued to rub, always shy of where she needed it, teasing and torturing.

She repeated his name, this new currency that would buy her untold pleasure. Callused finger pads rubbed through her wetness. *Wyatt.* He moved his lips higher, tripping tingles like live wires everywhere. *Wyatt.* Over and over, she said his name—*Wyatt, Wyatt*—giving him what he wanted to get what she needed.

"Feel how good that is?" He ran his beard along the soft skin of her inner thigh. She had no idea if he meant that texture against her skin or how his finger's slow stroke through her soaking sex was making her lose her mind.

"Wyatt."

He gently raised her ass, lowered that Viking jaw between her legs, and lapped at her.

Brain. Destroyed.

Strong hands held her in place, except to tip her up for a better angle as he licked her open.

"Feet over my shoulders, babe," he murmured, his voice's vibrations against her core giving her no choice but to obey. The position should have had her falling back on the kitchen table, but his peerless strength kept her at the perfect tilt to be pleasured like she had never been pleasured before.

Except with him. Only with him.

Cupping the back of his head, she tried her best not to get too greedy. After all, every luxurious swipe of his tongue was more than enough to ratchet up her desire. He alternated lovely, long licks with hard, spearing thrusts of his tongue, and she paid for each one gladly.

Wyatt Wyatt Wyatt.

Every scoop of moisture created more, and with it an ever-tightening coil of want. She lifted her hips in blatant appeal, craving, demanding every sensation he was giving her. Hot tongue, greedy lips, pirate jaw—the triple threat. And then his mouth sucked on her clit and she lost it, thrashing wildly as he pinned her hips in place.

As she gave herself over to her release, she might have squeezed his head so hard he grunted his discomfort. But by then she was floating on an orgasm cloud and she didn't give a damn. Even when he muttered what sounded like, "Fuckin' thighs of death."

He raised his eyes to hers, and the raw intensity she saw there made her gasp. Oh, God, if he didn't finish this properly—with him inside her—she would die.

She prayed to the god of safe sex he had a condom. The man was a walking wet dream, at risk of attack by nymphomaniacs at every turn. He should carry never-ending supplies of protection. He should have stock in Trojan. His hand went to his pocket, rummaged, and pulled out . . . yes, yes, *yes*?

A vibrating phone.

No.

He stared at it, blinked as though needing to bring what he saw on the screen into focus, and drew a breath.

"Kinsey got called into work suddenly, so Roni needs a ride."

The mention of Roni—of Wyatt's priority this summer—was like a waterfall of ice-cold water hurtling down on her head. Thoughts chased each other across his face as he worked that out for himself.

This could not happen again. No more slow kissing, comfort stroking, or mind-blowing orgasms. But it had sure been nice to get some after her two- . . . no, *three*-year drought.

"Hate to dine and dash, babe, but I need to get going."

"You did *not* just say dine and dash."

The corner of his mouth crinkled. Or she thought it did—the Thigh Tickler made it so difficult to know for sure.

He leaned in, but she did not need to be reminded

of how she tasted on his lips and how this would never, ever be enough. She placed a hand on his chest.

"Kitchen's closed, Marine."

His phone buzzed again, his groan filled the room, and before disappointment had a chance to settle, he curled a strong hand around the nape of her neck and kissed her. A thorough, deep, no-going-back kiss. Their tongues tangled, the taste of her pleasure triggering that pulse between her legs again.

He released her, looking pleasantly grumpy. "My balls don't like me much right now."

She coasted her hand away a few inches until she found what she was looking for. Over his erection, she draped the half-melted ice pack.

"Better, baby?"

His laugh was a mix of pain and amusement. Then on a soft kiss and a muttered "Evil," he left her a half-naked, quivering mess on Gage's kitchen table.

◆ CHAPTER TWELVE

"You've moved in with him?"

Molly held the phone away from her ear. At 6:05 in the morning, Cal's screech, as clear as if she was in the same room instead of five hundred miles away in Tennessee, was not helping her ease into the day.

"I've not moved in with him. I've stayed two nights with Gage and Brady next door while the leasing agent I hired works on finding me another place."

Because if she knew one thing with certainty, she could not remain here. It was bad enough witnessing the Marine's stoic consulting gig on the set. (Professional competence had always turned her on.) If she had to encounter the Wyatt Fox 'tude and badassery 24/7, she'd be a goner.

"I was really scared, Cal."

Her friend made a sympathetic cluck. "I knew you were faking it when I called last. What about the security team?"

"I gave them a couple of days off. It's best to not draw attention, at least until I'm in a new place." Given what had happened, that might sound counterintuitive, but nothing said X marks the famous person like tinted windows, dark suits, and security earpieces on quiet residential streets.

Cal hummed her agreement. "I'm trying to find out who leaked your location, but to be honest, it sounds like you are in the safest, most secure place possible."

Highly debatable.

"At least as far as your physical safety," Cal added, a smirk in her voice. There was a reason the woman was Molly's closest friend—she didn't miss a trick.

"Nothing's going to happen." That "nothing" had already happened on Gage Simpson's kitchen table yesterday morning was information Cal did not need to have right now. "I just want to get this movie done and work on those scripts we might green-light."

Heading out from Gage's guest room onto the second-floor landing, she slowed to peruse the gallery of family photos dotting the wall. One silver-framed photo in particular drew her focus: a clean-shaven Wyatt in his marine fatigues posing with Logan in bunker gear. Wyatt stared straight ahead, unsmiling, while Logan flirted with the camera. Side by side, the resemblance was striking, like two halves of the same heroic entity. Darkness and light.

In true dog-with-a-bone style, Cal asked, "So what are the sleeping arrangements like?"

"The guest room at Gage's is lovely." It was, all mellow yellow with fresh West Elm soft furnishings.

Cal snorted. "You guys have history of the boning variety and now he's next door, all neighborly and ready to take a bullet for you. Doesn't sound sexy at all."

It sounded like the plot of a Hallmark movie—or a porno. A sleazy electric guitar riff slithered through her brain. *Bow-chick-a-bow-bow* . . .

"I have work to do," Molly repeated. New scripts to read, calls to make, business to . . . business. Wyatt Fox need not take up any (more) of her mental real estate.

"A thin wall separates you from heavenly delights. You've been laying low for too long and now you owe it to your vag to get some action."

Action received, and Ms. Greedy was hungry for more.

Cal continued with her encouragement, and when she devolved to cheap quips about hose lengths, Molly hung up. She needed to get a move on. Where Gage and Brady lived in Andersonville, she was a few miles farther from the set than her Gold Coast summer place. This morning's burning question: how to play it. Should she knock on Wyatt's door and offer to carpool? What was the commuting protocol with the man who'd given her the most memorable orgasm in recent memory? In not-so-recent memory?

Duh, Mol. She couldn't be seen with him. If they showed up together, it would be grist for the gossip mill.

In the kitchen, she came across Gage standing at the counter, stirring his coffee. Every one of Molly's caffeine-deprived neurons stood to attention.

"Molly!"

"Oh, you're one of those. A morning person."

He grinned. "Sure am. Night owl, too. I don't need much sleep, and with how awesome my sex life is, that's probably for the best. Hope we didn't keep you up."

Laughing, she shook her head. "Heading into the firehouse?"

"Yeah, leaving in about thirty. Coffee?"

With a nod, she sat at the table—yes, *that* table—and watched as he played breakfast host. Conversation was jumping easily from topic to topic—Gage had strong opinions on the current season of *Big Brother*—when suddenly, the air shifted.

Wyatt walked in from the backyard. She hadn't seen him since his dine and dash yesterday, and her heart jumped at the sight of him in all his muscled glory.

Dumb heart.

"You see, this is how it works, Molly," Gage said. "Wy refuses to set foot inside a grocery store for fear he might be struck by a thunderbolt from the Whole Foods gods. He might pop into the bodega on the corner to grab half-and-half, but that's the extent of his domesticity, so every morning he visits chez Gage to avail himself of the pantry."

"I drop you a C-note a week to cover it," Wyatt said with a sniff. He helped himself to an Asiago cheese bagel from a box on the counter.

Gage went on. "And along with his raiding of the bounty, if I'm here, I'm expected to cook."

"You love it, shithead."

This double act the brothers had going on was too damn cute. With a martyr's sigh, Gage pushed Wyatt out of the way and rummaged in the fridge. A minute later, he was chopping and whisking and heating oil in a pan. Wyatt handed off a cup of coffee to Molly, complete with a carton of half-and-half and a selection of sweeteners, and then took a seat at the table. It should have been tense, but Gage's chatter wouldn't allow for any awkwardness.

"So what's the plan?" Gage asked Molly. "Not that we're trying to get rid of you, but I can't imagine this is what you had in mind for your summer."

"I've got a leasing agent on the case. He's showing me a place today after shooting's done."

Gage flicked a glance at Wyatt—and his dark, tan hand with knuckles popping pale as it gripped his coffee mug. Message received. He really did not want her here, contaminating the sacred Dempsey space.

"You could just stay here," Gage said, apparently oblivious to Wyatt's body language. "I won't harass you about giving me a part in the movie. Much."

"That's not it."

"Then what's the problem? Don't say the position of sassy gay friend is taken."

"I don't . . ." She slid a glance to Wyatt, who was watching her with his typical unreadable intensity. "I don't want to make things tougher for you all with Roni and her mom. If the press finds out I'm staying with you, then that brings heat on you when you don't need it."

"Holy shit, have you met us?" Gage shook his head. "We can handle whatever you bring. Apart from the bad-tempered teen, the moody Cajun chef, and the crabby lumberjack firefighter next door, we're actually fun to be around."

It all sounded so reasonable coming from Gage, yet she couldn't. First off, Wyatt. Second, oh, WYATT.

Gage was still making his case. "Besides, haven't you heard? I'm fucking the poorest example of gay-hood ever. I love him to death but he doesn't even know who Jennifer Lawrence is!"

That pulled a tension-relieving giggle from her. "The things I could tell you about her."

"See? You're meant to be here. And you won't have a better meal than what I serve up in this kitchen."

"Truth," Wyatt murmured. "No better eating than at this table."

Furious heat scalded her cheeks. Just when she thought Wyatt Fox longed to see the back of her, he made sexy incendiary comments like that. *Pick a lane, Marine.*

Gage divided a curious look between them and settled on Wyatt. "What's that on your face?"

"An overgrown mink, according to Alex."

"Well, yeah, but I meant the other thing. It's like this weird hook shape at one corner of your mouth and then it's . . ." He leaned forward and squinted theatrically. "It's matched on the other side. You see that, Molly?"

Eager to do anything that diverted attention away from her own acute embarrassment, she played along. "It looks like . . . but . . . it couldn't be. Is that a *smile*?"

"Cute," Wyatt said morosely. He motioned to the stove. "Still waiting on those eggs, Chef."

Molly's phone rang. Stephanie's grim countenance stared back at her from the screen. "Sorry, that's my agent." She moved to step outside into the backyard.

"Make it quick," Gage called out. "I'll have an egg-white omelette ready for you in five."

"You don't have to do that."

"Let him cook," Wyatt said. "It's the only thing that shuts him up."

Gage waggled his eyebrows. "Not the only thing."

Phone to her ear, Molly left the kitchen with Wyatt's eyes sealed to her very fine ass.

"Take a pic, bro. Might last longer."

"Shut it. And you shouldn't be asking her to stay. Luke's gonna go mental."

"Luke doesn't live here anymore. I decide who stays

and goes." Gage flipped a Denver omelette onto a plate and put it down before Wyatt. "You gonna tell me what's going on with you and our special guest star?"

"Nothin'."

Gage groaned. "Have you met the guy I'm currently shacked up with? Broody fucker, built like a linebacker, goes by the name of Brady Smith?"

Apparently this was rhetorical because Gage was now in full flight.

"As soon as he started opening up to me, good things happened. He smiled more, laughed on occasion, and now his sex life is off the charts. So how about you pry apart that tightwad mouth of yours and tell your favorite brother how you feel?"

To be honest, he did want to talk about it to someone, and Gage, despite his image of me-me-me, was actually a good listener with a heart that eclipsed even his gigantic ego. Of all the Dempseys, the kid was the most open, this big ball of puppy dog love from the minute he'd walked into this very kitchen when he was ten years old. Bold as brass, with Sean's strong hand on his shoulder, he'd announced he was gay before anyone could look at him crooked. Bravest little fucker Wyatt had ever met. The rest of them had been surprised when he fell ass-over-elbow for Brady, who was bound tighter than a fist, but not Wyatt. Gage's gift was to leave a room, having touched every person in it with his sunshine. He saw Brady's pain and wanted to make it better. Medic of the heart.

Wyatt did a quick recce on Molly's location out back, making sure she was out of earshot. He might have let his gaze linger on her sweet curves in those ass-hugging yoga pants that were going to be the death of him.

"I've met her before. Five years ago."

Gage's face almost split in half. "You sneaky little shit."

"Don't tell the others."

"Lips are zipped as far as telling tales go. But I need deets, bro."

"It was this brief thing before she moved to LA and hit it big. We didn't even know each other's names."

"Nameless sexing. Been there, got several T-shirts." He sounded wistful. "Must have been a real mind fuck when you saw her in the movies. So now she's here and there's all this sexy vibery, what are you waiting for?"

"It's not so simple."

"You two have enough chemistry to blow up a high school science lab. Why would you want to let that go to waste?"

"Not everyone leads with their dick, Gage. I have other things to consider. Like Roni." At least, that's what he was telling himself. He was most definitely not thinking about how he had let Molly go once and that he'd rather eat a bowl of rusty nails than put himself in that position again. Their lives did not mesh. She was Hollywood designer duds. He was Chicago Dumpster diving.

And he wanted her more than his next breath.

As for that dick he wasn't supposed to be leading with? All it wanted to do was point in Molly's direction, especially after what had happened yesterday on this table. Christ. Forbidden had never tasted so good. But more worrying was how her vulnerability had squeezed his heart and burrowed into dark, usually inaccessible places.

Yep. He was going to break that fucking rowing machine before the summer was through.

CHAPTER THIRTEEN

Molly eyed Roni sprawled on the patio sofa, her fingers orange-crusted with delicious fairy dust. Also known as Cheetos. The state of the teen's hands seemed to have no impact on her ability to text or whatever it was she was doing on her phone. Molly's mouth watered, but junk food was on her to-don't list.

Along with that batch of double chocolate chip cookies Gage had whipped up before heading into work at the Dempseys' bar and dangerous men who could glare her into orgasm . . . okay, back to clearing her mind and body with the power of yoga.

Twilight had thrown a dusky curtain over the sky and Molly inhaled as if she was breathing clear mountain air. This pocket sanctuary in Gage's backyard had that effect, and after her grueling day on the set, she needed to relax.

Molly switched to lotus and took three deep, chest-filling breaths. *Om.* Yoga was about the only thing placing on pause the images of Wyatt parting her thighs and rubbing that beard against her sensitive skin.

"You'd better not be taking photos of me," she said to Roni.

"As if there aren't enough of you out there." Roni

watched from beneath her bangs but quickly found her phone screen fascinating when Molly looked her square in the eye.

"You're welcome to join me."

"Lame."

"So you'd rather sit around all summer on your phone."

"I'd rather go downtown but Wyatt won't let me out alone."

Molly gave an unladylike snort. "You have a million relatives who'd take you anywhere."

"They don't want—" She caught herself with a shrug. "They have better things to do on their days off."

Molly's heart twanged. Did this girl really think her family would pass up a chance to become better acquainted with their new niece? Alex had filled Molly in on Roni's life pre-Dempsey, from the deadbeat dad-who-wasn't to the life-threatening illness. This kid had been through the wringer, so she was understandably wary of putting her heart in the line of fire, even with a sure bet like the Dempseys.

"So who are you texting?"

"My friend Lili back in Bloomington."

"About a boy?"

Another bored shrug, which Molly took for a yes. Usually accusations involving boys merited serious denial except when they were true.

"Lili's dating someone?"

"Trying to. The guy's playing it cool."

Unrequited. The worst. Molly detected a slightly plaintive note, and it wasn't there because Roni was worried about her friend's ability to attract a boy.

"Maybe she should be proactive. Who says she has to wait for the guy to make the first move?"

"Like you know anything about relationships."

From the mouths of babes . . .

Molly stretched and positioned herself for boat pose. Her hip flexors strained with the effort. *Om.*

"Yeah," she panted in response to Roni. "I'm a fine one to talk. I've made a sh—uh, a ton of mistakes, but I'd hate to think it's going to keep me from trying again."

The lie tasted like ash in her mouth. Trying again was not on her agenda. A woman in her position—rich, powerful, and hounded—wasn't likely to find a guy who was happy to play second fiddle to her career. She was done with bossy SOBs who had to control every aspect of the relationship. And even if she could find this magical unicorn of a man who didn't feel threatened by her new ball-busting persona, how could she trust her heart again?

No, darling, the prenup doesn't mean I don't trust you. This is Hollywood.

But Roni was young, not (entirely) jaded, and needed woman-to-woman advice. Molly was 99 percent sure the teen was not asking for a friend.

"I'd say she should ask him out, put herself out there," Molly said against her own innate instincts. "He might appreciate her honesty."

Roni appeared to consider this, then announced, "Or think she's a slut."

Or think she's a slut.

Om.

• • •

Ten minutes later, Roni had left to visit Darcy and Beck, leaving Molly to her thoughts and a huge pile of scripts. Her phone rang.

"Hey, hot stuff," Molly purred into her phone like a bad phone sex operator.

Cal laughed. "Hot stuff? Obviously you're not getting as much action as I'd hoped if you have to use those kinds of lines on me."

She moved the scripts on the patio sofa aside and readjusted the phone to her ear. "Never mind that. How's your gran?"

"Doing better. She's finally agreed to go into assisted living. I'd rather she moved in with me in LA, but she won't have it."

"Worried she'll cramp your style?"

"Hell no. Worried I'll cramp hers! She's such a ho."

Molly laughed. She'd missed Cal, though Gage was proving to be an awesome stand-in.

"So are you working your magic on any cute nurses?" Cal had always had a thing for women in scrubs. Something about the bossy/nurturing combo.

"Nurse Billy-Jo has made my heart flutter once or twice. And speaking of fluttering, how's Fire Mountain?"

"I can't keep track of the cavalcade of nicknames. I assume you mean my coworker Lieutenant Fox." *Stone Cold Fox,* she had been calling him in her head, *ThighTickler* on her phone, even if he was playing at beautiful stranger. "He's not quite as friendly as before."

"Uh-oh."

"I mean, it's okay. He's just been pretty cool toward me." It started this morning. After breakfast, he'd tailed her car to the set, still doing the protector bit, then proceeded to ignore her except for the bare-boned instructions necessary during filming. She supposed she should be glad that there was no one gossiping about them, but after the yoga flirtation and the intimacy of yesterday—welcome to your new digs, here's an orgasm!—she'd thought that there would be more flirty time with her gorgeous marine.

She wasn't sure what exactly had happened to send him from playful, or as playful as Wyatt Fox could get, to downright surly in the span of a few hours. Thankfully, she'd be out of here by tomorrow. She'd found an apartment near the set. Staying here was out of the question; as much as she loved the camaraderie of hanging with the Dempseys, this proximity to Wyatt was driving her mad. Sexy, stoic Wyatt was one thing. Surly-stoic could take a running jump.

"It's for the best. Told you, I'm on a man embargo."

Slight, disbelieving cough from her friend.

"I am!"

"Well, speaking of men, or one man in particular . . . I heard something."

Molly stiffened. "If it's about whatever prepubescent girl Ryan is banging I don't want to know."

Cal paused, the weight of it so heavy Molly felt it press on her across the miles. "It *is* about Ryan, but not what you think. It's about the photos."

A panicked flapping started in her chest. "What about them?"

"Bill Solberg called me." Bill had been Ryan's agent, but they'd parted on less-than-amicable terms after Ryan went against his advice and poured his money into a space opera that flopped at the box office.

"What did he have to say for himself?"

"That Ryan was behind the leak."

Molly's heart jolted. "Ryan's a power player, but even he wouldn't be behind a full-scale hack. It was traced to some server in Russia, Cal."

"Not the hack, the leak. Ryan used the hack to cover his tracks. He arranged for someone to release the photos and blamed it on the cloud service breach. According to Bill, those pics were never part of it. But—"

"I was in the middle of a bitter divorce and my husband saw an opportunity to make me suffer. He knew I'd fall apart. He—he . . ." The rest stuck in her throat, the full extent of Ryan's betrayal stinging her like hornets.

That. Penis.

"Maybe Bill's just trying to get payback on Ryan, but I don't think so. He knows what a poisonous snake his former client is and he thought you should know. I'm so sorry, hon."

Molly drew a shuddering breath. "Doesn't change the facts, Cal. He was always a dickweasel. Now he's a lying, petty, malicious dickweasel."

She pressed hard against the pain knotted behind her breastbone. She had thought there was nothing more her ex-husband could do to hurt her, but there you have it: Ryan Michaels, the gift that keeps on giving.

Those pictures had made her a target, fueling online vitriol from strangers and male smirks in studio meetings. Those pictures had brought her low and fucked her career. Those pictures had humiliated her grandmother to the point that she refused to speak to her only granddaughter or even share that she was dying of lung cancer.

Those pictures—*oh, God*. Had Ryan hated her that much?

"Molly, I'm sorry," Cal was saying, her voice muffled by Molly's thudding heart. "I thought you should know, but maybe I should have waited and told you in person."

"No. You did the right thing." She tried to inhale but her lungs were incapable of filling. "It's just a shock, is all. I—I need to go now."

"Okay," Cal said tentatively. She clearly hated the idea of dumping and dashing. "Call me later?"

"Sure." She clicked off.

And threw the phone clear across the yard, where it split into several pieces. Part of it landed in the herb garden. Another shard found a new home in the koi pond. Shit.

Shit shit SHIT.

She'd have to dig that out before the fish were poisoned. Fucking Ryan had dealt enough destruction already.

"Hey, Hollywood," a deep voice intoned. "No diva tantrums allowed."

CHAPTER FOURTEEN

Eyes that could put Wyatt six feet under twice snapped up, and too late, he realized that he might have made a mistake in being so flippant. Something was majorly off here.

"What's wrong?"

"Oh, nothing. Just me being my diva self," she snapped at Wyatt as she snatched at a pair of pink running shoes and stabbed her feet into them. Her eyes flickered to the remnants of the phone she'd chucked with a vengeance, and she seemed to waver before settling on a course of action. Sunglasses on, baseball cap pulled down, she marched to the gable of the house.

He was in her space in a CFD second. "Where do you think you're going?"

"Not that it's any of your business, but I'm heading out for a run."

He was sensing a little attitude here. At eight in the evening, the July sun was hanging low on the horizon. Darkness always crept up quicker than expected. "Little late for that."

"Don't care."

"Wait a minute. I'll change."

"Really, Wyatt?" She shook her head, her mouth

pinched in disgust. "Don't bother. You stay your same, surly self."

Okay, subtext thrown down, not in the least bit understood. The female brain was not his superpower. Protecting this woman was. He'd missed her. To the point that he'd taken on inventory and an extra shift at the bar last night so he wouldn't have to be reminded how much he missed her.

"Wait here," he ordered.

She chose to ignore him, but the view sure looked as good going as it did coming.

Ninety seconds later, dressed in shorts and running shoes, he was assessing the street where he lived. Tonight it was its usual tree-lined and car-packed self, but angry blonde–free. His next-door neighbor, Mrs. Gish, was sweeping her front porch. Cleanest spot on the block, bar none.

"Evenin', Mrs. G. See any short blondes running like their head's on fire?"

Mrs. G pointed her broomstick toward the lake, four blocks off. Made sense. Ideal place to put out the flames.

He caught up with her a block from the lake path, a V of sweat already painting the back of her shirt. Falling into step with her, he hauled labored breaths for a few. He'd sprinted to make up the distance.

She didn't acknowledge him, just kept that pin-you-to-the-wall focus he'd seen her display on the set. Her body maintained excellent form, economical in movement, nothing wasted. Her disguise kept her anonymous, and he let the pleasure of that soak in. Out in public together, but no one knew or cared. They were just a couple on a Thursday evening running along the lake in the most beautiful city in the world.

Molly might be pissed, but Wyatt was feeling pretty good. Like he was where he was supposed to be.

She stopped so quickly that he'd already run a few steps and had to course correct on a dime to face her. Hands on hips, chest heaving, she stared at her feet as if they had committed the cardinal sin of daring to be . . . feet.

Then she howled at them, a gut-wrenching bellow. A couple walking their dog backed up toward the relative safety of the large body of water.

Wyatt let her scream. Whatever was making her mad, it was best she let it out.

She paced a few steps forward, a few back. He would have loved to pull her into his arms, rip off her sunglasses, and see all that fire in her eyes. But she needed the mask.

Maybe they both did.

She poked the air between them with an accusatory finger. "If you say something about how cute I look when I'm angry, you will not live."

Wouldn't dream of it. If a woman had reason to be angry, then cute didn't enter into it.

Fists clenched on her hips, she stalked away from him, disgust in every step. Pivoted and stalked back. Getting her some time with the gym's punching bag moved up his list. For now, he was happy to stand in. Whatever she needed.

"If those pictures had been of a naked guy," she spat out, "he'd be getting claps on the back and compliments on the size of his dick. Not that it was anything to write home about. Definitely a shower, not a grower. Fucking double standards . . ." She growled and gripped her hips tight enough to bruise. "I'm sick of it. Of getting paid less, of having male studio executives look at me in horror when I express an opinion, of being punished because I trusted the wrong person."

The urge to touch her was overwhelming, but he resisted. There was a fair to decent chance she would bite his hand off. He could take that, but this was something she needed to work through, and pouring on the platitudes would not convince her. Protectiveness blazed in his chest, yet he made his arms like rods so they wouldn't enfold her.

With a nod of decision, she spun on those pink running shoes and started back the way they had come. And because it was his mission in life to protect her while torturing himself, he stayed with her, two steps behind, watching that Hollywood booty all the way.

Back at Gage's, Molly pushed her sunglasses to the top of her head and leaned against the porch. Wyatt stood a few feet off, stretching his calf muscles on his cooldown. And he had the gall to be shirtless. Boy, was she pissed as all hell at him and his glorious sunbaked chest and lickable copper-colored nipples. She knew he was just convenient, but she was spoiling for a fight.

Say something, asshole. Anything.

He obliged. "Want to tell me what has you hate-running?"

"Oh, it talks."

"Even at risk to my health."

The run had not calmed her down in the slightest. Fury was barging through her veins, frustration at all the assholes who had dared to cross her making her muscles rage beneath her skin. Missy Hickson, who wore the same red polka-dot dress to the tenth-grade harvest dance when she knew Molly had planned to wear hers. *Asshole*. The driver of the Bentley who cut her off on the 110 that time, forcing her to sideswipe another car and lose her waitress job. *Asshole*. Her parents, who died in that jeep crash while helping cure Zambian orphans of river blindness. *Assholes*. (Not the orphans, her parents. She really missed her parents.)

"You don't want to make me angry."

"You mean it could get worse? You scared people *into* the lake."

She was expected to smile at that, she supposed. *I'm fine, absolutely fabulous, never fucking better.* But she wasn't feeling much like America's Fallen Sweetheart today. She was feeling like a raging bitch.

"Watch you don't use up your word quota, Wyatt. Wouldn't want you to have some sort of aneurism with the effort it takes to communicate with me."

He didn't pretend to misunderstand her. "It's easier this way."

"It's easier when you act like a jerk with the name, rank, and serial number bit?"

"Easier for everyone if we don't do this."

"Do what? Be civil to each other? Friendly?" She stepped closer and touched his chest. Bad idea, because, *sizzle*. "Am I that much of a threat that a kind word to me might make you lose control and jump my bones?"

He covered her hand with his own, rough and warm against the glistening wall of his bare chest. This close to him, she inhaled clean sweat and male menace. Beneath her fingertips, his heart beat quick and vital.

The usual Wyatt Fox smoldering ensued. Gah! Fine, she'd say what was necessary. "I found a new place."

"Where?"

"It's a condo near the studio with beefed-up security. I'll be out of your way and you'll only have to put up with me for brief spurts on the set."

Those crystal-blue eyes flamed. "You think it's a chore for me to spend time with you, Molly?"

"You've made it clear I'm just your duty. Well, duty performed, Marine. You're off the hook."

He pushed her back toward the narrow passageway that separated his house from Gage's, and pinned her to the wall, huge and furious above her.

"Off the hook, Mol? Where you're concerned, there's no such thing."

His lips lowered to her mouth and took possession, and it seemed possession was catching. One hand cupped her ass, drew her up and against him. His other held her head in place for his deep, brutal kiss. She was drowning, and he was both pushing her under and keeping her afloat.

He drew back, his mouth harsh with lust. "Did that taste like duty?"

"Tasted like a kiss-off."

He clearly wanted to argue with her assessment—her lie—but he probably didn't want to give her any encouragement. His palm coasted down her sweat-drenched arm and locked with her hand. With a weirdly sexy bafflement, he looked at the clasp of their two palms together, as though he needed to convince himself of the possibilities in that small gesture.

Holding his hand, she felt the curious sensation of something fitting into place. Panicked, she jerked away, but he yanked back. In one swift movement, he lifted her against him and positioned her, straddling his hips.

She might have helped.

"C'mon, baby," he rasped, as graveled as the ground beneath their feet. "Give it to me good."

So she did. She kissed him angry, pouring the pain of that revelation about Ryan and the photos into her assault. She bit his lip, ate at his mouth, tugged at his beard. And he took it.

Shocked at her behavior, she drew back. This wasn't fair to him. He'd been her rock, and here she was treating him like a sex object.

"Wyatt, I—I'm sorry."

"I'm not."

Without realizing they had moved, she found her back flat against the back door to his kitchen. Which he pushed through and kicked closed, because apparently releasing her was not an option.

Her heart punched painfully against her ribs. She kissed him again, relishing his taste now that her fury was no longer ruining her appetite. He kissed back, all while continuing forward, ruthless, a man on a mission. Through the hall (decked out with a disturbing quantity of Cubs memorabilia), up the stairs, into the . . . bathroom?

Only then did he put her down. He rolled back the shower curtain—Cubs, again—and turned on the faucet.

"Wyatt, what the hell?"

"Just doing my duty." He unfurled her running top, like peeling a banana. His chest heaved and his nostrils flared at the sight of her breasts, though they weren't looking their best with Lycra dents scoring red bands across her skin.

Cupping her hips, he dragged her against his erection. "We can't do this, but hell if my brain can stay on that page."

"Well, that's usually how it works. Put a no-go sign on it and it lights up with 'do me.'"

"That's not what I meant. This isn't about you being forbidden fruit, Molly. It's about you having the ability to consume me, jumble every thought. I've been keeping you at a distance because I can't get involved with you. I owe it to my family not to get involved with you."

"I can't get involved with you, either," she offered in the weirdest presex negotiation ever. "I don't want to be splashed on gossip sites. Not after the last year." She'd tried going on a couple of dates post-Ryan. Men either were only interested in what an association with her could do for their careers or balked at the idea of a relationship with a woman shrouded in a toxic cloud. A public liaison would be impossible, bad for both her career and her heart.

They stared at each other. Arguments made and put forth. All very sensible, apart from the topless-in-his-delicious-arms thing.

His gaze dipped to her mouth, continued down to her breasts smashed against his chest. "So here we are, gorgeous girl. Not getting involved."

And then he smiled, that rare Wyatt slow burn, and she was gone.

She gentled his matted jaw and involved him in a kiss. He deepened it on a groan, and in that moment, she understood how hard this had been for him. But he didn't have the resources to express that well, being a man and all. The steam was rising in the shower, and as Wyatt pulled down her yoga pants, helping her remove them, the steam rose between them.

"Get in," he murmured, his gaze raking her nakedness approvingly. "I'll just be a second."

She obeyed, letting the hot water stream over her clammy skin and slough away any last-minute hesitancy. Within seconds, Wyatt was back with a square plastic packet.

They were doing this.

His chest to her back, he caged her in the embrace of a fully naked man.

They were definitely doing this.

She turned in his arms, needing to see all of him. It had been too long, and with his skin gleaming like satin, that blockbuster chest and goodie trail of hair arrowing down to a fully-aroused cock, he was even more beautiful than she remembered. "You've filled out, Marine. You were so scrawny before."

His lips raised in what could only be called a smile. She wanted to be the one who put that there all the time.

Better sign on to do more comedies, Mol, because that's your only shot at making him happy.

"Could say the same about you." His hands moved over her hips and her ass, a slow, sexy rhythm that quickened her pulse at every pounding point.

"You saying I've gotten fat?"

He raised an eyebrow and turned her away from him. "I'm saying you have grown into those sweet, soft curves. You are one fine-looking woman."

His appreciation warmed her better than the shower's pulsing spray. It had been a long time since she felt beautiful. She heard it the morning after an awards show, only to have the good feelings ripped apart by some hater who lived to bring her down. In her business, it was virtually impossible to let her self-worth not be determined by fashion magazines, vitriolic tweets, and whichever studio head controlled casting of the latest blockbuster. With Wyatt, there was no pretense. Plain speaking was his currency, and every deposit he made in her vault left her rich beyond belief.

"Just let me take care of these fine curves."

On a groan, she let him lead, because if one thing was certain, it was that Wyatt Fox knew exactly what he was doing when it came to taking care of her fine curves. His hands shaped and kneaded, circled and teased, slicking the warm, soapy lather over her skin. Sparks ignited in the wake of every touch. A well of want pooled deep in her belly, and when his fingers slipped between her legs, her knees melted.

Thankfully, he was holding her up.

He continued to stroke and madden, and lust seized her like a punch. Angling her head to face him, he fed her deep, luscious kisses. A tumble of sensation—that beard, those rough fingers, the steam—unleashed the pent-up desire in her body along with all the frustration of this day, the month, her year. God, how she needed this. How she needed him.

She let herself be pulled under by Wyatt's brand of wow.

Her body braced for bliss. Knew it was coming. Remembered and rejoiced. The orgasm slammed through her, like falling and flying at once. But of course, her Marine was there to catch her because saving her world was his job.

CHAPTER FIFTEEN

He was completely screwed.

Not in the best sense of the word—not yet—but Wyatt had gone and done exactly what he had sworn he would not do. Let the passions he claimed complete control over stage a freakin' coup. So much for clearheaded decision making. So much for putting the best interests of his family first.

None of that apparently mattered, because the one thing that had the ability to override all common sense was in his arms. Desire had erupted, leaving no room for sanity. Watching her come undone with his fingers inside her just about undid him, and now his cock pushed insistently against the inviting cleft of her ass, begging for its turn.

But first he needed to feel every single one of those beautiful curves. His hands roved and skimmed, cupped and plumped. Her ass was the Eighth Wonder, her breasts works of art. He tried to freeze a moment he thought would never arrive and hoped would never end.

Molly. The dream girl. Not because she was everyone's dream, but because first, she had been *his*.

"You waiting for an invitation, Marine?"

"Been a while. Once I'm inside you, I might not last."

"Stamina was never a problem before." Turning to face him, she gripped his erection, testing that statement. He clamped down on his lip, but a groan escaped nonetheless along with a ragged "Molly." Tentative at first, her strokes became tighter, rougher, more sure as he fucked her hand.

"Yeah, that's it. Work me good."

Soap-slick, her hand pumped while the other slipped underneath to cup his heavy balls.

"You used to like this," she whispered. "You liked when I stroked them, licked them, sucked them in my mouth."

He'd loved it. He loved everything she did then and everything she was doing now.

Pleasure built, fast rising, ever tightening, and he withdrew. "Inside you—need to—*fuck*."

Exclamation and intention.

He grabbed the condom, tore at the wrapper, and smoothed it on with a jerky motion and animalistic grunt. She was so short he'd need to lift her, which meant his shoulder would bitch and moan at him later. Whatever. These days he was used to everyone and everything being pissed at him, so his ticked-off muscles could get in line.

He went to hitch her up, but she moved out of his grasp. And turned around.

"You've been watching my ass for a while now, Wyatt. Figured you might appreciate this view."

Sweet fuck.

Below flared hips and a waist he could span with both hands, those perfect rounds sat up expectantly. Silky-smooth cheeks just waiting for him to spread apart and drill deep.

She placed both palms on the tiled wall, her right foot on the ledge of the tub, and hinged her hips at the most inviting angle to take her. Clearly thinking of his shoulder, and he supposed he should be glad of her consideration even if he didn't much like the idea she might not think him fully capable.

That world-class ass was helping him to deal.

Over her shoulder, she bit down on the fleshy pillow of her lip and raised one of those wild, sexy eyebrows. "Take me, Marine."

No need to ask twice. Hands on her hips, he rubbed his aching cock against the sweet, pink heaven she offered. Then he drove past the pearly gates into the hot clasp of her.

"Oh, God!" Fisting the tile, she pounded it once, twice. "That's—oh!"

His thoughts, exactly. He withdrew, plunged to the root, and filled her completely. The worry that he would blow as soon as he slipped inside her faded as remembrance of how their bodies worked together took over. Rarely had it been too fast; there had always been time, and that's how it was now. He slowed, stayed his pleasure to give hers a chance to build. Every inch inside her was torture, every one outside was pain.

Riveted, he watched where their bodies connected, the thick, sensual slide of his cock into the tight, velvet heat. Nothing had ever felt this good. No one had ever felt this good.

It had always been her.

Shoving that thought deep, he got to work on shoving his body deeper, particularly the hardest part of his anatomy into the softest part of hers. With every thrust, it became more difficult to leave her. The tight walls of her pussy clenched, held on tight, and without quite knowing how it happened, he had her pinned to the tile. Likely she had led him there with his cock embedded snugly inside her.

His hand fed around her body and grasped one silky tit, the other dipped to her swollen clit.

Still inside her, he slowed to a steady rock, needing to prolong this perfect, perfect moment. His mouth grazed her ear and kissed her softly.

She turned her head, her heavy-lidded gaze unable to mask the pleasure he was giving her. He stroked her clit and watched how her pupils blew wide with lust. In the grip of passion, her eyes ranged a rainbow of blues and violets. How had he forgotten that? Those subtle color changes heralding her rising pleasure. Silver sparks igniting. Another stroke of her clit turned them to a molten mercury. The next slippery brush brought sunset over a foreign desert. Beneath his fingertips, she bloomed to match the vibrantly colored desire in her eyes.

A squeeze of her silken muscles around his cock drew a loud groan from him. She licked the corner of his mouth. There was something a little dirty about it.

"You wanna play hardball, Molly?"

Her mouth curved, all vixen. "I think you need to come, Marine."

Yeah, but the challenge had been laid down.

Slowly, he set up a sensuous rhythm of pumping his cock, circling her clit, and kneading her breast. A trifecta of pleasure. She moved her hand to ring his neck, found purchase in his hair. It felt like every part of his body touched every part of hers, their nerve endings entwining, this connection he never wanted to cease. But he could feel the end in sight, the escalating desire in his groin about to graduate to an explosive orgasm.

He turned his index finger to the callused side and glanced it across her clit. Finally, she let go. That clamp of her hot little pussy around his shaft triggered his own much-needed release. On and on it went as she milked him so good his brain might have oozed out of his ears, as well.

Better with her than anyone. An observation that shouldn't grate, but did. He'd raised her up before, those six days of perfect pleasure the highlight of his sorry life. Now she was climbing the charts again.

He wanted more. Not only because sex this good should not be passed up, but to prove to himself that there was nothing more to it. She needed to be knocked off that pedestal and restored to a place of fond, distant memories. She needed to be that chick he balled in a hotel room five years ago—and not the woman who got away.

Wyatt had to practically lift her out of the tub she was so spent. Around her shoulders he draped a fluffy towel and rubbed softly against her skin.

His gaze ate her alive as if he hadn't already used up all his intensity in the shower. "You're staying, Molly. No need for you to move into a new place."

Where had that come from? "I can't. This—" She waved between them. "This can't happen again."

He pulled her close using the towel. "Promised I'd watch your ass."

"Then watch it while I leave you in the dust on a run."

"Best view in the city, but as long as you're living in Chicago, you're my responsibility."

Out of respect, she considered this for 2.5 seconds. "Don't be ridiculous, Wyatt. I'm a grown woman who can take care of myself." Or pay people vast sums of money to do so. A shiver ran through her. This was her life. Her well-being had a monetary value. These last couple of days, without her high-priced security, she had felt safe, cocooned, and best of all, normal.

"This isn't about you not being able to take care of yourself, Molly. This is about my peace of mind. Whether you're in this house or next door, it don't matter. This is happening."

"And what about this?" Again she motioned between them, feeling like a mime who had failed Mimeology 101. "Is *this* happening?"

"Course it is. You think one time is enough?" He leaned in, bending slightly because he was so much taller than her. "Five years ago, we couldn't get enough of each other. If I wasn't slipping inside you, caught between the dream of you and the fantasy in my arms, I was waking up to find your sweet lips wrapped around my cock, sucking me off like your next breath depended on it." He maneuvered her against the vanity. The towel fell from her shoulders as he rubbed his now-rehardened cock against her stomach. A quick lift brought them fully aligned. "Don't make out like we're done here, because that gorgeous body of yours is telling a whole other story."

"But—"

"But what?"

She threw up her hands, unable to verbalize. The soul of wit.

"Got a lot of talents, Mol. Mind reading ain't one of them." He swiped her lip with his thumb. His expression darkened. "Okay, I get it. You don't want to be seen with me. Well, that happens to work both ways."

Blunt, but then that was Wyatt. "In a nutshell."

"Sounds like a recipe for an illicit, under-the-radar fling. We'll be careful. No one has to know. And you're a great actor."

She wasn't that good. "I think you're going to be better at this than me."

Damn, she had already agreed. Wyatt Mind Trick.

"Answer this. Do you want me? Want what only I can give you?" His erection slip-slid through her soft, saturated flesh while he stared at her with those eyes. They searched inside her and locked on to something deep.

She nodded, feeling powerless to lie to him. That was the problem with magnets. Attraction wasn't a choice.

"That's all I need to know. There's a Starbucks nearby, a five-star chef next door, and I can give you tips on dodging the press. Just think, babe. We'll be craving each other"—a lusty suck on her lower lip—"sneaking around"—an unfairly sensuous rub of that weapon between his legs against her greedy center—"taking our pleasure where we can find it. Just for a few weeks. Now, don't that sound good?"

It sounded wonderful. A hot, secret summer affair with an ex—no, *former*—marine firefighter, who looked like a pirate and fucked like a dream. With a built-in expiration date, there'd be no awkward sep-aration. All upside.

Still, she felt compelled to point out the downside. "We can't be seen together at the set," she whispered, "and have you forgotten that you live with a teen-age girl and your family is pretty much *everywhere*?" Luckily, Roni was over at Beck's tonight, but they couldn't expect this level of privacy on a regular basis.

He looked invigorated by the challenge. "We'll figure out something. Just know this, Molly: I have to have you. And I'll feel better knowing you're here, safe and under my protection." And then he fell to his knees, his mouth seeking where she needed him most. Proving his point as only Wyatt could with his body, beard, and sheer force of will.

Her presence here might be giving him the peace of mind he needed, but it was doing sweet damn all for hers.

♠ CHAPTER SIXTEEN

Wyatt rounded the gable of the house, the sound of voices and laughter increasing with every step. His shoulder was sore after his PT appointment, and all he wanted was to kick back with the Cubs' game and maybe a soft woman curled into his side. Looked like neither would be happening.

Gage had invited people over for dinner. Family only, thank God. Alex was on shift at Engine 6 tonight and Luke and Beck were holding down the fort at the bar. Their better halves were sitting at the large communal table out back, bookending Roni. Darcy and Kinsey had taken her under their wings, for which Wyatt was more than grateful. Lights twinkled in the trees, casting a festive shimmer over the table laden with a feast of pastas and salads prepared by Gage. But the light that shone brightest was the star in their midst, Molly Cade.

Clichéd much?

It had been a week since she'd officially moved in with Gage and Brady, and the sneaking around had so far been only that. They'd connected a few times in his garage and made out like hormonal teenagers before he tailed her to the set each morning. She wanted more—hell, so did he—but he made sure to cut it short before it went too far. Molly deserved better than getting fucked on the hood of a Camaro.

He needed to figure out something, because if he didn't get inside her again soon, he was going to kill somebody.

No one had seen him yet, so he took a moment to drink it in. Molly, here in his home, or as good as. Getting along just fine with the family he loved.

Look up, babe. Know that I can't take my eyes off you.

"What the hell time do you call this?" he heard, all mock affront behind him.

He turned and took the Coke bottle Gage handed off.

"I cook all day to put food on your table and you show up at all hours and—"

"Yeah, yeah."

Nothing made his little brother happier than bringing everyone together, but there was something in Gage's eyes tonight hinting at strain. Usually, he only cooked this much when he was upset and—*shit*. Today was Gage's regular day to visit his mom at the nursing home in the suburbs. Struck with early onset Alzheimer's, she didn't know him, or remember how she had tortured him as a kid for being the fabulous little freak that he was. And yet Gage still made the weekly trek because his optimism had always outweighed his fear.

Wyatt usually let his family lead when it came to the emotional stuff. Butting into their lives or talking about his feelings or theirs was not his style, but maybe he needed to be more proactive. Show them that while he might never say it, they meant the world to him.

"You know, if you ever . . ." No sooner were the words out than a wave of doubt assailed him. Gage had no shortage of confidants.

"What, Wy?"

Wyatt exhaled, feeling dumber with every passing second. "You ever need anything, I'm here."

Gage could have deflected or made a joke but he didn't. Just took the offer as his due, because even though his childhood pre-Dempsey had been a shitfest, he never doubted that he was deserving of family and love. Not like Wyatt, whose biological dad had ingrained in his son a deep-seated inadequacy. In his father's profession of con man, charm was the prime ingredient, and he'd never let Wyatt forget his failings in not being a chip off the old block. Even now, after years with the Dempseys, doubt about his place was as inescapable as the sun rising in the east.

"There's hope for you yet," Gage muttered, his voice scratchy. He kissed Wyatt on the forehead. "Come eat, ya big lug."

The only open seat was beside Darcy and across from Molly. Good, because he had her beauty filling his field of vision and bad, because, ditto.

"We have a couple of new victims at our table tonight, so a toast is in order," Gage said, standing with a beer in hand. "She offered her honor, he honored her offer, and all night long he was—"

"Gage," Wyatt warned with a look at Roni.

"Oh, right. Innocent bunny ears."

Roni's mouth dropped open. "What? How does it go?"

"Never mind." Darcy raised her soda glass. "Here's

to the nights we'll never remember with the friends we'll never forget. Welcome, Roni and Molly. Our table is richer with you at it."

Everyone *aw*'ed the hell out of that. "And she's not even drunk," Kinsey joked.

"God, I wish," Darcy said with an accusing glare at her soda. "The first five months of not drinking have almost killed me, so I know the last four are going to send me over a cliff."

"And if you're breastfeeding . . ." Molly said with a sympathetic smile, which drew Darcy's groan. But she quickly recovered with a cheerful yelp as she grabbed Wyatt's hand and placed it over her belly. "He's kicking!"

Darcy's and Beck's excitement about their kid was infectious, but even if it wasn't, Wyatt would be enjoying the surprisingly strong taps against his palm. *Th-thunk, th-thunk.* Longing for something of his own making panged in his chest, and when he raised his gaze, he found Molly and those keen violet eyes sucking him in.

"Another boxer, for sure," he mumbled, and took a drink of his Coke.

The conversation continued with this and that, a good chunk of which Wyatt tuned out because there were horrifying descriptions of childbirth and cracked nipples and tearing in places no man wants to devote a brain cell to. Thankfully, the talk cycled past *Alien*-like, miracle-of-birth eruptions onto Gage's extravagant skill set.

"I can even do accents," Gage said, making his case yet again for a part in Molly's movie.

"Terribly," Wyatt cut in. "He went through a British phase when he was eleven. Asked for chips instead of fries, demanded lifts to soccer practice—"

"Which is known as football in my native land."

"And called Sean guv'nor for a month until Dad threatened to deport him back to his native land if he didn't quit."

"And I can sing," Gage continued, unfazed. He stood, but sat again when Kinsey lobbed half a bread roll at his big head. "I'm the only one in this family who can."

"That's true. Beck is just awful." Darcy rubbed her stomach and spoke to the growing life inside her. "Don't worry, little one. You have a fifty-fifty chance of getting my talent."

"Logan was the worst, though," Gage said. "Couldn't hold a tune to save his life. The karaoke had alley cats caterwauling throughout Chicagoland." He spoke to Roni. "What about you, niece of mine? You a bad singer like your dad?"

As quiet as Roni had been, Wyatt could tell from her watchful eyes and shy half smiles she was enjoying the ping-pong of conversation around the table. At Gage's query, she blushed. "I can't sing, so I guess . . ." She finished on a mumble.

"You've got the bad-singing gene," Gage confirmed confidently. "No worries, Wyatt's terrible, as well. Sounds like a rusty lawnmower crossed with a three-packs-a-day seal." Gage held his gaze with an artful smile Wyatt couldn't help but appreciate. Nicely done. His brother knew Wyatt was having a tough time with Roni.

"Molly's got a great set of pipes on her," Wyatt said absently.

"I do?" She cocked her head, those eyes like sunsets narrowing. "And how would you know that? I've never sung in any of my movies."

Shit. "Pretty sure I heard you somewhere." He shoveled in a mouthful of spaghetti carbonara to punctuate that epically bad cover job. He *had* heard her several times, live and in person, a fact she was not supposed to be aware of.

"Before I moved to LA, I did some musical theater. I was part of the traveling company for *The Who's Tommy*," Molly explained to the group. Wyatt could see her working that out, remembering that one of the company's stops was in Chicago. About five years ago.

Gage's eyes thinned on Wyatt. "Really? The Who is only Wyatt's favorite band."

"Among others."

"There's a reason I hate working shifts at the bar with him," Gage continued as if Wyatt hadn't spoken. "Other than the fact he can't flirt worth a damn and tips suck donkey balls when he's on, but he also plays the Who on the 'box all night. Bet Wy's seen *Tommy* a million times."

A million was overstating it. More like five. Not only because he did love the Who, and he was prepared to make a musical theater exception for Roger, Pete, and company, but because of one other excellent reason.

"Don't do musical theater." Just musical theater actresses.

"Okay to admit if you have a secret *Les Misérables* or *Miss Saigon* fetish, Lieutenant," Molly said with an arch smile.

"I'm sensing in that statement the rather stereotypical assumption that a guy like me would be uncomfortable admitting a love for musical theater. Well, I can affirm that I'm secure enough in my manhood to be fine with saying I love Broadway musicals, if that were actually a true statement."

"So no problem if I made you my plus one at a movie premiere for, say, a remake of *The Wizard of Oz,* and required you wear a pink dress shirt and, oh, a purple suit?" she continued, a mischievous twinkle in her eyes.

"Neck size eighteen, babe. Bring it." *Don't "babe" her, idiot.*

Gage's cough sounded suspiciously like "busted."

Darcy pointed at Wyatt. "Who's hotter? Chris Evans or Hugh Jackman?"

"This is the point where I'm supposed to feel threatened talking about another guy's hotness levels?"

"Or you could use the fact you don't know who they are as your out," Molly added. "We'd accept that."

Wyatt rubbed his beard. He really needed to trim it, but Molly liked how it felt between her legs. His mouth watered in memory and he turned so hard he could have lifted the table with his dick. "I'd say Wolverine's more rugged, while Captain America has the boy-next-door thing down. Both have a lot to offer to the ladies—"

Gage opened his mouth.

"And guys," Wyatt finished.

Gage shut it.

He could feel the entire table staring, though he only had eyes for the saucy grin of one Molly Cade. While Wyatt really had no problem talking up his love of pink or his fine-grained opinion of the hottest movie superheroes, he sure was glad none of the other guys were here to witness this vigorous defense of his masculinity.

Gage gave an incline of his head and a flourish of his hand. "We bow down to your unparalleled comfort levels with your sexuality and how darn tootin' evolved you are, Wy. In fact, you're a whole other species of het."

"Heteromaximus," Molly offered with a cheeky wink that only Wyatt saw.

Gage stood up and pounded the table. "Heteromaximus! We've found it, the missing link between Luke and Homo sapiens. It's Wyatt Fox."

The entire table cracked up, but only Molly's melodious giggle filtered through to harmonize with *Tommy*'s epic closing anthem in his head. *Listening to you, I hear the music . . .* He loved her laugh even when he was the butt of the joke.

She leaned toward the bread basket, giving him a prime view of the valley between her gorgeous breasts. *Groan.* "Gage has it all wrong, you know," she murmured, low enough that she couldn't be heard above the table's buzz of good cheer.

"Oh yeah?"

"You're not such a bad flirt."

Sneaking out of Gage's house, Molly closed the door quietly and did a quick check-in with her brain.

How old are you again?

Twenty-nine, an embarrassed voice offered weakly.

Yet here she was, using the light on her phone to illuminate a path so she could meet a guy for a spot of under-the-radar nookie. She was far too old and not nearly drunk enough for this.

The side door to Wyatt's garage opened and a strong hand yanked her inside.

"Evenin'," her captor murmured against her lips before covering them with that hot, sexy mouth of his. His body rocked hard against her, his need insistent. She let herself fall deep into the pleasure overloading her neurons.

He broke the kiss. "Hardest thing in the world to sit across from you at dinner and not lay hands all over you."

"I felt like you were touching me. The way you looked at me . . ." It was exciting in every possible way. The secrecy, the man, how fluttery she felt in his outsize presence. "But we have to be careful."

"Can't help how my body reacts around you, Molly. I'm like some horny teenager who can't stop staring at the girl I've got a crush on. And my cock knows what it wants—it wants in you. Wants to feel you tight and wet around me. It's just . . . I also want to respect you, and doing you in a dirty garage on top of a Camaro is not very respectful."

Was he serious? She drew back to check his expression, barely lit by the soft glow of a security light shining through the garage's window. Moonlight by ComEd. "Now, listen here, Wyatt Fox. When did we decide you choose the sex locations?"

"Mol . . ."

"Don't Mol me. It's been a week and this secret fling has failed to launch."

"I've been waiting for Roni to sleep over at one of the others'. She couldn't get enough of them before you moved in, now she's decided to be a homebody." She heard the guilt in his voice at the idea that he wanted to be rid of Roni so he could indulge in a bout of sexy high jinks with his hot-to-trot neighbor.

"Wyatt, I think you're missing the point of the illicit affair. It's supposed to be comprised of desperate quickies wherever we can find a flat surface. In waiting for it to be perfect, we are missing out on all the amazing, hot sex we should be having!"

He frowned at her outburst.

Must she do everything herself? She sidestepped him and opened the back door of the Camaro. "Like in here."

"You want to do it in the Camaro?"

"I do."

"You want to have sex in the backseat of my '69 Camaro?"

Sheesh, guys were so weird about their stupid cars.

"Maybe we could lay down a blanket or something."

He kissed the ever-loving stuffing out of her. "I must have been a saint in a previous life." Switching their positions, he maneuvered his big body into the backseat and flipped on the car's dome light. "Get out of my dreams and into my car."

Billy Ocean? Oh boy. Giggling like a schoolgirl, she climbed in. The dimly lit interior bathed them in a sepia-tinged soft focus. She leaned close, closer, *oh yeah*—strong fingers arrested her incline to bearded paradise.

"What the—?" He sat up and held her at arm's length. "What the hell are you wearing?"

She had to check. "My Cardinals shirt. I sleep in it."

"Let's have sex in the Camaro, Wy." His voice sounded different, sort of . . . higher.

"Are you imitating me? Badly?"

"Knew it was too good to be true. Funny, sexy, great ass, knows cars." He blew out an annoyed breath. "And a freakin' Cards fan."

She sat back in the seat, a move that displayed the butter-soft, overwashed Cards tee molding perfectly to braless breasts with puckered nipples. Puckered! She looked damn hot in this shirt, and yet the mere sight of it apparently pissed off the man who'd been looking at a sure thing until about ten seconds ago.

"Are you saying that me in this shirt is enough to give you a de-rection, Marine?"

"You could just take it off."

"I could just go back to bed and leave you with balls as blue as a Cubbies ball cap."

"Babe, that's just cruel." He reached for her hip and pulled her easily over him so she straddled his thighs. "It's okay. I'll just close my eyes and think of Wrigley."

She punched him in his annoyingly resistant chest. But in the muted glow, she caught . . . there it was, that slight upturn of his lips. "You need a light on your forehead signaling when Funny Guy Fox is in."

"Molly Cade, you could be wearing a White Sox shirt, a Yankees thong, and a Packers Cheesehead and I would still want to do you."

She sighed. "Such a romantic."

He slipped his hands under her skirt and coasted rough-hewn fingers along her inner thighs. Higher and higher until he reached . . . "Christ. You're already there."

Just the mere thought of him was enough to ready

her body, but his reverence tipped her over. The scent of her arousal filled the small space.

"Wyatt, please."

He stroked a thumb through her. Just one solitary stroke that liquefied every bone in her body.

"Kiss me, Mol," he whispered.

She did, softly at first, her hands framing his face so she could enjoy that beard on her palms, her lips, tickling her chin. He opened up to her slowly, as was his way. There was no rushing this man. Both large thumbs rubbed through her pulsing, wet flesh while his beautiful mouth seduced her with purpose.

The slow build fooled her, because within a minute, she was a bundle of pure sensation, her need clawing, her body not her own, and his thumb pressed to that nerve-packed nub of desire and she was gone, gone, gone.

And still they kissed. Through the wave, the fall, the soft landing. Most guys—again with the comparisons!—used the kiss as preparation and abandoned it when it no longer served its use. Not Wyatt. With this man, pleasure was the journey.

"Could kiss you all night, Marine."

He smiled against her mouth, light shining like flickering flames in his eyes. Such warmth and desire, and it was all for her.

"Then pucker up, Hollywood. By the time I'm finished with you, the neighbors are gonna need a cigarette."

"Doin' it in the Camaro," Molly said on a sated sigh. She lay in Wyatt's claiming embrace, her back against his chest, her body pleasure-stung and gorgeously used.

"If I had a better way . . ."

"No, no," she urged, turning in his arms. "This is wonderful." Who'd have thought Molly Cade would be getting her brains banged out in the backseat of a muscle car in a quiet residential Chicago neighborhood? Urban sanctuaries for the win. "We just have to be discreet. I can't give them any more ammunition."

"So you hate it, then. Being famous."

"I . . ." She paused, considering how to phrase it. "I hate it like I hate those last five pounds I can't lose from my ass. They happen to be the five pounds that sell me as Best Booty in Hollywood. They're necessary to keep me in the hearts and minds and porn stash of the movie-going public. Hating it is futile. It just is."

"Your life can't ever be normal."

"Define normal."

He waved around the car.

"This is normal?"

"It's close."

It's lovely. "If I retired, I suppose."

"But you love what you do." There was admiration in those words, maybe a touch of regret. Loving her job placed her life in another world from his. Parallel lines, not crossing, except for this brief intersection for a few hazy, lust-filled weeks.

"I plan to take on fewer projects, ones that are closer to my heart, and do more producing. Provided this movie is a hit." If it wasn't, she'd have a hard time funding any future projects. Less time in the public eye might take her fame footprint down a notch.

But her light would never be muted enough to work for a man as private as Wyatt Fox. And there she went again, regretting something that she didn't even want.

"I hate what happened to you," he whispered against her ear. "I wanted to kill someone—anyone—everyone when I heard about it."

Her heart turned molten. Wyatt always seemed so low key except when he wasn't. She couldn't speak, because talking about it, even thinking about it, reminded her of how it had come about.

Fucking Ryan.

Wyatt clearly took her silence for a different type of discomfort. "I know I have no right to feel that way. I didn't know you—"

"Except you did." He knew the real Molly, the one who was untainted by the tawdry business of making movies. Or perhaps she was just feeling nostalgic. Who really knows anyone after a six-day sex romp with no names exchanged?

"I'm not that different. Just a little older, a little jaded. But those pictures hurt me." At the time, she hadn't even realized how much. How it would be the final nail in the coffin of her already tenuous relationship with her grandmother, how it would change forever her outlook on relationships. "I know people say I deserved it for being so dumb to trust that my private business would remain secure. These days, keeping my business my own is the number-one priority, and neither do I want to expose anyone I'm involved with to that scrutiny. We both have too much to lose if we're seen together in public. Besides, I know how much you'd hate it. My research says so."

"Your research?"

"Only blurry pictures of you online. There isn't even a picture of you on the CFD site, and that site has photos of everyone looking hot in their dress blues. In the family portraits, you're always in the back." Plenty of them adorned the walls where she was staying, all showing an unsmiling Wyatt. With them, yet separate. A man apart.

But tonight at dinner, another side of him had revealed itself. Joking with Gage, taking the good-natured teasing of his sisters-in-law, his loving gaze never far from Roni. Mostly she'd noticed his expression softening when he'd laid a big palm on Darcy's belly. Awe and yearning overcame him for a moment. He wanted that for himself.

"Guess I'm the guy in the shadows."

"Deliberately."

"The headlines I leave to the rest of the family. They thrive on the attention, but that's not my bag. When I was a kid, I was pretty shy." The subsequent pause was as loud as a shout.

"What?"

He shook his head again, the friction of his beard against her temple delicious.

Her life was an open book; his was leather bound and locked. She needed to know something, anything personal about him. Turning, she cupped his pirate jaw. "Tell me."

"Didn't help that anytime I opened my mouth I sounded like a grunting animal. I stuttered, which was a real liability in my line of work."

"Your line of work as a kid?"

He gave one of those wry *I've said too much* smiles.

"Story for another day. Anyway, I had a hard time getting the words out, even my own name. The stress of having to talk to anyone I didn't know would just shut me down. First few months with the Dempseys, I talked to no one but Logan, and that was only when we were alone. But"—memories transformed the hard planes of his face into softness—"they wouldn't shut up. Gage and Beck weren't with us yet, but there was Sean and Mary, Luke and Logan, and Alex, the youngest and loudest of the lot. The noise was constant, and for some reason it soothed me, but still, I hardly said anything. Then Mary figured out I wanted to speak. Don't know how, but she and Sean had a sixth sense about those things. Knew when all of the kids needed a shoulder or a push. She said Alex wanted me to start reading to her, which was probably bull, but I grasped at it all the same. Mostly I'd sit and play with her. Dolls driving dump trucks—this was Alex after all— reading storybooks, shit like that. She was three years old and had a better vocabulary than me. I learned to communicate through my little sister."

Molly's heart almost imploded. She had never heard anything so amazing. "She must be so proud."

He huffed a short laugh. "She doesn't even remember, and don't mention it now or she'll never let me hear the end of it. She thought I was just playing with her, sounding out words she already knew when really she was saving my life, teaching me how to read and speak. How to be a Dempsey."

"And soon you were gobbling up Shakespeare and quoting it at unsuspecting girls in bars."

The curve of his mouth against her temple brought out her own smile. "Funny you remember that."

How could she forget the sexy Marine spouting the Bard? "If I hadn't already been doing you, that would have tipped you over into the win column. So are you still the shy, retiring one in the family?"

"Wouldn't say that." His grin was half wicked, half cocky. All sexy. "But I'm not one for drawing attention to myself. What you do, forever front and center, takes real guts, Molly."

Her warm fuzzies were replaced by panic. "You're taking a risk with me. If someone from the press saw us together—"

"I can handle that, Molly. I knew what I was getting into when I took on this job."

"I'm still a job?"

"Yeah, you're quite the chore, Cade." He kissed her shoulder and worked up the curve of her neck. "But I've always loved my work."

And then he proceeded to show her just how much.

CHAPTER SEVENTEEN

"How do you know if it's no good?"

Molly looked up to find Roni in her usual misunderstood-teen uniform of combat boots, leggings, and long-sleeved black tee with manga characters blinking big, expressive eyes. In one hand was her phone, in the other one of the comics she was never seen without. But today revealed an unexpected plot turn—her face was open and curious.

She sat down beside Molly on the patio sofa. "The script. How do you know if it's terrible?"

Like the junk Molly was reading right now? She really needed to employ a script reader, but she was having a hard time surrendering control. What if she missed the next big thing?

"It has to have three checks in its favor. An interesting conflict, the ability to surprise me, and my balls in a vise by page ten. Most scripts are about a hundred pages, so it's got ten percent to prove it's worth my time. Very few make it." She cast a dismissive glance at the pile of rejects. "I'm reading scripts by women or with strong female protagonists first."

"Sounds sexist."

"It's my production company, so I can be as sexist as I want. It also has to pass the Bechdel test."

Roni looked blank.

"There has to be at least one conversation between two women that's not about a man." She eyed the obviously interested teen. "What kind of movies or TV do you like?"

"Superheroes. Jessica Jones. Black Widow. Wonder Woman as long as she's not getting rescued by stupid Batman or Superman."

"Sometimes even tough girls need a little help."

Roni delivered her patented look of *Don't try to connect with me*. So fickle. "Must be handy having an ex-marine around to fight your battles."

"It's former marine, and I'm glad he was there."

On a desultory sniff, Roni turned to her comic. The cover portrayed a spiky-haired girl in an all-white clingy one-piece suit, silhouetted against a futuristic landscape. The title *Rocker Girl* blared in blocky letters.

"Who's Rocker Girl?"

"She's a teen cop." Roni looked up. "In the future," she added, explaining the obvious.

"Would you go see a movie about her?"

"You'd screw it up, so don't even try."

Next. Molly rifled nimble fingers through the scripts. "Could you do me a favor?"

Roni eyed the script in Molly's hand. Briefly, her eyes lit up with interest before dimming. Molly waited for the next predictable plot turn . . . *Bored shrug*.

"I have a script, but I don't know much about the source material. It's something about a group of girls who can change into creatures. *X-Men: First Class* meets *Twilight*."

"Like shifters?" Suspicious curiosity brightened her voice.

"Right." She supposed. "They're immortal and have to fight these beings that enter from other dimensions—"

"Sounds like *Animaux*." She leaned in, her body language completely transformed. Molly could sense her excitement, and it made Molly not a little excited, as well. "You have a chance to make a movie of *Animaux*?"

Molly acted her most blasé. "Is that a comic?"

"It's not really big," Roni said. "If they make a movie of it, it'll get bigger."

"That's a bad thing?"

"The worst." She motioned for the script and Molly handed it over. "I'll give it ten percent." She flipped to the first page, head already dipped so she never saw the smile that lifted Molly's lips.

Wyatt held up his set pass and a cop waved him through the barricade fifty feet from the entrance to Engine 6. Today's schedule featured location shooting, and his firehouse had been chosen for the exterior and bay shots. (*We decided it months ago,* Molly had insisted.) Over his shoulder, a mob of bystanders stood with phones at the ready, eager for a glimpse of Molly Cade.

"How long have they been here?" he asked the officer on duty. His badge said Ramirez.

"I came on shift two hours ago and most of them were already here." He gave a smartass smirk. "All they have to do is Google her name and they'll find all the pictures they want."

Wyatt balled his fists and counted to ten. Was this how it would always be whenever those photos were mentioned around him?

Officer Ramirez shifted his flat feet, probably wondering why he was getting the *I'm gonna kill you* stare-down. "Hey, don't you play hockey in the league?" he asked into the ever-lengthening silence.

"Yeah." Wyatt walked away, and Ramirez got to live another day.

Wyatt had been back to the house a couple of times to pick up paperwork for his leave but today's energy was different. Walking in, he breathed deep the scent of rubber, motor oil, and—sniff—last night's chicken cacciatore à la Gage. Cameras were already in position and the place was a flurry of activity; it hadn't seen this much action since that charity calendar was shot here over a year ago. Luke making a fool of himself while making eyes at Kinsey. Good times.

Wyatt stepped over cables, nodded at a few of the film crew, and headed to the lounge to say hello to any of his rubbernecking platoon who might have stuck around. Undoubtedly, Venti was practicing his intro to Molly in the latrine's mirror this very minute.

On turning a corner, he halted in surprise. His niece stood at the Wall of the Fallen, staring at a picture of her dad, and in that moment, a terrifying conclusion hit him with all the force of a 400 psi hose:

She could have died and he might never have met her.

Roni's mom had shown him photos of Wyatt's bald

and beautiful niece, taken as she battled leukemia six years ago. In every picture, bruised, weakened, and hairless, her eyes loomed large, like a message from her dad to take care of his girl. Guilt that he had deprived his family of her company for so long gnawed at him. Had he played it right? Should he have pushed Jen harder? He had no freakin' clue. What he did know was that he would do everything in his power to ensure nothing—whether it was a human enemy or the kind that tries to extinguish life from the inside—would ever hurt her again.

He stepped back, intending to give her space, but she'd already seen him. The vulnerable expression on her face gave way to her bored-teen mask. All she was missing were earbuds, a bubblegum snap, and a flip of the bird.

"Didn't know you were coming here today. I could have given you a ride."

"Aunt Alex brought me. She thought it would be fun to see where she works and visit a movie set at the same time."

He noticed she had a visitor's pass, probably set up by Molly. He also noticed that she had said where Alex works, not Wyatt. He pretended not to notice how his heart panged at that.

"Your dad was a big deal around here."

"People usually get a pass when they croak."

Harsh, but not wrong. If Logan were here, though, he'd be loving the hell out of her. Surely she knew that. If she'd learned a single thing about this family, it was that when they loved, they went all in.

"You already get the tour?"

"Yeah." She looked over her shoulder. "I'm going

to find Uncle Gage. He's still trying to work his way into the movie."

"God help us."

She laughed, and immediately clammed up when she realized her mistake.

"I'm not the enemy, Roni."

"No, you just look like him." She turned heel and left him standing there, astonished.

Was this the source of his niece's animosity? Sure, he and Logan resembled each other if you looked hard enough, but that's where it ended. If anything, Wyatt had been the dark angel to Logan's sunny nature. Apparently the blood connection that should have bound them closer was enough to put him on his niece's shit list, when all Dempseys not named Wyatt were making the fucking grade.

What did you expect, Fox? Every single one of them was a magnet, sucking the world into their bright orbits. Not good enough for Billy Fox. Not good enough to be Dempsey.

INTERIOR FIREHOUSE NO. 77, CHICAGO'S NORTH SIDE

Chase Macklin jumps off the fire truck, furious. Kelly Flynn follows him to the back of the engine.

                    KELLY
     Chase, you need to calm down.
     There's nothing you could have
     done.

```
              CHASE
              (loud)
    Not helpin', Flynn.


              KELLY
            (soothing)
    Sometimes the runs turn to crap. We
    can't save 'em all.


Chase turns and grabs Kelly by the
shoulders, pushes her against the fire
truck, and kisses her.
```

"Cut!"

Mother of God.

Molly's costar had actually torn his lips away from hers and called time on the scene.

"Gideon, mate," Mick called softly from the director's chair. "My job."

"What the hell was that, Molly?" Gideon spat out. "You're kissing me like a wet fish."

Mick loped over. "What's the problem here?"

Molly could feel the back of her neck redden with humiliation. No one appreciated their kissing technique being likened to a wet fish, especially while the crew looked on, projecting bored. But she knew better. They were filing it away for some later tell-all that would be attributed to an "inside source" on the set.

"Sorry, guys," Molly said. "Just nerves."

"Of course, darling. We all get them." He glared at Gideon, clearly not appreciating his unprofessional attitude in kiss-shaming his costar in front of the crew. "Perhaps you and Gideon could take a moment to discuss the blocking."

Blocking wasn't the problem, unless you counted her psychological block. Bottom line: Molly hated kissing and despised love scenes. Not only because it was embarrassing to have your bits flapping about while thirty blasé crew members watched or because you'd just had mac and cheese with your costar at craft services, and a pasta shell had somehow landed in his hair and fell onto your boob during filming (true story). For Molly, it ran deeper. A love scene had always meant that Ryan would go into one of his jealous rages.

Following the release of her last rom-com, before she was elevated to bubonic plague threat level by the studios, she'd received a few less-than-glowing reviews about her on-screen chemistry with her co-star. Essentially, she had been conditioned by her ex-husband to *in no way, don't even think about it* look like she might be enjoying a kiss with a fellow actor. The ones that were required by the script.

Ryan had always assumed she was banging everyone on the set.

So when it came to intimate scenes, she would go as stiff as a clapboard. Which meant there were several retakes and an ever-spiraling sense of failure in that aspect of her craft.

Today's scene was supposed to take place after a particularly tough run. Adrenaline high, spirits low, let's get it on.

And Wyatt was here.

She hadn't expected that. There wasn't anything scheduled that required a CFD consult, but it was his firehouse, so she supposed he had every right to be present. But now all she could think of was a jealous lover. Ryan questioning her when she got home about whom she had kissed that day on the set. He'd known everyone's schedule, had all the call sheets from her movies.

"Mind if we take five?" Molly asked Mick.

"No probs, darling."

She needed a moment to breathe, to think about how to play it, how to loosen her lips and her inhibitions. She looked around, and seeing no sign of Wyatt, insisted that disappointment felt close to relief. At least he hadn't witnessed her humiliation. The firehouse was empty, taken out of dispatch rotation for the shoot, so she walked through the unoccupied corridors, talking to herself and gathering her wits.

Possibly mutually exclusive endeavors.

A door opened and Wyatt stepped out. She tried to ignore the sunbeams of joy that burst in her chest. Failed spectacularly. "Hi—"

He grabbed her hand, walked her a few feet, and sexily manhandled her behind another door. It was a large walk-in closet smelling of rubber and testosterone, and filled with bunker gear and one verra sexy man.

"Babe."

"Wyatt, I have to get back. I'm supposed to be taking just five."

"Yeah, I saw it didn't go so well."

She groaned her embarrassment.

"I'm gonna pretend it's because the thought of kissing anyone but me turns your stomach."

"Well . . ."

"Have pity on my ego, Hollywood."

Laughing, she wrapped her arms around his solid trunk. He was so hard and strong and safe, and she'd give anything to stay inside this room. Inside all the bubbles he had created for her. Her home for the summer, the backseat of his Camaro, this world made for two.

"Don't like how he talked to you." He brushed his lips along the top of her head. "Made me want to talk to him."

"That's not necessary. I can handle it." By ignoring it. *Minimize, de-escalate, move on.* "I've been having problems with my love scenes for a while. I just get all wound up thinking about my ex."

She felt him stiffen. "What about him?"

"He assumed there was always something going on with my costars. He'd accuse me of ridiculous things."

Wyatt rubbed tight, soothing circles on her back. "Like what?"

"It was a lot of little stuff over the years. Small cuts that opened into bigger wounds. Petty jealousies that blossomed into divo rages. Instead of celebrating my success, he related everything to his own failures. We could never be up at the same time. He wanted an extension of himself, a trophy he could control, someone who fed into his image of superstar. Even the spooning was tyrannical."

The soothing back rub stopped. "Tyrannical spooning?"

"I hate spooning in bed. I get too hot and sweaty and uncomfortable, but Ryan insisted on it. He said it was a sign of our closeness and his need to protect me. You know, the strong, manly big spoon has to take care of the fragile, lady little spoon. The whole setup is riddled with patriarchal overtones."

Molly Cade, you have officially lost it.

Peeking up, she expected to find Wyatt mentally planning his getaway from the crazy lady in the firehouse. This is what she was like, a self-absorbed Hollywood nut job with so much baggage she needed a Sherpa to carry it around.

He wore an expression of tremendous gravity. Shocker. "I promise never to oppress you with spooning."

She laughed, feeling inordinately silly and completely seen.

"This guy of yours didn't trust you. You. The best thing to ever happen to him," Wyatt said, his gaze intent and true. "Idiot shouldn't have hooked up with an actor, then. He's not here, Molly. Your ex has no power over you anymore."

Oh, really? Those damn pictures said different. She wouldn't be surprised if Ryan encouraged his ex-agent to pass on the information about the leak to Cal. He'd have known how much it would throw her off her game. A year later, and he still had his claws in her.

"It's this Pavlovian thing. Lights, camera, kiss— and I turn into a statue."

Wyatt held her gaze, considering. She loved watching him work problems out.

"So, having been an enthusiastic participant in your original role-playing shenanigans, I happen to know you lead a vivid fantasy life."

Not what she expected, but okay.

"And you're an Oscar-nominated actor at the top of your game."

"I'll stipulate to that, Counselor."

"Close your eyes and think of me."

Say what, now? "You're recommending I fantasize about you while I kiss another man?"

"Better that than the other way around. This is work for you. I know that. Sure, maybe you have chemistry with some of your costars, but hell if I can see a spark of anything between you and Giddy-Up."

"Giddy-Up?"

"So christened by Gage. I know kissing that shithead is a chore, so I'm giving you permission to use all your hot fantasies about me to get it done."

She drew back and pressed a hand to her chest, endeavoring to cover her sudden tenderness for him with snark. "You'd do that for me?"

"For your art, babe. Now, how about somethin' to inspire you?" He captured her mouth with a slow, sultry Wyatt kiss. She had no other way to describe it. All him, focused on all her.

A minute later, she was a puddle of feeling in his arms, and still he continued. She felt him hard, pulsing against her belly, but he took it no further. Just made love to her mouth with deep, unhurried kisses. Hello-to-the-sun kisses. Her legs swayed like reeds but he was there with a hand on her butt, the other curled around her neck holding her in place for their mutual pleasure.

Normally, she'd be trying to move things along, restlessly rubbing her body to hint at her impatience, but with Wyatt, she let herself relax and enjoy the sensations exulting through her. He was swift when necessary in protecting her, but deliberate when it came to everything else. Clearly a proponent of the Slow Sex Movement.

She was fast becoming a big fan.

Several minutes passed in the solace of the bunker room, the only sounds their breathy sighs and whimpers of encouragement. Those soft lips framed by his beard hunted for the pulse at her throat and licked it. He roved over the curve of her neck, the line of her jaw, her beyond-sensitive earlobes. Kissing, biting, sucking.

Healing.

The heart that had hurt so much in the last year pried open, just a sliver. *There is a crack, a crack in everything. That's how the light gets in.* Leonard Cohen knew the score, and when you started quoting LC, you were in deep shit.

Spooked, she pulled away. "I—I should go."

He loosened his grip but still held her, giving her the choice to lengthen the distance. When it came time to end whatever was happening between them, she would be the one to leave. But not yet. She stepped away, meaning to go, *needing* to, and found herself back in his arms, sinking into his strength. Unable to get enough of this drug tearing through her veins.

Unable to get enough of Wyatt Fox.

CHAPTER EIGHTEEN

Molly pushed the buzzer for Darcy and Beck's condo in Andersonville, clutched tighter her copy of a *New York Times* best-seller billed as "the next *Girl on the Train*" along with a bottle of Cab Sauv—not too expensive so she wouldn't look showy—and waited to be admitted to the inner sanctum.

What was it about the Dempsey women that tied her knickers in knots? They had been nothing but pleasant so far, though she wondered if that would still be the case if they knew she was sneaking around for regular Camaro nookie with their brother. They were so crazily protective of each other; finding out about her past connection to Wyatt might draw accusations of using him for that Dempsey stamp of approval. And while it might have started out that way, now there were sultry kisses. Mind-melting orgasms.

The beard.

Darcy opened the door, her mom-to-be glow and vibrantly inked arms blinding. "Hey!"

"Hi," Molly said, suddenly shy. She held the wine aloft. "I know you can't imbibe, but I figure you can put it in your stash for when you can. And I also brought . . ." She rummaged in her Kate Spade tote and extracted edamame from Trader Joe's and salted caramels from Vosges. "Didn't know if you're feeling sweet or salty today."

"A bit of both," Darcy said, ushering her in. "Look, everyone, it's Molly. She brought much-needed supplies."

"And the book," Alex noted with a raised eyebrow. Her tee read: "You're sweet, but . . . No, I don't need help off the firetruck."

Molly hadn't enjoyed the book all that much, had only skimmed it, really. She'd always assumed reading was a cover for the real point of book club: massive alcohol consumption. "Was I not supposed to bring the book?"

Kinsey jumped up from the sofa and took the wine from Molly. "Love that tote, by the way, and yes, you were supposed to bring the book, though it's rare we actually get to discuss it. Usually, I'm the only person who's read it."

"I'm too busy kicking ass, saving lives, and having awesome sex fests to find time for reading," Alex commented, dry as sand.

Kinsey snorted. "And what's your excuse, D?"

"Ditto except replace 'saving lives' with 'making babies and creating artistic masterpieces.' If the demon kicks a lot while I'm reading, I take it as a sign that book's not for me. It was a freakin' earthquake down there when I read *Gone Girl*."

Everyone laughed.

"So, Molly, tell us to shut the hell up here, but . . ." Darcy threw a shifty look at the others. "We'd love to ask some questions about certain Hollywood personages. Is it completely basic to want all the down 'n' dirty details?"

"Completely." Molly sat on the sofa. "I'll need wine first."

An hour later, she'd wowed the girls and left them seriously agog at some of the gossip she'd shared.

"I can't believe they're able to keep that stuff out of the press," Darcy said, grabbing another salted caramel. "If one of Hollywood's finest is strung out on meth and chasing a Vietnamese pot-bellied pig down a Beverly Hills street, you'd think it might merit a mention on Page Six."

"When you're a double Oscar winner," Molly said, "you have great PR people."

"And I can't believe a certain notorious man whore is gay," Kinsey said. "Gage totally called that and I said he had to be wrong."

"Gage is never wrong about that," Alex said. "His dick is like a gaydar divining rod."

More giggles.

More wine.

More edamame, salted caramels, and cheesy-toasty things (scientific name, per Alex) that so hit the spot.

No book discussion.

Not that Molly minded. She was enjoying herself far too much. Kinsey was now trying to interpret her latest encounter with the bro code, but as she was on her third glass of Malbec, she was having problems nailing it down.

"I can understand the basics. If you borrow something gas-powered from a bro, it must be returned with the same amount of gas."

"Or full," Alex clarified.

"Or full," Kinsey agreed. "And if a bro helps you move, intergalactic bro law says you have to recip . . .

recip . . ." She dismissed with a wave her inability to shape that tongue twister. "Do the same for him."

Molly raised a hand to make a point of order. "Unless Moving Bro has not packed up his stuff before Helping Bro gets there."

Shouts of agreement greeted that. Bro code failure.

"But the groceries," Kinsey slurred.

Around her chewing of a caramel, possibly three, Darcy asked, "Wharaboudem?"

"All groceries go from the car to the house in one trip," Kinsey said in a deep baritone that Molly assumed was an impression of Luke. She counted off on her fingers. "It does not matter how many bags there are. It does not matter how heavy said bags are. It does not matter that you might dislocate something trying to carry them in."

Alex nodded in recognition. "Eli says that the sensation of losing all circulation in your thumb just as you reach the front door is the feeling of success."

Kinsey stood and pumped her fist. "Exactly!"

"Look, my brothers are the worst," Alex said. "And it amazes me how much Eli devolves every moment he's with them because he was a total fucking caveman before. I thought finding the loves of their lives would soften them up."

"Eli still sleeping in the guest room, then?" Kinsey asked with a grin.

"I let him in to sex me up, then send him on his way. The dog stays."

"The macho thing gets worse every day," Darcy said. "It's like they've acquired more territory, so they have to plant their flag. In everything." She rubbed her belly at that, drawing drunken giggles from the crowd.

Alex turned to Molly. "You'd think Wyatt would be the exception. He's usually so live-and-let-live, each to his own, but since he met you, he's no better than the rest of them. The chest-beating protectiveness, shadowing you everywhere."

"Well, he's always been a bossy guy," Molly said, then abruptly stopped talking because, *oops*. Cheeks flushing faster than she could blink, she looked down at her drink and damned it to hell.

"Always?" Darcy asked sweetly.

"Right. Since I met him." *Nicely covered,* tipsy Molly cheered. But *un*tipsy Molly, or the part of her brain that insisted she was not smashed, made a rookie mistake: unnecessary embellishment. "You know, a few weeks ago."

"Versus?" Kinsey, who was no longer slurring in the slightest, the trickster.

"I knew it!" Alex's green eyes glittered. "There was just something really familiar about how he was acting around you at the cookout, so not like our Wy at all. Did you know him . . . before?"

Hell, damnation, and a deep, deep breath. "We, uh, *might* have met a few years ago before I moved to LA."

Everyone not named Molly leaned forward.

"It was nothing, really."

Leaning at a forty-five-degree angle now.

"It was just a fling." Each admission spiked Molly's voice a couple of panicked octaves. "We hooked up in a hotel bar and had anonymous sex for a week," she finished on a breathy gush.

Three things happened simultaneously. Kinsey stood, swayed, and pointed like a deranged Marcel Marceau. Darcy clutched a hand to her throat, expecting to find . . . pearls? Alex knocked over an empty wineglass. They all screamed.

The condo's buzzer sounded. They screamed again.

Darcy wagged a menacing finger in Molly's direction. "Do not, I repeat, do not reveal anything about anything while I am out of the room."

Alex shuddered. "Maybe *I* should be out of the room. So don't want to hear about my brother's sexploits."

Molly laughed nervously as Darcy raced out, evidently terrified some great reveal would emerge during her absence. She slapped her forehead. "He's going to kill me if he knows I blabbed. You know what's he's like. Mr. Secretive."

"And look where that got him," Kinsey said. "Luke's still pissed. You are in the Circle here and your filthy little fling will not leave the Circle."

"Whose filthy little fling?" asked a new female voice. In walked a very sharply dressed woman sporting a Coco Chanel bob, a Dooney & Bourke purse, and vibes à la Anna Wintour.

"Molly and Wyatt had a dirty, no-names affair years ago before she hit the big time."

"Kinsey!" Molly protested.

The cool blonde motioned dismissively to the new arrival. "This is Madison. She's the embodiment of the Circle."

Molly recognized her now. Madison Maitland, owner of a prominent Chicago PR firm, Eli Cooper's former mayoral campaign manager—and his ex-wife. Who hung out at book club with his current fiancée? That was very . . . mature.

"Wyatt 'Incredible Arms' Fox?" A suspiciously rapt expression relaxed Madison's angular features. "Bet it must have felt amazing to be carried in them. Pity I was passed out."

A bolt of alarm shot through Molly, and she looked to the others for an explanation so she wouldn't be obliged to verbalize a request for same or go Hulkerina-Smash on Madison, who seemed to have a thing for Wyatt's incredible arms.

Alex saw Molly's face and grinned. "Cool yo jets, Crazy Eyes. Wyatt saved Madison's life in that hotel fire the same night I saved Eli's, before the bastard turned it around and saved me right back. He couldn't even give me that."

Darcy frowned at Alex. "We're getting off topic." As she poured a glass of wine for Madison, she said to Molly, "So you. Wyatt. All the sex, none of the names."

Acutely aware of how awkward this was for his sister, never mind for Molly herself, she held up the hand of no. "It happened. We parted ways. No drama."

"And now you've reconnected," Kinsey said. "So if you're keeping it on the down low, where's all this hot lovin' happening? Must be tough with so many Dempseys clit-blocking you."

Molly snagged her lip. "The backseat of the Camaro is surprisingly comfortable."

"*Fuck, no!*"

"*You're kidding!*"

"*Every teenage boy's wet dream!*"

Molly was having a tough time suppressing her giggles. "Guys, I'm serious," she said, though she couldn't keep a straight face. "Please don't tease him about it. Or even let on you know." Protectiveness for this amazing man sucked at her chest like a greedy surf. She knew how much he valued his privacy, even among the people he was so close to.

Darcy sighed contentedly. "We'll keep quiet. God, I love a good second-chance romance, but then I'm biased."

"She's our resident Disney queen," Kinsey said. "She'll have you down the aisle by Labor Day."

"So did anyone read the book?" Madison asked, only to be hushed by Darcy.

"Molly's about to compare current Wyatt with past Wyatt in the sack. And then both of them with her ex."

Molly laughed. "Am not!" She made a lips-zipped motion with her fingers, though the comparison could be summed up with two words: *no contest*.

"Hmm," Madison hummed with a long look at Molly.

"What?"

"Sounds like you deserve some fun after the year you've had." It wasn't said to pry; Molly intuited understanding in those words.

"I've been trying to put all that behind me. The divorce, the photos. I want the product to reflect who I am going forward."

Madison gave the slimmest of shrugs, took a sip of her wine, and remained silent. If that wasn't a challenge, Molly would eat every single one of those salted caramels. All serving sizes were wrong and stupid anyway.

"You don't think I handled it right."

"I'm sure your PR people are the best," she said with a diplomatic smile.

Kinsey's nod was wise. "That's Madison's way of saying 'If you were my client . . .'"

"I had a choice," Molly said, feeling a tad defensive. "Letting it die down seemed like the best option for my mental health."

"What happened to you," Alex cut in, "was a sexual assault. Sorry, I know it's none of my business, but it makes me so fucking angry that people just laugh and ogle when an actual crime occurred here."

Molly's heart thundered like a jet engine in her chest. "Once those pictures were out, there wasn't a whole lot I could do about it. After that, it's all damage control. I could choose either grace under pressure or whole-hog Xena Warrior Princess." She'd chosen the former, though she really wanted to go bat shit suing everyone into the grave: the cloud service with its security flaws, the anonymous Russian hacker who started it all, the gossip sites that spread the infection.

But by not making a fuss, she wouldn't be perpetuating the problem. *Minimize, de-escalate, move on.* It would eventually go away and she could refocus on the work, on what mattered. But a part of her had died the moment those pictures went viral. Adventurous Molly. Trusting Molly. Though in truth, that woman was being slowly smothered by Ryan's toxicity. And then to find out that this man she had once loved was the author of all her pain.

Molly should have slapped Ryan with an open

palm and a breach of privacy lawsuit the minute she heard about his involvement, but hell if she wanted to be the subject of more tawdry headlines.

"So many people had advice to give and most of it was about keeping my image sweet and pliant. Women who raise their voices in Hollywood are seen as difficult. Women who ask for equality in pay are seen as strident. Women who want are seen as bitches."

Nods of recognition all around. These women got it, each of them fighting for respect every day in their professional and personal lives.

God, she missed Cal. But how lucky was she to have landed in this circle, temporary as it was? Emotion clogging her chest, she took another pull of her wine, only to find it gone. Alex immediately jumped in with the refill, though Molly would have kept talking even on an empty glass. Now that she had opened up, she was finding it hard to stop.

"I felt violated, sick, in denial, angry as a bee swarm. I also felt weak, helpless, and impotent. Making this movie as awesome as I can is the only thing I can do to reclaim who I was." Losing herself in Wyatt Fox's strong arms, letting him shatter every inhibition and help rebuild her warrior heart—or the walls around it—was part of the cure, as well. But trusting her happiness to him or another man? Screw that.

"Throwing yourself into work?" Darcy asked.

"Yes, but more. Creating something that will stand the test of time, where I'll be remembered for being more than just a pair of tits or a big booty or the woman who made this exceptionally poor choice to allow her husband to take photos of her and keep them on his phone."

"But that choice is only poor because of what happened," Alex insisted. "You had every right to celebrate your body and take pride in how awesome you look by doing that. Yeah, maybe sharing it in a way that can never be deleted didn't turn out for the best, but why the hell should that choice be pissed on by the world?" She pointed a finger. "You should lay it out there, *Playboy* style. Show those haters you don't give a damn."

"Yeah, Hugh Hefner the hell out of it," Darcy said while everyone laughed.

Everyone but Madison.

Molly met her sharp blue gaze. "What do you think I should have done?"

"It doesn't matter now," Madison said, swirling the wine in her glass. "You've moved on."

Had she? Yes, she was making her comeback movie and running the show, but those pictures haunted her with their grainy, soft-porn focus and her corn-fed innocence sullied by every subsequent meme.

Madison seemed to pick up on Molly's ambivalence. "But if I had been advising you, I would have set up a photo shoot."

"*Playboy!*" From a drunker-by-the-second Alex.

"*Vanity Fair,*" Madison said. "Seminude, tasteful, classic poses exhibiting strength and pride. You control the message and the message is—"

"This is *my* body," Molly said. "And it's beautiful."

Satisfaction that Molly understood blazed in Madison's eyes, and a sharp flare of regret pulsed through Molly that she immediately tamped down. It was too late now, no use living in the what-ifs and if-onlys of the past. It was time to put it behind her and focus on the present. Make a great movie, embrace the new and slightly improved Molly, and enjoy all the hot lovin' with her sexy pirate.

• • •

HollywoodBooty: I'm hungry.
ThighTickler: My poorly stocked kitchen is yours to command.
HollywoodBooty: I want pregnant.
ThighTickler: Uh . . .
HollywoodBooty: PRINGLES!!! I WANT PRINGLES!
ThighTickler: ☺
HollywoodBooty: Blame autocorrect. And wine. Lovely wine.

Wyatt laughed, the sound strange in the echo of his empty kitchen, where he'd been sitting with a cup of steaming coffee—keeping a firefighter's schedule, caffeine had ceased to affect his sleep cycle a long time ago—and brooding over his recalcitrant niece, who was still insisting on pushing him to the margins of her life. Roni was sleeping upstairs, but it still didn't feel like she was living here. She spent more time out of the house than in, hanging with his brothers and sister. *Suffer patiently and patiently suffer.*

Molly's next text came in before he could respond: Meet me in the garage, big guy. Bring the goods.

A Hollywood booty call. Three minutes ago, he'd watched her wobble to the front door, scream "You ladies rawk!" at Darcy's car (containing one lady in total), and stumble into Gage's. He had planned to stop by and make sure she didn't pass out on the stairs when her diva demands to be fed came in. No

Pringles in the cupboard—Gage and Roni had taken to shopping together and she was more of a Cheetos girl—but there was a bag of Lays.

Very appropriate.

He grabbed the chips and a bottle of water, and headed out to the alley. Cicadas trilled the humid August air, competing with the tinny sound of a radio playing Mexican pop further on down the alley.

Molly stood—correction, slumped—against the garage door, one sandaled foot raised behind her. In her cute jean shorts and a low-cut top that barely contained her everything, she looked like a slice of Americana on a hot summer night.

"Hey, Marine."

"Hey, Hollywood."

"Good boy," she purred on spying the chips in his hand. "I'm pissed at you, by the way, but I want salt and sex, in that order, so I'm willing to put that aside for now." With a lusty giggle, she grabbed the bag, ripping it open on her way into the garage. Chips scattered in her wake.

Frowning, he followed. "Do I want to know what's got you mad at me, but not quite mad enough to stop you from using me for your salty-sexy needs?"

"I was reminded tonight of how bossy you are." Turning, she poked his chest with a potato chip. Predictably, it crumbled, yet she stared at it in rather adorable puzzlement. "How bossy all men are."

A special circle in hell existed for whoever had invented book clubs.

"So, taking you had a good night?"

"Positively *clit*-rary. Women talking about books and empowerment and important stuff."

"Baby, you're trashed."

"And it's your lucky day, buster."

Every day since the moment she'd walked back into his life had been his lucky day. Framing her face with his hands, he kissed her slow, sweet, deep, and wet. She tasted of wine and want and the woman he was a little bit crazy about.

A moan of pleasure escaped her. "You are an awesome kisser, Wyatt Fox. Bossy as hell, but an awesome kisser."

"Takes two, Mol." They kissed again, all that sweetness of her and the alcohol combining to make him dizzy.

"I needed that," she said against his lips.

"Me, too." God, he did. His troubles with Roni were starting to wear.

His body shook with the effort to keep this casual. Because he had needed it more, likely much more than her, and she was making it sound like he'd done her a favor. Just another thing that amazed him about this woman.

She looked up at him, her eyes glazed, her mouth parted expectantly. Desire shimmered between them, slippery, intangible.

"What else do you need?"

"My face between your thighs and those little sounds you make when I give it to you hard. But—"

"Butt? I've had a few, but you'd better not be thinking about a little sneaky backdoor action, Wyatt Fox!"

Well, he was now. "I was about to say I refuse to take advantage of a woman in your condition."

"You're not. You won't." She poked him in the

chest. "Drunk, sober, any state, I would be doin' you tonight, Mister. Lucky. That's what you are. A total BILF."

"BILF?"

"Beard I'd like to fuck." She fumbled with the back door of the Camaro and wrenched it open after a couple of tries. In she clambered, all legs and ass and giggles.

"Backseat. Into the bubble."

"Molly, we're not doing this."

She ignored his protests. Off came her jean shorts and the top with the thin spaghetti straps. Just beautiful Molly in a—*groan*—strapless bra, all white purity and sexy sin. Leaning back against the window, she propped one foot up on the front seat and spread her legs wide. She still wore underwear, but the scraps of virgin lace were more revealing than if she'd been wearing nothing. Hottest thing he'd ever seen.

The only sounds? His socks being knocked off and his dick climbing to full mast.

"Come and get it, Stone Cold Fox." And then she slipped a finger inside her panties, and he was lost.

Molly awoke with a start, her mouth dry, her head fuzzy. Slowly her eyes adjusted to the dark as consciousness stole up on her. She lay fluid in Wyatt's arms, cradled by his body, in the backseat of the Camaro. She was sobering up, though she resisted, preferring the hazy glow engulfing her body.

Alcohol, sex, Wyatt.

Her brain rewound and shone a fuzzy light on the three-letter word: Had there been sex? She'd enjoyed little enough of it in the last three years and plenty enough in the last three weeks that she knew when her body had been well used. This was not a body well used. She was in her underwear, though, and . . . she coasted her hand down Wyatt's chest to his waist. Hard as a wall, but still dressed.

So, no sex. Just . . . cuddling.

Uh-oh.

He nuzzled her temple. "Welcome back. You thirsty?"

She nodded, and he produced a bottle of water out of thin air. After sucking down half of it, she finally spoke.

"I offered myself on a platter and you didn't eat me up."

"Tempting as hell, Hollywood, but I draw the line at being used by a drunk-off-her-ass woman for salt *and* sex. I need to be wooed better than that."

"So . . ."

"We made out like teenagers and you fell asleep. A couple of hours ago."

Nope, not embarrassing at all. She only hoped she hadn't said something stupid about how his kisses were more addictive than a Class A drug or he made her ovaries scream to be mated.

She shifted. "You must be uncomfortable."

Against her temple she felt the curve of his lips, the scruff of his jaw, his breath warm and easy. "If this is what it takes to hold you all night, I'll happily surrender all feeling in my arms and legs."

A joke, with an undercurrent of something terrifying. Their nights together in olden times had been characterized by insatiable sex fests broken by brief dozes to refuel. Seeing a night through in each other's arms was an intimacy their earlier affair would never have allowed. But now they were increasingly entwined in each other's lives. Work, home, family.

This was dangerous. She needed to pull back and not allow this sanctuary of comfort and sex he'd created suck her in.

"I should go back to bed."

"I'll walk you back."

"No—no, it's fine." She fumbled and found her cami and shorts, balled in a lump at her feet.

"You got Tylenol at home?"

At home. It was just a figure of speech, but now everything was loaded. "Yeah, I do."

"Take two. Drink a couple of glasses of water."

He rubbed her back as she opened the door. She didn't dare look to see if he was disappointed that she didn't kiss him good-bye.

"Text me if you need anything."

She nodded, not knowing how to respond without cracking open and oozing out all over the garage floor. Her heart trip-hammered in her chest, forecasting the hangover that would likely hit her tomorrow. Hell, today.

And if she let Wyatt Fox invade her senses any more, she was going to have the mother of all hangovers when shooting on the movie wrapped. One a couple of Tylenol wouldn't be able to fix.

CHAPTER NINETEEN

The last thing Wyatt expected to find when he walked into Gage's kitchen on a coffee mission was his niece and Molly sitting at the table with a pile of what looked like scripts spread out between them.

"This one's on fleek," Roni was saying. "Time travel's popular right now. With *Outlander* and *Doctor Who*."

Molly picked up the script Roni had singled out. "On fleek?"

"It means awesome," Roni said, but she didn't sound her usual annoyed self when she had to explain something to the unhip adults.

Heading to the Keurig, Wyatt hovered and read over Molly's shoulder. A Post-it stuck to the title page of the script was covered in tidy writing:

Strong female protag. Great world building. Pirates. Drags a bit in the middle, but I marked where it could be tightened. Good pace in last quarter. B Test, yes.

More than a little confused, he continued his quest for coffee. Neither of them had acknowledged his presence.

"What about the May/December romance?" Molly picked through the stack. "This one?"

"Skeevy," Roni said with a lip curl of disgust. "But the writing's good. Passes the Bechdel test. Maybe if—"

"The woman was the older one in the relationship?" Molly finished, her finger to her lip and her brow scrunched tight. "Baby cougar."

"Yeah, the old ladies in your demo would love that." Roni softened that statement with a grin. A grin! Who the hell was this girl and what had she done with his niece?

"Mornin'," Wyatt said. "Anyone want coffee?"

"I'm good," Molly replied absently, her attention still on the script. Man, he loved watching her in the zone, even when it resulted in him being shoved out of it. "Susan Sarandon would be awesome."

Roni wrinkled her nose. "Who?"

"*Thelma and Louise*?" When Roni still looked blank, Molly prompted, "The ultimate 'bad girls sticking it to the man' movie?"

Wyatt was pretty sure the bad girls died when they drove their car into the Grand Canyon, so sticking it to the man was open to interpretation.

Molly was still trying to jog Roni's memory. "Young Brad Pitt as the hottest cowboy who ever lived?"

"That guy was young once?"

"I weep for your education. I'm going to assign a list of movies for you to watch. Inculcate the classics."

Wyatt hit the start button on the Keurig. "Here's all you need to know, Roni. *Planet of the Apes*? It was Earth all along. *The Sixth Sense*? Bruce Willis was dead the entire time. *The Empire Strikes Back*? Darth Vader won't be winning Father of the Year anytime soon."

"Don't forget to tell her the real identity of Keyser Söze and exactly how close Norman Bates was to his mother, spoilsport."

"As for *Thelma and Louise* . . ."

Molly's mouth fell open. "Who hurt you?"

He raised a villainous eyebrow. "It doesn't end well."

"God, you guys are totes adorbs. Just do it already." Roni made a gagging gesture in case the brick-thick sarcasm wasn't clear enough, but he could tell her heart wasn't in it. For once, she was acting like a human being and not a teenage pod person.

A blushing Molly lowered her head and tapped out a search on her phone. She showed Roni the screen.

His niece's eyes lit up in appreciation. "That's baby Brad Pitt? Okay, he's pretty cut."

"Standing right here," Wyatt interjected.

Molly turned on the mega-wattage grin and he melted under its power. "I'm trying to acquaint your niece with an earlier generation of hotness."

He squinted at Roni, and knowing it was a long shot, demanded gruffly, "Tell me you're not interested in boys yet."

Roni cocked her head. "Maybe I'm interested in girls."

Clearly said for pure shock value. Did she even know him?

"I *wish* you were interested in girls. At least then you wouldn't come crying to me with the news I'm going to be a great-uncle."

Roni's eyes—Logan's eyes—widened. Why had it taken him so long to figure out? Embarrassment, the ultimate weapon in the generation war. "You know it's okay if you like girls, sweetheart. Whatever makes you happy."

He caught Molly's eye and the smile she was doing her damnedest to hide. Evidently torn between mortification that Wyatt thought she liked girls and appreciation that he would be über cool with it if she did, Roni colored to fire-truck red.

"I'm coming out right now," she said indignantly. "As straight."

"Gage'll be crushed." He didn't laugh—far too risky, much too soon—and he could tell she was trying not to, either. Triumph at this brief connection howled in his chest.

"Now, about where babies come from—"

"Wyatt!" She finally let loose that laugh, and man, he almost buckled over at that beautiful sound. Her phone buzzed, and she stopped giggling. "That's Mom."

"Remember what I said," he warned.

She rolled her eyes in Molly's direction. "Yeah, I know. Big-ass secret. Emphasis on *big* and *ass*." Molly smiled serenely at that blatant insult while Roni took the phone outside.

Wyatt shook his head as he watched her leave. "That mouth. Spending too much time with Alex."

"Believe me, people have said a lot worse about my ass." Molly met his gaze with a saucy smile. "And news flash, Lieutenant. Lesbians can get pregnant, as well."

"Usually not because a condom broke. So when did my niece start working for a Hollywood production company?"

"She showed an interest a while back, so I thought

I'd do some market research. Figure out what the kids are into these days. She's got quite the eye." She patted the pile of scripts. "We agreed on all but one."

"Thanks for involving her in something, even if it does have the stench of child labor about it." Through the window, he watched Roni sprawled on the patio sofa. "Uh-huhs" and weight-of-the-world sighs filtered through as she listened to her mother.

Turning back to Molly, he let his gaze take her in properly. She wore a low-necked tee that showcased the tops of her lovely breasts. A hint of lace peeked above the border, inviting his gaze and turning him hard.

Somehow, he was sleeping with this goddess.

"C'mere," he said, his voice rougher than he'd intended.

"Wy—"

"Now."

Desire flared in her eyes and she walked over into his arms with no more arguments. He didn't kiss her yet, just tucked her under his chin, though really, he wanted to ask her how she thought their movie was going to end. *The Wyatt and Molly Story*. A predictable final third or shocking plot twist?

Her eagerness to flee last night after she had awoken in his arms should have been answer enough. Fade to black. A summer fling was all she was after, and that was only right because he wasn't the hero in this tale. Not to her, not to his niece. But he'd take any scrap Molly gave him because five seconds in her burning orbit was worth all the darkness to come.

"About last night," he said. "You okay?"

The question could be interpreted a number of ways. *Are you hungover? Freaked out? Ready to bail?*

She nodded. "I just wasn't expecting that."

Neither was he. Holding a smashed, half-naked, gently snoring Molly in his arms had been the strangest, most perfect version of heaven. He didn't consider himself a greedy man—being satisfied with his lot was a damn sight safer—but hell if he didn't want more of this woman.

"This has been an unexpected summer." His gaze strayed to Roni, his heart with it.

"She'll come around," she said quietly. "That girl needs you."

"Does she? 'Cause it seems like she's getting along just fine with everyone but me." Yep, petty jealousy was this year's black.

"You're the one who connected with her first. She's worried about getting close because losing *you*, her blood connection to her father, would be the hardest."

His sigh was borne of a year's frustration. "She's not gonna lose me. Any of us."

"She'll figure that out."

Tired of talking, he cupped her ass to lift her close, slanted his mouth over hers, and took what he needed. She surrendered, but only for a few seconds.

"Wyatt, your niece is literally a few feet away from us. Brady's upstairs. Not here."

This sneaking around was sexy but it was also exhausting. He was thirty-four years old, for fucking out loud.

"I need a night with you in a bed, where I can do unspeakably illegal things to you, not scraps in the backseat of a car on blocks in my garage."

"You'd better not be knocking the Camaro."

"Babe, you deserve better than a quick fumble."

She scoffed. "Quick? Ha! You are slower than a snail on top of a turtle. I've never met a guy who takes his time like you do."

He pinned her against the sink. "You're complainin'?"

"Merely making an observation."

She slipped out of his grasp, sat back at the table, and picked up a script. Peeking up at him through her lashes, she gave his body a thorough inventory. He'd been half hard with her in his arms; now he sprang to full mast under her scrutiny.

"This sucks," he muttered, sounding very like his fifteen-year-old niece.

Cue that impudent grin. "Guess you shouldn't have started the hot, illicit affair on your home turf, then, should you have?"

Cheeky. He went to lunge at her, but Brady walked in, and any hopes of escaping another day without the balls of blue scooted out the door.

• • •

ThighTickler: Tell Gage you have a friend in town tonight. You're staying at a hotel, good security.
HollywoodBooty: What's the plan, Marine?
ThighTickler: Wear something hot. A disguise.
HollywoodBooty: Mysterious. Where are we going?
ThighTickler: No more questions! Car will pick you up at eight. Stay fierce on the set, babe.

Wyatt walked into the bar and took a seat at the end. Busier than five years ago, its clientele appeared to consist mostly of out-of-town suits looking to get laid by other out-of-town suits. He checked his phone again. Two minutes early, but then he was never late.

Placing his palms on the bar, he popped his head up and sent a glance over the other barflies. No sign of her. He'd made sure there was no one around at home to see the car he'd arranged to pick her up—Roni was having a girls' night with her aunts; Brady and Gage were working. The planets were aligned. They might never get another chance like this.

He tried not to infuse too much meaning into those words.

A Coke bottle appeared before him.

"From the lady at the end of the bar." The bartender looked skeptical, as if the notion of laying a drink on a stranger in a crowded bar was the weirdest thing he'd ever come across. *You have much to learn, my friend.* He waited for Wyatt's nod of acceptance.

Wyatt raised the bottle to his lips and took a sip, the sweet nectar slipping down his throat easily. He loved the cool slide of the sugary sweetness better than any beer or scotch. He'd never been a drinker, preferring to remain in control. A Coke had always been his treat during those days on the grifters' road with Billy and Logan. Not that Billy would ever buy his son a treat, but Logan would slip him one when Billy wasn't looking.

Bottle in hand, he slid off the stool and took a stroll down the bar until he reached her usual spot.

Holy hotness, Batman. *Tonight, the role of rock chick will be played by Molly Cade.*

A sleek black wig, short leather skirt, sheer lace top, and spike-heeled boots made up a vision for the ages.

He gripped the back of the empty seat adjacent, the only way he could stop from touching her.

"Is this seat taken?"

She lifted . . . green-tinted eyes shining through long fake lashes. If he didn't know her intimately, he would never have guessed that one of the most famous women in the world was sitting in a hotel bar in Chicago trawling for a good time. A brief flare of panic pinged his chest at the notion that she might be discovered. Exposed. What they were doing was risky.

Sexy as hell, though.

She let her gaze catalog his appearance. Not his usual faded denim and tee look, but a button-down Oxford and dark-rinse jeans because he'd wanted to make an effort. Lights of appreciation popped in her eyes before she blanked to stranger.

"I'm waiting for someone," she said with just the right amount of attitude directed at either her tardy date or the boor with the sorry pickup lines.

He grabbed the purse holding the empty seat and slung it over the back. "His loss."

"As soon as he arrives, you'll have to leave."

"*If* he arrives." He settled in, adjusting his position to accommodate his hard-on. Ten seconds in her presence, and he was already sporting a plank in his pants.

"Are you always this bossy?"

"When I see something I want."

She practically disjointed her eyeballs trying not to roll them to the back of her head. So, it was clichéd. Wasn't that the point? Her snooty/surly act made him happy/horny.

It could only get better. "Are you from out of town?"

There it was, the pull of amusement on her mouth. She was having as much fun as he was.

"Passing through." She smoothed a hand along her skirt and let it rest on the bare band of thigh that the leather failed to cover. He had never wanted to touch something so badly.

So he did.

Knuckles first, a light graze over that peachy skin. Her breath hitched, she clamped down on her lower lip, and the quiet stretched between them, not uncomfortable but filled with delicious anticipation. One thing he liked about Molly was she wasn't a silence-filler.

"You in town with the convention?" Most of these guys looked like conventioneers.

"I'm actually with the band. I manage them."

Course the rock chick was with the band. "How do you do that?"

She shrugged, parted her thighs so his hand slid along of its own accord and dipped between her legs under the cover of the bar. "I'm all things to them. Den mother, whip cracker, confidante, lover. Fragile egos in the entertainment business. Takes a village."

"And you're a one-woman village." He bet the band just loved her.

"How about you?" she asked. "Do you live here?"

He moved his foot so it snagged the bottom rung of her stool. The bar was crowded, and the action raised his thigh and hid his wandering hand from any nosy patrons' gazes.

"I do now. Just completed my last tour with the marines."

Her eyes flashed. He'd gone off script and introduced an unexpected element: the truth. Or the truth as it had been five years ago.

"We're thankful for your service," she said with the perfect amount of sincerity.

He moved his hand higher, higher, *there,* until his knuckle brushed . . . oh Christ, she was bare. Her grip on the wineglass tightened.

"How thankful?"

She shifted in her seat, giving him better access, and inclined toward him. The plump curves of her breasts above the lacy bra cup strained perilously. "Isn't serving your country its own reward?"

"Not really. I joined up to score with chicks."

Her laugh was a blast of sun, its distinctive sound making his heart soar, his mind flail, and heads turn. It was too recognizable.

She pushed her body onto his knuckled index finger. Her eyes fluttered closed. Taking her pleasure, that's what she was doing, and he had never seen anything so hot.

But exciting as it was, he didn't want to share her. No one would see, but he wanted to capture her cry with his mouth when she came. Tonight would be for them alone.

He kept his voice low. "Not here."

She blinked, as if coming out of a trance. Things had escalated more quickly than he'd intended. Patience was usually his greatest asset. Waiting was ingrained in him—for the perfect target, the squad callout, the right moment to share Roni with his family—but with Molly, he didn't want to wait. He didn't want to play games anymore.

He just wanted her. Now.

This worried him. If he couldn't rely on his patience, what could he rely on?

He extracted his hand from her skirt, his billfold from his jeans, and slapped some bills down on the bar. He gave her the purse and clasped her hand, absorbing her shiver, enjoying the sheer rightness of it. How good it felt to claim her in public, even though they were both in disguise. What would that be like for real? Claiming *the* Molly Cade, telling the world she was his woman.

Crazy talk. She didn't want that because she couldn't handle the gossip or anything beyond a summer affair. The only difference from five years ago? Now she screamed his name when she came. Really, he was little more than a glorified bodyguard. Dressing up in a monkey suit to accompany the star to a movie premiere was not part of Wyatt's skill set.

Tonight, he would pretend.

Hand in hand, they walked through the crowd toward the lobby. One of those Art Deco jobs, it was recently refurbished and a lot more expensive than it was five years ago. He selected 12 on the panel and didn't dare look at her to see if she remembered—or didn't.

That would have killed him.

Once on the right floor, they headed to their room, that room, still holding hands, but not rushing like before. At the door, he put the card in the lock, and Molly placed her small hand over his knuckles.

"Wyatt," she said softly.

The last time they'd been here, she never said his name. She hadn't known it. He knew hers because he'd seen her in the show at the Ford Oriental Theatre around the corner. Desperate to escape himself and willing to suffer a musical to support his Who fandom, he had gone alone and surprisingly enjoyed it, captivated by the actress who played Tommy's mother. Her voice had rung sweet and strong, curling inside him and smoking through his blood. Later that night, wanting to embrace his solitude a little longer, he'd gone into a nearby hotel for a drink, and there she was at the end of the bar, swinging her leg and drawing him in. A quirk of fate.

Chatting up women was not in his wheelhouse. He'd landed stateside three weeks before and was thinking of re-upping. Too many memories of Logan and Sean driving him back to the desert, widening the chasm between Wyatt and the Dempseys. Every room, a photo. Every gathering, a story. Every bar, a song.

But not this bar. It was just Wyatt, the bartender, and the redhead he'd seen taking a bow not more than an hour ago. Molly Cade, the playbill had said, with a list of her credits, mostly dramas with titles that meant nothing to him.

He didn't talk to her that night.

But he did the next, after he had gone to see her show again. After he had summoned the courage to approach her. On one side of his ledger, he had kills; on the other, saves. Some people would say both sides required bravery, but none of that came close to the brass balls needed to walk up to a woman as beautiful as Molly Cade and speak.

"Wyatt," she said again, back in the present. Rock Chick Molly with her jet-black wig and fake eyelashes and green cat's eyes. This was easier when they didn't know each other; now every word and action was weighted with significance.

"I thought it would be the same," he murmured.

A shadow crossed her face. "That's what you want? What it was like before?"

Did he? It was certainly safer.

He cupped her neck and said what was in his heart. "I want you. Just you." The woman, not the part.

A small sound escaped her, impossible to decode, but he loved it. He wanted to drink that sound, imprint it on his soul, play it over and over. The games were fun and sexy, but stripped of their costumes, they were just two people with chemistry and a connection that had a mind and momentum of its own.

He pushed the door open and steered her inside. He didn't go for the lights, but the open curtains allowed a street-lit glow to permeate the room.

"The bathroom is—"

"I remember," she said, amusement warming her voice.

She went in and turned on the light, but left the door open. He sat on the bed, watching greedily as she changed from Rock Chick to Molly. *His* Molly. The wig, the contacts, the clothes—all of it fell away, and in its place, the real deal was revealed. There was something very intimate about watching a woman strip bare like that. Sure, she did it on the big screen for the more demanding roles, but here, now, in this room, he felt like he was witnessing a private moment. Her in the light, him in the shadows.

She strutted out of the bathroom and stood naked before him, a riot of heaven and curves.

"Nice shirt." Her fingers grazed the pink fabric. He

had wanted to look good, show her that he washed up well and she needn't be ashamed of him. As if a shower and a button-down shirt could make him worthy of this woman.

"Now, Marine. You've got the room, the bed, and the woman of your fantasies for the night. However are you going to use this time?"

CHAPTER TWENTY

He's wearing a pink shirt.

Molly was riding a helter-skelter of riotous emotions and Wyatt in his pink Oxford was not helping. A private joke that shouldn't mean a thing but signaled nuances in their relationship she wasn't ready to acknowledge.

She wanted to think his expression on seeing her dressed provocatively in a skirt so snug she had to walk downstairs sideways was garden-variety male desire. She wanted to think it as he slid his hand between her thighs and found her wet and wanting. But there had been something both protective and possessive about how he'd put a halt to the game and led her to the elevator, his hand wrapped around hers like they were a regular couple.

And when he said he wanted her, just her, and watched as she removed the mask, she wanted to think this was their real life. Desire and surprise and a sexy adventure with her rough-and-tumble warrior. He was doing it again. Creating a sanctuary from the crazy.

She placed her palms on his shoulders. "You planning to glare me into orgasm, Marine?"

"I don't glare. I smolder."

A ridiculously girly giggle escaped her. What was it about this man that sent joy barreling through her veins in equal amounts to lust?

He kept his gaze locked on her, hooded, watchful. Ablaze. She kissed the fine lines around his eyes. How did he get them if he so rarely laughed? His rough fingers snaked to the backs of her thighs, and all the while he stared at her with that blue-eyed intensity.

"I'm remembering some of your outfits from back then. Sexy librarian was a particular favorite." Heated fingertips grazed the curve of her ass, cutting a trail of desire across her skin. With what seemed like incredible restraint on his part, he refused to walk those fingers into more welcoming territory.

She needed more. Always more. Restless, she shifted against him. "And now rock chick?"

"Yeah, she's pretty hot but . . ."

"But?"

"You in your yoga gear. Hottest of all."

She raised a skeptical eyebrow.

"I mean it."

"Because you've been spying on me while I do downward-facing dog."

"I'm gonna assume that's related to yoga and not what I'd prefer to think it is." He gripped her ass and clasped her to his body with an almost lewd spread of her cheeks. The bite of the denim against her soft, damp nakedness felt divine. "Yeah, watching your ass is mighty pleasant, but that's not what I meant. I meant that it's my favorite outfit because it's all you. No role, no disguise, just Molly at peace, in her natural habitat."

Emotion pinged her chest and she sought to cover

with a cut to humor. "Where my natural habitat has my world-famous ass front and center."

"You so sick of compliments you can't take mine?"

Guilt replaced the yearning. "Not sick of them. But in my business I've learned to take them all with a grain of salt. Not a lot of sincerity in them."

"You think I'm not sincere?"

"I think you're trying to get into my yoga pants." His frown deepened, and she regretted her jokiness.

"I think you're the most beautiful woman I've ever seen, in costume or out, on a big-ass screen or at a backyard cookout. Molly, you slay me."

She believed him, and that was more shocking than the words he had just uttered. It had been so long since she believed a word anyone told her. Everyone had ulterior motives and *yes, ma'ams* on their tongues while they bowed and scraped before her. Cal was her best friend, and Molly questioned even how genuine that was, given she was also a paid employee. But every word out of Wyatt Fox's mouth was grounded in reality. His rock-solid gravity, devotion to family, and self-deprecation did it for her like no one else.

He did it for her like no one else.

Suddenly she didn't want to talk anymore, or she wanted to put her mouth—and his—to better use. Time to own this desire he had for her, and match it with her own. She framed his face with her hands and touched her lips to his. Their joint groans on that first contact echoed in the room, bouncing off the ceiling, finding a rhythmic feedback in their bodies. And how he tasted? His mouth hot and silken, like the only man who could ever taste this good, and hell if that wasn't the scariest notion alive.

What if she could never reach this peak with anyone else?

He pulled back, his nose nuzzling hers. "Time to get out of your head, babe. Don't overthink it."

Time to get *him* out of her head and just focus on her body as pure sensation.

"I need to see you." Fingers working feverishly, she pulled at the buttons of his shirt, and he obliged by shrugging it off his shoulders. Her blissful sigh emerged as a choked "Unh." The man was simply sublime with those broad shoulders that could carry the world and that hard chest made for her hands to explore.

Which they did.

Soon they were both breathing heavily as she smoothed her palms over his shoulders, pecs, biceps, lingering a moment on those badges of love for Sean and Logan. His jeans did nothing to cover his desire for her, and he wanted her to know that.

He paid her back tenfold with rough hands over the smooth skin of her naked breasts. One peaked nipple found its way into his mouth. Words died. Time stopped. Her heart stuttered, than started up with an insistent pulse of *yes yes yes*.

Every part of her vibrated like a plucked string, every beat in her body roared with the thrum of need his mouth and hands created. Moving over her ass, each knead and pass making her mindless with desire. Unable to stay still, she shifted against his denim-covered cock, seeking blessed relief.

He flipped her and pushed her back on the bed,

his body immobilizing her, the weight of him delicious. Lingering for a moment, he stared so hard it's a wonder she didn't come on the spot. Glare her into orgasm? It could happen.

Back up on his knees, he extracted a condom and lay it on the bed. Lovely sounds followed. The scrape of his zipper, the soft *whoosh* of his jeans and boxers shoved south just enough to release his rampant erection. He was so beautiful, his cock long and thick, already glistening with pre-come like a fat, shiny jewel. With one hand, he pumped, every stroke squeezing out more beads of beauty.

"Take me in your mouth," he said roughly, but she was already there, pouting and greedy. She closed her lips around him and let the thick vein on the underside of his cock imprint on her tongue. The pulse of it, all that life, shocked through her, making every cell in her body glitter. And his taste? Clean spice and musky man.

His hand shaped her skull and held her in place as she sucked. Loud, lusty groans, mixed with him calling her name, filled the room. Between her legs, her core pulsed, all feminine heat and sensual power. She could come like this, she was sure of it.

But she never got a chance to find out. Wyatt gentled her head back. "Condom, babe."

Dazed with desire, she tore at the packet and smoothed the condom onto his engorged length with shaky hands. She tugged at his jeans, still annoyingly on.

"Leave 'em," he muttered, and laying her back on the bed, he notched his cock at her opening and slid inside her in one, possessive thrust. He'd always fit so perfectly, and while everything else might have changed, that simple fact remained. She arched into him, trying to hurry him along, but it was pointless. Wyatt set the pace, rocked into her body, every stroke rooting deep and filling her completely. Reminded by the denim's friction between her thighs that he was half clothed while she was fully naked, she gasped at every long, luscious slide and return. Oh, this man knew how to surprise her. Each time different from the last, each moment ratcheting the sexual intensity.

With those trim hips pistoning between her thighs, he stretched her wider. His gaze fell to where their bodies connected, watching proudly as he slowly plundered, over and over. Her climax shimmered, always just out of reach.

"Every time, Mol," he murmured, and she heard the awe in it. "Every time."

As ever, he took it slow, and she studied his face, loving how expressive he became while he was lodged so deep she felt him all the way to her heart. In these charged moments of ecstasy, Wyatt Fox's truth shone bright. Unadorned, uncompromising, honest-to-God passion.

She grabbed his ass and dug her nails into his steely flesh, needing to see the emotion it produced. His eyes locked on hers. Terrifying. Relentless. And more: a sweet possession mixed with unexpected affection.

"That's right, baby. Scratch me up. Make your mark. I wanna look at my body later and know who I belong to."

So she did. She scored and clawed and bit, claiming him for her own. Each new attack drew his moan of pleasure, a deeper all-consuming thrust, and a niggling panic that she was in deep, deep trouble here.

Time waits for no man, except for *this* man, who must have sealed a devil's pact to slow the world to a standstill while he tested every inch of her limits. And when he finally let her come, and followed her over with a roar, she knew she might have made her mark on his body, but he had branded his on her soul.

"Room service."

"Be right there," Wyatt called out as he bent down to grab his jeans. (He'd *finally* taken them off and the world was now a better place.) Those incredible ass muscles bunched, and the sight of them incised with her marks of possession sent Molly's thigh muscles into a clench and her heart into a pitter-patter. She ran a hand over that slab of warm granite.

He glanced over his shoulder. "You gonna admire your handiwork all day or you gonna make yourself scarce?"

"What? Oh, right." There was danger at the door—and she didn't mean the fully loaded calorific threat of a hamburger with her name on it. The room service guy did not need to see a disheveled, well-fucked Molly Cade floating above the bed in a hazy, postorgasmic glow. Two hours since arriving in their bubble of iniquity, and they'd worked up quite the appetite.

Pulling a sheet off the bed for a spot of coquettish body coverage was never as easy as it looked in the movies. After a couple of tugs and no joy, she sighed.

"My overnight bag is in the bathroom," he said, amused. "Probably somethin' in there that'd fit you."

Acutely conscious of Wyatt's relentless gaze on her nakedness, she scurried to the bathroom and, once inside, rummaged through a black duffel bag she hadn't noticed before. Two blister-packed toothbrushes—*aw!*—toothpaste, a CFD tee (perfect for lounging around eating burgers with your marine firefighter pirate lover), yoga pants—

Yoga pants?

Heart thudding, she searched some more and found tennis shoes, socks, underwear, and . . . her Cardinals shirt. He had packed morning-after clothes for her. Even more amazing, he had sullied his hands with an emblem of the age-old enemy.

Oh boy.

Her thudding heart went ballistic. Deep breaths, deep breaths, deep . . . *fuck*. Each precious word from this man, every thoughtful gesture was piling on to the point she was having a hard time seeing straight. She stared in the mirror, annoyed to find she was glowing. If she weren't so terrified, she would think she looked happy.

It's just the amazing sex. Best skin-care regimen ever.

Outside, a soft snick announced that they were alone once more. Peeling on Wyatt's CFD shirt, she padded back in, inhaling the aroma of cooked meat and—hallelujah—french fries.

Wyatt drank her in and she returned the favor. He'd left his top jeans button undone and God, was he bringing sexy back.

He chewed on a fry. "Look good in my shirt, babe."

"You brought me stuff to wear."

"Figured you'd like to be comfortable on your way home."

Strangely, the word *home* didn't trigger the usual panic. "Instead of looking like a two-bit hooker on a wobbly walk of shame?"

He smiled, that Wyatt Fox slow burn that melted *everything*. "After a night in my bed, it's a walk of glory. And ain't nothin' two-bit about you, either, Hollywood."

But still looking like a hooker. Oh well, that's what she was going for. She flattened both hands on his broad, naked, *hot damn* chest. "Do I want to think of you poking through my drawers choosing my lulu-lemons?"

Sexy brow crumple.

"My yoga pants," she translated.

"I sent Gage in."

"Coward." The full force of that hit her. "So Gage knows about this? About us?" Her landlord had looked smugger than usual when she mentioned her visiting "friend" from out of town.

"Yeah, and about before." He looked a little wary of her reaction, so it was only fair she confess her own sins.

"Your sister and sisters-in-law know, as well. And about before." She grimaced. "Book club."

"Special circle in hell," he muttered, whatever that meant. "Guess neither of us have careers as James Bond in our future."

She giggled her relief. "Worst secret agent ever,

telling everyone his name. Bond, James Bond. It's a wonder he wasn't whacked years ago with that level of stupidity."

He gave an amused, sexy-as-all-get-out grin. "He's doing all right with the ladies, though."

"Yeah, *he* is. The lucky ladies all die horribly after he fucks 'em. If I saw James Bond, I'd run a mile in the other direction."

"No, you wouldn't."

She laughed. "No, I wouldn't. I've met Daniel Craig and he is smokin' in a tux." Hmm, Wyatt in a tux . . . that would probably kill her dead.

He kissed her forehead. "You don't have to worry about my family talking about your business. Or about the press finding out that you're getting your kicks with a blue-collar guy like me."

Okay. Did Wyatt really think he wasn't good enough for her to be seen in public with him? That this was the reasoning behind her preference for privacy?

Before she had time to defend herself against the implied accusation, he patted her ass. "Let's eat. Gotta keep your strength up for what I got planned."

"It stunk something awful."

Bellies full, and surrounded by the ruins of their room service feast, Molly had just finished telling Wyatt about the body farm where she did research for her role as an FBI agent in *Deadly Pursuit,* a thriller she starred in a couple of years ago.

"Yeah, well, dead bodies'll do that." He'd seen his fair share, after all.

Against the headboard, he lay with an arm behind his head, watching Molly sitting cross-legged on the bed in his CFD tee. No small amount of satisfaction heated his chest at the view. "So how long did it take you to learn to ride a horse for that one about the rodeo?"

"Two months," she said, making a face. Fucking adorable. "Two long, painful months with my butt and thighs screaming that they'd get their revenge. They made a pact with Ben and Jerry and loaded on twenty pounds once we wrapped."

"Then you lost it for the sci-fi film."

Whip-fast, she straddled him and splayed her hands on his chest. "Wyatt Fox, have you seen every one of my movies?"

There was a reason why he kept the chat to a minimum.

"Wyatt . . ." she warned when he refused to answer. "Fess up now."

"Movie theaters are usually the coolest places in summer."

"Oh. My. God." Her mouth fell open in genuine wonder. "You're a fan."

"Wouldn't go that far."

She grabbed a pillow and whacked him hard on the head. "Admit it. You are a fan!"

They tussled for a moment, though he maintained the gentlest hold possible as he pinned her and maneuvered between her legs. Best place on Earth.

"Yeah, I'm a fan," he admitted. "Sitting in the dark with a bunch of strangers, I'd look up at that big screen, riveted by the way you move and smile and talk and that little crinkle you get at the side of your mouth when you're callin' bullshit. I know her, I'd think. I've been inside her body, felt her tight and wet and hot around me. I had this secret, this moment in time that belonged to me. A few days with a goddess when I forgot my shitty life and my responsibilities and what lay behind and ahead. When it was just me and her."

She was breathing heavily, her CFD tee–covered breasts rising and falling, rising and falling. *When it was just me and her.* Like now.

If she had devoted a single thought to him over the years, she didn't say so, and he was glad of it. He wouldn't want phony conciliation thrown out merely to make him feel less alone in his nostalgia.

"I'm not a goddess," she whispered. "Just a regular girl. Or trying to be."

"Goddess/mortal determinations exist only in the eye of the beholder."

His gaze fell on her plump, kissable lips. He had a lot of favorite parts when it came to Molly, but her mouth was definitely top three. A wicked little miracle.

Now it curved in query. "Where did you come from, Marine?"

"I arrived fully assembled, like GI Joe. Just changed my marine threads to firefighter ones."

"So I can move your legs and arms and dick-less torso around for my pleasure?"

"Yours to use and abuse, babe."

She held his gaze, staring at him, into him. Maybe it was some acting trick to make your scene partner feel important, like the center of the universe. Whatever it was, it worked. Probably because he wanted to be tricked.

"Before the Dempseys, I spent a lot of time on the road. Billy—my dad—wasn't really a straight-and-narrow kind of guy." He inhaled a sharp breath. "He was a con man and we were part of his schemes. Me and Logan."

Her brow furrowed. "What kind of schemes?"

"Shills and scams. You name it, Billy did it. He'd put us to work buttering up anyone who would listen. Logan, really, because he had the gift. Could talk to anyone."

"Did your dad get arrested? Is that how you ended up with the Dempseys?"

Not quite. "We were running a Murphy Game. Selling knockoff phones from the back of a van. You show the mark the working one, then switch it out for a dud. We were careful to never go back to the same neighborhood twice, but someone recognized us. Called the police. Dad and Logan got away, but I was caught and put into juvie."

He'd been in a thousand objectively more terrifying situations since: desert bunkers surrounded by enemy fire, airless basements with his oxygen tank on zero, working up the courage to talk to the most beautiful woman he'd ever laid eyes on. But none of them held a candle to that first night in juvie. The smell of Clorox and body odor, sex and violence. The knowledge that even if you made it through the night without getting shanked, the days were no safer.

She rubbed his chest, right over the knotted ache behind his breastbone. "How old were you?"

"Had just turned ten."

"But they knew about your dad? How it was his fault?"

"Yeah, but he didn't step forward to explain or claim me or anything, not when it would have placed his own ass in danger." He felt a brief stab. After all this time. "Logan was the useful one. Could charm the dogs off the meat truck, always had a way with the old ladies. I was just another mouth to feed." And a stuttering one, at that.

"But Logan wasn't his son."

Just the son he'd wished he had. "No. His stepson, my half brother. We had the same mom but she died of a drug overdose when I was nine. Billy never stayed in one place too long, so we had no chance to go to school. I was pretty behind by the time I got to the Dempseys."

Those big eyes, like something out of a children's storybook, held him on lockdown. "How long were you in juvie?"

"A couple of months. Thought I was left for good with all these big kids who would as soon crack a slap across your head as look at you. You know what Logan did? Got himself caught so he could protect me. He knew I'd be beaten stupid because I was pretty scrawny back then. Saved my life. Then Sean and Mary saved it again." Most foster parents had no use for a weirdo who could barely mouth a greeting, but Logan would insist they were a package deal. Miracle of miracles, the Dempseys were drawn to the fuck-ups who needed them most. A match made in heaven.

He wasn't saying this for sympathy. He just needed to share with her something he hadn't told anyone else. His family knew the broad brush strokes, but not what Logan had sacrificed. Not how Wyatt owed him for everything.

"What happened to your father? To Billy?"

"They found him dead in an alley about three years ago. He'd been beaten and robbed. A lifetime of bad decisions caught up with him at last." That could have been Wyatt—his slow reflexes as a ten-year-old had probably saved his life, putting him on the path to the Dempseys. He knew how Roni felt, how the failure of the people who were supposed to watch over you could keep you from making that leap.

Molly stared at him, soul-penetrating, and Wyatt embraced the intimacy of the moment. Let it warm him right through.

"Told you I was trouble, babe."

"No, you didn't."

"Well, I should have. Is it too late?"

Because it was for him. He'd already fallen hard for this woman. As if she knew the crazy stream of thoughts running through his head and wasn't quite ready to deal, she lay down in the crook of his shoulder and snugged in tight. He closed his eyes. Pretended he was worthy.

"Roni won't say it, but I can feel her curiosity about her dad," he whispered in her hair. "It's just hard for her to get the words out." Funny how his niece was more like Wyatt than Logan in that way.

"I think she'd like to hear about the father who loved his baby brother so much he got himself arrested so he could watch over him."

He had no words, nothing left to give but his arms and chest and cock, so he pulled her tighter into the hold of his body. All he'd wanted was a night to worship her the way a quality woman like this deserved.

Now he was completely and utterly—what was the word?—*hosed*.

His mind wandered back to his confession about being a fan of Molly Cade, the woman on the big screen. Seeing the face that launched a thousand hard-ons up there a couple of times a year had kept a piece of her close inside, and though he wouldn't expect it from her, he had to ask.

"Did you think of me sometimes?"

Her body sighed into his, and it was a few seconds before she answered.

"Some days less than others."

He didn't believe her, but it sure was nice to hear.

♦ CHAPTER TWENTY-ONE

"Cut!"

Mick rolled his eyes and gestured to his chest. "Gideon, mate, we've been through this. Me, director. You, actor. Which means I'm the only one who gets to yell that."

Gideon squared his admittedly impressive shoulders and jerked a chin at Molly, his signal for *private meeting, now*. She walked with him off the set of the firehouse locker room to Mick's director chair.

"What now, Gideon?" Mick asked with a sigh.

"He keeps ogling me."

"Who, mate?"

Gideon threw a nervy glance over his shoulder to where Gage Simpson stood gloriously shirtless, mysteriously sheened, and looking hot enough to burn down the set. "The firefighter extra. The gay guy." He whispered that last phrase because even Gideon was self-aware enough to know that rumors of homophobia would tank his career.

"In your dreams, Gideon," Molly said, though she silently conceded that her nitwit costar was right. Gage had definitely been checking Gideon out in the scene where the firefighters change out of their bunker gear and head to the showers. The guy was an equal opportunity flirt, and as he had told Molly earlier, "I'm in a monogamous relationship with a guy I'd walk through fire for, but neither am I dead."

Mick turned to Molly. "Just have a quick word in the firefighter supermodel's ear, darling."

Part of her job as producer involved keeping the talent happy, so back she went to Gage, who was busy explaining something to Wyatt with a lot of hand gestures. As usual, Wyatt remained his sexy-stoic self until finally raising an unconvinced brow at the conclusion to the story.

"So. Gage," Molly said.

"Molly!" A puckish gleam brightened his eyes. "What's got Giddy-Up's boxers in a twist?"

"You know full well. Could you stop leering long enough for us to get this scene done?"

Gage's grin shifted to all sexy affront. "I've never leered in my life. Lechers leer. Perverts leer. I *flirt* with my beautiful eyes."

Wyatt growled. "Gage, quit fucking around. Some of us want to go home tonight."

"Is that all you kids ever think about? Okay. Must not flirt with hot movie star. Must not flirt with hot movie star." He winked at Molly. "You can bring Giddy-Up back. I'm ready for my close-up."

Off the set, Molly watched while Wyatt headed over to talk to Roni. A regular visitor of late, today she sat near the catering service, Beats on, head down, while she alternated between checking Facebook and reading scripts for Cade Productions. Wyatt said something, and a moment of unchecked joy overcame her before she caught herself and returned to her task.

His loving gaze lifted and sought out Molly, and the smile he hit her with knocked her sideways. Not because of its rarity, though that was a shock in itself, but because he smiled at her like they were old lovers who had known each other for years.

Heart punch.

She'd gone to that downtown hotel, playing yet another role, and left feeling more like herself than she had in years. Connected to her body and mind in a way she had forgotten was possible. Listening to Wyatt sharing his pain had drawn her closer to this brooding man. Dangerously closer.

"Cut!" Gideon again.

Wyatt's sexy shrug—and only this man could make shrugging sexy—said it all.

This is what happens when you get involved with those damn Dempseys.

How about with one damn Dempsey?

An hour and a half later, a scene that should have taken fifteen minutes to film was in the can, and Molly was still chuckling as she threw open the door of her trailer and stepped inside.

She froze.

Something about the air was different, a pungent sting to her nostrils. Dolce & Gabbana Velvet cologne, the preferred scent of assholes everywhere.

"Hey, honey. I'm home."

Her blood turned to ice. The man who had almost destroyed her sat on the sofa of her trailer wearing an Ermenegildo Zegna suit and a smile so smug it sickened her. Knowing Ryan, he would choose to interpret her shock as heart-stopping awe at how gosh-darn handsome he was.

"Ryan," she said, regrouping and affecting bore-dom. "To what do I owe the pleasure?"

He chuckled, a sound that used to send sexy shiv-ers through her but now just curdled her stomach. "My sister lives here, remember?"

She did remember, but that didn't answer her ques-tion. He recognized this. Smirked.

Eager to take him down a notch and put them on equal footing right off the bat, Molly went for the jugular. "Worried about your release next week?" she asked sweetly. "I hear they're not screening it for reviewers."

His face darkened. Bull's-eye. It was a well-known fact that a movie not made available for pre-release reviews was considered a dud by the studio. The head honchos didn't want to risk the bad press, so they hoped to slide it by an unsuspecting public. As the public was pretty much in on this, no one was fooled.

"Thought I'd take you to dinner, Molly. For old times' sake."

"Somewhere private and romantic where, shocker, the paps appear out of nowhere to see RyMo in a cozy tête-à-tête. Is reconciliation in the air?"

"So suspicious," he said with the grin that made millions. It made her furious. Anger hurtled through her veins, unblocking those frozen streams of ice.

"I know what you did."

"You'll have to be more specific, Molly. According to your lawyers, I inflicted pain and suffering that more or less approximated the value of the house in Malibu. Tell me. What else did I do after plucking you out of obscurity and making your goddamn career?"

A twitch in the vein on his forehead confirmed that he knew exactly what she was talking about. Nevertheless, she'd spell it out because saying it aloud was necessary.

"Your agent clued me in that you were behind the photo leak."

Not one iota of surprise registered on his face, though she was happy to note he was finally looking his age. "Because he's always wanted to do you. He'd say anything to get in your panties." He stood and approached, his hand reaching for her jaw before she could pull away.

"You piggy-backed onto the hacking scandal to humiliate me, Ryan. You put those photos out into the ether to win points."

His expression hardened. "You were supposed to come back to me, Molly. Run into my arms so we could weather the crisis together."

Breath whooshed out of her. She hadn't expected him to come clean so quickly. Every concession had always been so hard won. "You. Fucking. Prick."

He passed over her observation. "No one seems to know where you're staying. Don't know how you managed to go off grid, but it shouldn't be too hard to find out."

"I'll make sure to pump a few extra thousand volts into the fence. A little welcome for when you come visit."

Ryan winked. "Aw, honey, I've missed this. None of them can hold a candle to you."

"Well, when you hook up with bimbos who can't pick out Canada on a map, your dinnertime conversation is probably going to be lacking." As for this conversation, it wasn't getting her any closer to what she needed to know. Praying that her voice wouldn't crack with the hurt of what he had done, she asked, "Why, Ryan? Did you hate me so much?"

He blanched, evidently surprised at her question. He truly had no idea how much pain he'd inflicted. Several attempts at calling up various emotions ensued before he settled on a particularly terrible approximation of sorrow.

Poor Ryan. Botox had played havoc with his range.

"We okay here?" Words carved out of a granite cliff face entered the room, soon followed by the hard body of the movie's CFD tech consultant. Two seconds was all it took for him to assess. Three seconds more and he was in her personal space.

"Is this your bodyguard?" Ryan asked in that voice he reserved for the help.

Wyatt sniffed. "Just one of my jobs." He pulled her into his body and—oh, God—patted her ass. Like he owned it.

Which he did, but so not the point.

"Moved onto rough, honey?" Ryan asked, though really he should keep his mouth closed because the seething rage that was Wyatt Fox was like a fourth person in the room. Ryan divided a look between Wyatt and Molly, awareness dawning.

"So this is the Hooded Avenger? I've seen you in action, man. Thanks for taking care of my wife."

"Your ex-wife," Molly corrected.

Ignoring her, Ryan addressed Wyatt, bro to bro. "We have a Taylor-Burton thing going on, and you know what happened with those two. Married twice.

Couldn't stay away from each other." His gaze slipped to where Wyatt's fingers were digging into Molly's hip, and she saw it: the familiar green tinge of his overly tanned skin.

Though furious at the pissing contest with her at risk of being pissed on, still she resisted pulling away from Wyatt. Ryan would not get any satisfaction from her.

"Think you should go, Ryan," she gritted out.

"Sure, honey. I'll leave my number here. I've misplaced yours since we started going through legal proxies." He dropped a card on the vanity and left the trailer.

Only then did she pull away from Wyatt. "What the hell was that?"

"That's me taking care of what's mine," he said, demonstrating evolved male at not misunderstanding the reason for her annoyance by uttering the most unevolved statement she had ever heard.

"I am not yours."

Wy-brows rose, but no words were spoken. Infuriating man.

"Listen, Cro-Mag, I've had it up to here with men thinking I'm property. Studios, agents, Ryan, you. I didn't ask you to step in with your alpha pain-in-the-ass shtick."

"Didn't need to ask. Just did what had to be done." Frowning, he picked up the card Ryan had left. "You want this?"

"What? No, I don't want that."

She expected him to crumple it. Instead he stared at it for a good five seconds. "Reckon it might take you a few to hash out this pissy thing. Later, babe."

And then, goddamn him, he left the trailer.

• • •

Wyatt would never claim to be an expert on the female mind, but he knew this much: Molly was not going to calm down until he'd given her space to get there. He'd thought about stripping her naked and running his tongue all over her body because her in that hissy fit would have made for some mighty fine bed sport, but he figured he'd play it safe.

And in a manner that protected his junk.

Her ex hadn't moved far. Two trailers over, he held court with a few of the assistants facing him in a horseshoe of admiration. On his approach, Wyatt gave the girls what Alex called his "badass resting face." They got the message and left.

Ryan examined his manicure and Wyatt, in that order. "Did Molly send you out to get me?"

Fuck, this guy needed to be high-fived in the face with a chair. With great restraint, Wyatt put the card in the breast pocket of his sharp suit. "You forgot this. Also somethin' else you forgot."

"Oh yeah?" To think Wyatt had actually wasted some of his hard-earned dollars seeing this guy in a movie. Just one, though. That first time where he and Molly had paired up to save the world from the nuke threat, the movie that had propelled Molly to stardom. The one where they had supposedly fallen in love during filming.

"You forgot that you had your chance to treat her right but you fucked up. A quality woman like that needs a lot of attention from her man. She needs to be told early and often that she's the center of his universe." He leaned in, using his size to intimidate. "That sweet little body of hers is like a song, y'know. Gotta play the notes right. Hit it up high, take it down low. Don't know where you went wrong and don't need to. All you need to know is that your time has passed."

"I could have you fired," Ryan sputtered. "Black-listed. *Destroyed*."

Wyatt's laugh was mirthless. "People have tried before you and they'll keep on trying. I've survived enemy fire, flames all around, the world against me and my family. Bring it if you don't value your moneymaker. I see you near Molly again and there'll be no more talking, only doing. Consider this your last warning."

Done with speechifying, he lifted his gaze and found the entire cast and crew, including Gage and Roni, staring at him.

Good job keeping your hot fling under the radar, Fox.

Wyatt left Ryan and the black storm on his face, and headed back to Molly's trailer. Gage fell into step with him, pretty jaunty with it, too.

"Bro, you are so screwed."

Wyatt grunted. "That guy? Please." He reached Molly's trailer, pulled on the door . . . and found it locked. Shit.

His brother shook his head pityingly, the begin-nings of a smile teasing his smart mouth. "Like I said. Screwed."

As usual, Gage was right. Wyatt might have survived enemy fire and flames all around. He would likely survive the threat of being Hollywood blacklisted by a dickweed like Ryan Michaels.

But the odds on him surviving Molly Cade were dropping with every passing second.

CHAPTER TWENTY-TWO

"I thought I did awesome." Gage grinned at Molly. "Tell him how good I was."

Molly delayed the moment by taking a sip of her wine and giving the flames in the fire pit on Gage's patio a thoughtful stare. She chose her next words carefully. "I'm seeing an Oscar nod for . . . best special effects."

Gage sat up, wounded. "What the hell does that mean?"

"It means that those abs of yours could win an award, but you're really too pretty to be taken seriously as an actor." She caught Brady's eye. The hulking chef was doing his best not to laugh. "Ryan Reynolds has the exact same problem. It's a compliment, Gage. Truly."

Brady threw his arm around Gage's chest and drew him into a claiming clasp. "I don't want to lose you to the bright lights, Golden. Stay in the sticks with me."

Gage sighed. "This face and bod, both a blessing and a curse. We'll see what the people demand. When does the movie come out?"

"Next year." She didn't have the heart to tell him his small walk-on part in the firehouse locker room might end up on the cutting room floor in post.

Postproduction, post-Chicago, post-Wyatt.

Although after that ridiculous stunt he'd pulled with Ryan, Molly honestly couldn't say whether that was a good thing or a bad one.

"So your ex visited the set," Gage said. "Must be fun seeing the men in your life getting along so well."

Molly took another sip of her wine. The August night had turned cooler and sitting so close to the fire, she should have felt warm. But it seemed the only heat she could draw depended on Wyatt, who was working tonight at the family's bar. Not that she cared, because she wasn't talking to him after his caveman antics on the set. She'd been running searches all day—something she never, ever did—trying to determine if the gossip mill of a love triangle had started its grind. Nothing had surfaced yet, but her naked photos were enjoying new Photoshopped life now that she had officially crawled out of her cave. Molly wearing a firefighter's helmet, and nothing else, while climbing a ladder. Molly spread-eagled on the mound at Wrigley Field. Molly perched in a very uncomfortable manner on top of the Sears Tower.

There was a reason she had Cal as her buffer.

She looked up to find Gage watching her intently.

"Shooting wraps in a week," he said.

"It does."

"Have you talked to Wyatt?" His voice was graver than usual. "And don't say about what."

"We're just having fun."

"So that's why you look like someone just stole your gelato." Gage sat up straight. "Lots of people do the long-distance thing, and it seems to me a woman of your means can live anywhere she wants. Unless this isn't grand enough for you."

"Gage—"

"I'm kidding. But not really. I'm not just talking about how this might be ten steps down for a woman with a twenty-mil mansion in Malibu. Wyatt's not really Hollywood, is he?"

Absurdly, she felt insulted. Wyatt was about as far from Hollywood as she was from shopping at the Gap for sexy undies, but she didn't care about that.

"I don't want to hurt him," was all she could manage. And it was true. She suspected that's all she would do if she tried to entwine him further in her world. She had no idea what Wyatt said to Ryan today, but she had heard Ryan's loud response from the confines of her trailer: *Blacklisted. Destroyed.*

He had the power to make things difficult for people. Look what he'd done to her.

Gage's expression softened. "I know you don't. Thing is, today, Wyatt did something I've never seen him do. He put himself out there and claimed you in front of a bunch of strangers. He's in pretty deep, and if you're not going to make a go of it, then you need to let him down."

Brady growled. "Stay out of it, Gage."

"He's my brother. And everyone thinks he's this tough guy automaton who doesn't care about stuff, but that's wrong. He cares too much."

"I care about him, too," Molly said. Damn, she more than cared. She lo—

She loved him. Oh, God, she was in love with that hot, hunky, bearded Neanderthal former marine firefighter. He was the best she'd ever had—at everything—and she loved him. But how could she bring all the crazy that followed her around into this pocket of peace? As much as she craved a normal life, she'd made her bed in Hollywood, and Wyatt would not enjoy lying in it.

Gage looked sympathetic to her plight. Could he tell that her internal organs were currently switching places inside her chest cavity? "I don't mean to interfere—"

Brady snorted and got an elbow in the ribs for his trouble.

"But Wyatt is a meat-and-potatoes kind of guy. He wouldn't enjoy being anyone's arm candy, and a life in the spotlight would kill him."

"Gage," Brady warned again.

"I know. I know. MYOB."

Brady stood and held out his hand. "Come on, for once we both have the same night off. Let's get busy."

Gage grinned. "And they said romance was dead." He turned back to Molly as he stood and leaned in to kiss her on the cheek.

"We still friends?"

She smiled, though inside her heart and lungs were flying apart. "Always."

Watching them walk into the house, arms around each other, eyes locked in love, Molly considered Gage's warning. This was most definitely a case of love not being enough to conquer all, though she had no idea if Wyatt felt even one iota of what she felt for him. Gage's words echoed in her muddled brain: *He put himself out there and claimed you in front of a bunch of strangers.* Was that Wyatt's way of declaring his feelings? The man was a doer to the core.

But their lives were not on the same path. He had a relationship to build with his niece, a family to protect, and a life at the firehouse to return to post-rehab. The shoot would end in a week and there would be no reason for her to stick around. No reason at all.

Her phone buzzed and she frowned in surprise at the name that popped up on her screen.

"Roni?"

"Molly, are you alone right now?" Her whisper competed with considerable background noise. Music and laughter. Tonight, Roni was hanging with Darcy at the tattoo shop, with clear instructions from Wyatt not to come home with so much as a dot of ink on her skin.

"Is everything okay?"

"Could you come get me?"

Panic bolted through Molly's chest. "Are you not with Darcy?"

"No, I . . ." She lowered her voice. "I went to a party and now I need a ride home. But please don't tell the others."

"Where are you? Gage and I can come pick you up—"

"No! Don't get Gage involved. Just you. Please."

Damn, Molly had been drinking, so she couldn't drive. With her phone attached to her ear, she headed to her room to grab her purse and debated whether she should disturb Gage and Brady. She paused outside their bedroom door. Low murmurs, what sounded like a slap, and a throaty "Aw, yeah" made the decision for her.

She opened the Uber app on her phone.

"Roni, are you in danger right now? Because if you are, you need to call 911."

"No, I just need a ride." Something like fear colored her voice, and Molly's heart plummeted into her stomach. She hoped the girl had the common sense to recognize the different types of fear.

"Give me the address."

Ten minutes later, Molly clambered out of an Uber car in front of a nice ranch house in Evanston, a middle-class suburb just north of Chicago and home to Northwestern University.

"Would you mind waiting?" she asked the driver. *Boom-boom* bass and raucous revelry echoed onto the street. No sign of Roni, but this was definitely the right place.

She approached the front door, ready to knock, though she doubted anyone would hear it above the music, when it was flung open and a man was flung outward. She stepped aside just in time to avoid his projectile hurl all over the porch.

"Watch the hydrangeas, dude!" a voice called out from the foyer. "My mom'll kill me if you frack those flowers." A blond kid, no older than eighteen, stood in the entrance. His hazy focus semi-sharpened on seeing Molly. "My parents know about this."

She had no time for this nonsense. "I'm here for Roni."

"Who?"

She pushed past him. "Roni? Purple hair, multiple piercings, surly."

"Half the chicks here, lady."

The house was your typical underage partying and boozing nightmare, but Molly could tell this crowd was slightly older than Roni. As tempting as it was to call the police to break it up, she would much rather find Roni first, because once the police became involved, it would descend to untold levels of crazy. Meaning a night in lockup and multiple pissed-off Dempseys. She pushed through swaying teens, searching alcoves and corners. Checking her phone again, she tried calling Roni but it went straight to voice mail.

With an impending sense of dread, she pounded up the stairs, throwing open doors, shouting out Roni's name. Nothing but youthful bodies in various states of undress. She headed downstairs again, frantically searching, until she came to the back porch and— *thank God*. Roni. Who was not alone.

A tall figure loomed over her, imposing his brute masculinity with a tire-sized bicep positioned above her head. He might have been protecting or threatening her, and though Roni wasn't pulling away, her body language was shrinking. Molly was fluent in that particular dialect. Minimize, de-escalate, do whatever was necessary to keep the peace. Another bulker blocked her exit—or escape.

"Roni!" Molly called out, increasing her frenzied pace. Once she had closed the gap, she gathered the girl into her arms. "Are you okay?" Molly searched the teen's face for signs of injury. All she saw was heartache and trepidation.

At the foundation of this problem was a man. *Surprise, fucking surprise.*

She turned to the man. A boy, really, but definitely older than Roni. Molly's label-sensitive eye recognized the Diesel jeans, Burberry shirt, and Prada sunglasses perched perfectly on sun-bleached hair. Must be slumming it from one of the wealthier suburbs on the North Shore.

"Who the hell are you?" she snapped.

"This is Dean," Roni answered, her voice unsteady. "He's my . . . boyfriend."

"Ex-boyfriend," he said with a sneer.

"Yeah, 'cause I won't put out."

Rage tore through Molly. How dare anyone hurt this lovely and amazing girl? Shoving Roni behind her, she got all up in Dean's personal space. "She's only fifteen."

"Which I just found out. Told me she was sixteen."

"Which is still underage, you limp-dicked asshole."

The sidekick stepped in. "You watch your mouth, lady."

"Or what? Are you going to knock me out with your halitosis? Yeah, that's a multisyllabic word, Groot. Look it up."

He might prefer to snap her in two. She barely came up to his Northwestern Wildcats tee-covered pecs.

"Molly, let's just leave," Roni said.

Dean did a double take. "Molly? You're . . . huh, I thought you looked familiar. Probably would've recognized you sooner if you were in the buff."

"Good one, *Dean*. You know who I am and I know who you are. Know what else I know? I've got enough money, influence, and lady rage to bury your suburban ass in the middle of the lake. And this girl has a bunch of berserker firefighter uncles, but they're not the ones you should be worried about. It's her kickass firefighter aunt, Alexandra Dempsey, who you might recall made national news last year when a guy really, really pissed her off. That moron got off easy with only his car shredded. She'll probably remove your pea-sized nuts with the Jaws of Life and feed them to tree squirrels. You come near Roni again and I'll make it my personal mission to ensure your pretty-boy face isn't so pretty anymore."

"And if she doesn't, I will," a deep bass sounded behind her.

All heads turned and Molly sealed gazes with a very still, very pissed Wyatt Fox.

Wyatt had arrived in time to hear Molly giving a speech worthy of one of her movies. His woman defending his girl.

Proud. As. Hell.

But that pride was now being crowded out in his chest by a few other blood-boiling emotions. Not least of which was fury, equally divided between his niece and this POS who'd thought he could touch her.

Who might already have.

He rounded Molly, stepped in front of her, and gripped the asshole's throat. "What did you do?"

Through a strangled gasp, he shook his head. "Noth—nothing! I didn't lay a finger on her."

"Wyatt, please!" Roni screamed. "He didn't do anything. I promise." She grabbed his arm but someone pulled her back. Molly.

"I swear, man," the kid sputtered. "I met her online, on Facebook. She said she was older."

"It's true!" Roni cried out. "It's not his fault."

A crowd had gathered around them, their energy fueling Wyatt when it should have warned him of the dangers of being seen. Filmed. Vilified. But he didn't care. This was his family, and no one fucked with his family.

He unhinged his paw from the kid's windpipe. Old enough to know better, but still just a kid.

Molly stood back, her arms wrapped around his niece, protecting her. Watching him. Her eyes flashed with pride, though whether it was because he had stepped in or dialed it down, he didn't know.

To the kid now holding his throat, Wyatt said, "Gimme your driver's license."

"What?" At Wyatt's subtle lunge, the *what* quickly became *yes, sir, right away, sir* as he fumbled with his wallet and handed it over.

Wyatt noted the name and address. Almost nineteen, the same age as Logan when he knocked up Molly's mom. Just another dumb fucking kid. This one had signed up to be an organ donor. He'd get to keep his heart and lungs for now.

"You gonna fuck with me or my family again?"

"No. God, no." He looked at Roni, his eyes the color of regret. "We're good."

Wyatt wasn't so sure about that, but wordlessly, he led Molly and Roni out to the street and his illegally parked truck. He stood on the passenger side and held Roni by her shoulders, directing her chin up to face him. Tears streamed from black-rimmed eyes, down painted cheeks, and over red-stained lips.

"You met him online?"

She nodded.

"When?"

"A—a few months ago."

"That's why you came to Chicago."

She shook her head. "Grams sent me. Because I was trouble."

"Because you *made* trouble." Deliberately. And he

had thought she'd planned it to meet her family. She'd played him for a fool. "How many times have you seen him?"

"A couple." Her eyes slid to Molly and she bit down on her lip. "Four or five."

"What did he do to you?"

Her cheeks reddened, glowing through the black rivulets. "Nothing. Just kissing. I didn't want to . . ." She tapered off, but at Wyatt's squeeze of her shoulders, she continued. "Tonight, he invited me to this party and he wanted more. I got scared and called Molly."

"It's okay, Roni," Molly said. "You did the right thing."

His gaze snapped to Molly and she returned it with challenge. Yes, she'd done the right thing, but dammit, she should not have been in that situation in the first place. This was why she'd come to Chicago. Not to visit with her family, but to hook up with some guy. The Summer of Roni was exactly that—all about her.

Molly squeezed Roni's arm. "Did you send him any photos or videos? Anything you wouldn't want shared or seen online?"

He hadn't even thought of that.

"No," Roni said with a panicked look at Wyatt. "I didn't. Nothing, I promise."

"Okay," Molly said, her relief palpable.

"Wy—" Roni started, but he cut her off.

"In the truck."

"But—"

"Won't say it again."

Sad eyes turned up to the max, she got into the

truck's backseat. Molly was clearly trying her best to bite her tongue as she waved the idling Uber driver away, which was good, because the second she opened her mouth, he was going to go ballistic.

He walked twenty feet down the sidewalk, needing the space before he drove them home. *Home.* Fuck that. That's not how Roni saw it. Fury blistered inside him, waging a war against disappointment in his chest. The muted bass coming from the party house roused him to action. He made a call, snitched those boozy teens out, and returned to his truck.

Luke, Gage, and Brady were waiting out front as Wyatt pulled up.

"Wyatt," Roni started again. She'd been using the quiet time on the ride home to shine up her story, he assumed. Well, he'd run out of fucks to give.

"Not talking to you right now, girl. Go use your excuses on the rest of 'em."

He heard a hissed breath from Molly, but she wisely kept her counsel.

"I'm sorry," Roni said, her voice small and lost, and Wyatt almost reached for her, but anger stayed his hand.

She hopped out of the truck and rushed into Luke's arms, and Wyatt tried not to be hurt by that, even though he'd driven her there. He sucked ass at this whole family thing, and this night was the proof of it. All this time, she had been going behind his back. Probably planned it from the start. Pissed off her gran so she could land in the Big Smoke and meet this guy who'd almost raped her tonight.

Watching as they took his niece inside, forgiving arms around her like she hadn't just put them through hell, he tightened his grip on the steering wheel and started a ten-count.

About the time he got to four, Molly spoke his name. Soft, but not so soft that he felt she was trying to pander. He'd say that about Molly—she didn't tip-toe around anything.

"You go on in, too."

"And leave you to marinate in your guilt?"

"I'm not—" He started over. "She's my responsibility and tonight I screwed up."

"You can't monitor her 24/7, Wyatt. She's surrounded by people who love her, but she's a kid and will still make dumb choices. Tonight, she made up for it with a good choice. She called someone."

"She called you." Another bitter accusation, but this one tasted all wrong. He knew Molly and Roni had been getting close. He loved that they were, so he had no right to go all sad panda now.

"She's terrified of disappointing everyone, but especially you. Maybe this summer started out with different intentions, but she's been getting closer to all of you. And with what she went through when she was sick and that piece of crap she thought was her dad, the idea that you might abandon her is the scariest thing she can imagine."

He knew that. He'd lived with that fear his entire childhood, even years after being taken in by the Dempseys. He wasn't funny like Gage or Beck. He didn't wear his heart on his sleeve like Luke or Alex. He was the stutterer in the shadows, the odd one out, nothing to tie him to the Dempseys but his desperation to belong.

It had taken a while to figure out that their love for him wasn't dependent on his performance. Surely Roni knew that their love was unconditional. No need to win it, she was already in it.

Each of them would die for her.

Which got him thinking of who else he might die for, and the danger she'd put herself in tonight.

"You should have called me." But the words sounded less harsh than in his head.

"It was a split-second decision, Wyatt. You were thirty minutes away and I was ten. By the time you got there, it could have been too late. So how did you even know where she was?"

He got out of the truck and scooted around to the other side to open it, then pulled Molly down and into his arms.

"Darcy called me at the bar to ask if Roni was feeling better. She'd bailed on hanging with her and Beck because she claimed she was sick. I've got a tracker on her phone. When I got there and found you there, too . . . well, damn. Won't forget it."

"What?"

"All five-four of badass Molly Cade fronting with those pissants."

"No fronting about it. I meant every word."

She did. This pint-sized beauty with the warrior heart too big for her chest put herself in the line of fire for the one person who meant more to Wyatt than anything.

"Don't like that you had to do that. It was dumb and brave and crazy. That's my girl you took care of and that goes a long way with me."

He framed her face in his hands and kissed her, pouring his frustration and need into it. Maybe more. His wishes that he was a better man. The best uncle for Roni, the right guy for this woman of his dreams.

He had no clue what to do about that, so he kept on with the only language he could speak with any eloquence. Kissing her, opening her up to his demanding mouth, mapping her with his tongue. Tonight, it wasn't just his fear of losing Roni that had slapped him in the gut, it was that crazy panic that Molly could be hurt and terror—yeah, terror—that he'd fallen hard for this woman.

He was definitely punching above his weight here, but what man ever thought he was worthy of his woman? So goes the first commandment of relationships. And the second? Whether you're wrong or you're right, say sorry early and often.

"About what happened at the set."

"When you figuratively whipped out your dick and had a sword fight with my ex-husband?"

"Probably not my finest moment. But I couldn't *not* do anything, Molly."

She arched an eyebrow.

"I know he didn't treat you right and then he waltzes in and puts the moves on you. I'm not going to take that lying down."

Her expression darkened. "You think I can't handle Ryan? I've been handling him for five years. And I certainly don't need this alpha dog act of yours in front of the rest of the cast and crew. Have you any idea how dangerous that is? How one slip from an insider source places me slap-bang in the middle of a love triangle on TMZ?"

"Says the woman who just got all up in the face of those pricks at that party. You don't think someone grabbed footage of that?"

"That's different. Roni needed my defense. I don't need yours."

At one time, he might have believed that—at least, about himself. He'd spent most of his life thinking he didn't need anyone, always maintaining a buffer between him and the people in his life. But lately, he'd come to realize that was wrong. Humans weren't supposed to be Teflon-coated robots, repelling all the love coming their way. If you found a bunch of people or a special someone you connected with, then shout it out. Tell the fucking world.

That's probably what he should have said next.

Instead, there was this gem: "I refuse to say sorry for defending what's mine."

Surprise widened her violet-hazed eyes. *What's mine.* Even he hadn't expected those words to fall from his mouth. Neither had he expected how goddamned right they felt.

Apparently, he was the only one who felt this way.

"I'm not your property, Wyatt. I already had a bossy control freak for a lover once. I don't need another."

"Everything I do is with you as the focus."

"That's what he said."

Shit, that stung. No guy enjoyed comparisons to the bad news his woman had eighty-sixed in a previous lifetime.

He stepped back and folded his arms because really, there wasn't anything he could add to that. She'd decided those walls of hers were impervious to his sledgehammer, and who was he to convince her otherwise?

That miracle mouth of hers worked, but she seemed to realize that her last statement was a conversation ender and headed into Gage's.

CHAPTER TWENTY-THREE

Wyatt didn't do introspection. He didn't do emotion. And he was trying not to do regrets.

But he did self-recrimination pretty well.

He had failed Roni. She clearly didn't want a relationship with him, and he wasn't sure he had it in him to try anymore. They were blood but what the hell did that matter? Billy Fox had been blood, too, but Wyatt had been nothing but an obligation to his father, a tie forced on him by societal norms and legal duty. He'd had to grow up fast, and maybe he expected too much from his niece.

This morning, he couldn't bear to look at her, so deep was his disgust—not for her, but for himself. For thinking he had it in him to be a normal family guy. At the breakfast table, she had opened her mouth to say something, her father's eyes imploring him, and shut it down at whatever she saw on his face.

The door slam? Spectacular.

Ten minutes later, a loud, *I mean business* rap on the back door pulled him out of his Cocoa Puffs laced with self-pity.

Wyatt opened his back door to find Molly standing there with her fist raised, ready to knock again. Dressed in her sexy yoga gear, her body language stiff, she looked like inner peace was not going to come easy today. She also looked beautiful.

"I'm not talking to you," she snapped.

"Pretty sure I heard you say something. To me."

"I'm here to tell you to stop being a jerk to your niece." She waved a finger. "Yeah, I know, she's your niece and it's none of my business, and I get that you're furious about the danger she was in, but she's just a kid. A kid who did something really dumb, and you're going to have to be the grown-up here and stop taking what she did as a personal insult."

"I'm not—"

"You are. She's a sneaky teenager, something you know a helluva lot about, Mr. Let's-Screw-in-the-Camaro—"

"Which was your idea."

Her eyes promised instant death if he dared challenge her again.

"She wants nothing more than to know you. You're the closest thing she has to a dad."

Contradiction was on the tip of his tongue, but she puffed up to what seemed like twice her size and held up a hand of *shut-it*.

"Oh . . . what's that sound?" She cocked an ear dramatically. Freakin' actors.

He was about to say he didn't hear anything but he suspected it was a trap.

"I believe it's the sound of your Terminator programming telling you to get your head out of your ass and man up."

And with that, she twitched her shapely hips off to Gage's backyard.

• • •

YMan: I'm a jerk.

The longest minute of his life later . . .

Roni: Tell me something I don't know.
YMan: I think you don't know how much I love you.
Roni: Lame.
Roni: ;)
YMan: Come back home. Not doing this with an
      audience.

Before Wyatt hit send on that last message, the door to the kitchen opened. His beautiful niece stood there, flushed, red-eyed, looking a whole lot younger than fifteen. His heart seized and terror hurtled through his veins as the memory of last night tried to take hold. He could have lost her, and his wounded pride had almost destroyed what they were building.

"Let's go for a ride."

Her big eyes welled. "Sho—should I get my stuff?"

"What stuff?"

"You're driving me back early, right? To Bloomington. I'll miss the party."

He was supposed to drive her home tomorrow, but first the family was coming over tonight to give her a proper send-off. He shook his head. "No stuff. Just you."

Fifteen minutes later, Wyatt turned the truck into Roseland Cemetery. They parked and walked a couple of hundred feet to the grave in the northeast corner, the final resting place of Sean and Mary Dempsey and their eldest son, Logan Keyes. It'd been a while since he visited, but fresh gerbera daisies, his mom's favorite flower, smiled back at them. Beck liked to tend it on a regular basis.

He let Roni take a moment to absorb where she was. When the silence became taut enough to squeeze the breath from his lungs and the words from this throat, he spoke.

"You look so like your dad, Roni. Hurts sometimes to rest my eyes on you." Shit, it came out sounding like an accusation. "Sorry."

"It's okay. You look like him, too, and sometimes that makes me a bitch."

She stared at Logan's tombstone and its epitaph, "Beloved Husband, Son, Brother, and Hero." "Mom didn't tell me about him until after I was recovered, and I was so angry. About the cancer and being behind in school and feeling tired all the time. That she married the wrong guy and he treated her like shit and the cancer again because without it, I would never have known the truth, I could have, like . . . just kept my life. Gerry was a crappy drunk of a dad, but until they did those tests, he was *my* crappy drunk of a dad. Instead, I get sick and lose two dads. One's dead and one doesn't want to know. When you showed up after, like, fourteen years, I was pissed. Really, really pissed. He wasn't here, but you looked exactly like him, and I . . . I didn't know what to do with all of that."

He reached for her, any fleeting worry that touching her might result in his hand being bitten off vanishing into the ether as she curled her soft fingers around his.

Molly's words echoed. *I think Roni would like to hear about the father who loved his baby brother so much . . .*

"When I was a kid, I did something dumb and was put into juvenile detention. I was pretty scared and thought I was all alone. But Logan showed up one day, not to visit but to stay. He got caught on purpose. To protect me."

Tears filled in her eyes. "He did that?"

"Family meant everything to him, Roni." He wasn't trying to make her feel worse, but he needed her to understand. If Logan had known about her, he would have moved skyscrapers to be with his daughter. It wasn't fair. It just was.

Tears trickled down her cheeks. "I wish I'd met him."

He threw an arm around her shoulder and tucked her into his chest. "I wish you had, too, but we can't change that. We can only look to the future. I've got his girl under my wing. You don't just have Logan's blood runnin' through your veins, Roni, you have mine. You know what that means?"

She sniffled. "That I'm never going to have a boyfriend again."

"Damn straight."

A burst of tension-busting laughter left her throat. "I'm so sorry for what I did. I met Dean online and yeah, with Mom gone I saw this opportunity. But I did want to meet you all. That's the truth. Then when I got here that day at the cookout and you didn't look like you wanted me there, I felt like I was butting in."

"Sweetheart." He squeezed her shoulders tighter. "Surely you realize by now that my pleased face and my pissed face are practically one and the same."

"Uh, starting to get that."

"There was never a question of me not being happy to see you. You, here in my city with my family—with *our* family—is all I've ever wanted. My life is a million times better with you in it."

"Really?"

"God, yes." He hugged her so tight that squeezing the life out of her was a real possibility. Never wanting to let go, he loosened up enough to allow her to draw a breath, but she grasped tighter and buried her face in his neck.

"So the Dempseys have a motto, Roni. Sean used to say that fire is stronger than blood and defend the people you love to the last ember."

"Because you're not related by blood and you're all firefighters," she said, her voice muffled from where it was buried in his skin.

"Right. We were chosen by Sean and Mary to be Dempseys, all of us, but some us are also blood. You and me and Logan, we are blood, and that doesn't just mean something. It means everything."

She nodded against his neck. He felt her tears against his skin, the vibration of her soft sobs and sniffles. A few moments passed until she spoke, her voice a rusty whisper. "We're blood but I also choose. I choose to be Dempsey."

His heart shattered into a million shards. There was a reason he did not do emotion. This cuttingly painful joy in his chest was the reason.

"I love you," she whispered. "I love you all."

"I know, sweetheart. And we love you. So much."

One day he'd tell her the rest, about the scams and the hurts and the childhood on the lam. For now, all she needed to know was how her dad got his start in the lifesaving business when he showed up that day in juvie. How she had been Dempsey from her first drawn breath.

Feeling more than a little glum about her fight with Wyatt, Molly wandered into Gage's backyard after a day on the set and found planning in progress. Gage was rolling a giant TV out to the center of the patio. Just as it looked like it might topple, Molly reached forward to steady it.

"Thanks. You Hollywood divas sure are worth every penny they pay you."

"Oh, shut up," she said, intending that to come off as good-natured but not quite making the grade.

"Uh-oh, what's eating you? Other than—"

"Do not dare say his name. He's asshole non grata right now."

"Well, he's made up with Roni. They went downtown for some uncle-niece time. You wouldn't have anything to do with that, would you?"

Her heart cheered at this happy conclusion, but for Gage's question, she redirected. "What's with the TV?"

"PJ party for Roni's last night. Wy's driving her home to Bloomington tomorrow, so we're going to stay up all night and watch movies. Everyone's coming over." He crossed his arms. "You, too, Cade."

"I've got work to do. Scripts to read." This was Dempsey family time and she'd rather let them get on with it. Better acclimatize to a life without their rambunctious cheer. Her heart squeezed, thinking about Wyatt and how much he would miss Roni. It didn't squeeze hard enough to forgive him for doing the caveman club-and-drag on the set, but she understood it would be tough for him. For them all.

Gage threw an arm around Molly. "You won't want to miss it. We're watching the great feminist manifestos of cinema."

"*The Hours* and *Frida*?"

"*Pretty in Pink* and *Grease*. And I've got the perfect onesie for you. Been saving it for special." He wiggled his eyebrows. "You're coming. End of."

Several hours later, Molly was cursing Gage Simpson's ability to talk anyone into anything. She looked in the mirror, sighed at what she saw, and headed downstairs.

Brady was pulling a tray of minipizzas out of the oven. On seeing her, a crooked grin split his face in two.

"Lookin' good, Molly."

"Hey, you're not wearing one," she protested. Brady wore plaid PJs and a black tee that shaped his broad chest and made him look the opposite of hot mess.

Screw this. She went to turn only to feel her progress arrested with a hand on her arm.

"You look awesome." Gage wore a SpongeBob onesie. Okay, she didn't feel quite so ridiculous. "Come on, everyone's here."

"I can't believe I let you brainwash me like this." Out in the twilight-shaded yard, the entire complement of Dempseys was gathered—living, laughing, and loving. Thankfully, she and Gage weren't the only ones dressed up. A combination of superheroes and film characters greeted her, including Roni dressed as some unrecognizable animal-vegetable-mineral that probably came from manga.

Molly's hungry gaze shifted to the table set up for the snacks, which also happened to be where Wyatt stood, dressed in a— She blinked. *Oh wow.*

St. Louis Cardinals PJs.

His unnerving gaze softened to appreciative at the sight of her gussied up like—may the Cards forgive her—a Cubs fan. "Welcome to the Dark Side, Cade," he murmured.

Damn Gage. Or, perhaps damn Wyatt. There was an element of Stone Cold Fox deliberation about this. As if she weren't mad enough at him.

He covered the distance between them with silky marine speed. She crossed her arms over the offensive logo, not ready to give up the real good mad she was holding on to.

"Is there a point to this?"

"Trying to walk a mile, Molly. Also trying to tell you I screwed up."

"You're admitting you're wrong?"

"It happens."

"Hold on." She unpocketed her phone. "I need to time-stamp this."

"Funny." He took her face in both hands, holding her still so there was nowhere to hide. She had missed his touch so much, and that was just one day without it. How the hell was she going to manage when the shoot wrapped in a week and she was back in LA?

"I'm apologizing here, babe. I saw him all over you and the next thing I saw was red. I wasn't thinking of how it might look to the rest of the crew. I wasn't thinking that you're weak and I'm the only one who can defend you. I wasn't thinking at all. That's what happens when I'm around you. My brain shuts down."

Speaking of organ failure—her heart and lungs had stopped working.

He'd stood up for her at the set against Ryan, something that maybe she wished she could have done for herself. True, she hadn't asked for it, but werewolf protectiveness was entrenched in his DNA. Instead of seeing this as Wyatt flexing his dick, perhaps she should look at it as an example of his need to protect.

What woman wouldn't count herself lucky to fall under Wyatt Fox's giant wingspan?

"Forgive me," he said, his eyes burning holes in her heart, his voice low and rough with things unsaid.

"Yes."

And that was that. She didn't need long speeches or heartfelt monologues. Wyatt Fox's brand of communication was enough, each precious word loaded with significance.

Someone groaned. "For God's sake, just kiss her," called out Luke.

Wy-brows rose. That carnal mouth curved. He kissed her, a lazy, languorous smooch in front of his entire family. Claiming her just as he had on the set. On and on he plundered and unraveled her, showing no sign of stopping, even when she heard a few high-pitched whistles and Beck say something about how they were embarrassing the koi.

It was up to her to break the kiss because Wyatt showed no intention of doing so.

She murmured against his sensuous lips, "That outfit of yours is really much too tight for this to continue, Marine."

He looked down to the space between them, now

filling with . . . oh dear. "You walk in front," he muttered.

"Maybe a visit to the kitchen for a hot dog?" She was having a hard time keeping a straight face. Another glance down, and she lost it. "Perhaps some Polish sausage?"

"Sizing not quite right, but you're getting there." He pulled at her hand with the clear intention of taking her inside the house.

"Don't even think about it," Luke said with a side glance at Roni. "Pretty sure that ground rule number one was thou shalt not sneak off to have S-E-X during family gatherings, Wy."

Roni looked annoyed. "Uncle Luke, I'm fifteen, not five. Molly, sit with me." This from the girl who could barely shrug a greeting a month ago.

Molly grabbed a beer from the cooler, the hand of her honey, and sat down beside Roni. "So what's first on the bill?"

"*Pretty in Pink*," Beck sang in a deep-graveled voice to match the Psychedelic Furs' soundtrack. Sure enough, the original Molly—La Ringwald—was already on screen rocking her red tresses and hand-sewn clothes, and rolling her eyes at Duckie's adorable jokes.

Wyatt sat on Roni's other side, his arm along the top of the sofa, his hand massaging the nape of Molly's neck. After that kiss in front of everyone, her brain was spinning, her heart was pounding, and her sex was throbbing, so she took out her pent-up frustration with popcorn hurled at the screen every time Andrew McCarthy fed one of his vacant, doe-eyed stares to Molly Ringwald.

"I hate that she ends up with Blane," Darcy said, shaking her head. "Should have been Duckie."

"Should have been Steff," Alex countered as Andie and Blane PG-13 kissed in the parking lot after prom. "Spader was a total stud in the eighties."

"But Duckie was so cute," Roni argued.

"Yeah, but the Duckies of this world don't win," Molly commented. "The bland frat guys and the hot rich guys do. Blane didn't deserve her, wouldn't even stand up for her until the end. Jerk." She squeezed Roni's hand covertly. She'd had her heart broken by a boy but she'd get over it. She just needed someone as strong and solid as her uncle. Wyatt slid her a glance over Roni's head, and the affection she saw there cut her in half.

But there was more. Somehow she had become part of this rich and thriving ecosystem, the Dempseys and their boundless love for each other.

Annoying tears stung the backs of her eyelids. She would miss them all so much.

By the time *Grease* was over, and Sandy and Danny had flown away—literally—in a magic car to their happily-ever-after, Roni had cheered up enough to list the movie's shortcomings. It'd always been suspect from several points of view, not least of which was credibility. The high school students look like thirty-year-olds. The academic year whizzes by in the space of a week.

"So Sandy wears skintight pants, gets a perm, and starts smoking to win Danny," Roni said thoughtfully.

This one *was* pretty troubling. "Maybe we should see it as her making a choice to rebrand herself as the woman who goes after what she wants."

Wyatt grunted. "She took up a life-threatening habit for a guy who was a jerk to her throughout the whole movie and he makes it up to her by putting on a cardigan. Roni, any guy who treats a woman with such little respect is not a real man."

Life lessons from Wyatt Fox.

"Marine, you have clearly thought long and hard about this," Molly said.

His grin could wipe out the national debt and end wars. "Told you. I watch a lot of movies."

Less than five minutes after *Grease*'s closing credits, ground rule number one was about 95 percent of the way to being smashed to smithereens. Molly and Wyatt covered the stairs to her room with either indecent or Olympic speed, depending on your perspective. Barely inside, he pounced and ripped off her traitor's garb. Buttons flying, zippers tearing, seams rending. Fast and furious, not Wyatt's usual MO at all. He was out of control, primitive and feral, rougher than ever before.

She loved it.

Urging him on, she raked his back with her nails, breaking skin, marking him up good. Claiming this man for her own.

In seconds, he was inside her, the weight of him perfect, the feel of him addictive. This wasn't their usual slow, rapturous joining. This was desperate, zombie-apocalypse, we-might-die-tomorrow sex where nothing existed outside this moment, just their soul-deep connection and the need to affirm it. Her body was so primed that the barest friction was enough to send her over, and her clamp on his beautiful cock triggered his own howling release.

Then nothing but the silence of their bodies speaking more than words could say.

Feeling ransacked, she cradled him close. He lay still, spent, as if every ounce of his life force had left him and entered her bloodstream. With each subsequent night together, he gave more and more of himself. In his arms, she was lost and finally found again.

She shifted.

"Hurtin' you?"

"No. Just wanted to make sure you were still with us."

His warm chuckle against her neck felt like the most treasured gift. "Barely," then softly, "Every time, Mol. Every single time."

Oh, God.

"It gets deeper with you. Find it harder to leave your body." His breath was hot against her ear, pulsing shivers through her to match those words. "Find it harder to keep it straight. Keep us straight."

She didn't know what he meant—she didn't *want* to know what he meant. Because it sounded like he was opening his soul to her, and the preciousness of it squeezed her heart to a fist.

He lifted his head, his body with it, and eased his solid weight from her. Air and a distance she hated rushed into the space between them.

"But you've put me straight about Roni. About a lot of things. Five years ago and this summer."

"Back in that hotel room, there was no putting anything straight, Marine. It was dirty, hot, and kinky."

He laughed quietly and kissed her nose. Rolling

back, he gathered her into his side. "You have no idea, do you?"

She shook her head slowly.

"Back then, I'd just finished a tour and was thinking about re-upping."

"What happened?"

"You."

Her heart jerked in her chest. "What?"

"Luke, Beck, and Gage were already in CFD. Alex was an EMT, waiting her turn. For four years since Logan and Sean died, I'd been keeping my distance from them. Just seemed better that way. If something happened to me or to them, those miles I placed between us, physical and emotional, would keep the hurt to manageable levels."

"Did you really believe that?"

"Made myself believe it. When Logan and Sean died, I locked myself in this black space. The two men who had saved me were gone, wiped out of existence, and I didn't think I could survive my heart shattering again. So I convinced myself this was easier on the rest of my family. If I died in the desert, they'd mourn me and move on."

He thought he wouldn't be missed. That he could control the situation in such a way that his passing, God forbid it should happen, would mean less to the family that adored him.

"Then came you," he said, low and jagged. "That week with you, I realized that I felt more of a connection to a stranger I'd just met than I did to my own family. That was my fault. I needed to fix it. Day after you left, I put in my application to CFD. Was called up six months later."

Her heart hammered triple-time. "I'm the reason you're a firefighter."

"You're the reason for a lot of things, Molly. But it didn't quite work to bring me closer to them. I still kept my distance, because every day at the firehouse I'm reminded of what I lost. Being a firefighter, being a Dempsey, is a double-edged sword."

"How so?" Her throat was thick with unshed tears.

"It's the best, and because it's the best, you realize how much you have to lose if something goes wrong. You tried to tell me that once when you were explaining Roni's detachment. How her getting close is a lot for her heart to risk."

This man. Gage was right. Wyatt felt as much or more than any of them. He just locked it down to protect himself in case it all went wrong.

"But I'm sick of holding that in. They're my people. Roni's my girl. And if I don't let them know what's up, then it'll be too late if something happens. And yeah, if it goes FUBAR, whether it's me taking the dirt nap or one of them, at least they'll know I didn't hold back. Instead I held on. To the good and the bad."

Did that include her? Did he want to hold on to her through good times and bad?

He stroked the side of her face. "Got you to thank, Mol. With everyone else, I feel like there's all this stuff deep down that I can't pull out. But with you, it's right below the surface. One slice across my chest, and it's exposed. Raw and open. With you, it's necessary."

Wyatt Fox had just told her he loved her, not with three little words but in a declaration that came straight from his soul.

She was shaking, her emotions reaching critical

mass, the moment profound and tangible between them.

"We're gonna need to talk about how this is gonna work," he said quietly.

Bluff it out. She needed time to think. "How what's going to work?"

His answer was to stare at her, like that could make her get on the same page, or quit playing at dummy. He eased his big body out of the bed and sat with his back to her. Reaching down, he pulled at the clothing on the floor. He grabbed hers, put it on the bed, and resumed the search for his own.

A minute passed. Then two. Wyatt redressed in the Cardinals PJs.

"Wyatt . . ."

"I'm giving you time."

"For what?"

"To think on what I said. About how it's gonna work."

"I'm too tired to crack the dude code. Any chance you could give me the layperson's version?"

Turning, he held her gaze with heart-wrenching intent.

"The 'it' is us. For a while, I've wanted to think it only existed in the backseat of my Camaro or that hotel room, then and now. But it's bigger than you and me; it's graduated into an 'us,' and now we need to figure out how to navigate this new information."

Her heart clattered madly. *Us.* They were an us. But that's not what she wanted, was it? Her life was already a list of suffocating rules and prescriptions, how to act in public, how to ensure that no boats were rocked. A man like Wyatt Fox wouldn't enjoy those constraints, the level of scrutiny his life would become subject to. He was such a straight shooter, no artifice, no double-talk. In the land of fakery and no one meaning a word they said, he'd stand out. He would eventually come to hate it—and her with it.

"Wyatt, I can't deny there's some strong pull between us—"

"Then don't."

She scowled her annoyance because he was right. "But you've seen what my life is like. I'm hounded and picked over, and you have your family to think of. Roni to consider. You said yourself your privacy means more than anything. You want to give that up?"

"Have you met my family?"

"It's not the same."

"Not much different. And Roni might have been a valid excuse before. Kept us both safe, thinking we had good reason to stay on the down low." He stood, slipped his tee over his head, and sat down on the bed again. "What've you been looking for this summer, Molly?"

Her self-respect, a way back to the woman she once was. But love? Not at all.

Sometimes it just whacks you over the head anyway.

"Sanctuary," she whispered.

Slivers of moonlight shone through the window, illuminating the shadows painting his face. He drew a finger in a sensuous line across her jaw. Didn't say a word. He didn't have to, because he'd already laid it out in his no-nonsense Wyatt Fox way. And then he left the room, giving her the time to think that he'd promised.

She'd finally found safe harbor, and that was down

to Wyatt. This man was her sanctuary. This man was her home.

The word should have filled her with dread. LA had never felt like home, and after her gran died, there was no going back to New Haven, Missouri. Neither had she found a connection in the countless places she'd lived or filmed in. But these last few weeks staying with the Dempseys had been the closest she felt to belonging somewhere in a long time.

With Wyatt's demand that she consider their future, she realized she had to puzzle out how exactly this relationship might work. He hadn't said he wouldn't come to LA, but reason should rule. She could live anywhere—and if Wyatt was with her, who cared how big or small the house was? She could be living in a fifty-thousand-square-foot mansion and Wyatt's virility, solidity, and unabashed maleness would dwarf every room.

He would want to be close to his family. To Roni. To the job he loved. So many reasons not to do this, but they meant nothing in the face of the one reason why they should.

She loved him and she was pretty damn sure he loved her.

◐ CHAPTER TWENTY-FOUR

Distracted by the sound of a distinctly feminine gasp, Wyatt looked up from the tomato, onion, and feta frittata in the skillet. Molly stood at the back door, wearing that yoga outfit he loved almost as much as he loved his dick. He'd texted her a few minutes ago on the pretext that Roni was leaving soon and Molly should stop in and say good-bye.

"Mornin'."

She pointed. "What in the name of all that is holy are you doing?"

"What's it look like?"

"You're cooking." She said the word like she might say *smoking* or *watching carny porn*. "But you can't cook."

"Never said that."

Hands on her hips, she surveyed the kitchen as the delicious aroma drew her into his web. "Am I being pranked? Will Gage jump out any second and shout 'gotcha'?"

He circled her waist with one arm and nuzzled her cute nose, all while keeping his eye on the bubbling egg-and-veggie mixture. "I never said I couldn't cook. I choose not to because it makes Gage feel useful."

"How noble. What else don't I know about you?"

That I love you. That I can't imagine my life without you. That I refuse *to imagine it.*

"Isn't it nice to find out that there's more to learn about someone?"

Her smile was shy. That had been a very futuristic sort of thing to say.

She cleared her throat. "Where's Her Highness?"

"She wanted a caramel mochacino or something, so she headed over to Starbucks."

"At 7 a.m.?" Roni was not known for greeting the sun.

"I think she wanted to take a walk around the neighborhood one last time." This afternoon, he would drive her home to Bloomington so she'd be there when her mom's flight from Seattle arrived later. He would stick around to tell Jen about Roni's online boyfriend, because if he didn't, the universe would find a way to make sure she found out and blamed Wyatt. No more secrets. No more lies. Jen would be pissed, but hell, when was she anything else?

"You're going to miss her."

More than he could express in words. "Yeah, but it's not so far. We'll make it work."

He may as well have been talking about his future with a certain Hollywood superstar. Last night he'd laid it out there. He felt the truth of what was happening between them in every kiss, every thrust, every precious moment they spent together.

Now it was her call. She knew what his life was like and he knew a good deal about hers. If she wanted this to happen, then he would do whatever it took to make it work.

"We need to talk," she said.

He cheered a mental touchdown. "Hasn't always been our strong point, but probably a good idea."

The door blew open, Gage with it. Christ on a cracker, his brother's timing was exquisite.

"Wy, we have a prob—" He stopped, blinked, turned, and left the kitchen. One second later, he was back. "Alternate universe, perhaps?"

Molly giggled. "Apparently your brother's some sort of secret culinary ninja."

Gage looked over his shoulder. "That my recipe?"

"Nope."

His brother shook his head in amazement. "Well, this is fascinating and completely worthy of closer examination later, but we have something more pressing. Literally." He divided a worried look between them both. "The press is here."

"Here?" Molly's eyes widened. "Outside?"

Gage nodded. "I was headed into work when I spotted a couple of guys with cameras in the alley. They didn't recognize me." His attention-loving brother sounded ever so slightly peeved about that. "When I hit the street in front of the house, I saw more. Probably five or six, hanging on the sidewalk."

City property, so they couldn't be touched.

Wyatt moved the perfectly done eggs to the unlit back burner. "It was bound to happen eventually," he said to Molly, feeling strangely calm. He needed to be like this with her, so she understood that he understood. "We'll handle it."

"Wyatt, what about Roni?"

Shit. She was out there on the streets. "I'll call her and tell her to stay away. Gage can go pick her up and take her to Luke's."

He went to grab his phone when the door opened again. This time, his niece stood there, face flushed, eyes large, Starbucks in hand.

"The paparazzi are here."

Wyatt put his arm around her. "Did they see you?"

"Uh, yeah." She laughed, but it left her throat in a shaky wobble. "And they took photos."

Wyatt had known it might come to this. After all, if he was going to be Molly's man, then certain unpleasantness came with the territory. Such as asshole ex-husbands and crazed admirers and the surrender of his privacy. He'd hate it (especially the ex-husband asshole part), but it would be good to set some ground rules with the vultures wielding cameras.

No time like the present.

He strode toward the group clustered on the sidewalk outside his house, a couple of whom he recognized from the stalker-fan neutralization incident.

"How's Molly doing, Wyatt?"

So they knew his name, something else he'd have to get used to.

"Fine, as far as I know. Gonna have to ask that you leave."

"Can Molly come out? Give us a photo of the two of you together?"

He sucked in a breath. How nice did he have to be here? "If you don't leave, I'll be calling the police."

"Not breaking the law," said one guy in a Nike tee. He raised his camera and clicked.

"You think the cops are in your corner?" one wag tossed out. "Your brother Luke beat up on that detective last year. The former mayor threatened another detective with the sack because of your sister."

All true. So CPD might not be in a hurry to come to the aid of the Dempseys.

Back to trying reason. "I'd like you to delete the photo of the girl you saw walking in here a minute ago."

No impact. If anything, it seemed to spur them on to taking as many more photos as they could.

Done with playing nice, he hardened his tone. "Delete. The. Photo."

The nearest photographer held the camera at chest level, obviously with no intention of removing anything.

"I get you have a living to make and that I'm fair game. But kids are not. That photo needs to be erased or I'm gonna erase your existence."

"We're within our righ—"

Wyatt grabbed the photographer's shirt before he could complain about his rights or how they were about to get trampled on.

"Photo. Now."

Of course he meant the one of Roni, but the other leeches took it as an order to shoot—and shoot they did. A TMZ-worthy pic of Wyatt manhandling one of the weasels who dared to intrude on the personal life of his niece.

In for a penny. He ripped the camera from weasel number one's hands and turned it over, looking for the smart card slot. Found it, popped it, removed the card. But they all had cameras and it seemed unlikely they'd just line up and delete-on-demand. This was . . . shit, this couldn't get worse. Or so he thought.

He shoved the camera back into the scavenger's chest and pushed him so hard, he fell back on his ass.

That was probably worse.

"Wyatt!"

Or this. In all the commotion, he hadn't noticed a cab pulling up. Standing there with a suitcase and a look on her face that would have frosted hell was Roni's mom, Jen.

"Mom!" Inside the relative safety of Wyatt's house, Roni ran into her mother's arms and let herself be enveloped in a hug. "I thought I wouldn't see you until tonight."

"I got the red-eye from Seattle into O'Hare and figured I'd drive back with you instead of picking up the connection to Bloomington." Jen kissed the top of her daughter's head. "I can't believe how you've grown in two months. What have they been feeding you?"

"Gage never stops stuffing my face. He's the best cook."

Jen drew back and assessed her daughter, love and concern shining off her equally. "I missed you so much. And now I need to talk to Wyatt. Alone."

Roni frowned. "It's not his fault. He was just protecting me. All of us." Her gaze flickered over Molly, who stood near the kitchen entrance, looking acutely embarrassed. "Molly, I didn't tell anyone, I swear."

"I know you didn't, honey."

Jen visibly stiffened at Molly's endearment. "Go get your things."

"Mom—"

"Just—just do it."

Roni's eyes welled and her gaze met Wyatt's, shock and pain lurking there. He wanted to hug her and pull her close, this girl he loved not only because she was his flesh and blood, but because she was one of a kind. A Dempsey, through and through. He gave her a tight smile to let her know it would be okay.

So what if it made him a liar?

Roni trudged up the stairs. Once she was out of earshot, Jen turned to Wyatt.

"Do they have pictures of my daughter?"

"Yes. That's why I was talking to them."

Her mouth firmed even further at the word *talking,* and she redirected her focus to Molly.

"I assume you're the reason why my daughter's uncle is involved in a brawl that'll splash her name and face all over the Internet."

"I'm sorry. They weren't supposed to be here."

"Are *you* supposed to be here?" Jen's voice was comically quiet-loud. She was trying not to lose it but clearly on the cusp.

Molly looked to Wyatt, and what he saw crushed him. The doubt about whether she should be here, about how maybe this had all been a mistake. *They* were a mistake.

One fire at a time.

Molly muttered, "I'll let you talk in private," and headed upstairs after Roni.

Shaking her head, Jen put her hands on her hips and nailed Wyatt with a world-class glare. "Are you going to pull that big-quiet-man crap on me now?"

"Why say anything? You've clearly already made up your mind about what you saw, Jen."

"I told you to keep her safe. No drama. None of the bullshit your family is always pulling."

"They're her family, as well," he said quietly. "They always will be, bullshit drama and all." He scrubbed his mouth. "We're not the villains here. You had a bad time of it with your ex, and maybe from the outside, we don't look much better, but—"

"From the outside?" Jen hissed, cutting him off. "I just saw you brawling with a stranger in the street. There's nothing outside about it. You are no different than my ex."

"The difference is I was protecting Roni. Protecting what's mine."

She scoffed. "She doesn't need that sort of protection. You weren't there when she was so sick she couldn't hold any food down or move an arm to read one of her comics. You weren't there when he left her and broke her heart."

And whose fault was that? Christ, there was nothing worse than being punished for another man's sins.

"Jen, she needs her family. All of her family."

Her mouth worked, but he knew before she spoke it would be the same old party line. "She needs stability. She doesn't need you or that crowd of louts you call family. I gave you a pass because you're Logan's real brother, but the rest of them . . ." She waved a hand dismissively. "All she needs is her mother."

And that was it. All his rage had been expended on those dickwads out front. He could let Jen rip Roni out of Wyatt's arms, harden his niece's heart against her mother, but that wasn't his way. And he certainly wasn't going to engage in a headline-grabbing custody battle with the world watching.

"At least let me drive you home."

"We'll take the train."

Fine. Anger dogging every step, he took the stairs two at a time and stuck his head around the door of Roni's room. She sat on the bed, hugging Molly as they said their good-byes.

"You're always welcome in LA, honey," Molly was saying. "And I'm serious when I say you have a really good eye for scripts."

"You don't know that," Roni said on a sniff. "I bet someone thought *Jem and the Holograms* was an amazing idea."

Wyatt coughed, clearing the emotion from his throat. "Your mom's waiting, Roni."

Her eyes snapped to his, accusing, brimming with hurt. Seemed he could never escape being the bad guy.

"I'm sorry about what happened out there. You shouldn't have seen that. It's not who I am."

"You were protecting me. That's exactly who you are."

He looked to Molly, who watched with those violet eyes that saw everything.

"Yes."

"And now you're sending me away."

"This summer was always going to come to an end. So your mom's here a few hours early, that's all." Still pissed, still mouthing off about his family. But he refused to rip this mother-daughter relationship apart so he could make his with Roni stronger. In a couple of years, Roni could make up her own mind. Maybe she already had. If she still wanted to be in their lives, he would welcome her back with a big Dempsey hug and he wouldn't let go.

He grabbed her bag and stepped outside while Molly hugged Roni again. The clog of misery in his throat threatened to choke him. He ducked into his room to compose himself a minute, and when he emerged, they were standing at the top of the stairs waiting for him.

"I know you don't understand right now, Roni, but one day I hope you do."

"I'm fifteen, Wyatt, not five," she muttered.

Okay, so maybe she understood more than he gave her credit for, but understanding didn't make it hurt less. He took her small palm and placed in it the one thing he had of Logan's that held any value. Apart from her.

"This is your dad's badge. Keep it safe." Folding her in his arms, he embraced her hard enough to imprint his love on her. Sure, it was just a few hours early, but he'd wanted to use the drive back to Bloomington to tell her stories and learn about hers. To say all the things he'd left unsaid.

Now they'd run out of time, and he prayed that one day he'd get another chance.

CHAPTER TWENTY-FIVE

Molly had been living on borrowed time, thinking she could fake normal and wouldn't infect everyone around her with the craziness that was her life.

Furtively, she watched from an upstairs window as Wyatt walked his family past the gauntlet for which she was to blame and put his niece and her mom in a cab. Cameras that should have been aimed at her probed and pointed at them. Wyatt shielded them the best he could and stayed for a moment, watching the car until it turned the corner at the end of the block.

She knew exactly what tomorrow's headline would say: "Molly Cade: Home Wrecker."

Not true, yet Molly felt like she had destroyed something here.

She met him at the bottom of the stairs. "I'm sorry," she said, the words sounding heartbreakingly hollow and alarmingly inadequate.

He didn't acknowledge her, just pressed the heel of his hand to his forehead as if that could hold in his pain.

"I should leave," Molly said after the silence had strained to the tautness of a stretched rubber band. "It's the only way they'll go."

"Do not dare use this as an excuse to pull away here," he ground out.

"It was Ryan. I just know it was." She was pacing now, pounding panicked steps up and down Wyatt's hallway as her brain figured it out. "He put two and two together and sicced those mad dogs on you and your family. First, the photos, now this." Was she ever going to be free of him?

His head snapped back. "The photos?"

She should not have said that—or maybe she should have. Maybe he needed to know the depths that an association with her could descend to. "I found out from Cal that Ryan used the hack to cover a photo leak. He deliberately put those photos he took of me out there to punish me during our divorce. Revenge porn."

For a moment, she thought he hadn't heard her. His eyes glazed over, his entire body stilled, and it looked like the nearest wall was going to get an introduction to his fist.

"How long have you known?"

"I found out the day . . . the day we first . . . got together. It's what had me so upset during the run." That made it sound as though she'd used him to work out her anger. Well, she had, hadn't she? She hurried on. "I wasn't completely sure, but then he more or less admitted it when he visited the set. He wouldn't have liked you standing up to him. He would have found out who you are and sent them here." With each damning realization, her voice rose in panic. She would never be free of Ryan, and she refused to let his poison contaminate the best thing to ever happen to her.

Wyatt and his wonderful family did not deserve this.

"You should have told me, Molly."

This was what bothered him? "It wasn't your problem. And talking wasn't really—"

"What we were about?" He huffed a low laugh. "Jesus. And I thought I had communication problems. You couldn't even trust me with that."

She couldn't even burden him with that. There was a difference.

"I should leave."

"Thought you were made of sterner stuff."

Whatever made him think that? "I can't do this."

"You can't do my humble hovel?" His query emerged with an eerie calm.

"That's not what I meant—"

"Then say what you mean. Let's both say it. Cut through the excuses and the layers and expose the root. Those vultures out there? An excuse. Getting photographed whenever we go out to eat? An excuse. The threat to my relationship with Roni? An excuse. Take all that away and you're left with you, me, and how we feel about each other."

"It's not as simple as that."

"Isn't it?"

He had only experienced it in microcosm. The macro view was a hundred times more terrifying. "All those things you labeled as excuses? They're my reality. Those vultures out there? My permanent biographers. Getting photographed whenever I go out to eat? The reason why I can't. The threat to your relationship with Roni? It will always be there. They're what I have to live with, day in, day out. And the last thing I need is you making it worse by getting into public spats with my ex and the press!"

Those blue-gray eyes heated. "I will protect what's mine. And if that means dressin' down your ex and shovin' a paparazzi camera where the sun don't shine, then so be it."

The man who was usually the soul of restraint had transformed into a rabid dog. This is what she'd turned him into. "There's an unwritten pact here, Wyatt. I let them take a few photos and they don't call me a bitch on TMZ. I play nice with my ex in public and the studio green-lights my next project. I smile and simper, I lie back and think of Hollywood. These are the rules." Different for women in the business than men, but still the rules. *Minimize, de-escalate, move on.* "And I can't have you going rogue because you refuse to play the game."

"The game? So those fuckers take photos of my niece, get all up in the business of my woman, and I'm supposed to accept that? No fuckin' way."

"I'm not saying you should! If I'm not around, you and Roni won't be targets. Problem solved."

"Back to that?" He shook his head, exasperated. "I know you're scared, Molly. After all that shit you went through, you kept your head down and no one would fault you for playing it that way. You have it in that beautiful skull of yours that you belong to them. Your public. Your critics. The only person you belong to is you."

He was wrong. She belonged to him. Utterly, completely.

His big, coarse hands cupped her face. "Baby, I've never met a strong person with an easy past. But you can't hide forever or rely on making a good movie to be your only statement. Inside here"—he touched gentle fingertips above her breast—"is the heart of a warrior. The mama bear who protected Roni. The woman who scratches and claws to mark her man. So your ex did a number on you. That's why he's ex. But if you let the bullshit mask the good stuff, he wins."

He didn't understand. The warrior heart, the mama bear, the Hollywood producer—all an act. Roles she slipped into when the part required it. She wasn't as strong as this man before her and she sure as hell couldn't live up to his standards in a mate. Eventually he would tire of the brutal slog. Of repelling the wolves from his door.

Every day she lived it, and she was exhausted.

"It's not just that me being in your life turns your normal world upside down, Wyatt, but there's the other side. You in mine." Gage's words of warning came back to her. *A life in the spotlight would kill him.*

His hands fell away. "You think I don't belong in your world, Molly?"

Not as it was currently crafted, and she could never belong in his without tainting it forever. She let her silence be the answer. Set the bar so high that not even her badass marine firefighter could reach it.

None of this was supposed to happen. She hadn't expected love.

She hadn't expected Wyatt.

There were a million ways she could have hurt him, but implying he wouldn't fit her life was the deepest cut of all. Clueing him in was the only way she could make him understand. Those bubbles of sex and comfort he'd created for her had to burst eventually.

He searched her face, looking for some sign that the words she left unsaid might not match the intent in her heart. Unable to bear the furious pain she saw there, she reached for him, but he drew back, the hurt on his face a stab to her heart.

"We're not doin' comfort hugs or good-bye kisses, Molly. I can't stop you from rewinding to the memories we've already created, but you'll get no more from me. I won't fill that well you'll draw from for your next big role."

He made her sound like a leech, an incubus who survives by feeding on others' emotions. She opened her mouth to defend herself, but she had zilch. He was hurt, he was right, and there was nothing she could say that would make this better.

In case she had any doubts that they could emerge from this horror with some semblance of goodwill existing between them, he asked, "You need a ride?"

She shook her head, her agony mirroring his. She knew he didn't want to cause her pain, but he had to manage his own the best way he could. Dazed, she headed toward the door.

"Use the kitchen," he said with a gruff softness. "Safer."

He walked her out, back to Gage's house, staying a couple of steps behind. Molly could already tell how this would go down: Once she had packed up, he would escort her to the rented Lexus parked beside his Camaro in the garage. He'd load her luggage into the trunk and check to make sure she was wearing her seat belt. He'd stand with hands shoved deep in his jean pockets, watching with those unholy blue eyes as she snuck out of the alley and through the gauntlet.

This man had had her back from the beginning. He would protect her to the last.

Right until she drove out of his life, her coward's heart in pieces.

CHAPTER TWENTY-SIX

The doorbell chimed. Wyatt waited. A full minute passed before it was opened by Judy, Roni's grandmother.

"Look what the cat dragged in," she said around the cigarette dangling from her lips. "Jen's at work. Guess you know that."

"I'm here to talk to my niece."

"Wyatt?" Roni's voice echoed from above. She came into view halfway down the stairs and his heart stuttered to a stop thinking of how much he loved and missed her. It had been a hellborn week, a nightmare without her and the woman he loved.

He held his breath. Anxiously waiting. Slowly dying. Would she even care?

She ran the rest of the way down, threw her arms around his torso, and snuggled in close. "You're here."

"Damn right I am. Not givin' up on you." He kissed the top of her head and raised her chin to face him. "Got time for lunch with your uncool, embarrassing uncle?"

She looked at her gran, who gave a heavy sigh. "Go get your phone, so I don't have to listen to that beeping while you're gone."

Grinning, Roni went inside.

"Try your best not to abduct her. My daughter will never let me hear the end of it."

Wyatt snorted. "Surprised she's even letting you near Roni after the stunt you pulled dropping her off in Chicago."

Judy's smile was sly. "I love my Jen, but I didn't agree with how she was handling things. Something had to be done."

An unexpected ally. In the haze of all that had happened this last year, Judy had walked a fine line through this whole mess. She was the one who'd contacted him initially, who'd gone over Jen's head and let him know he had another human being with his blood in her veins.

Sometimes he forgot he had people on his side.

They went to Applebee's because Roni said the chicken fajita roll-up was "to die." Once the server had taken their order, Roni fixed Wyatt with a strong, unflinching gaze, like she'd grown into a woman since he'd seen her last.

"Molly texted me."

Three little words that sliced right through him.

"She's being really encouraging about film school. I'm thinking about Columbia."

His heart twanged. "New York."

"Chicago," she said with a shy smile. "I'd like to major in cinema art and science, focusing on screenwriting. I'd start in two years, assuming my grades are good enough."

"They will be. Or I'll kick your ass."

Smiling, she tweaked her earring. "Might need a place to live. Keep my costs down."

"No shortage of Dempseys who'll put you up."

"I'd rather live with you, if that's okay."

His tongue felt too thick for his mouth. "I won't rent out your room, then."

The server brought their drinks, and Wyatt was grateful for the interruption. It was getting a little heavy there.

But it could always get heavier, because the people he loved were nothing if not dramatic. Roni sucked on her straw and raised her gaze to him, now looking close to tears. "It's my fault you and Molly aren't together. If the paparazzi hadn't taken that photo of me—"

"Girl, your career as a screenwriter will be over before it starts if you think that tired old cliché is going to work." Mercifully, no photos of Roni had seen the light of day. Why bother when they had a much better shot of Molly Cade's is-he-or-isn't-he lover losing his ever-loving shit on a photographer? "You're not to blame. Molly and I are worlds apart. It's not just a distance thing, it's the way our lives are playing out."

"Wy, you guys are great together, like Sandy and Danny. Like Andi and Blane, though it should have been Duckie." Jesus wept. Far too much time spent with Alex and Gage. "Like Thelma and Louise!"

"They drove off a cliff."

"You know what I mean. An unbreakable team."

Except Molly wasn't looking for another player to travel that journey with her.

"Roni, a woman like Molly needs someone larger-than-life, someone who'll reflect all her light back on her. That's not me." Some people were doomed to their roles. Charmless son, silent protector, killer in the shadows.

He'd spent his entire life in the background. It was where people expected to find him and he liked it there. With a woman like Molly, it was all or nothing.

"You don't want to wear a tux and be her plus one at all those premieres?"

"Could you see that?"

Her smile was sad and beautiful. "Yeah, I could. And not just as her stone-faced bodyguard with a finger in your ear and an eye on the crowd looking for weirdos. Not two steps behind, letting her absorb all the light because you're such a freakin' vampire you can't handle the attention."

"Roni—"

"Her life isn't all galas and premieres and hot co-stars. That's just a small piece of it. The rest is hanging with friends and family, doing stupid yoga, and dropping everything to get dumbass teens out of trouble." She squeezed his hand. "That's what's real. That's what matters."

"You should be a screenwriter."

"Stop deflecting."

"Or a psychotherapist."

"Wyatt!" Her raised voice drew the attention of diners five tables over. "Oh, sorry," she mocked. "Am I making a scene? Is your skin getting all vampire-tingly because the world might be watching?"

Yes, and hell yes. "Roni, she's got her life, and coming home to my hovel between jaunts around the world is not on her agenda."

The divide ran deeper than whether he was willing

to suffer the attention that followed her everywhere, play the game of star versus paparazzi. Threaded through her rejection was the inescapable conclusion that he was good enough for a secret fling in a hotel room, a bout of backseat action in his Camaro, but not ready for prime time. She didn't want him dulling the edge of her glittering life, and that hurt more than he could have ever imagined.

"Do you love her?"

"Roni," he warned.

His all-knowing, old-soul niece stared him down like a Dempsey. "Do you love her?"

"The whole world loves her." Of course he did. Why the hell would he be different from every other loser in every darkened theater around the world? You could adore the moon and stars from afar, but they weren't going to love you back. "She's up there, shining bright, and yeah, your vampire uncle doesn't want to get burned. Me loving her is not the issue. How could I not?"

The food arrived, so neither of them was forced to consider that.

"You told him he didn't belong in your world?"

Cal almost did a spectacular spit-take of her Pinot all over Molly's Jonathan Adler white leather sofa. Maybe Molly was tempting fate by (a) letting her friend drink red wine in the pristine living room of her Malibu beach house and (b) telling her about her last conversation with Wyatt, which admittedly was a doozie. She could afford to reupholster, but her Midwestern values would go apeshit.

"Perhaps we should move this outside." The September air was sea-breeze balmy, but she'd resisted spending time on her deck since she'd come back to LA. It was just so big and lonely and Dempsey-free. No immaculate koi pond, no Gage flipping burgers in an X-rated apron.

No Wyatt staring into her soul from across a food-laden patio table.

For the last two months, she'd had no shortage of company, whether it was Roni while they binge watched *Jessica Jones*, Gage and Brady's easy companionship over a cheese and charcuterie board, or Alex giving her the insider scoop about taking no prisoners in the CFD. And Wyatt's solid and sensual presence the foundation of it all.

The memory of him lingered inside her, an incurable ache.

At the Chicago wrap party for *Into the Blaze* ten days ago, she'd spent the entire night fending off a drunken Gideon while willing a certain CFD tech consult to walk through the door. He never came. (And after Molly had spread a little rumor about her costar's "shortcomings," neither did Gideon.) If someone had told her at the beginning of the summer that the worst of her problems during her first movie production would be wrangling her man-child costar, she would have smiled serenely and said, "Bring it!" Now she had a great product, a movie she was so damn proud of, but where was the sense of accomplishment? The joy at achieving exactly what she'd set out to do? Falling miserably in love apparently made all the good stuff taste like crap.

Well, screw love and the horse it rode in on!

Cal curled her legs under her body. "Let's talk about how you're feeling."

"Should I lie down? Maybe think back to the time my parents wouldn't let me get a dog?"

Cal snorted. "You had three dogs. Dogs are not the problem here. It's you."

"You're blunter than my last therapist." She sighed. "He said my ex did a number on me."

"Your therapist?

Molly frowned. "Yes. But also Wyatt."

"Wyatt did a number on you?"

Have another glass of wine, Cal. "No, well, yes, but that's not what I meant. Wyatt said my ex did a number on me."

"True," Cal said with the wisdom of the almost-drunk.

"He also said if I let the bullshit mask the good stuff, Ryan wins."

"Also true."

Molly sipped her wine. "The thing is, I spent the summer living Wyatt's life and he loves it the way it is." She had loved it, too. So much that her heart pined for it. For him. "He adores his family, his job, tinkering with his car. I'm not saying he'd have to give any of that up, but if we were to be together, and I mean really be together, as a unit, he would have to come into this world sometimes and he'd hate it." She looked around the beautifully appointed room, a million times removed from Wyatt's cozy bubble. It left her cold. "He says he'd be okay with the reporters and the attention, but I've seen how he reacts. It'd eventually chip away at him. At us. He'll want to defend me, I'll tell him that it's part of the game, and he'll get pissed off and leave."

"Wow, you're already headed to divorce court?" Cal let out a low whistle. "Hope he signed a prenup."

"You know what I mean. I already went over the rainbow and it's a one-way trip. I can't go back into his world and he'd hate it in mine."

Cal looked disgusted. "You're worried that he'll trust his happiness to you and that somehow you'll fail him because your life is as nutty as it looks from the outside? Molly, there'll always be reporters. There'll always be crazy, mouth-breathing stalkers who want to sniff your panties."

"Eww!" But true.

"There'll always be those photos. And that's what it comes down to. Ryan fucked you over, emotionally and literally. He was your first major relationship and he set the blueprint for all your future relationships. And that blueprint is like an Escher drawing. It's filled with impossible stairs and corridors that go nowhere and pathways that fold in on themselves. It's twisted like the man is twisted."

She paused for a breath and a sip of wine.

"You have to take control, Molly. Stop letting Ryan and those photos overshadow everything. Stop allowing the press to dictate how you're going to live your life. Fight back and take what's rightfully yours."

Wyatt. He was hers. It started all those years ago and transformed into something unexpected. Something absolute and real.

Knowing her friend was right didn't make it easier, only more frustrating than ever. Molly was mired in that Escher drawing with its infinite loops. One minute she'd been running toward Wyatt and then the stair hung a left just before she reached her goal. Happiness was just over that next hill, then fear had set a booby trap that blew up in her face.

But Cal wasn't right about everything. Ryan wasn't her first major relationship; he was just the most public one. Before Ryan, before the crazy, there had been someone else. Sexy, strong, a straight talker, brave on so many fronts.

Her blue-eyed, badass Marine.

She had a warrior heart beating inside her chest, yet she had failed the one person who had healed it and made her whole again. She'd let the bullshit mask the good stuff. Raised a white flag to the haters.

The realization was empowering, but not nearly enough.

Something big needed to happen, the narrative changed, a statement made. She was a product of Hollywood, after all. She needed to take a page from the Book of Wyatt and put that warrior heart to use.

And hope to God she wasn't too late.

CHAPTER TWENTY-SEVEN

The view from the upper hitting deck at Diversey Harbor included the lake, Lincoln Park, and teasing glimpses of Chicago's skyline, but it wasn't quite spectacular enough to compensate for what you had to do to enjoy said view.

Play golf.

Or, more specifically, bang the shit out of a bucket of small balls on the driving range.

"Set your feet farther apart," Eli instructed as Wyatt prepared to line drive a ball into the lake. Given the distance and the net set up to catch balls that made it to the edge of the range, that would have been technically impossible, but at this moment he suspected his rage might give him superhuman strength.

He planted his feet closer together than Eli suggested, because these days, he was furious at everyone and hell-bent on being a contrary asshole, and struck the ball. It landed about half the distance of Brady's shot. Cue a raspy huff of laughter from the big chef sitting behind him.

"I hate golf," Wyatt griped, and sat down on the bench three feet away from the strike zone.

"Only because you suck at it," Gage called out from the hitting mat one spot over, where he was paired up with Beck.

"Besides, it's good for your shoulder," Luke said as he readied for his shot. That would be the same Luke who Wyatt knew also hated golf because it was the kind of "white-glove-country-club crap" that people like Eli indulged in. His brother drove his ball perfectly down the fairway and celebrated with a triumphant whoop. "That's how it's done."

Wyatt glared at his brother's back. *Asshole.*

For all the Dempsey men to have the same night off was as rare as unicorn shit—and Wyatt wasn't buying it. Some serious favors must have been called in at the firehouse and the bar so everyone could be here, ensuring that Wyatt didn't slip into more-than-average moroseness, he supposed.

Or, he assumed this was the plan until Brady asked, "How's Roni doing?"

"Fine," Luke said before Wyatt could speak. "Course, would have been nice to get a chance to say good-bye in person before her mom rushed her off like that."

Wyatt's chest tightened. "You wanna do this now?"

"What? Talk about how you screwed things up?" Luke took a seat on the bench, a foot apart from Wyatt. "Sure, bring it."

"Gentlemen," Eli cautioned. "Not during golf, if you please."

Wyatt ignored him. "Getting a bit sick of your holier-than-thou 'tude, Luke. So this won't go down as a banner year for decision making in my life, but to

364 • KATE MEADER

hear the guy whose motto is 'Hit first, forgiveness never' criticize how I played it with those reporters is more than I can stomach right now."

Luke looked taken aback. "I'm not criticizing that. Hell, if I'd been there, I'd have whaled on those pricks with everything I had. So I wasn't too happy with how things went down with Roni at first, but spending time with her this summer more than made up for it. And we'll see her again. That's not the problem here."

Wyatt glanced up at Eli and Brady. Back to Luke. "Then what?"

"What in the fuckity fuck of all that is fucking fucked did you do to drive your woman away?"

"You're assuming it was my fault?" Gage and Beck had ambled over to take part in what was starting to look like . . . shit, an intervention? The expressions of the rest of the guys appeared to concur with Luke. "Women are capable of screwing up, too."

This statement was found to be uniformly hilarious.

Eli shook his head. "That's what I imagine is the first of many errors in your judgment, Lieutenant. It does not matter who is technically at fault. It does not matter that your lady got out of bed on the wrong side and started grumbling at you because the coffee you'd prepared for her is five degrees cooler than she likes it. And it certainly does not matter that every decision you have ever made has been with her as the central focus, yet she still thinks you're, and I quote, 'an unscrupulous pigfucker.' What you must accept is that by virtue of being born with a dick, you are always, always wrong in these matters, and that your only mission in life is to make it right."

Luke waved a hand at Eli. "What he said."

"Hey, don't be so hard on him," Beck said. "Knowing what a woman wants is a learned skill."

Gage's brows hitched high. "So much simpler when you like dick."

Luke rolled his eyes at Gage and redirected his attention back to Wyatt. "Remember this time last year when you told me to get down off my cross and go get my girl? How chicks need the big gesture?"

Was his brother fucking with him? Advice like that was always easier to give than to receive. "Sure do. I also remember that she shut your ass down and sent you packing back to Chicago."

"Yeah, it sucked golf balls at the time, but Kinsey needed to see me coming for her. She's not one for snap decisions, so she had to think on it and figure out what it meant for her, and once she did that, the rest was history."

Was there anything more self-satisfied than a man hitched for life to the woman of his dreams? Wherever had Wyatt stashed his smug-wipes?

"I laid it all out on the table. Told her the press, her ex, all that shit means nothing to me because all that matters is us. So when you do that for a woman, when you"—*open a vein and bleed your heart out on the hallway rug*—"lay it out there and she still doesn't want you, then I think you have to recognize that it's time to call the game for darkness."

His declaration threw a pall over the group. There was nothing that he would have done differently. He was cracked open, a gaping wound, and Molly was the salt and the suture. Gage, recognizing that alcohol might be the only thing that could improve the collective mood, moved off to the bar to pick up another bucket of beers.

Times like this Wyatt wished he drank. Sick to blazes of his own misery, he turned to Brady. "So when're you gonna make an honest man of my brother?"

Brady glanced over his shoulder to make sure Gage was out of hearing range. "Thinkin' of asking him soon, maybe next week. Our one-year anniversary."

No effen way. Only trying to redirect the conversation, Wyatt hadn't expected that Brady would actually have a plan. He'd always assumed Gage would be the one doing the asking, but hey, those two loved each other, so why shouldn't low-key Brady be the one to go big?

"That okay with you guys?" Brady asked the Dempsey contingent, which was pretty damn cute, to be honest. Eli didn't look in the least bit surprised, but then he and Brady were tight.

Luke grinned. "Like we'd say no. It's not as if you're a dickhead like Cooper here."

"Yet you've welcomed me with open arms, Almeida," Eli said drily.

"Only because my sister terrifies the bejesus out of me. Your happiness is incidental." Luke and Eli exchanged knowing smiles. They'd come a long way in the last six months.

Brady and Gage tying the knot shouldn't have changed a thing, but somehow it did. Four of the Dempseys hitched, and the last holdout, the man on the sidelines, was still Wyatt.

Gage returned with beers and eyes narrowed

to curious slits. "You guys were talking about me, right?"

"We talk of nothing else, Short Stack," Luke said with a friendly head rub for their baby bro and a sly look at Wyatt. They were on the same page again, and that eased ever so slightly the hollow ache in his chest. This was good. Back to normal, simpatico with his family, and even if he wasn't mate material, he had this.

The best people, and the people who knew him best.

Beck's phone rang. Almost immediately, both Luke's and Eli's phones joined the party, earning dirty looks from other driving range patrons. Wyatt shot back a dirty look of his own. Hardly the cathedral of St. Andrews here.

"Yeah, he's here," Beck muttered into his phone.

Thirty seconds and a series of grunts later, all of them were now staring at him with expressions ranging from discomfort to superlevels of discomfort. He shared a puzzled glance with Gage and Brady, both of whom merely lifted shoulders of not-a-clue.

"What's wrong?"

After a couple of screen taps, Beck passed his phone over to Wyatt. "You need to read this."

The banner of *Vanity Fair* blazed at the top of a Web page labeled "Suck It, Haters, or How I Learned to Get Over Mean Girls, Bad Boys, and Myself."

By Molly Cade.

What the hell had she done? He lifted his gaze to his crew, who watched him warily. If they were expecting him to regale them with a bedtime story by reading this shit aloud, they'd be a long time on the hook. Inhaling deep, he turned back to the phone.

I thought about addressing this letter to the world, but that seems a bit on the pretentious side, so I'll dial down my diva and say, "Hey, whoever you are, thanks for reading."

My name is Molly and I'm an actor. Yeah, I'm throwing that out there like an addict admitting her addiction. But that's true. I'm addicted to my job, to the lights, to the rush in my veins when I nail a performance. And like all addictions, there's a downside. I know, I'm famous, I need to get over myself. Drought over, here are all of America's tears.

But I have a right to a private life and so do the people I care about. I have a right to go about my regular day unmolested. And I have a right not to have nude photos of myself posted and shared for your jerking-off pleasure. Come the revolution, the person responsible will get his, and I'll be offering him a blindfold and a last cigarette. Because I'm classy like that.

To the people who viewed, I don't blame you. But to those of you who decided to body-shame me with opinions on my size, shape, and general unworthiness to be a deposit in your boyfriend's spank bank, think on this. There are a lot of photos of me out there in Dior and Givenchy, in yoga pants and sweats, in bikinis and perfectly draped bed linens. I get it. That's part of the territory. I wear clothes for my job, for photo shoots, and so I don't break public indecency

laws when I step outside my door. Guess what?
I'm naked underneath all those clothes. Does
it surprise you that I don't have green scales?
That my nipples are a particular shade of dusty
pink? That I probably should implement a more
regular bikini wax cycle? Well, it shouldn't. I
am possessed of a woman's body with human
imperfections. Why the obsession with this body,
these breasts, this ass? When it's a man with his
jiggly bits out for all the world to see, no one
blinks an eye except to compliment him on the
size of his equipment. The rules are different
for us humans with vaginas. The consequences
certainly are.

Do you think you can shame me into silence?
Do you think I'll slink away like the good little
woman, having learned my lesson not to indulge in
a little consensual, in-the-privacy-of-my-own-home
naughtiness?

Think again!

This body is strong and beautiful and so damn
sexy that strangers think it's worth jerking off
to. And while those pictures might belong to the
world, my body belongs to me. Don't ever forget
that.

If you've read this far, I thank you. Now you
have a choice, or perhaps you're one of the people
who have already made it, like a kid going straight
for the present instead of doing the polite thing
and opening the birthday card first. (That's okay,
I was that kid, too.) There's a link following this
letter that will take you to a Molly Cade–approved
glamour shot. If you're the kind of person who

reads Playboy *for the articles, then it might not interest you. I don't mind if you click, don't mind if you don't. That's not the point. The take-home here is that I, Molly Cade, chose to share* this *photo on the Internet. That choice was denied me before.*

Enjoy this titty pic, world!

> *With love from my warrior heart,*
> *Molly Cade*

<u>Click here</u>

Holy. Hell.

Stunned, Wyatt waited for the rest of them to catch up. For his brain to untangle. A good thirty seconds of ominous quiet passed, except for the distant whack of golf balls and the thud of Wyatt's overfull heart.

Eli broke the silence. "I've just made it back into the master bedroom. Why do I feel like my fiancée is testing me?"

"Yep," Luke said. "My better half has sent me an article where another woman has given me permission to look at her naked. Am I supposed to accept that at face value or do I risk the eternal wrath of my wife?"

"Not just your wife," Wyatt muttered. If one of them so much as dared to click that link in his presence, they would have a death-by-golf-club situation on their hands.

Needing a moment, he stood and walked to the edge of the hitting area. Butterflies dive-bombed in his belly, his hands tingled with the effort to keep them from shaking. His visceral reaction made no sense. Her curves were as well known to him as the lines on his face. He could trace them from memory, had mapped every intimate corner with his tongue, and yet the thought of this photo out in the ether terrified him.

Anyone could see her. *Everyone* could see her.

But this was her body. Her choice to share with the world. And he respected the hell out of that.

He took a breath and clicked the link.

There she was. Beautiful, brave, and grinning, as if to say, *The joke's on you, suckers*. Taken in profile, it was one of those in-the-mirror selfies with her arm banded across her gorgeous breasts, but not so much that a peek of nipple couldn't be seen. More tantalizing and sexy than a total reveal. A skimpy thong prevented full-frontal nudity, but she had twisted and tilted her ass at a jaunty angle so your eyes couldn't help but be drawn to those lush curves—and the message branded on them.

Tattooed across the ass that dethroned JLo was the rather cheeky declaration:

CUBS SUCK

Oh no, you didn't.

The laugh he loosed lifted the weight from his chest. With love from her warrior heart, indeed.

The guys watched as he passed the phone back to Beck, who eyed him expectantly. Only when Wyatt nodded his permission did he look down at the screen. A blinding grin broke out on his brother's face.

"Now, that's what I'd call a big gesture."

Cosigned. Molly Cade had just won the Internet.

"I wish you were here," Molly said into her phone as she adjusted the strap on her Louboutins. Red with a heart-shaped rhinestone buckle.

Cal chuckled softly. "I can see the headline now: 'Molly Cade Driven to Lesbianism at Charity Gala—Again!' You can walk down a red carpet by yourself, hon."

"If these shoes don't send me crashing."

"It's my first date in over a year," Cal said, for the tenth time today. Molly would never begrudge her friend a chance at actual, in-person nookie, so it was really bad form to make it all about her.

"I know, sorry. Just being a diva bitch."

The background noise on Cal's phone had picked up. It sounded like the restaurant she was in was crowded. "Hey, no one's more thrilled than me that the diva bitch is back. Oh, here's my date. Wonder if I should tell her that she's getting lucky no matter what?"

Molly giggled. "Sure, who needs all that awkward flirting and will-she-won't-she crap?"

"Exactly. Night, Mol, and good luck."

"Night, Cal."

Her phone's subsequent silence taunted her, though it had been ringing nonstop since the letter had posted to the *Vanity Fair* website yesterday afternoon. Just not with a call from the one person whose voice she needed to hear. Had he read it? Had he seen her warrior heart beating on the screen, her apology shining off her ass?

A smile tugged at her lips as she recalled the body artist's expression on hearing her requirements.

The smile vanished. It had made no difference. Her message's intended target never responded, the blow she'd dealt him apparently too painful to overcome.

The limo stopped outside the Wilshire Ebell Theatre, where Molly would present an award at the LGBT Youth in Crisis gala. She practiced her game face in her compact because, even with her recent bout of honesty still buzzing through the press outlets and every five-star restaurant in LA, there was only so much shooting from the hip Hollywood could handle.

An usher opened the limo door and the noisy cheers burst her bubble of quiet. The mere thought of that word—*bubble*—ripped her brain open, as she thought of all the bubbles he had created for her. How he had made her feel safe and wanted and loved.

Archive, Molly. Shove it into the file cabinet of Wyatt Fox memories that would eventually acquire dust.

Extending one golden leg, underscored by the sexy thigh-high slit of her white Alexander McQueen dress, she took the usher's outstretched hand.

And almost fainted clean away.

A zing of recognition had sizzled up her arm, forcing her to stare at her hand and the one that dwarfed it. She knew it well. It had pleasured and protected her. It could fell paparazzi like bowling pins.

And knock the heels off one jaded farm girl from Missouri.

"Evenin', Hollywood."

She raised her eyes to meet the stark, relentless, so—damn—blue gaze of Lieutenant Wyatt Fox.

Who had shaved.

And was wearing a suit.

A *suit*.

How fine he looked in black, as handsome as Lucifer, the clean lines of Tom Ford struggling to contain his blatant masculinity. Forget the shoes as her demise; her jellied legs would surely give out any second.

Gently, he took charge, pulling her forward and closing the door to allow the limo to move on because her shocked standstill was holding up the next arrival.

"Ready?" he asked, as if that were a perfectly normal question. As if his presence here should pass without comment or meltdown. He held her hand and repositioned it, subtly measuring his large hand against her small one, another thing he'd done that always made her feel sheltered and loved.

"Security at this event is really slipping," she murmured.

The quirk of that carnal mouth was easier to see now that he was beard-free. "Work now, banter later."

The red gauntlet was a blur as she walked it, stopping on occasion to sign autographs and take selfies with the fans. She had to let Wyatt's hand go for some of that, but ever protective, he still found a way to stay connected to her. A hand on her back, his fingers light but unyielding on her waist. By the time they reached the press line, the phony-bright smile she usually kept fixed in place for such occasions had transformed into something joyfully genuine.

He was here, in the open, at her side.

How he must hate it.

How he must love her.

"Molly." Billy Bush from *Access Hollywood* leaned in and kissed her lightly on the cheek, careful not to mess up her makeup. Though she had to wonder if the glare Wyatt was laying on him had anything to do with the barely there smooch.

After the requisite "Who are you wearing?" and "Tell us why this cause means so much to you," Billy braved a glance at Wyatt.

"So, Wyatt, it looked like you surprised Molly back there at the bottom of the red carpet."

Wyatt paused for a couple of seconds, an age in Hollywood time, and ignoring Billy, turned to Molly. "She didn't know I was coming. But this is an important night for her and this great cause, and I wouldn't miss it for the world."

Oh, he was good. How did he get so good?

"And what did you think of Molly's letter in *Vanity Fair*?"

Wyatt squeezed her waist, a gesture of support that meant more than any words. Those unholy blue eyes tore her heart out and held it aloft in victory.

It was his. He owned it.

"Never been prouder, though I do have a bone to pick with her." He raised a Wy-brow. "Can't be dissing the Cubbies, babe."

She laughed. "I knew if the ass didn't get your attention, a direct attack on your hometown team might do the trick."

"The ass has *always* had my attention." And as if he knew the protocol for a red-carpet interview—keep it under two minutes, don't reveal anything you care about, leave 'em wanting more—Wyatt subtly steered her to the next vulture waiting to eviscerate her.

Stepping inside the gala venue ten minutes later, she leaned in and inhaled that heady mix of soap and pirate. "Have you been taking lessons in handling the red carpet?"

"Kinsey and Madison gave me a few pointers. And I might have spent the whole flight boning up on YouTube."

Poor Wyatt. She smothered a giggle. How was she going to manage two hours of speeches and small talk with her fellow table guests, unable to have a real, God's-honest conversation with this man? Only then did she realize that they weren't entering the ballroom, but had turned down a corridor. One of the security personnel nodded at Wyatt—as if he knew him!—and opened a door.

"Best I could do on short notice," Wyatt said, shutting the door behind him. Disinfectant stung her nostrils. Mops and brushes would be their witnesses.

"How did this happen?" Awareness struck. "Cal."

"I had planned to get here earlier, but my flight was delayed. Miss Johnson arranged a car, a suit, and cleared it with security." He sounded ever so slightly vexed.

"You think it was too easy to get by security, don't you?"

Eyebrow lift of doom. "I could've been anyone, but I'll give them a pass this once because I'm not just anyone."

"So who are you exactly?"

She'd thrown it out there, intending it as part of their glib banter, not ready for it to get real. It emerged sharper than she'd meant it to, but as always, Wyatt took it in his stride.

"I'm the man in the shadows, Molly, who doesn't do the limelight or drama or diva shit. Who's lived his whole life on the margins because it was easier than coming in from the cold. Except . . ."

She jumped on that crumb, her hand gripping the lapel of his suit hard enough to rumple. "Except?"

"Except I'm more than that man. Sometimes I'm the guy who saves people trapped in fires or mangled wreckage or capsized boats. Sometimes I go nuts on assholes who threaten the people I love. I usually do it with a whole lot more class and efficiency than Luke, but I do it all the same. Because I've absorbed everything about being a Dempsey and learned that love requires big choices, bold moves, and on occasion, a little bit of drama."

That—it—does.

He blew out a breath. "Don't know how Brady puts up with Gage talking this much. You sick of me yet?"

Tears pressed, but she held on by the thinnest of sniffly threads. "Never. Could listen to you all day."

"Gonna hold you to that. Now, I know you got scared. There was a lot happening at once with Roni, Jen, the reporters, and I wasn't making it any easier getting all bossy and demanding you make a call."

Her heart was brimming over. This man knew her intimately, down to her insecure diva toes. Trusting herself was something she'd had to relearn this past summer, and even now, she needed remedial classes. Who better a teacher than Wyatt Fox?

"I panicked," she confessed. "Everything with you

is turned up to the max, and although my instincts were telling me you were what I needed, I've had problems trusting them lately."

Wry smile. "Thing is, Molly, you're not the only one who's been second-guessing what's for the best. I didn't think I had it in me to be the guy you needed, the one who steps out on your arm and guides you through all that shit." He waved his hand, presumably in the direction of "all that shit" on the red carpet. "I'll be honest and say I didn't like that one bit, but if you need a date, I will always be here for you. And when you don't need a date"—he pulled her close and leaned his forehead against hers and she thanked her stars she was wearing these heels after all—"when you need your man and some peace and a place to rest that beautiful head of yours, then I'll be here for you, as well. Wherever you need that to be."

She closed her eyes, soaked in those heart-healing words. "And Roni?"

"I told you those were excuses when you brought that up before, but in truth, I let you get away with using them because it was easier not to fight. All my life, I've kept my distance from makings things too personal. Until I met you and you undid the knots inside. Unraveled me completely. As for the attention, Roni can handle it better than any of us, and her mom's gonna have to understand that her daughter is a Dempsey and with that comes a certain amount of drama and a whole lot of sun. Kid wants an invite to the Golden Globes, by the way."

"Not the Oscars?"

"She says TV and Netflix are where it's at."

Clever girl.

Joy bubbled up inside her. Uncontrollable, crazy, ebullient joy. She wanted to scream. She wanted everyone to know how happy she was.

But for now, the only person who needed that information stood in front of her.

"I know I'm not the easiest woman to handle, but you've been unbelievably patient so far, putting up with my diva crap. I hope you're up for more, because you're the only one I want. The only one I trust to keep me safe, grounded, and protected. I love you, Wyatt Fox. So much."

He closed his eyes as if he wanted to hold on to this moment, and when he opened them again, deep blue emotion shone back at her.

"I'll be your reality check and you can be what you've always been."

"What's that?"

"The woman of my dreams. Falling in love with you was the easiest thing I've ever done. Falling is easy. Staying that way is hard. But I've been choosing hard all my life, so why the hell would the life I make with the woman who completes me be any different? I love you like a madman. You're the air I breathe, my next heartbeat, and I'm never letting go."

Her warrior heart kicked hard. This man. This beautiful, scene-stealing man.

And then he kissed her, a Wyatt Fox special. Her entire body sighed into his, and she let him ruin her makeup while he used that wicked pirate mouth to tell her everything in his heart.

When he broke the kiss, she coasted fingertips along his smooth-shaven cheeks. "I miss the beard."

He smiled against her lips, a smile she dissolved

into, and she realized she didn't miss the beard after all. Because here he was, the guy she loved, losing the mask and leaving the shadows.

Her protector, her lover, her soul.

"There *is* something I need to ask you, though, Molly. And our future depends on the answer to this question."

That sounded ominous. "What happened to 'the air I breathe' and 'my next heartbeat'?"

His big, blunt hand skimmed her hip and cradled her ass professionally. "That tattoo—can I assume it was temporary? Because while I can put up with the Cards tee, only, and I repeat only, because it does amazing things for your breasts, any further besmirching—"

"Besmirching?"

"Besmirching of the Cubs' name is an absolute deal breaker."

She thought on this a moment and cast a sneaky glance toward the closed door.

"That, Marine, is something you're going to have to find out for yourself."

Needless to say, they were late for the gala.

🔥 EPILOGUE

"Does anyone else think this is a terrible way to cook a turkey?"

Gage shot Kinsey a condemning look over his shoulder. "Listen, Cali girl, just because you believe lettuce is the foundation of a well-balanced meal, there's no need to piss on our carnivore ways. And it's not a mere turkey, it's a royal turducken."

"N'Awlins style," Brady added as he lowered the Frankensteined bird into the outdoor fryer set up on the patio. An ear-splitting sizzle went up as the virgin meat hit the oil, followed by a big cheer from everyone present for a Dempsey family Thanksgiving.

With his chest warmed by her back, Wyatt wrapped his arms tighter around Molly and buried his chin in the tender skin of her neck. It was hard to believe that almost three months had passed since he'd claimed her on that red carpet.

Currently in postproduction, *Into the Blaze* was scheduled for a big summer release and was expected to be huge. (The trailer was sitting at fifteen million views and counting and had knocked Alex's luxury car slice-and-dice YouTube video off its perch, much to his sister's annoyance.) Meanwhile, Molly was fo-cusing on lining up projects for her production company, but she had signed on for a ten-week movie shoot in Vancouver starting in January. It would be their first big test of being apart. More attention brought more paparazzi out of the woodwork, but he was trying to keep his cool.

Except when he had Molly in his bed. Only then did he unleash his primal hunger, his raging desire, his unquenchable thirst for the woman who had coaxed him into the light.

"Okay, we're looking at T-minus ninety minutes," Kinsey said, "so before everyone gets sloppy drunk on the rum-spiked eggnog, we're doing holiday card photos."

"I have more than enough ugly sweaters for everyone," Gage added with a grin. "But I call dibs on Santa with a light saber, riding a unicorn."

"Sounds like we have time," Wyatt murmured in Molly's ear.

Her entire body relaxed in his arms like a smile. "Sneaking away during a family gathering. Which Dempsey commandment are we breaking again?"

"Number one, babe. It's always number one."

As everyone else trickled back into the house, Wyatt caught Roni's arm and pulled her in for a hug. These days he refused to hold back his love for his people, even though his niece risked dislocating her eyeballs with every eye roll.

"I'm going to start charging you for every one of those, y'know. Get my college fund in good shape."

She wouldn't have to worry about that. "Just glad you're here, Roni. All of you." Her mom and grandmother had joined them for the holiday, an invitation he'd gladly extended, not expecting acceptance. Sure, it was a touch awkward, but these blended-family situations often took time while they fumbled their way through the dysfunction on the path to harmony. Jen needed to see how awesome Logan's family was and how much they all loved her daughter.

Molly had taken advantage of his moment's distraction to inhale deeply from baby Ella, resting peacefully in her papa's arms. She couldn't get enough of Beck and Darcy's newborn, one week old today. "Love that new-baby smell," she murmured.

Beck indulged her for a minute before heading back into the warmth with the sage advice, "Get your man to give you one of your own, Molly."

Wyatt had added that to his New Year's resolutions.

Beneath a star-spangled sky that had been spitting out the odd snow flurry all afternoon, he led Molly to the yard next door, but at the last moment switched to the alley. Her soft giggle told him she knew exactly what he was up to. In the garage, the Camaro was still on blocks. He was tempted to leave it that way, a shrine to their illicit affair, but come the spring, he'd return to making it whole again.

Tonight, however, it was the perfect spot for a furtive, fevered fumble in the dark—or would have been, if he hadn't taken a few moments to festivize the garage. Icicle lights streamed on the brick walls, their cheery glow illuminating Molly's surprise.

"Wyatt," she gasped.

Chuckles and sighs were their soundtrack as they maneuvered their bodies into position in the backseat, warm breath and heated skin keeping the temperature inside a few degrees above the November chill.

He still couldn't believe his luck—the brusque firefighter and the Hollywood superstar.

They saw her on the screen, that beautiful smile a promise they'd forget their worries for a couple of hours. But no one saw her the way he did. Vulnerable, open, in bloom, new layers revealed with every moment he held her.

"Gettin' it on in the Camaro." Her fingers stroked his jaw, at once loving and inciting. "Do you think maybe—"

"I could grow back the beard?" Surprise, surprise. "How 'bout I dress as Santa in the next couple of weeks?"

"Spice things up with a sexy stranger?"

"Gotta keep you interested. Not sure that redecorating our home will be enough." He wouldn't allow her to contribute to the mortgage—and he was fully aware of how ridiculous that was when Molly could wipe it out with the click of a bank transfer—but he'd given her free rein to spruce the place up to her designer heart's content. Outside, it would be your typical Chicago brownstone, inside a palace befitting his queen.

"Our home," she murmured against his lips. "I like that."

"So do I." And then he kissed her the way they both liked it, fiendishly slow, taking his time to get her primed. In the dark, he listened to her body, waiting for those sweet sounds that told him she was close. Her language of sighs and moans was as fluent to him as the shape of her hand-filling curves, and when he slipped inside her at last—*ah*. He'd never tire of that gasp of surprise while he filled and stretched her.

Just the sheer miracle of this woman sent his heart and blood soaring into the cold, starry night above their heads.

Every time, Molly. Every time.

"I know, Marine," she whispered in answer to his unspoken affirmation, and then, like always, their bodies finished the conversation.

ACKNOWLEDGMENTS

So many people have helped to make the Hot in Chicago series the awesome world that it turned out to be. Captain Jerry Hughes at Truck 33 in Chicago lent his expertise whenever I had a question about the Chicago Fire Department. Movie business maven and author Abby Green answered my queries about film shoots and scripts. My agent, Nicole Resciniti, told me what to fix. My editors at Pocket, Elana Cohen and Lauren McKenna, crafted great stories from the word lumps I sent them. Copy editor Faren Bachelis kept me honest. Melissa and Jean Anne in publicity at Gallery/Pocket did a fantastic job getting the word out. As for the art department—just look at my smokin' covers: need I say more?

Thanks to Monique Headley and Lauren Layne, who read early drafts of the various entries in the series and provided incalculable advice. Several other authors went out of their way to recommend the series and help readers discover the Dempseys, and their support makes me feel warm and blessed: Eloisa James, Sophie Jordan, and especially Sarah MacLean, who told everyone, including whomever she was standing next to in line at the grocery store and her UPS lady, that they should read all about these sexy firefighters.

I'm so grateful to my readers' group, Kate's Kittens, for loving my books and spreading the word. Several of the kittens are bloggers and reviewers who've been with the series (and me) from the start. Thanks to Slick, Laurie, Kim, Maria, Michelle, Missy, Beth, Gretchen, Jaime, Angy, Miranda, Elizabeth, Misty, and CL (phew!) for all their support.

To Jimmie—you know what you did!

Finally, thanks to the brave men and women of CFD and fire departments everywhere for the work you do and the lives you've saved. With such amazing source material, creating stories based on what these heroes see as "just their jobs" makes *my* job the best in the world.

Find the love you've been looking for with bestselling romance from Pocket Books!

Pick up or download your copies today!

XOXOAfterDark.com

 POCKET BOOKS
An Imprint of Simon & Schuster
A CBS COMPANY

49067